THE YOUNGER GODS

By David Eddings

By David and Leigh Eddings

Voyager

DAVID AND LEIGH
EDDINGS

THE YOUNGER GODS

Book Four of The Dreamers

HarperCollins*Publishers*

Voyager
An Imprint of HarperCollins*Publishers*
77–85 Fulham Palace Road,
Hammersmith, London W6 8JB

www.voyager-books.com

Published by *Voyager* 2006
1

A catalogue record for this book
is available from the British Library

ISBN-13 978 0 00 715767 6 (hardback)
ISBN-10 0 00 715767 3
ISBN-13 978 0 00 715768 6 (trade paperback)
ISBN-10 0 00 715768 1

Set in Janson by Palimpsest Book Production Limited,
Polmont, Stirlingshire

Printed and bound in Great Britain by
Clays Ltd, St Ives plc

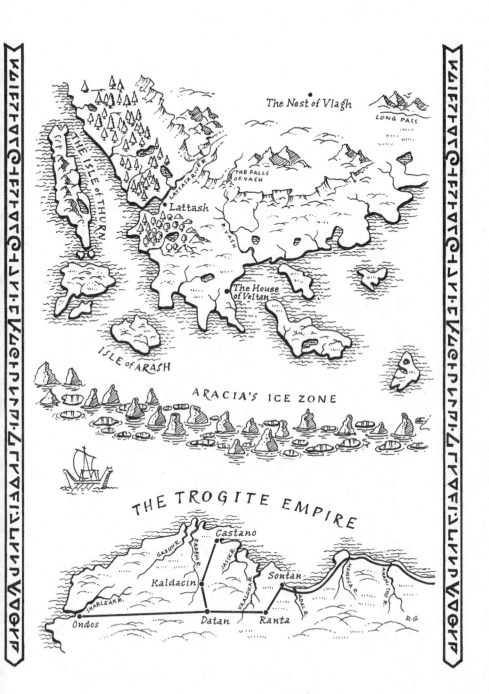

The Nest of Vlagh

LONG PASS

THE FALLS
OF VASH

THE ISLE of THORN

LATTASH RIVER

Lattash

VASH

The House
of Veltan

ISLE of ARASH

ARACIA'S ICE ZONE

THE TROGITE EMPIRE

Castano

GAZUN R.

ERDEM R.

JASIVR.

Kaldacin

VAALOKAR

Sontan

MHONOS R.

ADAL R.

ARAMTHO R.

SHARLEAH R.

Ondos

Datan

Ranta

R.G.

PREFACE

Those of us who devote our lives to the care of mother were greatly concerned by her rage after the disaster of 'blue fire' which had consumed so many of her warrior children. It is the duty of the warrior children to die if it is necessary to achieve that which mother wants, but deaths beyond counting reduce our numbers and weaken the overmind which guides us all. And, truly, the weakening of the overmind lessens all of us who live but to serve our beloved mother.

We are told by those who came before us that mother had been content in the nest which shelters us all until – in times long past – the weather changed and in each season there was less to eat than there had been in previous seasons. It had been then that mother had sent forth those servants we call 'the seekers of knowledge,' and in time they returned and told mother that beyond the high hills that surround our homeland there was much to eat. And this warmed mother's heart. It came to her that should those who search for things to eat go beyond the high hills and bring back much to eat, she could spawn yet more children – and then even more – and soon our numbers would be so great that no other mothers would dare to send *their* children out to fight with us for things-to-eat, since we would destroy their children and soon they would be alone in their nests screaming in despair.

And so it was that mother began to alter the children which would go forth from the nest to search for things-to-eat in the lands beyond the high hills. And many were her alterations, for the man-things that dwelt in the lands beyond the high hills were very clever and they used weapons that were *not* parts of their bodies.

And this gave mother great concern, for it is most unnatural for *any* creature to take up things that are not parts of their bodies to use as weapons. Then it came to mother that if the man-things could do this, could not *her* children do so as well? She sent forth more of the seekers of knowledge to find creatures who had unusual parts of their bodies that gave them advantages in the search for things-to-eat.

And the seekers of knowledge returned in time with much that mother might find useful. There were creatures without legs that had long, sharp teeth that could instantly kill anything the creature without legs saw as something-to-eat. There were other creatures who had eight legs rather than six who could turn the insides of things-to-eat into liquid that the eight-legged creature could conveniently drink. There were creatures with hard shells that covered and protected their bodies, and there were still other creatures with hard, sharp mouth-parts that could cut pieces off the thing that was being eaten.

The more dear mother considered it, the more she thought that the teeth of the creature that had no legs might be the most effective.

Then, in seasons beyond counting, mother put generation after generation to work on the high hills that stood between our nest and the land of the sunset. There were burrows that would safely take mother's children beyond the peaks of the high hills, and there were many flat stones piled on the slope of the high hill that appeared to have once been nests of the man-things, and it seemed that the empty nests might be useful to deceive the man-things.

In time, all was complete, and mother waited as the elder divinities grew older and less responsive. Then, in the springtime of this present year, all was ready, and mother commanded the children to attack the man-things clustered near the top of that particular high hill.

And great was the consternation of the man-things when the servants of our mother crossed the empty ground to attack the pile of rocks the man-things had gathered at the top of that high hill. But the man-things knew not that most of the servants of dear mother were creeping through burrows that went beneath that high hill to come out in various rock-piles lying on the sunset side of the high hills.

And mother rejoiced, for victory was now in her grasp.

But it was not to be, for disaster came down on the servants in the burrows. Two of the high hills did most suddenly burst into flame, hurling liquid fire high into the spring sky. It was not the liquid fire in the sky that brought grief to mother, however. It was the liquid fire that ran down through the burrows that made the servants of dear mother vanish as if they had never been.

And when word of this reached mother, she shrieked in agony, and all who lived but to serve her shrieked as well, for our over-mind was made less by this disaster.

Now the seekers of knowledge had spent much time over generations in the lands of the man-things, and they had come to learn the way by which the man-things used noises to communicate with each other. And many of the seekers of knowledge had learned how to make the noises the man-things called 'speech.' And so it was that when our beloved mother decided that we should go down into the land of longer summers where there was much to eat, the seekers went up the slope of the high hills to gather information about the man-things of that region.

And while the seekers worked on this task, beloved mother brought forth many new forms for the warrior children. The new forms were well-designed to overcome the many advantages the man-things appeared to have had in the land of the sunset.

And when the seekers returned, they were sorely discontented, for the man-things had told them many things that were not true. In truth it would appear that the man-things said more things that were *not* true than were truly true. The seekers had discovered *one* thing that they felt to be most important, however. Although that which ruled the land of longer summers was called Veltan, there was another man-thing called Omago, who had far, far more power than did the one called Veltan. The Omago thing was not yet fully aware of this power, and it had never used it. There was yet another man-thing called Ara, however, who shared this knowledge with the Omago thing, but it never spoke with the Omago thing about that power.

As the new hatch of the warrior servants matured, beloved mother sent them toward the land of longer summers, and we all believed that our warrior servants would most easily overcome the man-things, and the land of longer summers would be ours before the seasons changed.

But it was not so, for many man-things had come to the land of longer summers, and they had piled up endless stacks of flat stones to impede our progress toward what was rightfully ours. And once again, the cursed man-things used things that were *not* parts of their bodies as weapons. We had encountered the flying sticks before, though none of us had been able to understand just *how* the man-things could make the sticks fly. Some of us were quite sure that the sticks were live things that were controlled by various man-things. When the man-thing said 'fly,' the stick obeyed. Then, when the stick was in mid-flight, the man-thing spoke again and said 'kill.' And the stick did that.

We searched and searched for sticks that would obey commands, but we found them not.

The man-things had used other weapons as well. The long stick did not fly, but it was nearly as cruel as were the flying sticks. The long sticks had wide points that were alien, having no relation to the stick itself. The points were very sharp, and they easily penetrated the bodies of the warrior servants.

It came to us that many of the man-things we had encountered were not related to the man-things that occupied the land of the sunset and now the land of longer summers.

The struggle on the slope was long and difficult, and our beloved mother sent many new-form servants into the struggle, but they could not overcome the man-things who hid themselves behind their protective rock-piles, rising to their feet only to kill those of us who were attacking.

Much disturbed were those of us who are the *true* servants of beloved mother when she insisted that we should take her from the nest to the region where the conflict was taking place. *Her* safety must always be our first obligation, but mother saw no reason to be concerned. She is immortal, of course, but the conflict was raging in the land of longer summers. The nest was safe, but the region of conflict was not.

She *was* mother, however, so we had no choice but to obey her.

Then yet another group of man-things came rushing up from far down in the land of longer summers, and that particular group appeared to have some other goal than the defeat of mother's warrior servants. There were many reports from the seekers that the man-things which had been fighting mother's warrior servants were stepping aside to let the new group pass through without restraint.

And the new group of man-things rushed to the top of the slope that led down to mother's region and then they ran on down that slope – almost as if they could not even see mother's warrior servants. We have learned – much to our sorrow – that most of the man-things are extremely clever, but the new group of man-things seemed to have little or no thought as they blindly rushed down the slope toward something which only they could see.

And mother's warrior servants of several altered forms killed the mindless man-things by the thousands, but the other mindless man-things paid no heed to the fate of their companions, but continued their rush down the slope toward that which only they could see.

And then it was that enormous amounts of water burst forth from the upper face of the high hill above us, and mother's warrior servants and the mindless man-things alike were engulfed in water and carried down the slope to certain destruction.

And mother screamed in anguish even as those of us who live but to serve her carried her back toward the safety of the nest, for it was now clear that water could be as deadly as fire, and that the land of longer summers was now and forever beyond our reach.

Great was the grief of our beloved mother, but in time the seekers of knowledge persuaded her that there were still two regions beyond the high hills that were not now and forever blocked off from us. There was the land of the sunrise and the land of shorter summers. Many were the arguments between those warrior servants who favored the land of shorter summers and those who favored the land of the sunrise, and those arguments became more heated until those who preferred shorter summers and those who favored sunrise began to kill each other.

And finally, to prevent more of the killing, beloved mother chose shorter summers, and once she had chosen, the killing stopped.

The seekers were much interested in a low-tree that flickered and put out light and dark clouds which lay close to the ground or rose high up into the sky, for they saw that low-tree as a way to kill the man-things from a long way off, and that would put none of the servants of our beloved mother in peril.

And the seekers were much pleased when they discovered that the low-tree was most generous, and freely it shared its flickers and clouds with other low trees of its own kind.

Now other seekers had gone into the high hills that blocked off the land of shorter summers, and they soon found a narrow pathway that went through the high hills and emerged in a well-concealed manner in the land of shorter summers.

Cautious was our beloved mother, however, and she sent forth servants that could make the noises of the man-things to deceive the man-things and to set them at war one with the other, for it had come to the overmind that the man-things on occasion hated each other even more than they hated us, and gladly would they kill each other, and that would make things easier for mother's warrior servants.

We proceeded across the flat place where there are no things-to-eat and came at last to the narrow pathway that led from mother's region to the land of shorter summers. Much were we discontented when we arrived there, however, for the man-things had once more piled flat rocks on top of other flat rocks to block our path.

We now had a means to drive them away, however. The seekers entered several nesting places in the high hills below the flat rock-pile of the man-things, there to make piles of the low-trees that flicker inside the nesting places, and dense black clouds passed over their rock-pile, and then the man-things turned and fled, leaving the pathway open to the warrior servants.

Beloved mother rejoiced and told the warrior servants to move rapidly along the narrow pathway toward the land of shorter summers, for now the low-trees – which almost certainly loved mother almost as much as do we who serve and protect her – continued to drive the man-things away.

And so it was that the warrior servants swarmed up the narrow pathway with victory almost certainly within their reach.

But then a man-thing that was *not* a breeder as most of the man-things are, unleashed something that no one has ever seen before. We, the servants of beloved mother, have encountered the fires of the man-things before, but the man-thing who was not a breeder sent a huge wave of fire that was *not* yellow down the pathway. The fire was blue instead, and it consumed warrior servants uncounted as it rushed on down the narrow path and even beyond.

That in itself was horrid beyond anything we had yet encountered, but then the man-thing which was *not* a breeder called forth yet another blue fire at the foot of our narrow path. And *that* blue fire rose higher than the pile of flat rocks the man-things had built, and it showed no indication that it would ever stop burning.

And yet once again, our beloved mother screamed in agony, and we who serve her also screamed.

So great was mother's fury that she listened to a suggestion of one of the seekers – a suggestion she would not even have considered had she been more calm. The seeker declared that since there was only one part of this land that was *not* blocked, the man-things would certainly know that mother's warrior servants would attack them from that direction, and their numbers would be enormous. 'You will need many, many warrior servants to overcome the man-things, beloved Vlagh,' she said. 'Can you possibly spawn out more this time than you did when we attacked the other directions?'

'Many, many more,' dear mother replied. 'I will bury the man-things in freshly hatched spawn. I *will* have the land of the sunrise, and my children will feed on the remains of all the man-things that contaminate this entire land that is – and always will be – *mine*.'

We did not wish to remind beloved mother that a spawn of that size would severely reduce any future spawns to the point that there would hardly be enough new care-givers to see to her needs, and seasons uncountable would pass before she could spawn more. We tried as best we could to bring this to her attention, but she paid little heed and commanded us to carry her straight-way to the spawning chamber. And, since it is required, we did as she commanded.

Should disaster come again, however, the children of future spawns will be so limited that as the seasons plod on by, the nest of our beloved mother will have few – if any – care-givers to see to her needs, and in time, it may be that she will dwell here alone.

MOUNT SHRAK

1

⬩►◄⬩

I t was well past midnight, and Zelana was standing alone on the balcony of what big brother Dahlaine called his 'War Chamber.' It seemed to Zelana that those fancy names had always been one of Dahlaine's failings. For some reason he seemed to feel a need to give almost *everything* some kind of stupendous title. If he'd spend as much time *solving* a problem as he usually spent coming up with a name for it, things might go a bit smoother for him.

Right now, however, Zelana was trying to swallow some very peculiar events. It seemed that they had a mysterious helper who could pull miracles out of her hat – or sleeve – without any kind of warning at all.

Down in baby brother Veltan's Domain, Longbow had been plagued with a series of very peculiar dreams which were being rammed into his mind by an entity he always called 'our unknown friend,' despite the fact that he'd told Zelana and the others that he recognized the voice – but he couldn't quite attach a name to the speaker. Zelana knew that Longbow's mind was too sharp to start getting fuzzy about something *that* important, so it was quite obvious that 'unknown friend' had been tampering with him in ways Zelana could not even begin to comprehend.

There was one thing that was abundantly clear, however. Not only could 'unknown friend' erase memories, she could also break – or just ignore – some very important rules. Zelana and her family were *not* permitted to kill things. 'Unknown friend,' however, had manipulated the members of the Trogite Church with her 'sea of gold' and lured them into a confrontation with the Creatures of the Wasteland. Then, when the two enemy forces were locked in what would almost certainly have turned out to be a war of mutual extinction, 'unknown friend' had obliterated them *all* with an enormous wall of water that she'd pulled up from about six miles down below the face of the earth.

It seemed that their friend had powers that Zelana could not even imagine, although she was almost positive that their friend was using the Dreamers to assist her.

The more Zelana thought about it, the more certain she became that Eleria's flood and Yaltar's twin volcanos had *also* originated in the mind and imagination of 'unknown friend.'

The involvement of the Dreamers had been confirmed when the children's shared vision had mentioned 'a fire unlike any fire we have ever seen,' which had produced the blue inferno that had obliterated what had almost certainly been an entire hatch of the Vlagh.

That, of course, brought Aracia's idiotic attempt to conceal Lillabeth's Dream right out into the open. Aracia had always been obsessed with her own divinity, but now – probably because of the overdone adoration of those assorted indolents who had identified themselves as her clergy – Aracia's mind had begun to slip, and she seemed to be convinced that she was now the most important creature in the entire universe. Her absurd attempt to conceal Lillabeth's Dream had been a clear indication that sister Aracia's mind was starting to come apart.

The more that Zelana thought about it, though, the more she remembered that Aracia had *always* been more than a little unwilling to go to sleep and relinquish her Domain to Enalla. It seemed that deep down, Zelana's sister *hated* Enalla. The length of their sleep-cycle made change inevitable. Zelana ruefully recalled the time in the distant past when she'd awakened to find her Domain covered with ice that must have been at least two miles deep. It had taken Dahlaine weeks to explain *that* to Zelana's satisfaction. He'd assured her that the inevitable thaw had already begun, but it had been almost five centuries before the ice was gone, and Zelana's Domain didn't look at all the way it had when she'd drifted off to sleep. Perhaps even more disturbing had been the fact that the creatures she'd come to know in her previous cycle were all gone, and strange new animals had arrived to replace them. Dahlaine had used the term 'extinction,' and that had chilled Zelana all the way down to her bones. She'd had almost no contact with Aracia during that particular cycle, but she was almost positive that her sister had somehow twisted things around in her mind so that she could blame Enalla for those eons of ice and the disappearance of almost all of the creatures that had been present in her Domain when she'd gone to sleep.

Something like that *was* the sort of thing Aracia would do.

Zelana was growing more and more weary now, and she'd be more than willing to hand the responsibilities of the Domain of the West to Balacenia – the adult version of Eleria – but she was almost positive that Aracia wouldn't see things that way at all, *and* her priesthood was probably in a state of near-panic by now. Whether they liked it or not, Aracia *would* go to sleep very soon, and Enalla would replace her. Zelana had caught a few hints from Eleria that Enalla – the *real* version of Lillabeth – had some plans that Aracia's priests wouldn't like very much at all.

'It might almost be worth staying awake long enough to watch,' she murmured to herself. '*Almost*,' she added, 'but not quite.' As closely as she could determine, 'sleep-time' was no more than a few months away. She'd long since decided that the pink grotto on the Isle of Thurn would be the place where she'd sleep this time. The pink dolphins would sing her to sleep, and she might even have dreams of her own this time – dreams of a Land of Dhrall without a Vlagh, and a land where her friends did not grow old and pass away, and where she could sing and write poetry, and where it was always spring and the flowers never wilted. Now *that* might be the best of dreams.

'I *thought* I could feel your presence here, dear sister,' Dahlaine said as he joined Zelana on the balcony over the 'lumpy map' of his Domain. 'You seem to be troubled. What's bothering you so much?'

'Aracia, of course,' Zelana replied. 'I think her mind is slipping even more than it was when she tried to conceal Lillabeth's Dream. I wish that there was some way that we could put her to sleep a few months early this time. Then we could all concentrate on the Vlagh and stop worrying about our sister.'

'It probably *would* make things a lot easier.'

'What *is* it about Aracia that makes her start to go to pieces at the end of every cycle?' Zelana demanded. 'I was thinking back, and as closely as I can remember, Aracia's never once gone off to sleep without fighting it every step of the way. Why does she *do* that?'

Dahlaine shrugged. 'Inferiority, most likely. When you include our alternates, there are eight of us altogether, and as closely as I've been able to determine, our alternates trade off authority in the same way that we do. That suggests that Aracia's the dominant one for only twenty-five thousand years. Then she has to wait for a hundred and seventy-five eons for dominance to return. For some reason, she just can't *stand* that. She yearns to be at the center of the entire universe. If I remember correctly – and I usually do – the last time she was dominant, she literally wallowed in her position. Of course there weren't any developed humans around back then, so *she* was the only one around who could adore her, but as I remember, her self-adoration was more than a little extreme.'

Zelana smiled. 'Maybe you and I should join Veltan when our next waking cycle rolls around. I'm sure he was just trying to make a joke of it – we all know how much Veltan enjoys jokes – but he told me on one occasion that he might just go back and camp out on the moon when Aracia's next cycle of dominance comes along, and I think he was about half-serious when he said it.'

'That's our baby brother for you. Any time responsibility comes along, Veltan runs away.' Dahlaine scratched his cheek. 'It probably wouldn't have made much difference in eons past, but there are humans in our various Domains now. I don't know about *you*, dear sister, but I will *not* permit Aracia to run roughshod over the people of *my* Domain.'

'You almost sound like you're thinking about declaring war on our sister.'

'I'd hardly call it a war, Zelana. Aracia's people are supposed to spend every waking moment adoring her, so they wouldn't pose much of a threat.'

'You're putting our sister in the same category as holy – but crazy – Azakan of the Atazak Nation of your own Domain, big brother,' Zelana said. Then she frowned. 'There *are* quite a few similarities, though, aren't there?'

'Except that Aracia actually *has* the power to make things happen. Poor Azakan spent most of his time ordering the earth and sky to obey him, but I don't think they paid very much attention. Aracia, however, has a certain amount of power, so she *can* make things happen if she feels the need.'

'Maybe so, but none of us are permitted to *use* that power if killing things is going to be involved. If Aracia steps over that line, she'll probably vanish right then and there,' Zelana suggested. 'And if *Aracia* vanishes, will *we* still be here? There's a linkage between the four of us, Dahlaine, and if *one* of us ceases to exist, isn't it quite possible that we'll *all* just vanish?'

'You're starting to give me a headache, Zelana.'

'At least it's still there to ache, mighty brother.'

'I think we've had *one* stroke of good luck, Zelana. Your pirate chief has persuaded Commander Narasan not to just pack up and go home. We're going to need forts in Long-Pass, and when someone says "forts," he's usually talking about Trogites. Did *you* have anything to do with Sorgan's little scheme?'

'No, big brother. As closely as I can determine, Hook-Beak came up with that all by himself. Of course, the likelihood that he'll be able to swindle a lot of gold out of Aracia probably played a large part in his decision, but right up beside his greed is his friendship for Narasan. He'll keep Aracia so flustered that she probably won't even remember that Narasan exists. He'll go on down to Aracia's absurdly overdone temple and persuade our none too bright sister that he'll be more than happy to defend her – *if* she'll give him enough gold.'

'What's he going to defend her *against*?' Dahlaine asked. 'The servants of the Vlagh will be coming down Long-Pass, so they won't be anywhere *near* Aracia's temple.'

Zelana smiled. 'If I know Sorgan – and I *do* – he'll come up with ways to keep Aracia – and her clergy – so terrified that they won't even *think* about sending anybody up Long-Pass to pester Narasan while he's building forts.'

It wasn't much later when the door to Dahlaine's map room opened slightly, and Eleria looked in. 'Ah, *there* you are, Beloved,' she said to Zelana. 'We should have guessed that you'd be in here conferring with dear old Grey-Beard.'

'Mind your manners, Eleria,' Zelana chided her Dreamer.

'I'm sorry, Old Grey-Beard,' Eleria said with one of her mischievous grins. 'We've been looking for you and the Beloved for hours now.'

'We?' Dahlaine asked curiously.

'Big-Me and I. Mother wants us to talk with you.'

'Mother?' Zelana asked, feeling suddenly baffled.

'We *all* have a mother, you know, Beloved. Big-Me can explain it much better than I can, I'm sure.' Then Eleria came on inside the large room, and immediately behind her was an extremely beautiful lady.

Dahlaine gasped. 'What are you *doing*, Balacenia?' he demanded. 'You're not supposed to be awake yet.'

'Grow up, Dahlaine,' the lady replied. 'Your little game almost tore the world apart. We've had a lot of trouble smoothing things over, and we're not even supposed to be awake yet.'

Zelana was staring at the lady. 'Are you *really*—' she almost choked at that point.

'Yes, Beloved, I *am* your alternate. Our Domain is still under your control, however. I promise that I won't tamper – unless Mother tells me – us – to.' She put her hand on Eleria's shoulder.

'This can be terribly confusing sometimes. This is Little-Me. You know her as Eleria, which is sort of all right, I suppose. She makes me laugh quite often, and laughter's good for the soul – or so I've been told. There *is* something I've been curious about, though. Where in the world did she come up with her hugs and kisses ploy? She has poor Vash so confused that he doesn't know exactly what to do.'

Zelana suddenly smiled. 'The idea came to Eleria back in the pink grotto when she was very, very young. She can kiss a pink dolphin into submission in no time at all.' Then she looked rather closely at Balacenia, her alternate. 'The resemblances are definitely there, Balacenia. You *are*, in fact, a grown-up version of Eleria the Dreamer. How is it that the two of you can both be in the same place at the same time?'

'It's just a little complex, Beloved. Actually, we're *not* here at the same time. Actually, I'm not even really here. I'm still sound asleep, and what we're all seeing right now is *my* Dream.'

'That's not possible!' Dahlaine protested.

'Why – and how – am I here, then?' Balacenia demanded. 'Your little game was very clever, Dahlaine, but it got away from you almost right at the beginning. You *thought* that you could step around us with your "infant" hoax, but it started to come apart when Eleria had her first Dream. That was the one when she saw the very beginning of this world. Then, a little later in the Land of Maag she had a variety of Dream that you didn't even anticipate. She had what *we* call a "warning dream," and it was *that* Dream that saved Longbow and his friends from the intentions of the Maag called Kajak. *You* might not have been aware of what that Dream suggested to *us*. Dreams can be warnings as well as predictions.'

'That *did* startle me just a bit,' Dahlaine admitted. 'I'd sort of believed that *I* might have some control over the Dreams, but the children keep slipping around me.'

'Actually, it's Mother who's guiding the Dreamers. She picked up your little game, and she's doing things with it that you couldn't even imagine.'

'Mother?' Dahlaine sounded startled. 'We don't *have* a mother.'

'Where did we come from, then?' Balacenia demanded.

'You'll really like her, Dahlaine,' Eleria said. 'She can do all kinds of fun things. She was the one who took me down under the sea so that I could pick up my pink pearl. That's what started all this, remember?'

'She's the mother of the whole universe, Dahlaine,' Balacenia added, 'and she's more than a little peeved with you right now. The outlanders are all right, I suppose, but Mother was – and still is – dealing with it in her own way.'

'That will do, Balacenia,' a melodious voice came through the open doorway. 'Why don't you let *me* deal with this?' Then a misty sort of form that seemed to be pure light came through the open doorway. 'What were you thinking of when you hired all those out-landers to come here and fight this war for you, Dahlaine?'

'You *do* know that we have limitations, don't you?' Dahlaine demanded. 'Now that I think about it, if you're who Balacenia says you are, *you're* probably the one who came up with them. You may have forgotten, but we aren't permitted to kill things – even when they're attacking us. We needed armies, so we went out into the world to hire outlanders to do the killing for us.'

'That particular limitation might just be a little outdated,' the glowing presence conceded. 'Right at first, there were very few living things here, and we didn't want to lose any of them – at least not until the populations had grown to the point that extinction was no longer a distinct possibility. When the incursions by the Creatures of the Wasteland began, I was going to take care of it myself, but before I could even start, the whole Land of Dhrall was crawling with outlanders. You've got to learn to trust me, Dahlaine.'

'Longbow suggested something you might want to consider, though,' Zelana stepped in. 'The assorted outlanders *are* helping us to hold back the Creatures of the Wasteland, but Longbow seems to think that it's much more important that the more greedy out-landers come to realize that the people of the Land of Dhrall are quite capable of making life very unpleasant for *any* invaders. The outlanders are helping, but they're also learning. The greed of the Amarite Church down in the Trogite Empire was almost legendary, but *you* dealt with that in a way that advised *all* outlanders that an attempted invasion of our part of the world could be a ghastly mistake.'

'And your blue fire in Crystal Gorge made it more obvious,' Dahlaine added. 'Nobody in his right mind walks into fire. Some of the more greedy outlanders might *want* to come back, but I don't think they will.' He hesitated. 'You seem to be very attached to us, for some reason,' he said rather carefully.

'You *are* my children,' the glowing form replied, 'and I *will* protect you. You've come a long, long way, but you might want to go back a bit and have a look at where – and when – this began.'

Zelana's mind suddenly reeled as memories came rushing back from so far in the distant past that there was no word for that many years. The suggestion of the hazy figure of glowing light had seemed to set off bells inside Zelana's mind.

Dahlaine's eyes suddenly went very wide as – evidently – the same memories came flooding over him.

'All in all, you did quite well, my son,' Misty Lady continued. 'Your notion of the Dreamers was brilliant, and it's worked almost perfectly – except that you'll have to come up with a way to persuade the Dreamers to reunite with their previous identities. Things are just a little touchy this time, however, so I want all of you children to back away and let *me* deal with the situation in Aracia's Domain. It's almost reached the point that she'd rather die than hand her Domain over to Enalla. We've *got* to get her under control, because she's getting very close to total insanity. If she crosses that line, we'll lose her, and that will lead to a disaster – not immediately maybe – but if she's a raving lunatic when she wakes up from her sleep-cycle, the entire Land of Dhrall will be at risk – and *that* risk will make the invasion of the Creatures of the Wasteland look like some child's game by comparison.'

2

Zelana was certain that it was just after sunrise when the commanders of the outlander forces, led by the bleak-faced Longbow, came through the door and out onto the balcony that encircled Dahlaine's map room.

'The map seems to have changed a bit,' Longbow said, looking down at the map Dahlaine had put in place after Balacenia and the strange, mist-covered figure of 'Mother' had left.

Dahlaine shrugged. 'We've finished here in my part of the Land of Dhrall,' he explained, 'so I laid out a "lumpy map" of sister Aracia's Domain. Ordinarily, we'd have relied on Aracia for a map, but her view of her Domain is just a bit vague, since she almost never leaves her temple.'

'Being worshiped *would* probably take quite a bit of time,' Sorgan Hook-Beak said, peering down at the well-illuminated map. 'Just exactly where *is* this "temple-town" that's got everybody so worked up?'

Dahlaine reached out with his hand, and a bright beam of light came from his forefinger and illuminated a spot on the representation of the east coast.

'That's a useful idea there, Lord Dahlaine,' Sorgan said,

'particularly when we're all standing ten feet or so above the map.'

'It *does* seem to work fairly well,' Dahlaine replied modestly.

'And where's this "Long-Pass" that everybody keeps on talking about?'

Dahlaine's glowing little spot of light moved along the eastern edge of the map to a sizeable replica of a bay with a fairly wide river running down to it.

'Then the river's not in any way connected to your sister's temple-town?' Sorgan asked.

Dahlaine shook his head. 'The east coast of the Land of Dhrall gets some savage floods almost every year,' he explained. 'Aracia didn't want her temple destroyed that often, so she had her servants build it farther south where there aren't any major rivers coming down out of the mountains. The ground's sort of marshy, but Aracia's workers laid in a substantial base before they started construction.'

'How long ago was it when they built the temple?' Keselo asked.

'Eight – maybe ten – centuries ago, wouldn't you say, Zelana?' Dahlaine asked.

'You couldn't prove that by me, brother mine,' Zelana replied. 'I was living in my grotto on the Isle of Thurn then.'

'Do all those priests who worship your sister plant crops of any kind near the temple?' Sorgan asked.

Dahlaine shook his head. 'The farmers of Aracia's Domain deliver large amounts of food to keep most of our sister's priests quite fat, at least.'

'Fat seems to show up quite often in the world of priests,' Longbow observed.

'Professional hazard, wouldn't you say, big brother?' Zelana suggested. 'Priests spend much of their time stuffing food into their mouths.'

'And that makes them so fat that their hearts wear out and they fall over dead,' Dahlaine added.

'Now *there's* an idea,' Rabbit said. 'If we just happened to pile twenty or thirty tons of food on the steps of sister Aracia's temple, her priests would eat themselves to death inside a week.'

'I *like* that notion, brother,' Zelana said. 'We wouldn't violate our limitations by providing food for dear Aracia's priests, would we? And if they ate too much and fell over dead, it wouldn't be *our* fault, would it?'

Dahlaine squinted at the ceiling. 'You might want to take that up with Mother, Zelana. If we feed Aracia's priests too much and they die as a result, wouldn't that almost be the same as poisoning them?'

'Spoilsport,' Zelana grumbled. 'Can you imagine how much screaming would come from Aracia's temple if she woke up one morning to discover that all of her priests had died during the night?'

'We'll keep the idea in reserve, dear sister,' Dahlaine said. 'Let's push on, though.' He looked at Narasan. 'Who would you say is the head of sister Aracia's priesthood?'

'They call him Takal Bersla,' Narasan replied, 'and he's almost as fat as Adnari Estarg of the Amarite Church was – before that overgrown spider had him for lunch. Bersla has made a career out of oration. He spends hours every day telling your sister how holy she is, and Aracia's almost paralyzed by Bersla's overdone speeches. Padan kept track one day not long after we'd arrived at Aracia's temple, and Bersla talked to your sister for six straight hours. Then he ate lunch – a lunch that would have overstuffed four or five normal people – and then he stood up and orated for another five or six hours. The man's a talking machine, but your sister can't seem to get enough of all that tedious adoration.'

'It sounds to me like she's getting even worse, Dahlaine,' Zelana observed. 'She drinks in adoration in almost the same way that a drunkard pours beer into his mouth.'

'It's not a good sign, Lord Dahlaine,' Sorgan said. 'If her mind has slipped *that* far, getting her attention might be a little difficult.'

'Not necessarily, cousin,' Torl disagreed. 'If this Bersla priest is the main adorer in Lady Aracia's temple, and he wound up dead some morning, you could probably get her immediate attention.'

'Maybe so, Torl,' Sorgan agreed, 'but how do we know that he'll die at any time in the near future?'

Torl slid his hand down into the top of his boot and pulled out a long, slender dagger. 'I can almost guarantee that, cousin,' he said, flourishing his dagger.

'It *has* got some possibilities, Lord Dahlaine,' Sorgan said. 'If your sister's sitting on her throne some morning and several of her priests drag the body of her favorite underling into her throne room to show her that somebody – or some *thing* – slipped into her temple and butchered her head priest, she'd go to pieces. Then, if I tell her that the stab-wounds in Bersla's body were almost certainly caused by the teeth of one of the bug-people, she'd start paying very close attention to anything I said. I could feed her all kinds of wild stories about bug-people creeping around through the halls of her temple killing off her priests by the dozens.'

'Wouldn't she demand to see the bodies?'

Sorgan shrugged. 'If she wants to look at bodies, we'll *show* her bodies. Torl might have to sharpen his dagger six or eight times a day, but that's all right.'

'Thanks, cousin,' Torl said sourly.

'Don't mention it, Torl,' Sorgan replied with a broad grin.

*　　*　　*

'I'd say that the separation of Long-Pass from Aracia's temple will work out very well for you,' Longbow suggested to Sorgan and Narasan a bit later. 'You can sail on down to that river-mouth, and those of you who'll be going on up Long-Pass can go ashore while Sorgan goes on down to pacify Aracia. She and her servants won't even know that you're anywhere in that pass, so she won't be issuing commands for you to rush on down south to defend *her*.'

'That's a very good idea, Longbow,' Narasan agreed. 'I'm sure that the only thing that interests Bersla will be the defense of the temple. He doesn't care at all about what happens to the ordinary people of Aracia's Domain. He wouldn't so much as turn a hair if all the rest of Aracia's Domain was overrun by the bug-people.'

'There's a thought, Captain Hook-Beak,' Keselo said. 'If you send out some scouts and they report back that the bug-men are eating all of the peasants, the priests will be afraid to come out of the temple and take a look for themselves. They'll hole up inside the temple itself – almost as if they were prisoners.'

'It *would* keep them out from underfoot,' Sorgan agreed. Then he looked at his friend Narasan. 'You've been there, but I haven't,' he said. 'Did you see anything at all like building material near the temple? Rocks or logs or anything like that? If we're going to go through the motions of *looking* like we're building a defensive wall of some kind, we'll need to put up something that *looks* like a fort.'

'You're not going to find anything like rocks – or even logs – in marshy country, Sorgan,' Narasan replied.

'Ah, well,' Sorgan said, 'the temple's there anyway. It shouldn't be *too* hard to knock it down so that we can build a fort.'

'Our sister will come apart at the seams if you do that, Sorgan,' Zelana told him.

'And you'll be able to hear her priests screaming from ten miles away,' Dahlaine added.

'Not after my scouts come back and report that the bug-people are eating the farmers alive, I won't,' Sorgan disagreed. 'When the fat ones hear *that*, they might even offer to help. Just how big would you say that temple is, Narasan?'

'About a mile or so square,' Narasan replied.

'You're not serious!'

'The priesthood's been building Aracia's temple for centuries, Sorgan,' Dahlaine said.

'You should be able to build quite a wall with that much stone, Sorgan,' the warrior queen Trenicia said.

'The screaming's likely to go on for a long time, though,' Veltan added.

'Not if the stories my scouts bring back from the countryside are awful enough, it won't,' Sorgan disagreed. 'If the priests hear about a bug that's twelve feet tall and rips out a man's liver when it gets hungry, they'll run for cover and tell us to do whatever's necessary to hold back the monsters – *and* they'll be hiding so far back in the temple that they won't see daylight for at least a month.'

'I *like* it!' Narasan said enthusiastically.

'That's the way we'll do 'er then, old friend,' Sorgan replied with a broad grin.

Zelana smiled. The unlikely-seeming friendship between Sorgan and Narasan seemed to be growing stronger and stronger, and now it appeared that they'd do almost anything to help each other.

While their men were preparing for the long march to the east coast of Dahlaine's part of the Land of Dhrall, Sorgan, Narasan and several others spent most of their time carefully studying the map.

'I'm going to need those ships as soon as you unload your men down in Aracia's temple-town, Sorgan,' Narasan reminded his friend. 'I'll still have more than half of my army sitting on that beach on the east coast.'

'No problem,' Sorgan replied. 'The ships would only clutter up the harbor of temple-town anyway. Then too, if Aracia's priests look at your ships *too* long, they might decide that they want a navy so that they can go out to sea to preach to the fish.' He frowned slightly. 'Do the people down there actually call their city "temple-town"? Most places have fancier names.'

'The priests – and Aracia herself – never refer to the place as a town, Sorgan,' Narasan explained. 'The people who live out beyond the walls might have a different name, I suppose, but the people you'll be dealing with just speak of "the temple." It's entirely possible, I guess, that *most* of the priests aren't even aware of the buildings and houses outside the temple walls. For them, the temple is the whole world.'

'That's stupid,' Sorgan said.

'I think that's the word most people use when they're talking about *any* priesthood, Sorgan,' Narasan said with a faint smile.

Longbow had been studying the map, and he gestured to Sorgan.

The Maag captain joined him. 'Do you see anything that might go wrong?' he asked.

'Not *so* far, friend Sorgan. It just came to me, though, that most of *your* fleet is still sitting in the bay over there.'

'They'd *better* be,' Sorgan replied. 'I sent Skell over there to keep a tight grip on them.'

'I'm sure that more archers will be very useful once we're in

Long-Pass, and it's only a few days south of where your ships are anchored to the village of Old-Bear, where hundreds of archers are sitting around telling stories to each other. If Skell picked them up and carried them on up to that fishing village on the coast, they'd only be a few days behind us, and they'll probably reach the upper mouth of Long-Pass before the bug-people come storming out of the Wasteland.'

'That's not a bad idea at all, Longbow,' Sorgan approved. 'It'll keep the sailors busy, and it'll give Narasan some help when he's likely to need it.'

'I definitely approve,' Narasan said, 'and I'll take all the help I can get.'

Longbow continued to stare at Dahlaine's replication of Eastern Dhrall. 'There's this range of low, rounded hills running down along the east side of the Land of Dhrall. I think that when we reach that range, I'll lead the archers of Tonthakan on down that way, and Old-Bear's archers won't be *too* far behind us. We'll most likely be at the upper end of Long-Pass even before Narasan's fort-builders get there. We can make sure that there won't be any surprises for the Trogites when they go up there to build forts.'

'I'll get word to Skell,' Sorgan said. Then he looked over at his friend. 'How many forts were you planning to build?' he asked Narasan.

'As many as the Vlagh gives me time to build,' Narasan replied. 'I'd go for one fort every mile or so down that pass if I've got enough time. The bug-people don't like forts, so I'll make things as unpleasant for them as I possibly can.'

'How are you going to keep the bugs from smoking you out again like they did down in Crystal Gorge?' Rabbit asked.

'Veltan and I can take care of that if it's necessary,' Dahlaine said, 'but I don't think the bugs will try that again. The prevailing wind down there comes in out of the east, and if they tried greasy smoke again, that wind would blow it right back in their faces.'

'The Vlagh almost has to be desperate this time, big brother,' Veltan said. 'The other three regions have been blocked off, so this is the only way left. If she doesn't win *this* time, she'll spend the rest of eternity trapped out there in the Wasteland. She'll do almost anything to get her servants past you.'

'We'll have to make sure that she doesn't succeed then, little brother,' Dahlaine said quite firmly.

It was somewhat later, and all of the outlanders had gone to their beds. Zelana and her brothers lingered in the map room, however. All three of them were quite certain that they'd soon be getting more instructions. Longbow had also remained behind, but he didn't say exactly why.

It was perhaps midnight when the door opened and Balacenia and her glowing, mist-covered companion joined them on the balcony. 'One of you will have to go to sister Aracia's temple with Sorgan,' the misty lady told them.

'I'll take care of that,' Veltan volunteered. 'Aracia thinks of me as an immature creature without much of a brain, so she won't pay any attention to me.'

'That's not a bad idea, Veltan,' the lady said. 'Keep a very close eye on Aracia. She's right on the verge of going to pieces, and if her brain flies apart, you'll need to tell Zelana and Dahlaine about it. The three of you might need to step on her to keep her from breaking the rules. We *don't* want to lose her.'

Longbow was standing off to one side, and he had a peculiarly startled expression on his face.

Then, after Balacenia and her glowing companion had left the large room, the usually grim-faced archer suddenly began to laugh.

'What's so funny, Longbow?' Zelana asked.

'Nothing all that important,' he replied. But then he laughed again.

Zelana found that to be very irritating, but she wasn't sure just exactly why.

3

Early the next morning the assorted armies were preparing to march, and Longbow joined Zelana near the mouth of Dahlaine's cave. 'It might save a bit of time if Chief Old-Bear knows that the Maag longships are coming,' he suggested.

Zelana smiled. 'You'd like to have me fly on down there to let him know, I take it?'

'If it's not too much trouble,' Longbow replied.

'And if it is?'

'Do it anyway.'

'Longbow!' Zelana exclaimed. 'Are you actually giving me orders now?'

'Let's just call it a strong suggestion.'

'That means the same thing, doesn't it?'

'Approximately, yes, but it's more polite.'

'Things might go more smoothly for you if you'd learn how to smile.'

'The air's very cold right now, Zelana,' he replied. 'Smiling when it's cold is hard on one's teeth.'

'Did Dahlaine have time to take a look at that worn-down mountain range off to the east for you?'

Longbow nodded. 'His thunderbolt took him on down there at first light this morning,' he said. 'When he came back, he told us that we wouldn't have any trouble.'

'Who are you taking with you when you veer off from the main army?'

'Mostly the local hunters,' he replied. 'Kathlak will lead the Tonthankans, and Two-Hands will bring the Matans. Ekial and the Malavi horse-soldiers will go with us as well. Actually, that was Narasan's suggestion. He's going to need his ships to carry his army down to the mouth of Long-Pass, and the Malavi don't like to ride in ships. They'll probably be more useful at the upper end of Long-Pass anyway.'

'Things should go quite smoothly for you and your people,' Zelana said. 'That's unless you get caught in a blizzard, of course.'

'I think your older brother's going to take care of that,' Longbow replied. 'He's very good at dealing with the weather.'

'How far is it from where you and your men will turn south to the upper end of Long-Pass?' Zelana asked.

'If Dahlaine's map is accurate, it's about a hundred and sixty miles,' Longbow said. 'I'm sure we'll be able to cover thirty miles a day, and that puts us about five and a half days out. We'll be there before Narasan's ships drop him off at the lower end of the pass. I'm sure that we'll be able to keep the Creatures of the Wasteland out of the upper end of the pass.'

'That's all that really matters, I suppose,' Zelana said.

Just then Sorgan and Narasan came out of Dahlaine's cave. 'Don't worry about a thing, Narasan,' Sorgan was saying. 'I'll keep Lady Zelana's sister so busy that the notion of causing you any problems won't even cross her mind.'

'I appreciate that, my friend,' Narasan replied. 'If I never *see*

Lady Zelana's sister again, it'll be about six weeks too soon.'

Sorgan grinned. 'The nice part of this is that she's going to *pay* me to keep her out of your hair.'

Then Eleria's adult person came out of the cave with the warrior queen Trenicia. 'Are we almost ready, Beloved?' Balacenia asked Zelana.

'Beloved?' Zelana asked, slightly startled.

'A lot of Eleria's been rubbing off on me,' Balacenia replied.

'She's good at that.'

Trenicia had joined Narasan and Sorgan, and Balacenia stepped closer to Zelana. 'I've been catching a few hints that Trenicia's becoming very attached to Narasan,' she said quietly.

'She *wants* him,' Zelana replied. 'I spoke with her about that after she and Narasan walked out on Aracia. In many ways Trenicia doesn't think – or behave – like a woman. I made a few suggestions, and she seems to be following them.'

'Do you really think she'll catch him?'

'Probably. She can be quite charming when she sets her mind to it.' Zelana smiled. 'It might sound a bit peculiar, but I've noticed over the years that women who want to catch a man use themselves as bait. I don't know if Trenicia's managed to hook Narasan yet, but it probably won't take her much longer.' Then Zelana yawned. 'Sorry,' she said. 'I'm getting to the point that I can barely keep my eyes open.'

'I'm sure that this silly war will end very soon,' Balacenia said, 'and when it does, Eleria and I'll take you home and put you to bed.' Then she paused and her expression suddenly became very, very familiar. 'Won't that be neat?' she said, using one of Eleria's favorite remarks.

Zelana laughed and took her alternate in her arms. 'Eleria calls this a "hug",' she explained.

'Yes,' Balacenia agreed, 'and now I see why she likes them so much. Any time you feel like hugging, Beloved, I'll be right here.'

Zelana laughed, and then she yawned again.

THE JOURNEY

1

Sub-Commander Andar was more than a little grateful that Chief Two-Hands of the Matan Nation had given him one of the thickly-furred bison-hide cloaks as Commander Narasan's army began the march from Mount Shrak to the east coast of the Land of Dhrall. It was early winter now, and it was bitterly cold in the grassland of Matakan. Andar had grown up in Kaldacin, the capital city of the Trogite Empire, and sometimes during the winter months there it grew chilly enough to put a thin layer of ice on the nearby ponds, but Andar had never before seen a lake or pond that had been frozen solid from the surface all the way down to the bottom in a huge block of solid ice. 'How do you people find water to drink when it's this cold, Tlindan?' he asked one of the nearby Matans.

'There's quite a bit of water in that pond,' Tlindan replied.

'It's frozen solid,' Andar pointed out.

'You'd have to melt it,' Tlindan said. 'Most of the time we melt snow when we need water, but ice *will* melt if you're really thirsty and there's no snow nearby.' The fur-cloaked Matan squinted across the browned grass toward the horizon. 'We don't usually spend much time outdoors during the winter. We sort of hole up in our lodges instead. If a man inside his lodge keeps his fire going, it's fairly warm inside, and a pot-full of snow will melt down in an hour or so. Ice takes longer, but it *will* melt – eventually. Most of us don't care all that much for ice. It takes quite a while to melt, even if the lodge is very warm.'

'How do you melt it when you're out in the open and it's very cold?'

'The best way I've found is to chip the ice with a hand-axe. If you tried to use an axe with a handle, you'd probably break it up into small pieces. You want very tiny chips of ice, since bigger ones take longer to melt. Then, when you've got what looks like enough, you scoop them into a pot. Then you scrape together a fair sized heap of dried grass, put your pot in the middle of the heap and then set fire to the grass. You'll have water to drink in almost no time at all.'

'Isn't the water a bit hot for drinking?'

Tlindan shrugged. 'Add some more ice to cool it down. In the winter-time, I sort of like to drink warm water. Your stomach will spread the warmth around, and you'll feel better all over – except for your feet, of course. Everybody's feet are cold in the winter.'

'How can *anybody* live in a place like this?'

Tlindan spread out his hands. 'The hunting's very good, and winter doesn't really last all that long. We don't usually spend much time out of our lodges in the winter-time. It's a very good time to catch up on your sleep. Twelve-hour naps are sort of nice when there's nothing going on outside. A man who takes twelve-hour naps feels all rested when spring arrives.'

Andar looked up at the grey clouds rolling off toward the east. 'Is it cloudy like this all winter long?' he asked the native.

'Fairly often, yes. Dahlaine's playing with the clouds this year, though. Usually we get blizzards here during the winter season.'

'Blizzards?'

'Heavy snowstorms. A good blizzard can put twelve feet of snow down in about a day and a half. When that happens, *nobody* goes outside. They're not really *bad* things, though. When the snow melts off in the spring, the grass gets *lots* of water, and it grows very fast. That gives the bison herds plenty to eat, and they're nice and fat when we go hunting. Weather works *for* you, if you know how to get along with it.' Then he squinted up at the sky. 'We'll probably have to stop and set up camp fairly soon. It'll be dark before much longer.'

'It's just barely past noon,' Andar protested.

'That's one of the things you should know about the north country. In the winter-time up here, the days are only six or seven hours long, and nighttime comes very fast.'

Andar frowned. 'We can talk more later,' he said. 'I think I'd better go warn Commander Narasan that night's almost here.' He walked rapidly toward the front of the column. 'I think we might have a bit of a problem, Commander,' he said.

'Now what?' Narasan demanded in a peevish-sounding voice.

'It's going to start getting dark before long. One of the Matans warned me about that. We aren't going to have daylight for much longer.'

'It's only a few hours past noon, Andar.'

'The Matan told me that there's no more than six or seven hours of daylight up here in the winter-time.'

Narasan scowled. 'I think we'd better go have a chat with Lord Dahlaine, Andar. We've got a long way to go to reach the east coast, and we're going to need longer days – or it'll be summer before we reach the coast.'

*   *   *

'It's not really all that much of a problem, Narasan,' Dahlaine said. 'I'm sure you remember my toy sun. She – and sister Zelana's fogbank – helped us quite a bit down in Veltan's Domain.'

'I should have remembered that,' Narasan said. 'How many extra hours a day would you say she'll be able to give us?'

'How many do you want? She enjoys putting out light, so she'll give you as many extra hours of light as you want.'

Narasan squinted across the frozen grassland. 'She puts out heat as well as light, doesn't she?'

'She kept the inside of my cave warm and cozy when Ashad was just a baby.'

'That might even be more valuable than light,' Narasan said. Then he looked at Dahlaine. 'This isn't really any of my business,' he said, 'but you don't feel hot and cold in the same way that we do, do you?'

'I know that they exist,' Dahlaine replied. 'I think I see where you're going with this, Narasan. It's not a bad idea, now that you mention it. If my pet gives you and your men light *and* heat, you'll be able to go much farther each day, won't you?'

'I'd say at least an extra five miles,' Narasan estimated. 'Possibly even an extra seven or eight.' Then he winced. 'That *might* just disturb my men quite a bit, though.'

'I didn't quite follow you there, Narasan.'

'Ten miles a day is one of the articles of faith in a Trogite army, Lord Dahlaine. Individual soldiers could exceed that, I'm sure, but when they're marching together, ten miles is the limit. Anything any farther is viewed as an abomination. It's a custom, and we Trogites are big on customs.' He shrugged. 'It actually grows out of the inevitable delays that keep cropping up when you're moving a hundred thousand men.'

'Wouldn't you say that "rest time" has something to do with the ten miles a day limitation, Commander?' Andar suggested.

'Rest time?' Dahlaine asked.

'Another custom, Lord Dahlaine,' Narasan explained. 'We're expected to give our men a quarter of each hour spent marching to catch their breath. It makes a certain amount of sense in mountain country, but it's a bit foolish on flat land.' His eyes hardened. 'I think it might just be time to abolish that foolishness. If we can add an extra few miles to each day's march, we'll almost certainly reach the east coast of your Domain several days earlier than we'd originally planned. I'd say that it's worth a try. Then too, if it's warmer, we won't have to worry too much about blizzards, will we?'

Dahlaine grinned. 'It might make them a little sulky,' he said, 'but I think I'll be able to make them quit pouting. Let's see how far my pet can go. I don't think we'll want mid-summer, but early autumn might be sort of nice.'

'Whatever you think best, Lord Dahlaine,' Narasan said.

'You're very good at putting all sorts of things together, Narasan,' Dahlaine observed.

'That's what an army-commander is supposed to do, Lord Dahlaine. Our people come up with all kinds of ideas, and we're supposed to fit them together to construct a plan that might work. There are many people in my army who are much more clever than I am, but that doesn't hurt my feelings very much. *My* job involves putting their assorted ideas together to come up with something that'll work and won't get *too* many of my men killed.'

'Aren't you just a little bit out of uniform, Padan?' Andar asked his friend as they set out early the following day.

'I'm supposed to look like a Maag,' Padan explained. 'Narasan suggested it to Sorgan. The Maags aren't too good at defending cities – burning, yes; defending, no. I'll stay in the background so Aracia's priesthood won't recognize me, and I'll give Sorgan details when he needs them. The idea is to have us put something together that'll *look* enough like a fort to deceive the priests into believing that we've come up with something impregnable. I'm not as good as Gunda when it comes to building forts, but I should be able to come up with something that *looks* like a fort.'

'Right up until the wind starts blowing,' Andar said.

'Be nice,' Padan said. Then he scratched at his cheek.

'Problems?' Andar asked.

'Sorgan suggested that I should let my whiskers grow. He said that most Maags wear beards, and if I want to *look* Maagish, I should get a bit more shaggy. He didn't bother to tell me that the thing itches all the time.'

'Maags might not notice that, Padan,' Andar replied with a faint smile. 'You'd think that people who live out at sea would bathe more often. I'd almost be willing to bet that the Maags are the native home of fleas and lice.'

'You're in a grumpy sort of mood today, Andar.'

'Homesick, I suppose,' Andar admitted. 'I miss Kaldacin. It's corrupt and it doesn't smell too good, but it *is* home.'

'If Lord Dahlaine's correct, this will be the last war here in the Land of Dhrall. There's only one path left open to the creatures of the Wasteland. Once this last one's closed off, we'll all be able to go on back home and sit around counting all the lovely money we've picked up here.'

'It'll be a lot cleaner now that the Church of Amar has been eliminated,' Andar added. 'I don't know if you noticed the similarities between the priests of "Holy Aracia" and the high-ranking clergymen of the Church of Amar.'

'They're all fat, if that's what you mean,' Padan agreed. 'Did I ever get around to congratulating you for that horror story you foisted off on the fat priest called Bersla?'

'There *was* a certain amount of truth involved, Padan,' Andar protested. 'We've all heard stories about the famines that show up every so often. When people are starving, they *do* sometimes revert to cannibalism – except that they'll eat people who are already dead. I was fairly sure that the prospect of being eaten alive might frighten Bersla enough that he'd start paying attention to what was happening out in the real world.'

'The fact that his hair was standing straight up and his eyes were bulging out of their sockets sort of hints that he was getting your point.'

'We can hope, I suppose. His sense of his own superiority rubbed me the wrong way. He behaves as if the common people of Aracia's Domain were nothing more than cattle whose only purpose in life is to feed *him*, and Aracia's mind has slipped so far that she believes just about anything he ever tells her.'

'I hate to admit this – again—' Padan said, 'but I think Keselo's scheme might be the best one any of us will ever come up with. If Sorgan sends out scouts and they report back that the bug-people are coming and that they're *awful*, I'm fairly sure that all those fat priests will try to take cover, and they'll all be so far down in the basement that they won't have any idea of what's *really* happening. If they're all busy hiding, they won't even *know* that Sorgan's been tearing down certain parts of the temple to build that wall.'

*   *   *

Now that Dahlaine's little toy sun was giving them much more daylight – as well as warmer weather – the combined armies were making much better time than they'd made during that first dreadful day, so they reached the low mountain range off to the east much sooner than any of them had thought possible.

The worn-down range of mountains had a familiar quality that Andar found rather pleasant. In many ways they were very much like the mountains off to the south of Kaldacin, so Andar found them to be quite beautiful. They weren't as rugged and imposing as the mountains in the Domains of Zelana, Veltan and Dahlaine had been. The young scholar, Keselo, had told them that mountains were much like people. As they grew older, their rough edges were worn down by the passing years, and they were much gentler.

'I think this is far enough for today,' Commander Narasan announced. 'Put the men to work setting up camp. We'll be splitting up tomorrow, so it might not be a bad idea to talk things over before we're separated.'

'Good idea,' Dahlaine agreed. 'Longbow told us that he was going to lead the Tonthakans, Matans, and the Malavi horse-soldiers south along this mountain range to the upper end of Long-Pass while the Trogites and Maags go over to the coast to sail south. That's the way we decided to do this back at Mount Shrak, and I don't see any reason to change things.'

'You didn't tell him, I take it,' Ekial the Malavi said to the bleak-faced Longbow.

'I didn't really want to alarm him – or his sister, Zelana,' Longbow replied.

'Alarm?' Zelana asked the archer. 'What are you up to now?'

'I *will* be leading the others, Zelana,' Longbow replied, 'but I'll be quite some distance ahead of them. Kathlak, Ekial, and Two-

Hands know where they're going, so they won't need me around to keep pointing them south. I'll go on ahead and make sure that the creatures of the Wasteland haven't reached these mountains yet. Then I'll go on down Long-Pass to the sea. I'll probably be there when the ships arrive, and I'll be able to pass along anything I've seen to our friends.'

'That's too much of a risk,' Zelana declared. 'You can't just run around by yourself like that.'

'You can come along, if you'd like,' Longbow told her with a faint smile. 'Somebody has to go ahead – somebody who knows enough about the servants of the Vlagh to know what he's looking for. That means *me*, Zelana. I know more about the Creatures of the Wasteland than anybody else does, and I know exactly what I'll have to do to stay out of their sight. I've been doing this for a long, long time, Zelana, so I won't be in any real danger.'

'You're going to insist, I take it?' Zelana said.

'I thought I just did. You worry too much, Zelana. It'll make you old if you're not careful.'

'I'm already old,' she snapped.

'But you don't want it to show, now do you? I'll be just fine, Zelana. I know *what* has to be done and *how* to do it. Nobody else does, so I'll have to do it myself.' He looked around at the others. 'I know that many of you would like to help, but you'd just be in my way. I'll see you down at the mouth of Long-Pass in a few days, my friends,' he said, and then he turned and ran smoothly off to the south. Andar was quite certain that Longbow's decision had grown perhaps more out of his desire to be alone. Longbow didn't really like – or need – other people around him. He was definitely the most solitary man Andar had ever encountered.

2

Andar had been careful to keep his opinion of the warrior queen Trenicia strictly to himself, of course, but she was always there when he needed to speak with the Commander. It wasn't that she ever interfered or anything like that, but just her presence made Andar uncomfortable.

It *might* have been the massive sword she had belted to her waist that disturbed Andar so much. Women were not *supposed* to carry weapons like that. Women were supposed to be soft and gentle – and subservient, of course. It seemed to Andar that Trenicia's very *existence* was a violation of some natural law dating back to the beginning of time.

Of course Andar had never even *heard* of the Isle of Akala until the Trogite fleet had reached the temple of Lady Zelana's sister early last autumn. The notion of a place where women were dominant was so unnatural that Andar was almost positive that it was some kind of hoax. He was quite certain that a *man* was the true leader on the isle, and that Trenicia was nothing more than an elaborate deception.

But she could run for at least a half a day, and her shoulders were even larger than Andar's were. She had all of the characteristics of a warrior – except that she was a woman. Commander

Narasan treated her with respect, and the two of them seemed to get along quite well.

As the army continued the march to the east, Andar continued his private argument with himself. Queen Trenicia wasn't really supposed to be with them – but she was. Queen Trenicia was supposed to be in some fancy palace surrounded by servants who were supposed to respond to her every whim – but she wasn't.

Andar's whole world seemed to be turning upside down, and he didn't like that at all. 'I really wish that we'd stayed home,' he muttered to himself.

They reached the coast several days later, and the Trogite ships were still anchored where they'd been when Commander Narasan's army had disembarked to begin the long march to Mount Shrak.

Then Sorgan Hook-Beak rowed over to the *Victory*, and Narasan was already standing at the rail waiting for him. 'We need to talk, Narasan,' Hook-Beak called.

'Of course,' Narasan replied. 'The weather, maybe?'

'Very funny,' Sorgan said without smiling. 'Can we get down to business?'

'Sorry,' Narasan apologized.

'I've been talking with several of the men who were with you when you arrived at the temple of Lady Zelana's crazy sister. I gather from what your men told me that the priests aren't any too bright. If I was going to be dealing with people who had something beside air between their ears, I *might* be able to get away with an advance force, but from what I've heard, the "Holies" down there wouldn't even know what I was talking about. I'm going to have to make it simple for them by putting my whole army down on the beach at the same time. Then I'll be able to persuade Lady

Zelana's stupid sister that I've got enough men to protect her and her "holy of holies" when the bugs attack her precious temple.'

'*And* to find out how much gold she'll be willing to pay?' Narasan asked.

'That *is* sort of important, Narasan. Anyway, if we agree that putting my entire army ashore will be the best way to go, I'm going to need about a hundred of those wallowing tubs of yours to get me and my people in place.'

'It makes sense, friend Sorgan. As soon as you get your men ashore, though, release those ships. I've got a lot of men who'll still be camped here, and I'm fairly sure I'm going to need them when the Creatures of the Wasteland come storming in.' He looked rather speculatively at his friend. 'Would it bother you if I made a few suggestions about dealing with Lady Zelana's sister?'

'Not one little bit, Narasan. You know her and I don't.'

'First off,' Narasan said, 'push up your price just a bit. Money doesn't mean anything to Aracia, so she probably won't pay any attention. When you talk with her, act sort of arbitrary. Tell her that if she doesn't agree to do things your way, you'll take your men back to the ships and sail away. She *will* pay what you ask and agree to keep her priests from interfering, but agreeing with everything you say will make her feel a bit on the defensive side. You'll need to use any lies or ideas you can think of to keep her that way. If she believes that you've got the upper hand, she'll do just about anything you demand of her. Always be abrupt – and even arbitrary – particularly when you announce that you're going to tear down a major part of her temple to get the material you'll need to build a fort. Don't ask her; *tell* her. Her fat head-priest will probably start screaming as soon as you announce that you're going to dismantle a major part of her temple. I don't know if I'd kill him right there on the spot, but you can make a few threats – draw your sword or hit him in the mouth with your fist. Always keep Aracia off balance if you possibly can.'

'You can be a very nasty fellow when you set your mind to it, old friend,' Sorgan said with a broad grin.

'That's where I made my mistake when *I* was there, friend Sorgan. I avoided "nasty" because I was trying to be polite. "Polite" doesn't work when you're dealing with someone like Aracia. Push her – and keep pushing. Don't give her time to object.'

'A suggestion, if I may?' Andar said, stepping in.

'I'll take all the help that I can get,' Sorgan declared.

'I'd say that Keselo came up with the best answer,' Andar said. 'Pick out the best liars in your army and send them out into the countryside to pretend that they're scouting. When they come back, you'll want them to start telling stories about all the terrible things the bug-people are doing to the ordinary peasants – eating them alive, pulling out their livers, having their eyeballs for dessert – that sort of thing. If Aracia's priesthood is totally terrorized, Aracia will do almost anything you tell her to do.'

'You're even nastier than Narasan,' Sorgan noted.

'I received my training from the best, Captain Hook-Beak,' Andar replied modestly.

'We'll try it your way then,' Sorgan declared. Then he grinned. 'I've got a hunch that I'm going to have a lot more fun than you two will. You'll have to face *real* bugs. All I'll have to do is deal with imaginary ones to make sure that big sister's frightened enough to do just about anything I tell her to do.'

'I think you'll do just fine, friend Sorgan,' Commander Narasan said with an answering grin.

*   *   *

It took several days to load the Maags on board the ships Sorgan had borrowed, and then, when all was ready, the burly Maag joined Narasan and the others on board the *Victory*. 'We're just about ready to start,' he advised. 'If it's all right, I'll go on ahead. It won't take long to unload my men, and then I'll send the ships back here to pick up the rest of Narasan's men and take them on down to the mouth of Long-Pass. 'I'll send word of how things are going from time to time, but I don't really expect much in the way of trouble.'

'Keep our sister off balance as much as you can, Sorgan,' Zelana told him. Then she looked at Dahlaine. 'I've found that the un-expected always seems to startle Aracia,' she said.

'I pretty much agree with the scheme to drop horror stories on Aracia – and her priesthood,' Dahlaine replied. 'If it goes the way I *think* it will, the priests will be so frightened that they won't be able to deliver all those flattering orations, and that alone will shake Aracia right down to her roots.'

'Your sister has roots, Dahlaine?' the beautiful lady called Ara asked with a sly smile. 'If she does, then maybe we could trans-plant her – in the middle of the night, probably. When her priests wake up and find that she's gone, they won't have any idea at all about where she's gone – or why – and it's likely that their minds will shut down.'

'I'm not at all sure that something like that would work, dear lady,' Dahlaine replied. 'Aracia's priests spend all their time grov-eling in her throne room whether she's there or not. Groveling is an art-form among the priests of Aracia.'

'Doesn't that make them sort of meaningless?' Ara's husband suggested.

For the life of him, Andar could not think of any reason at all just *why* the two neighbors of Lord Veltan were present here on the *Victory* – except, perhaps, for the glorious food Ara presented to Narasan and his friends when meal time arrived. Without a doubt, Ara was probably the finest cook in the whole world, but why did she and her husband always participate in these serious meetings?

'Build good forts, friend Narasan,' Sorgan said then. 'I *don't* want the bug-people sneaking up behind me when I'm busy swindling holy old Aracia.'

'We'll do the best we can, Sorgan,' Narasan replied with a grin. 'Swindle away for all you're worth, and we'll keep the bug-people out of your hair.'

The weather was holding – probably because Dahlaine told her to – so the remaining ships in the fleet made good time as they sailed on down to the mouth of Long-Pass. The ships that had carried Sorgan's Maags down to Aracia's temple had turned around and they'd passed Narasan's fleet two days ago, and they were probably picking up the numerous cohorts that had stayed behind. It wouldn't be much longer before the entire army would be reunited and marching up the pass toward whoever – or whatever – would soon be invading.

THE TEMPLE OF ARACIA

1

It was late afternoon when the hundred Trogite tubs Sorgan had borrowed from Narasan hauled into the harbor of the temple-town of Zelana's elder sister. Sorgan, Veltan, and Padan were standing in the bow of the *Ascension*, the lead ship, and Sorgan was more than a little astonished by the enormity of the temple. Narasan had told him that the silly thing was about a mile square – which might be easy to say – but Sorgan realized that saying and seeing were altogether different. 'It seems to go on forever,' he said to Veltan in an awed sort of voice.

'I'm sure that Aracia likes to think so,' Veltan replied.

'Most of it's empty, though,' Padan advised. 'It's not what I'd call jam-packed with priests and her church hangers-on. I nosed about when we first arrived last autumn, and there aren't really that many people living there.'

'Fat Takal Bersla was probably responsible for the overdone size of the silly thing,' Veltan added. 'It's one of the many myths he's foisted off on my big sister. He *claims* that there are thousands and thousands of priests living in that absurdity. Aracia's absolutely certain that she has worshipers beyond counting living here, but she never bothers to look. There might be thousands

and thousands of creatures living here, but most of them are probably mice.'

'Or spiders,' Padan added. 'I roamed around in that foolishness
last fall, and *most* of the corridors in "Holy Temple" are jammed
to the ceiling with cobwebs.'

'It's nothing but a hoax, then?' Sorgan asked.

'A "holy hoax," Captain Hook-Beak,' Veltan corrected. 'Aracia
devoutly believes that the absurdity her priests have foisted off on
her is a sign of her overwhelming importance.'

'That's pathetic,' Sorgan declared.

'That's a fair description of my sister, yes,' Veltan agreed.

'We've got company coming,' Padan said, pointing across the
bay. 'I'd say that it's most probably fat old Bersla coming out here
to find out what we want.'

'That thing doesn't look at all like Longbow's canoe,' Sorgan
observed.

'It's not really the same thing, Sorgan,' Veltan agreed. 'Longbow's
canoe is designed to carry one man. The ugly thing coming out
here to meet us is designed for show. Bersla yearns to be important, and he thinks that having hundreds of men paddling him out
here makes him *look* important.'

Sorgan squinted at the approaching boat. 'It looks to me like it
was made out of a single tree-trunk.'

'That's fairly common here in the Land of Dhrall,' Veltan said.
'They're called "dugouts," probably because making them involves
scraping out most of the log with sharp stones. I've never actually
seen one built before, but I'm told that most of them are partially
hollowed out with fire – very well-controlled fire, of course. There
are certain advantages, though. A boat made from a single log
wouldn't leak, would it?'

'Maybe not,' Sorgan said, 'but if it doesn't have a keel, it'll probably roll over any time one of the paddlers sneezes or hiccups.'

'That *has* happened here fairly often, Captain Hook-Beak,' Veltan said, grinning broadly. 'Stately – but not very bright – Bersla doesn't understand *why* just yet but it might come to him – eventually.'

'That's pure stupidity!' Sorgan declared.

'I'd say that's a fair description of Bersla, yes. You've already met Aracia herself back in *my* Domain, so you don't really need Bersla to introduce you to her. He's terribly impressed with himself. He'll demand to know why you're here, but I'd suggest that you tell him that you're here to see Aracia herself, not some servant.'

'Won't that offend him?'

'Probably, yes. I'd say that you should tell him that you're too important to talk to servants. When we reach the temple, I'll introduce you to my sister and tell her that you'll defend her temple *if* she'll pay you enough.'

'That sounds good to me,' Sorgan replied. 'How should I behave? Am I supposed to bow to her or any of that other nonsense?'

'A certain amount of arrogance wouldn't hurt. Tell her that you're the mightiest warrior in the world, so you're worth your weight in gold – that sort of thing. One thing you should always remember. *Don't* let her give you orders. Tell her that you'll do what's necessary to defend her, and you don't want any interference from her or her priesthood. Get that established right away. You're going to be tearing down a large part of her temple, so there'll be a lot of screaming from the priests. Tell them that you have her permission, and that they should mind their own business. Pull out your sword, if you have to.'

'Or maybe even if I don't, right?'

'Now you're getting the idea. I think you'll do just fine, but you'll have to push my sister back into a corner as well, and that might take a few days.'

'It'd better not, Veltan,' Padan said. 'Captain Hook-Beak *has* to persuade your sister to let him do things *his* way, but he can't drag it out for *too* long. They'll have to reach an agreement *before* he unloads his men and frees up all the ships here in the harbor. Those ships are vital to Narasan, because half of his army is still sitting on that beach up in Lord Dahlaine's territory.'

'He *does* have a point there, Veltan,' Sorgan said. 'I promised Narasan that I'd release his ships as soon as possible, and I don't lie to my friends.'

'I can manipulate a few things,' Veltan said, frowning slightly. 'A good following wind *would* recover a day or two. We can give you that much time to manipulate my sister if you need to. After that, you might have to be sort of arbitrary in your dealings with Aracia.'

'I don't see much of a problem there, Veltan,' Sorgan declared. 'I *am* a Maag, after all, and we *invented* arbitrary.'

The obviously unstable log-boat pulled alongside the *Ascension*, and the grossly fat priest rose to his feet to stand in the bow – which struck Sorgan as an act of sheer stupidity. 'We have beheld your approach to the temple of Holy Aracia,' he declared in a rolling sort of voice, 'and we must know of your purpose here.'

Veltan stepped forward. 'I am Veltan,' he said, 'the younger brother of she who guides you.'

'I have not heard of you,' Bersla declared in a haughty tone of voice. 'Surely Holy Aracia would have advised me that she has a brother beside Mighty Dahlaine.'

'I wouldn't depend on Aracia very much if I were you, fat man. Her mind isn't all that stable anymore.'

'Blasphemy!' Bersla exclaimed in a shocked tone.

'Not if it's true, it isn't,' Veltan disagreed. 'I see that you're going to need some convincing. Watch closely, fat man, and pay close attention. This is your only chance to avoid my resentment.' Then Veltan slowly rose up into the empty air above the *Ascension* to stand on nothing but air.

Fat Bersla went pale, and his eyes bulged almost out of their sockets.

'I can go higher, if you'd like,' Veltan said. 'I could even take you up into the air with me, if that would convince you. I am unlimited, Takal Bersla. If need be, I can carry you all the way up to the moon – but I don't think you'd like that very much. There's nothing to eat on the moon, and no air to breathe, so you'd probably die almost immediately.'

'I believe you!' Bersla declared in a shrill voice. 'I believe you!'

'Isn't he just the nicest fellow?' Veltan mildly asked the others.

It took the trembling Bersla a while to recover. 'I pray you, Lord Veltan,' he said, 'why have you come here?'

'It should be obvious, priest of my sister,' Veltan replied. 'The Creatures of the Wasteland will soon invade my dear sister's Domain, and I have brought fearless warriors to drive them away.'

'Eternally grateful shall we be if you succeed, Lord Veltan.'

'Were you planning to live eternally, High Priest Bersla?' Veltan asked with feigned astonishment.

'Ah – we will pass this on to generations as yet unborn, timeless Veltan,' Bersla amended. 'May I speak now with the chieftain of these mighty warriors who have come from afar to defend our Holy Aracia?'

'I don't waste my time speaking with servants,' Sorgan declared as roughly as he could. 'Let's go talk with your sister, Veltan.'

'That cannot *be*!' Bersla protested. 'Holy Aracia's time is all filled for this day. As you may know, however, *I* speak for Divine Aracia when it seems necessary.'

'Not to *me*, you don't,' Sorgan declared. 'I only talk with those who have gold.'

Sorgan and Veltan conferred briefly, and then a sailor with nothing else to do untied a rope that held a well-built skiff in place, and then he lowered it over the side.

'That is not permitted!' Bersla declared. 'No alien ships or boats may go ashore in Holy Aracia's Domain.'

'You don't think for one minute that I'm going to ride to the beach in that unstable canoe of yours, do you?'

'It is perfectly sound,' Bersla declared.

'Of course it is, Sorgan replied sarcastically. 'At least it might be as long as you leave it on the beach. It's when you push it out into the bay that it tends to roll over without much warning. How many times has that happened so far this month?'

Bersla began to splutter a denial, but there was a muscular oarsman sitting just behind the fat priest, and he held one hand up with the fingers stretched wide and two fingers of his other hand clearly visible. Then he winked at Sorgan.

'Let me guess,' Sorgan said to Bersla then. 'I've got a strong hunch that your tree-stump tub has rolled out from under you seven times already this month.'

Bersla's eyes went wide. 'How did you – ?' Then he broke off.

'Instinct, fat man,' Sorgan replied. 'I've spent most of my life at sea, so I know a lot about things that happen out on the water.

Logs *always* roll over in the water when you don't want them to, and seven's a lucky – or unlucky – number, be it logs or dice.' He made a slight gesture to the muscular oarsman, and the fellow nodded. 'Let's go hit the beach, Veltan,' Sorgan said then. 'I want to meet your sister, and then I'll look around. If I'm going to defend her territory, there are a lot of things I'll need to know.'

'How in the *world* did you know that Bersla's log-canoe had rolled over seven times already this month?' Veltan asked as Sorgan rowed the skiff toward the beach.

'You weren't watching very closely if you missed it,' Sorgan replied with a broad grin. 'When I asked the fat priest how many times his log-boat had rolled over, one of the oarsmen held up seven fingers.'

'Why would he do that?'

'I haven't got any idea. I'm going to talk with him later and find out, though. It's entirely possible that he might turn out to be very useful later on.'

'Does he know that you want to talk with him?'

'Of course he does. I don't want to hurt your feelings, Veltan, but you don't pay very close attention to what's going on around you. That oarsman gave me a wink when he held up his fingers, and I pointed at my mouth after I threw "seven" into the fat priest's face. Pointing your finger at your mouth can mean two things – "let's eat" or "let's talk." Everybody knows that.'

'It *does* make sense, I suppose.'

'Are we going to have any trouble getting in to see your sister?'

'Probably not,' Veltan replied. 'Aracia knows who I am, after all, and as soon as she sees me, she'll know that I've got some information for her. I'll introduce you to her, and then we can get down to business.'

It had seemed to Sorgan when he'd been on board the Trogite ship out in the bay that there'd been a kind of coherence about Aracia's temple, but as the skiff came closer to shore he began to see some glaring inconsistencies. 'I don't want to sound critical or anything, Veltan,' he said, 'but there's a sort of slapdash quality about your big sister's palace. Didn't the people who were building it ever get together and establish some rules? In some places, the stones are very smooth, but in others they're rough and lumpy.'

'There *do* seem to be quite a few inconsistencies,' Veltan agreed. 'I'd say that the assorted work crews didn't have anything to do with each other. Some of them appear to have spent a great deal of time polishing the stones, while others concentrated on piling up more rocks.'

'Something on the order of "prettier" or "bigger", you mean?'

'That probably comes very close, Sorgan. I don't imagine that Aracia really cared much one way or the other. As long as her temple kept growing, she was probably quite happy.'

'She's not really very bright, is she?'

'I wouldn't go quite *that* far. Aracia has different needs than the rest of us do. She desperately needs adoration, and her priests spend all of their time adoring her. I'm fairly sure that they didn't spend *much* of that vital time telling the work crews who were building the temple how to proceed, and that's what probably led to these inconsistencies.'

'It's possible, I guess.' Sorgan turned and looked a bit more closely at the beach. 'No piers,' he grumbled.

'Building piers would take the work crews away from expanding big sister's temple,' Veltan explained.

'We'll have to climb all over her right away,' Sorgan said.

'I didn't quite follow that.'

'We'll need piers when we unload the people from about a hundred Trogite tubs, Veltan,' Sorgan declared. 'They *won't* be willing to swim in the dead of winter, you know.'

'Good point there,' Veltan said. 'I think I'll have to cheat,' he added glumly.

'Cheat?'

'I'll make the piers myself. I know what they look like, and I'll be able to set them up much faster than the temple work crews possibly could. Then, too, if *I* do it, we won't have to listen to all the sniveling and complaining we'd get if we pulled the crews away from their "Holy" task of expanding my sister's temple until it's fifty or a hundred miles square.'

'Which probably won't take them much more than a few hundred years,' Sorgan added.

They pulled the skiff up onto the beach and then walked directly up to Aracia's temple.

When they reached the entrance, however, Sorgan's heart almost stopped beating. 'Is that door made out of what I *think* it is?' he gasped.

'Oh, yes,' Veltan replied. 'There might be a bit of bracing here and there, but most of it *is* gold.'

'There must be a ton of it!' Sorgan exclaimed.

'More than that, I'd say,' Veltan replied. 'Gold is very heavy, and that's quite a large door.'

'Are you saying that your sister just leaves it right out in the open like that?'

'It's fairly safe, Sorgan. I doubt if a hundred men – or even two hundred – would be able to pick it up and carry it. Let's go on inside and have our little chat with my sister, shall we?'

'Who are you, and why have you profaned the temple of Holy Aracia with your presence?' an officious-sounding young lady demanded as Veltan and Sorgan entered the corridor beyond the golden door.

'My name is Veltan,' Sorgan's friend replied. 'You may have heard of me – assuming that my sister remembers the rest of her family. You can go tell her that I'm here – or step aside and I'll go tell her myself.'

'You would not dare. I am Alcevan, the priestess of Holy Aracia, and I speak for her in all matters.'

'Aracia has women priests now?' Veltan said, sounding more than a little startled. 'Does Bersla know about this?'

The young lady sneered. 'Fat Bersla only knows what Holy Aracia and I want him to know. He might *think* that he's the most important person in Aracia's Domain, but that's no longer true. *I* am the one who speaks for Holy Aracia now, for I am her High Priestess and always will be.'

'That's very nice, I suppose,' Sorgan told her, 'but you're going to be a doormat if you don't get out of the way.' He put his hand on his sword-hilt in a threatening gesture.

Her eyes went very wide, and she turned and fled.

'Now *that's* something I wouldn't have expected,' Veltan said. 'It seems that things are getting more and more complicated here in Aracia's Domain.'

'The little lady *could* have been just making this up,' Sorgan said.

'It's possible, maybe,' Veltan replied. 'I think we'd better keep our eyes open, though. If the young woman was telling us the truth,

Aracia's playing a different game now.' He squinted slightly. 'I think maybe you should hold onto this attitude you just threw into Alcevan's face. Be sort of rough and abrupt. Let's keep Aracia off balance if we possibly can.'

Sorgan was somewhat startled by the sheer size of the room at the end of the corridor. At the very center, of course, was a massive marble pedestal topped by a golden throne and backed with dark red drapes. Zelana's sister was sitting on the throne, and the little lady Alcevan was kneeling before her and babbling.

Veltan went directly to the pedestal. 'I wouldn't pay too much attention to anything the young lady's telling you, dear sister,' he said. 'We had a slight misunderstanding out in the corridor. I wasn't aware of the fact that you were now accepting women as members of your priesthood.'

Aracia straightened, glaring at her younger brother. 'Who is this pagan, Veltan?' she demanded. 'And why have you profaned my holy temple with his presence?'

'You know who I am, sister of Zelana,' Sorgan declared. 'We met in Veltan's Domain last summer. He brought me here to defend you and your people when the bug-things invade, but since you and your stupid priests don't appreciate that, I'll just go back out to the harbor and sail away. From what I've seen so far here in the Land of Dhrall, I'd imagine that the Vlagh will have you for breakfast some day very soon.' And then he stormed out of the room, winking at Veltan as he went by.

'Maybe just a trifle extreme there, Sorgan,' Veltan's voice came softly out of nowhere.

'I think maybe I got carried away just a bit,' Sorgan admitted. 'Your sister and that uppity lady-priest of hers irritated me more than a little.'

Veltan's laugh came out of nowhere. 'On second thought, Sorgan, don't change a thing. I'm quite sure that my sister will come around fairly soon. Go on back out to your ship and wait. I'm almost certain that she'll send someone out to talk with you before long.'

'I hope you're right, Veltan,' Sorgan replied. 'I didn't leave myself very much room to wiggle out of this.'

2

The husky oarsman from Bersla's log-canoe was leaning over the rail of the *Ascension* when Sorgan rowed his skiff out from the beach. 'How did things go in the silly temple?' he asked when Sorgan pulled the skiff neatly in beside the ship.

'Things are sort of up in the air right now,' Sorgan replied.

'If I understood what your signal meant a while back, you wanted to talk with me about something.'

'I'll be right with you,' Sorgan replied starting up the rope ladder hanging down from the rail.

'This is a real fancy boat you've got here,' the native said.

'It's not mine,' Sorgan replied, swinging his leg over the rail. 'I borrowed it from a friend.' Then he squinted at the beefy native. 'I'm just guessing here,' he said, 'but I take it that you don't have much use for that fat priest.'

'He might make pretty good bait if I wanted to go fishing for sharks.'

'It'd take a very big shark to eat that much,' Sorgan said with a grin. 'If that's the way you feel about him, why did you go to work for him?'

'Free food. I don't have to work very hard, and Fat Bersla makes sure that we get fed regularly. We don't eat as much as *he* does, but nobody else in the whole world eats as much as Bersla does.'

'It definitely shows,' Sorgan agreed. 'You seem to keep track of how often that log-canoe of his rolls over.'

'That's only natural, since I'm the one who rolls it.'

'Do you want to run that past me again? I didn't quite follow you.'

'It's the easiest thing in the world to do,' the native said with a broad grin. 'All I have to do to get poor fat Bersla soaking wet is lean toward one side or the other. As long as everybody is sitting up straight, the canoe will keep on sitting upright in the water. One quick lean toward one side or the other rolls that thing in the blink of an eye. Any time Bersla starts to relax, I tip his canoe over.'

'What for?'

'I don't like him. Nobody *really* likes him. If *I* don't roll his canoe every now and then, one of the other paddlers *will*. Bersla hasn't gone home dry for about three years now. *We* get wet, too, but our clothes dry in a hurry. Bersla's clothes are thick and fancy, so they take at least a week to dry out. That's a big part of what this is all about. He has to keep on giving us food to eat, whether he goes out in his canoe or not.'

'You and I are going to get along just fine,' Sorgan said with a broad grin. 'What's your favorite kind of food?'

'Meat. Everybody likes meat.'

'I'll see what I can do to chase down some meat for you.'

'What will you want in exchange?'

'Information, my friend. Information. What's your name, anyway?'

'Platch,' the native replied. 'What's yours?'

'Sorgan Hook-Beak.'

'How did you *ever* get a name like that?'

'I had to work for it a long time ago. Let's go have something to eat, shall we?'

'I thought you'd never ask,' Platch replied with a broad grin.

Veltan came into the large cabin at the stern of the *Ascension* early the following morning. 'It took me a while, but I managed to calm my sister just a bit. I explained some of the peculiarities of the Maag culture to her – *after* she'd sent the priestess Alcevan off on some meaningless errand. I made quite a big issue of what good warriors your people are. Aracia's very arrogant, but she *does* know that her priests would be useless in a confrontation with the Creatures of the Wasteland.'

'Unless the bugs happen to be hungry,' Sorgan added with a broad grin.

'I mentioned that, yes. When you get right down to it, though, it's very unlikely that Aracia or any of her servants will even *see* any of the servants of the Vlagh. Your scouts will tell the assorted priests that the bugs are out there and that they're living on a steady diet of people, but all that we're *really* doing is diverting their attention from the *real* invasion – the one that's pointed at Long-Pass.'

'How would you say I should approach your sister?' Sorgan asked. 'I might have been just a little too rough yesterday.'

Veltan squinted at the cabin ceiling. 'You might want to be a bit more polite today – not *too* polite, of course. Swagger a bit and brag about what a great warrior you are and how you defeated the servants of the Vlagh back in sister Zelana's Domain and helped Narasan in *mine*. Then tell her that you want to talk about gold. Gold doesn't mean anything to Aracia, but she'll probably try to make you lower your price. That's when you should storm out

73

again and come back out to this ship. Try to make it look like you're just about ready to sail off and leave her here to fight her own war. This is *very* important, Sorgan. Don't ever back down when you're dealing with Aracia. She *will* come around when she realizes that you mean what you say.'

'You people play very rough games with each other, don't you?'

'Indeed we do,' Veltan agreed. Then he smiled slyly. 'Fun though,' he added.

Sorgan rowed the skiff back to the beach. Veltan offered to take up a set of oars to help, but Sorgan said 'no' quite firmly. 'I'm not trying to offend you, Veltan, but things go much more smoothly if there's only one man rowing. We'd both look sort of silly if we were soaking wet when we went back into that throne room. If we happened to do something wrong, we could tip this skiff over *almost* as fast as Platch can roll Bersla's log canoe.'

'Did he ever tell you why he does that every so often?' Veltan asked.

'It takes the wind out of the fat man's sails,' Sorgan replied with a chuckle. 'A man who's soaking wet and dribbling water all over the floor doesn't look very important. Platch despises Bersla, so he keeps him wet most of the time.'

Sorgan rowed the skiff up onto the same beach where he had beached her the previous day, and then he and Veltan went on up through the assorted buildings lying outside the temple.

Sorgan looked longingly at the ornate temple door. 'I don't suppose—' he left it hanging.

Veltan shook his head. 'Sister Aracia wouldn't hold still for that, Sorgan. We *might* encounter the same objections when we tell my sister that we're going to have to tear down some of the outer reaches of her temple, but that door is much too important in my sister's eyes for her to agree to it as your price. Then too, how would you move it? It weighs tons, and even if you managed to get your hands on it, the sheer weight would sink any ship you could bring into the harbor. Stick to the gold blocks, Sorgan. They're much more convenient.'

They passed through the long corridor and entered the throne room. Fat Bersla was delivering a flowery speech, comparing Zelana's sister to a sunrise, a hurricane, and an earthquake. Aracia's attention, however, seemed to be a bit divided, since the young priestess Alcevan was standing beside the throne whispering on and on. Sorgan sensed a certain competition there. It seemed that Bersla and Alcevan were each doing everything they could think of to get Aracia's attention.

Sorgan walked up to the marble pedestal and looked Aracia right in the face – which was probably against all the rules. 'Well now,' he said. 'Veltan tells me that you're ready to listen to what I say.'

'Not right now,' Aracia replied with a note of irritation in her voice. 'Takal Bersla is addressing me now.'

Sorgan drew his sword. 'That's not really much of a problem, you know. He'll stop talking just as soon as I kill him.'

'You wouldn't *dare*!' Aracia exclaimed.

'Watch me,' Sorgan suggested in an offhand sort of way. 'You've got a problem, and I'm here to solve it. Let's dispense with all this foolishness and get down to business.' He purposefully crossed the marble floor to where Bersla had just stopped talking. The word 'kill' seemed to have gotten his attention.

'You *have* finished your speech, haven't you?' Sorgan asked, moving the point of his sword back and forth about six inches from Bersla's face.

Bersla nervously backed away. 'Holy Aracia will protect me,' he declared, still backing up.

'How?' Sorgan asked. 'You *did* know that she's not permitted to kill things, didn't you? I don't have those restrictions. I can kill anything – or anybody – whenever I feel like it. You've got a very simple choice, fat man. What it all boils down to is shut up or die. The choice is entirely yours, though, but you'd better hurry. My sword's very thirsty right now.'

Bersla flinched back, and then he ran out of the room.

Veltan was smiling. 'I'd say that there's a certain charm to Hook-Beak's directness, wouldn't you, dear sister?'

'I will not tolerate this!' Aracia almost screamed.

'I think you'd better,' Sorgan said bluntly. 'I came here to protect you and your people – for money, of course – so let's get down to business. I'll start protecting right after you pay me.'

'*I* will decide when – and how much,' Aracia declared. She was obviously trying to regain control in this situation.

'That might be very true, Lady Aracia,' Sorgan said, 'but *I'm* the one who'll say yes or no. Be nice to me, lady, because *I'm* the only one willing to protect you. You've offended your big brother *and* your sister, so they won't have anything to do with you. That sort of says that *I'm* the most important person in the whole wide world, wouldn't you say?'

Aracia gave him a cold, superior sort of look. 'How much do you want?' she asked.

'Oh, I don't know,' Sorgan replied. 'How does one hundred blocks of pure gold sound to you?'

'That's absurd!'

'It is, isn't it? Let's make it *two* hundred, then.'

She stared at him, her eyes suddenly gone wide.

'It's entirely up to you, lady. That's the price. Take it or leave it.' Then he turned and walked toward the door, not even bothering to look back.

'I'll pay! I'll pay!' Aracia almost screamed.

'That's more like it,' Sorgan said. 'Now you can see just how easy I am to get along with.'

'He leaned on her, Padan,' Veltan told their friend the next morning. 'Very, very hard.'

'I wish I'd been there to see that,' Padan said with an evil sort of grin.

'Your whiskers aren't quite long enough to make it safe for you to roam around in the temple, Padan,' Sorgan told the Trogite. 'Give them another week before you visit that holy absurdity. You're not wearing your Trogite uniform, and that *might* be enough, but let's not take any chances yet. We want you to look entirely different before you start making any public appearances.' He scratched his cheek. 'I think maybe you and Rabbit should talk this over. Rabbit's got a fair idea of the horror-stories he's going to tell Veltan's sister, but I think you might want to add a few other stories as well. We've seen quite a few different varieties of the bug-people, and we'll want to throw them all in Aracia's face – in bits and pieces, of course. Let's say that the first time you'll sorta concentrate on the snake-bugs that we encountered in Zelana's Domain. Then move on to the bug-bats and the turtle-shell bugs. Hold off on the spider-bugs for quite some time. *That's* the *really* scary one. I still have nightmares about people having their insides turned into a liquid that the spider drinks right out of them.'

'It *did* eliminate Jalkan and Adnari Estarg, Captain Hook-Beak,' Padan said. 'A lot of us in Commander Narasan's army are quite sure that was the nicest thing anybody – or any*thing* – could have done for us.'

Sorgan smiled. 'If I remember right, Gunda wanted to make that a national holiday down in Trog-land. I'll be sending Ox, Ham-Hand, and Torl out as well. Maybe you should all get together and decide which awful each one of you should present to Aracia and her assorted priests. Each one of you should have a different story to wave in Aracia's face. Remember that she *was* down in Veltan's Domain, so she knows about *most* of the varieties of bugs. Let's add a few new ones, though – bird-bugs, maybe, or wolf-bugs and lion-bugs. Maybe the group of you should get together and decide how you're going to spread these stories out and make them sound real. The whole idea is to give them *new* awfuls every so often, and each awful should be worse than the previous ones. We want to make Aracia's priests so terrified that they'll be afraid to come out of the temple to see the awfuls themselves.' Then he had a sudden idea, and he looked at Veltan. 'You know how to make images of things that aren't really there, don't you?'

'More or less,' Veltan admitted. 'Where are we going here?'

'Let's say that our scouts come back with stories about some ter-rifying varieties of bugs. Then, maybe a day or so later, the priests and other servants actually *see* those very same bugs.'

'I can do that, yes,' Veltan admitted. 'I'll need to stay quite a ways away from Aracia when I do it, though. If I'm too close to her, she'll be able to feel what I'm doing.'

'We'll probably be out along the west side of her temple. That's quite some distance from the main temple here. The higher-ranking priests will probably be hiding out in cellars and what-not, but I'm sure we'll be able to come up with some reason for a few of the lower-ranking priests to be out there with us. If you whip up some nasty images, they'll probably run back to Aracia yelping and squealing. Let's keep your sister so terrified that she can't think straight. We want her to order all of her priests to come home to the temple to join up with the ones already here. We don't want *any* of her priests out there catching whiffs of the invasion of Long-Pass. Let's make sure that Narasan can get his job done without any interference from your sister or her overweight priests.'

'You're getting very good at this sort of thing, Sorgan.'

'Practice, Veltan, practice. And if worse comes to worse, we can borrow a few of the children. I'm almost positive that Eleria could scare your older sister into convulsions, if that's what we really need. We're pulling off a hoax here, but let's make it seem so real that *nobody* who works for your sister will even dare to come out of the temple to have a look for themselves.'

UP FROM THE BEACH

1

It was late afternoon on a cold, grey winter day when the *Victory* hauled into a narrow bay where a sluggish-looking river came down through a range of low, rounded mountains.

'This must be the place, Andar,' Gunda said to his friend as the sailors lowered the sails of the *Victory* and dropped the anchor. 'Lord Dahlaine's map only showed one river coming down out of the mountains along this stretch of the east coast.'

'It looks to be quite a bit wider than the streams and rivers we encountered off to the west,' Andar observed.

'And fairly quiet as well,' Gunda added. 'That doesn't particularly hurt my feelings, though. Waterfalls and rapids are pretty to look at, but trying to get around them isn't much fun at all.'

'I *knew* it,' Andar said.

'Knew what?'

'Longbow said he'd be waiting for us here, and there he is.'

'I don't—' Gunda started, but then he too saw the leather-clad archer sitting on a log not far from the river-mouth. 'That's Longbow, all right,' he said. 'If he says he's going to do something or be someplace, you might as well believe him. I learned never to argue with him during that first war in Lady Zelana's Domain.'

'If I was reading Lord Dahlaine's map right, he had hundreds of miles ahead of him when he led the Malavi and those natives down along that mountain range,' Andar said, sounding more than a little baffled.

'The first rule when you're dealing with Longbow is always to believe him when he tells you something,' Gunda said with a slight smile. 'It may not be true when he says it, but it *will* turn out to be true in the long run. If Lady Zelana doesn't wiggle her fingers to make things happen, Longbow's *other* friend – the one who conjures up tidal waves on dry land or sets fire to a mountain range when she gets irritated – *will*. Don't *ever* cross Longbow if you can possibly avoid it. That's the best way I know of to stay alive.'

Narasan and the overly clever Keselo came out of the cabin at the stern of the *Victory*, and they joined Gunda and Andar at the starboard rail. 'I'd say that we made good time,' Narasan observed.

'Not *too* bad,' Gunda agreed, 'but Longbow outdid us. He's camped on the beach, and he's probably been waiting for us for a month or so at least.'

'I see that you're filling in for Padan in the funny remarks department,' Narasan said in a sour tone. 'If you are, you'd better practice just a bit. Padan would have added all sorts of irritating comments to *that* one.'

'Give me a little time, Narasan,' Gunda replied. 'My sense of humor's sort of rusty – the weather, no doubt.'

'Longbow should be able to tell us if the bug-people are coming up out of the Wasteland,' Keselo said. 'That's what we *really* need to know.'

Gunda squinted at the narrow bay. 'I was sort of hoping that we'd be able to get closer to the beach,' he said. 'If the men have to row ashore from this far out, it'll take us several days to get everybody on shore.'

'We won't be going anywhere for several days anyway, Gunda,' Narasan said. 'Half of the army's still camped on that beach up in Dahlaine country. Sorgan's scheme *should* keep Aracia out of my hair, but when he borrowed half of the fleet, he slowed things down for us quite a bit. Let's go ashore and have a little chat with Longbow. We really need to know if the bugs are moving yet.'

'How far would you say it is to the top of Long-Pass from here?' Narasan asked when several Trogites met with the archer.

'About a hundred and twenty miles, Narasan,' Longbow replied. 'Dahlaine's map was fairly accurate.'

Narasan winced. 'That's not exactly good news, Longbow,' he said. 'At ten miles a day, that's twelve days at least.'

'Is ten miles a day some sort of religious obligation?' Longbow asked the commander.

'No, not really,' Narasan replied. 'It's based on reality. One man alone can cover much more ground, but when you're dealing with an army of a hundred thousand, ten miles a day is about the best you can hope for.'

'But your fort-builders wouldn't *really* have to move that slowly, Narasan,' Longbow declared. 'Friend Gunda here is the expert, so he'll know how many of your men we'll need to get the job done. If I were to guide – or maybe lead – your fort-builders up the pass, I'm sure that I'd have them up there in four days, and they could have *most* of the work finished by the time you and the rest of your army reached the top.'

'It's just not done like that, Longbow,' Gunda protested. 'An army's not an army if it gets all split up like that.'

'Don't be in such a rush, Gunda,' Andar suggested. 'It's very likely that we're going to *need* those forts and we'll definitely need them *before* the bug-people come charging across the Wasteland. I suppose we could give some thought to blocking them off somewhere about half-way down the pass, but I'd say that blocking them right up at the top of the pass would work better.'

'He's got a point there, Gunda,' Narasan agreed. 'We're not fighting an ordinary enemy, and we *don't* want them to get into the pass if we can possibly come up with a way to keep them out.' Then he looked at Longbow. 'Can you *really* get the fort crew to the head of the pass in just four days?' he asked.

'Not all of them maybe,' Longbow replied, 'but enough of them to get started. The Tonthakans, Matans and the Malavi can hold our enemies back for a while, but I'm sure that forts are absolutely essential.'

'I see your point,' Narasan agreed. 'All right, then, take the fort crews on up to the head of the pass as quickly as you possibly can. If we don't block off Long-Pass, there's a fair chance that poor old Sorgan will be facing *real* bug-people instead of assorted imaginary ones.'

Gunda shrugged. 'If that's the way you want it, glorious leader, that's the way we'll do it.' Then he squinted at Andar. 'Are you feeling up to a long hike in short time?' he asked.

'That's up to the commander, Gunda,' Andar replied. 'If he wants me to go along, I'll go, and we could turn it into a race, if you'd like. I can probably run at least as fast as you can.'

Gunda was seriously discontented by Longbow's scheme to rush the building crews up to the head of the pass. Spreading the army out in potentially hostile territory wasn't a good idea at all, and he was highly skeptical when Longbow announced that he could march the construction gangs to the top of the pass in a mere four days. Longbow himself probably wouldn't have any trouble covering that much ground in four days, but Longbow wasn't familiar with all the delays that can crop up when several thousand men are moving in the same direction. Gunda's years in Narasan's army had taught him a fairly simple rule – 'Always expect the worst, and you'll seldom be disappointed.'

The grumbling and complaining began before they even started up the pass the following morning. When Longbow said 'at first light' he meant it, and that didn't sit too well with most of the men in the construction crews.

It didn't take Gunda very long to put his finger on the source of much of their problem. Longbow was a tall man, and Trogites, for the most part, were significantly shorter. Gunda didn't bother to keep count, but he was almost positive that he had to take two steps for every one of Longbow's. Most Trogites, it appeared, almost had to run to keep up with the archer.

'He moves very fast, doesn't he?' the farmer Omago suggested.

Gunda wasn't sure just why Omago had joined them, but he decided not to ask any questions just now. 'He steps right along,' he agreed. 'If somebody happened to take six or eight inches off each one of his legs, things might be a lot more pleasant for the rest of us.'

'I think it might have something to do with the fact that he's a hunter,' Omago said. 'From what I've heard, all hunters move fast, because they don't eat if they just plod along.'

'That probably has a lot to do with it,' Gunda agreed.

'Hunting might be exciting,' Omago said, 'but turnips don't run away, so we don't have to chase them.'

'I've never been involved in farming or hunting,' Gunda said. 'Down in the Empire, we just buy our food. We don't have to grow it or chase it down to shoot it full of arrows.'

'Did I hear correctly?' Omago asked then. 'Somebody told me that Trogite soldiers are born and raised in those forts down there.'

'Not quite *all* of us,' Gunda replied. 'It's mostly just the officers. We start out playing soldier, but then we move on to being real ones.'

'Isn't it sort of dangerous to hand real weapons to little children?'

Gunda smiled. 'We don't get *real* weapons until we're older,' he replied. 'We start out with wooden swords, and there are quite a few old veterans keeping an eye on us. Then, when the weather's bad, they tell us war-stories. There was an old sergeant named Wilmer who could spend hours telling us stories about wars the army had fought in the past. I'd say he was probably one of the greatest story-tellers who've ever lived. He could keep us sitting on the edge of our chairs for hours.'

'The stories the older farmers tell *us* when we're little boys aren't really very exciting,' Omago said. 'Stories about bugs eating our crops used to show up quite often.'

'That's what *this* war is all about, though, wouldn't you say? Of course, this one's just a little different. This time, the bugs are eating *people*, not just crops.' Then he saw something quite interesting. 'Excuse me a minute, Omago,' he said. 'I need to mark something.' He went to a fair-sized oak tree and tied a length of red string around it. 'A good spot for a fort,' he explained. 'Narasan told me to keep my eyes open while we're going through the pass and mark any place that might be a good spot for a fort.'

'Are you saying that you're going to build forts *this* far down the pass.'

'Only if the bug-people give us enough time, Omago. If things work out right, we'll build a fort every mile or so. If the bug-people *do* decide to come down this way, we'll be able to make it *very* expensive for them.'

'You Trogites are most certainly the finest soldiers in the world,' Omago declared. 'We're very lucky that Veltan was able to persuade Commander Narasan to come here and help us. I keep hearing stories that your commander had given up soldiering and had taken up begging instead.'

Gunda shrugged. 'He made a blunder in a war, and his nephew was killed. Narasan couldn't live with that – until Veltan came along and told him that it was time to go to work again.'

Omago smiled. 'Veltan can be very persuasive when he needs to be.'

'He is indeed,' Gunda agreed. 'He threw some things at Narasan that jerked our commander out of his gloom, that's for sure. Narasan was sure that the world was coming to an end, and time would stop. Veltan told him that time didn't, and never would, have an end – or a beginning either.'

'He was wrong there,' Omago said. 'Time may never have an end, but it definitely had a beginning. There was a time when the universe wasn't, but it suddenly appeared. *That* was when time began.'

'Just when did that happen?' Gunda asked curiously.

'It's very hard to say,' Omago replied. 'It was before the world – or the sun – came into existence, so Veltan wasn't around.'

'Where did you pick up this story, Omago?'

Omago frowned. 'I'm not really sure,' he admitted. 'I just somehow know that it happened that way. Isn't that odd?'

'This Land of Dhrall is the native home of odd, Omago,' Gunda said. 'We'd better pick up our pace, my friend,' he suggested. 'Longbow's getting a fair distance ahead of us, and if we don't keep up, he'll get very grouchy. If we keep strolling along like this, he might send us to bed without supper.'

Omago laughed, and they both began to walk faster.

The sun was setting off to the west when Longbow decided that they'd gone far enough. Gunda breathed a sigh of relief at that point. He was fairly sure that he didn't have another mile left in him.

'We'll need to go a little farther tomorrow,' Longbow said.

'*Farther?*' Gunda protested. 'I'm not sure I'll be able to stand up tomorrow morning, much less walk more than a mile.'

'You spend too much time lying around when you're riding on boats, Gunda,' Longbow replied. 'You'll be in much better shape when we reach the head of the pass.' Then he looked back down the pass where the last of the Trogites were stumbling up toward where they'd soon be setting up their night's camp. 'Did Narasan happen to tell you why he sent so many men?' he asked.

'Narasan doesn't explain too many things to me anymore, Longbow. All it does is confuse me.'

'But ten thousand men to build one fort?'

'That might depend on just how big a fort we're talking about.'

They had beans for supper, of course, but Gunda was sure that he could eat almost anything by then. He put out guards and then fell asleep almost immediately.

2

—◆—

Longbow had been quite obviously not at all pleased when Commander Narasan designated some ten thousand of his men as 'fort-builders.' Andar had privately agreed with the archer, but he chose not to make an issue of it. The more he thought about it, though, the more he realized that the idea might have some merit.

He went looking for Longbow and found him still awake. 'I take it that you aren't too happy with the commander's generosity, Longbow.'

'I wouldn't call foisting that many people off on me "generosity," Andar,' Longbow replied in a sour sort of voice.

'There *is* something we might want to consider, though,' Andar said.

'Oh?'

'About how wide would you say that the upper end of this pass is?'

'I'd say fifty feet at the most.'

'That would put almost two hundred men to work on every foot of our projected fort, wouldn't it?'

'I'm not sure that building a fort out of people would be a very good idea, Andar.'

'It might be just a little difficult to feed them if they're piled up on top of each other,' Andar agreed. 'But since we've got a surplus of people, we *could* put the extra ones to work building a second fort a mile or so on down the pass. That way, there'd only be five thousand standing on top of each other in each fort.'

'That's *still* going to be badly crowded.'

'If it seems that way when we get up there, we could build even *more* forts. If we've got four solid, well-made forts blocking off the creatures of the Wasteland, life might start to become very unpleasant for them, wouldn't you say? We'll have archers and spear-men standing on top of those forts and Malavi horse-soldiers slashing at them from both sides. I'd say that each fort could cost them a half-million or so of their companions. If we keep on erecting new forts every mile or so, the Vlagh's likely to run out of warriors before her army even gets half-way down the pass.'

'Maybe sending ten thousand fort-builders up the pass wasn't such a bad idea after all,' Longbow agreed. 'Do you think Gunda will go along with us on this?'

'Not right at first, maybe, but after a day or so of watching his men falling over each other, he'll probably listen to our suggestion.'

Longbow looked at Andar in a speculative way. 'I've noticed several times that you're more clever – and practical – than either Gunda or Padan. Why does Narasan pay so much attention to those two and ignore you?'

'It has to do with our childhood, Longbow,' Andar explained. 'We were all children in the army compound in Kaldacin, but we didn't all live in the same barracks. Narasan, Gunda, and Padan were childhood friends, because they all lived in the same barracks. Brigadier Danal and I lived in a different barracks, so Narasan didn't know us as well as he knew Gunda and Padan.' Andar smiled briefly. 'In a way I'm *earning* my position while Gunda and Padan get theirs for free. Narasan's perceptive enough to know that I'm not a dunce. These wars here in the Land of Dhrall have been most useful for me. It's reached the point that Narasan depends on me almost as much as he depends on Gunda and Padan.' He glanced off to the east. 'The sun's coming up,' he noted, 'the *real* one, I think. Dahlaine's toy might still be asleep. I think you might want to start out now, and I'll tell Gunda that it's time to go. If you step right along, you'll get farther and farther ahead of him. Gunda should get the point in an hour or so, and he'll start pushing the men. They like him, so they'll do as he tells them.'

'They don't like you as much as they like Gunda, do they?'

Andar shrugged. 'Being liked isn't that important, Longbow. It's getting the job done that counts.'

The river that had carved out Long-Pass over the extended eons was wider and more gentle than the frothy, tumbling brooks in the more rugged mountain ranges in other parts of the Land of Dhrall. In some ways the river rather closely resembled the streams in the southern region of the Trogite Empire. Andar pulled his mind back from that particular comparison, since it reminded him of the death of Commander Narasan's gifted young nephew Astal. Narasan had never come right out and admitted it, but Andar was fairly sure that he'd been secretly pleased when word reached him that Gunda and Padan had arranged to have Astal's murderers assassinated by a number of professional killers.

It seemed to Andar that the river that flowed down through Long-Pass was wider than it should be. The unseasonable warmth caused by Dahlaine's pet sun appeared to be melting ice and snow farther on up the pass. Had anyone ever told him when he'd still been living in Kaldacin that it might be possible to have a glowing little sun as a house pet, he was quite sure that he'd have had *that* particular informant sent off to some lunatic establishment.

Longbow, who evidently could get by on very little sleep, roused them before daybreak the following morning. It was bitterly cold, and Gunda saw something that was very rare down in the Empire. Any time somebody spoke, a cloud of steam came out of his mouth to accompany the words. 'I thought we were far enough to the south that we wouldn't blow out steam when we talked,' he said when he and his friends were eating breakfast.

'It happens up in the mountains fairly often,' Longbow said. 'It can be quite useful when you're hunting – or fighting a war. It's fairly easy to find out just where the animals – or your enemies – are.'

'Do the bugs blow out steam when they talk to each other in the same way that people do?'

Longbow shook his head. 'Most bugs don't talk with words the way we do,' he said. 'They talk with touch instead. Most bugs don't even *have* voices.'

'They *do* make noises, Longbow.'

Longbow nodded. 'They rub their legs together to *make* the noises you've heard, Gunda, and the noises they make aren't words. Bugs don't *need* words. They all know what they're supposed to be doing, so they don't have to talk about it.'

'Were you able to see the Wasteland when you came down that mountain range, Longbow?' Keselo asked their friend.

'Fairly often, yes.'

'Are the bugs moving out there yet?'

'I saw a few – quite a long way out in the Wasteland. I'd say that the ones I saw are probably scouts. The overmind needs to know whether we're here or not and how many of us there are. The main force is probably quite a way behind the scouts.'

'How far behind you would you say that the Tonthakans, Matans and Malavi are?'

'Just a few days would be about all. The Malavi would be quite a bit farther south, of course.'

'But you *still* outran them, didn't you?'

'Probably,' Longbow replied with a shrug. 'Horses get tired after a while.'

'But you don't, do you? You can run all day long, can't you.' Keselo's voice was strangely intense.

'If necessary, yes. You seem to be concerned, Keselo. What's bothering you so much?'

'There are times, friend Longbow, when I'm not absolutely sure that you're human.'

'We don't live the same kind of lives, Keselo,' Longbow replied. 'I almost never walk. I run instead. Your body gets used to doing things the way you want it to. I've trained my body to run. When you get down to it, walking tires me much more than running does.' He looked off to the east. 'It's almost daylight,' he told them. 'You'd better tell your men to get started, Gunda. Days don't last very long in the winter-time.'

It was about mid-morning that day when they rounded a turn in the pass and came to something that noticeably brightened Gunda's day. Andar waded across the now-shallow river and rubbed his hand down a weather-worn rock face.

'Well?' Gunda called.

'It's granite, all right,' Andar called back. 'It's been worn down

95

until it's quite smooth, but there are cracks here and there, so we should be able to pry quite a bit of it free.'

'You Trogites seem to be very fond of that particular variety of stone,' Omago said.

'It's the very best that there is,' Gunda replied. 'If you want something to last for a long, long time, build it out of granite. It's heavy and hard, and if you know what you're doing, you can chip it into blocks. If we have access to granite, and the bug-people aren't right on top of us when we get to the head of the pass, we'll be able to build a fort that *nobody* will be able to get past. A well-built overhang makes it almost impossible to climb up the outer face, and the archers and spearmen will delete "almost." Give me and my crew about three days, and the bug invasion will stop right there at the head of the pass, and that sort of translates into "we just won another war," wouldn't you say?'

'That's what this is all about,' Omago agreed.

Then Longbow came back down the pass. 'Why have we stopped?' he asked Gunda.

'We just came across a sizeable deposit of the best building material in the whole world,' Gunda replied smugly. 'Give my men and me a few days and we'll have an impregnable fort at the head of the pass.'

'We're talking about that grey rock, aren't we?'

'That's it.'

'We might as well move along, then,' Longbow suggested. 'Almost all of the rock at the head of the pass is the same as that rock face on the other side of the river. Your men won't have to come down here and dig up building material. It's laying all over the ground up at the head of the pass.'

'Let's move right along, then, Longbow,' Gunda said concealing a broad grin. 'All this shilly-shallying around is just wasting time.'

Longbow gave him a hard look and then he turned around and continued his hike.

'Wasn't that just a little bit—?' Omago started.

'It's good for Longbow, friend Omago,' Gunda said with a broad grin. 'It'll take some of the wind out of his sails.'

They made camp for the night as dusk settled down over the pass, and Gunda was quite happy when he came to realize that his legs and back weren't aching nearly as badly as they'd been the previous evening.

He slept very well that night, and he even woke up before Longbow came around to rouse him. 'You're already up and moving?' the archer said. 'What an amazing thing.'

'Don't beat me over the head with it,' Gunda replied. 'When do you think we'll reach the head of the pass?'

'Late tomorrow,' Longbow said, 'or early the following day.' Then he smiled, and that slightly startled Gunda. Longbow almost never smiled. 'We have company,' he announced.

'Way out here?' Gunda demanded. 'Who's foolish enough to join us out here in the wilderness?'

'Zelana herself,' Longbow replied. 'She has some information for us.'

'Let's go see what she has to say,' Gunda said, throwing back his blankets.

Zelana was sitting near the river bank, and she looked rather pensive. Gunda, as always, was more than a little awed by her presence. Lady Zelana was by far the most beautiful woman Gunda had ever seen, and just her presence set him to trembling. He reminded himself over and over that she was *not* a woman in the usual sense of that word. She was an immortal goddess instead, and she was quite probably at least a million years old.

'Are you all right?' Longbow asked her. 'You seem to be a little unhappy about something.'

'It's nothing important, Longbow,' she replied. 'I'm approaching sleep-time, is all. There were many, many things I wanted to do during this cycle, but I seem to be running out of time.' Then she stretched up her arms and yawned. 'It's getting closer,' she said. 'My nap seems to be creeping up on me from behind.' Then she straightened. 'Let's get down to business. I rode the wind out over the Wasteland late yesterday to see what the Vlagh is up to. She's sent out many of her servants to nose around and find out what we're up to, and I don't think she likes what they've been telling her. She doesn't really have very many choices this time. Long-Pass here is her only possible invasion route, and I'm sure that she knows that you're coming up the pass to block her off, and she doesn't like that one little bit.'

'What a shame,' Longbow said with no hint of a smile.

'It stops being funny right about now, Longbow,' Zelana told him. 'After I'd had a look at the Vlagh's scouts, I drifted farther out into the Wasteland, and from what I saw, I'd say that the Vlagh's throwing everything she's got at us this time. There are limitations on just how many eggs she can lay at any one time. She's *supposed* to hold enough back to maintain the population of her nest. I'd say that she's ignoring that this time. From what I was able to see, she has close to five times as many warriors as she's had during the previous wars, and they're all coming this way.'

'How long would you say it's likely to take for her children to reach us up here?' Gunda asked.

'Five or six days anyway.'

'That's probably all that I'm going to need,' Gunda said. 'We'll have the fort erected and manned before the Vlagh gets here. From what Longbow told me, the head of the pass isn't very wide, and I'm sure that our fort will be complete before the Vlagh even gets close. Once that fort's complete and well-manned, the Vlagh can stand out there beating her head against it until next summer, but she won't get past – no matter how many of her children she sends to attack.'

ALARMING NEWS

1

It took the better part of two days to get Sorgan's army ashore, and then Sorgan and Padan rowed over to the *Victory* to speak with Brigadier Danal.

'That takes care of things here, Danal,' Sorgan told the lean, stubborn officer. 'Convey my thanks to Narasan, and tell him that I'll stay in touch.'

'I'll do that, Captain,' Danal replied.

'How long would you say it's going to take you to get the rest of his army down to the mouth of Long-Pass?'

Danal squinted. 'The ships will be empty when we go north,' he said, 'and that should save us a day. Loading the troops on these ships will take a couple of days, and then four days to the mouth of the pass. Then two more days to unload. I make it to be twelve days to two weeks. Even if the bug-men have reached this side of the Wasteland, the Malavi and those archers from the North will be able to hold them off until Gunda's got some forts in place.' Then he smiled slightly. 'You don't necessarily have to tell Narasan that I said this, but your little side-trip gave me a wonderful opportunity to avoid all that tedious business of building forts.'

'That's what friends are for, Danal,' Sorgan said with a grin. 'If you happen to meet Lady Zelana up there, tell her that I said hello.'

'I'll do that, Captain Hook-Beak.'

'Oh, and tell Narasan that I'll keep the *Ascension* here. I'm going to need a private place to confer with my men. I don't want one of Lady Aracia's fat priests eavesdropping when I'm telling my men what to do.'

'I'm sure he'll understand, Captain,' Danal replied. 'You have a nice war now.'

'I'd hardly call what we're going to do here a war, Danal. It's just going to be an imitation.'

'Those are the very best kind,' Danal said with a grin.

Sorgan and Padan climbed down the rope ladder to their skiff. 'I like that man, Padan,' Sorgan said. 'We get along just fine.'

'He's a very good soldier,' Padan agreed.

They rowed across to the *Ascension* and joined several Maags in the rear cabin.

'All right, then,' Sorgan said. 'The Trogite fleet will sail at first light tomorrow, and they'll pick up the rest of Narasan's men and take them on down to the mouth of Long-Pass to fight the *real* war. In the meantime, we'll get started on the imitation war here. I don't *think* Aracia has any people up in that vicinity, but we'll want to make sure that no word of what's happening up there reaches her. I don't think she'd pay much attention to anything that's not going on here in the vicinity of her temple, but we should probably block off any roads or trails coming down here from up in the Long-Pass region.'

'I'll send some men up there to take care of that, cousin,' Torl said.

'Good,' Hook-Beak said approvingly.

'Have you worked out a plan yet?' Padan asked the Maag.

Sorgan grinned. 'Oh, yes,' he replied. 'I'm going to take some men to Aracia's throne room. I'll tell her that they're scouts, and they'll find out what they can about the upcoming invasion of the bug-people. Then I'll tell her how dangerous things are going to be for those scouts and make a big issue of how many varieties of invaders we'll come up against. Then I'll send the men on their way, and they'll march out about a mile or so and then set up camp in some fairly well-concealed place.'

'Wouldn't you say that a mile is just a little too close?' Padan asked.

Sorgan shook his head. 'I want them to be close enough to be able to hear the sound of a horn. I'm going to work on Aracia to build up her fright. Then, when she's filled to the brim with terror, I'll send word out to the west side of her temple, and one of the men there will toot a horn. When the imitation scouts hear it, they'll come running back and start piling "awful" all over Aracia and the fat ones who worship her.' He squinted. 'Torl,' he said to his cousin, 'I'll send Rabbit out there with you. He's very clever, and between the two of you, you should be able to come up with stories that'll send Aracia and her fat priests screaming and searching for safe places to hide. I'd say that you two should put things together so that this non-existent invasion by the bug-people starts out with moderately awful and then builds up to pure horror. You'll have several days to work on these stories, so use lots of imagination. Then too, I think you all might want to practice looking frightened. Bulge out your eyes, shiver like crazy, and scream once in a while. The whole idea here is to frighten everybody to the point that they'd sooner die than go outside the temple and have a look for themselves. *If* we can scare them enough, the notion of going north to pester Narasan will never occur to any of them. They won't know that Narasan's there anyway, but I want those priests to be so frightened that they won't even *consider* following an order to go anywhere away from this central temple. We'll use terror instead of bars, but this silly temple *will* be a prison if we do this right.'

Padan was just a bit surprised by the level of sophistication Sorgan's scheme indicated. 'Maags aren't supposed to be that clever,' he murmured to himself.

'I think you'd better come along, Padan,' Sorgan said when they went out onto the deck of the *Ascension*. 'I'm going to be playing a game of sorts, so I might miss a few reactions of Aracia or her assorted priests. If you happen to notice any degree of scepticism, let me know immediately. We *don't* want any doubts floating around at this point.' Then he turned to his cousin. 'Gather up the men who'll be going with you and come along. I'll give you your marching orders right there in the temple. I want Aracia and her priests to see you leave so that they'll recognize you when you come back. Try to look brave and strong when I send you out, and frightened and timid when you come back. I'll make an issue of how skilled you are as warriors when you march out. Then, when you come back whimpering, Aracia will believe just about every-thing you tell her about all the awful-awful you've witnessed.'

'This is a side of you I don't think I've ever seen before, cousin,' Torl said. 'You're an excellent deceiver, aren't you?'

'I'm probably the best,' Sorgan replied. 'Let's go frighten Zelana's sister for an hour or so, and then *I* can come back to the *Ascension* and rest for a while. I've been running steadily for about three days now.'

They rowed on to the beach just below Aracia's temple and then walked on up to the golden door. Evidently word had gotten out, and no priest – or priestess – tried to interfere as they marched on along the corridor that led to the throne room.

The fat priest Bersla was delivering another oration of praise when they entered Aracia's throne room. His majestic voice faltered when Sorgan marched in, however.

'Are you just about through?' Sorgan asked in a flat, unfriendly tone of voice.

'I was just about to leave, mighty Sorgan.'

'No,' Sorgan said abruptly, 'stay. There's something I want you to see.'

'As you wish, mighty Sorgan,' Bersla replied in a squeaky sort of voice.

Sorgan approached the throne. 'I've looked around your temple here, Lady Aracia,' he said, 'and we've got a lot of work ahead of us, I think, but for right now we need information – what kind of bugs are coming this way, anything new and unusual approaching, how close they are to where we are right now.' Then he gestured at Rabbit and Torl. 'These men are the best, so they'll be leading the scouting parties. I'm *hoping* that some of them will live long enough to bring back the information we need. There are many different varieties of bug-people. We know about quite a few of those, but there might be others as well. If there are, I want to know about them. We *don't* want any surprises. We already know that bugs can come at us from under the ground, from up in trees, and even out of the empty air. There's one variety that's part bug and part bat, and it flies around biting people, and the people die immediately.'

Aracia shuddered. 'How in the world did these things come into existence?'

Sorgan shrugged. 'Their queen – the one called "the Vlagh" – comes up with the idea for these various creatures, and then she lays eggs. When the eggs hatch, there's a whole new variety of bug. Worse yet, she lays those eggs by the thousands.'

'They'd only be infants,' the priestess Alcevan said. 'They wouldn't be much of a danger for quite some time.'

'I see that you've never spent much time around bugs,' Sorgan said. 'Bugs only live for about six weeks, and then they die. The infancy of a bug only lasts for three or four days, and then it's a full-grown adult, and it'll kill anything the Vlagh wants it to kill. They're not intelligent enough to be afraid of anything. I've seen two or three of them still attacking a fort after we've killed thousands of their friends. They just keep coming until they die.'

'That's absurd!' Bersla declared.

'You'd better be ready for *lots* of absurd when the bug-people attack,' Torl said. 'About the only thing we've found that gets their attention is fire. When you set fire to something, it tends to get a little confused.'

Then Sorgan gestured toward the door. 'Take your men and go out there and see what you can find out. Don't get *too* many of your men killed by taking chances. I need information, not dead friends. Find out what you can and then hurry back, and be very careful. You can die some other time. *This* time I want live men who can tell me what I need to know.'

Sorgan had moved his main force to the far western side of Aracia's temple. 'If there really *was* going to be an invasion by the bug-people, they'd reach this part of Aracia's temple first,' he told Padan. 'That means that we'll need some kind of fort here to persuade Aracia and her priests that we *are* going to protect them. It won't have to be *too* close to a real fort. The temple itself isn't really that well-built, so the priests wouldn't recognize *real* construction even if it walked up and bit them on the nose. We'll move a few of the building blocks and maybe knock down a tower or two. Then we'll have the men pretend to be building some kind of fort and let it go at that. What we'll *really* be doing will be terrifying Aracia and her priests to the point that they'll be afraid to come out of the central temple.'

'If this works out the way we want it to, we'll have pulled off one of the greatest hoaxes of all time, Captain,' Padan said.

'Naturally,' Sorgan boasted. 'No matter what I do, I'm always the best.' Then he laughed. 'Sorry, Padan,' he said then. 'It was just too good an opportunity to let slip by.'

'Where's Veltan?' Padan asked. 'I haven't seen him for the last few days.'

'He's nosing around over in the main temple,' Sorgan replied. 'I need to know how much of our silly story the priests – and Aracia, of course – have swallowed whole. If there are any doubts over there, we might have to play some more exotic games.' Then he shivered. 'Let's get in out of the weather, Padan,' he said. 'I *hate* winter.'

They went on back inside to a room that had a stove, and it wasn't too much later when Veltan joined them.

'Well, Sorgan,' he said, 'you've managed to terrify my sister's priesthood.'

'That was sort of what we had in mind, wasn't it?' Sorgan asked. 'That's why we've been waving bugs around every time we're near any priest.'

'It's *you*, not the bugs, that has them worried, Sorgan. They're desperately trying to come up with some way to reduce your grip on Aracia. They're afraid of you, and they hate you. It seems that you've got a tighter grip on Aracia than even *we* could imagine. I think it all goes back to Bersla. He had Aracia wrapped around his little finger with those stupid orations of his. Then you came along and pushed him back into a corner and threatened to kill him if he said one more word. He's had Aracia under his control for years now, and then you walked in and took her away from him in just a day or so. Aracia had the title, but Bersla had the power. Now he doesn't anymore.'

'Poor, poor Fat Bersla,' Sorgan murmured smugly.

'Now we come to the interesting part, Sorgan,' Veltan said. 'Bersla wants to kill you – or persuade some lesser priest to do the job for him.'

'They don't even have weapons, Veltan,' Sorgan scoffed.

'They *do* have knives, you know. They're made of stone, but a good hard stab in the back with a stone knife will penetrate your skin and go in far enough to do very serious damage to your vital organs. Bersla's doing everything he can think of to persuade some minor priest to stab you in the back. Quite a few of them are very interested by the offers Bersla has been waving in their faces. Instant promotion to the higher priesthood sounds very nice to young, ambitious priests who don't stand too high in the Church of Aracia.'

'It sort of sounds like I should have borrowed one of those iron breastplates from Narasan before I even came down here,' Sorgan muttered.

2

After a bit of thought, Hook-Beak spoke briefly with his first and second mates, Ox and Ham-Hand, and after that, the two big Maags followed their captain wherever he went in Aracia's temple. Ox was carrying his huge battle-axe, and any time Hook-Beak spoke with one of Aracia's overfed priests, the hulking Maag touched up the already razor-sharp axe-blade with a hefty whetstone that made a shrill sound as Ox drew it across the axe-blade.

The priests of Aracia got the point almost immediately.

Veltan, who had frequently demonstrated his ability to listen without being seen, advised Sorgan that the priests of Aracia had stumbled over a truth in their desperate search for some way to loosen Sorgan's grasp on Aracia. They had taken to denouncing Hook-Beak and his men as opportunistic swindlers. 'They keep telling each other that there's no such thing as a bug-man, Sorgan,' Veltan reported. 'They're claiming that you and your men are waving "bug-men" around as a way to leech more and more gold out of Aracia.'

'That's ridiculous, Veltan,' Sorgan protested. 'I know for a fact that Lady Aracia has actually *seen* the bug-people. I was standing right beside her down in your Domain when the bug-people and the Trogite priests were busy killing each other.'

'I know,' Veltan replied. 'I think big sister has been keeping that to herself. The last thing she wants here is to have all of her priests come down with panic. If they run away, she'll be all alone here.'

'We're going to have to do something about this, Veltan,' Sorgan said. 'The priests are obviously scraping this off the wall, but it looks to me like they've accidentally stumbled over the truth. Bug people are real, but they aren't coming through *this* part of Aracia's country.' Then he looked speculatively at Veltan. 'Maybe it's time for you to start making people believe that they're seeing something that's not really there, can't you?' he asked.

'If it's absolutely necessary,' Veltan replied. 'I don't want to do it too soon, though. She *can* sense things like that if I leave the illusions in place for too long.'

'I think a few brief glimpses might serve our purpose, Veltan. We want to confirm Aracia's belief that the bug-men are invading *this* part of her Domain, *and* to persuade the priests that I'm not lying and that Aracia *knows* that I'm not. I think I'll go have a little talk with Torl and Rabbit. If they come running out of that farm-land off to the west and there are images of several huge bugs right behind them, Aracia will probably go into hiding and this scheme the priests came up with will fall apart right then and there, wouldn't you say?'

'I think it's worth a try, Sorgan,' Veltan agreed. 'I've briefly touched Aracia's mind a few times since we arrived, and she's absolutely convinced that the Vlagh is out to get *her* personally. She's sure that the Vlagh wants to kill her, and she's terrified.'

'She can't actually die, can she? I mean she's immortal, isn't she?'

'Yes, she is, but she's drifting toward senility, so she's not sure of *anything* anymore. This has happened several times before. All of us get a little vague when we're approaching the end of one of our cycles, but Aracia tends to take it to extremes.'

'I had a talk with Torl and Rabbit last night,' Sorgan said the next morning in the cabin of the *Ascension*. 'Now they know about Veltan's illusions, and they'll make some show of fighting them off. The only problem we might have is that Aracia has to *see* this imitation skirmish, and she almost never comes out of that silly throne room of hers.'

'We've got some time to play with, Sorgan,' Padan said. 'You might want to have your men get started on the fort. Then, when its base is in place, you could invite holy Aracia to come out and have a look.' Padan scratched his bearded cheek. 'I suppose that technically you'll need her permission to continue, so a visit would be very appropriate. If Veltan and your scouts know when she'll be there, they'll be able to put on a show for her that'll send her running for cover – *and*, after that, she'll dismiss any priest who tries to tell her that you're a swindler.' Then he laughed as he remembered something that had happened in Kaldacin several years ago.

'What's so funny?' Sorgan asked.

'The Church of Amar down in the Empire has a fair number of dungeons scattered about. When a priest blunders and insults one of his superiors, they lock him in a hole in the ground and throw away the key. I'd imagine that Bersla would lose quite a bit of weight if Aracia had him locked up in a dungeon where all he had to eat would be bread and water.'

Sorgan frowned slightly. 'I wonder if we could get away with that,' he murmured.

*   *   *

The Maags were busy knocking down walls that afternoon. Padan saw that they were very good at destroying things. Building, however, might cause them a few problems.

A young priest came scurrying out of the central temple with a look of horror on his face. 'What are you *doing*?' he screamed.

'We need a fort to hold off the bug-people,' Sorgan replied. 'When we saw that nobody lives here in this part of the temple, we decided to modify it just a bit. There are quite a few similarities between forts and temples. Did you ever notice that? Anyway, things are going along fairly well. Give us a week or so, and the invasion of the bugs will stop right here.' Then he looked rather speculatively at the young priest. 'He looks pretty husky to me, Padan. If Lady Aracia wants this fort in place to defend her temple, she might just order all of her priests to come here and lend us a hand. The exercise would probably be good for them, wouldn't you say?'

'I'm sure it would,' Padan agreed. 'If we were to sweat some of the fat off them, they'd probably live longer.' He looked at the now horrified young priest. 'If you were to step in and lend us a hand with our fort here, you *might* even live past your thirtieth birthday. And if you were to *really* bear down, you *might* even live to be forty. Look at all the extra life you'll get out of a few weeks of hard work.'

The young priest turned and fled at that point.

Sorgan laughed. 'I think that might eliminate any further objections,' he said. 'The notion of doing *real* work doesn't seem to sit very well with Aracia's priesthood.'

'What an amazing thing,' Padan agreed.

Their imitation fort was coming along quite well now that Sorgan had leaned on his men and ordered them to follow Padan's instructions. They had what *looked* like a solid base about ten feet tall running along the west side of Aracia's temple.

'It's not really all that substantial, Sorgan,' Padan admitted, 'but Aracia wouldn't even recognize a *real* fort. I don't know that you want to wait too much longer. I'm sure that her priests are trying everything they can think of to discredit you. Let's not give them *too* much more time before she sees the skirmish between your men and the imitation bugs Veltan's going to conjure up. That's going to verify our scam and scare Aracia's stockings off. After that, we'll be home free.'

'You're probably right, Padan. I'll have a quick talk with Veltan, and he can go on out and start Torl and Rabbit this way while you and I go to the throne room and tell Aracia that we want to show her what we've accomplished so far.'

'What are you going to do if she refuses to come out here?'

Sorgan shrugged. 'I'll tell her that all work stops until she comes out here and approves of what we've done so far. No matter what her priests have been telling her, she's still terrified by the Vlagh, so she won't take any chances. She knows that her priests would be useless in a war, so she'll do just about anything to stay on the good side of me.'

Bersla was orating again, but for once Aracia didn't even seem to be listening.

'Where have you been?' she demanded of Sorgan when he entered the opulent throne room.

'Off on the west side of your temple, Lady,' Sorgan replied. 'My men have been building a fort to hold off the bug-people. It looks fairly good to me so far, but maybe you should come there and take a look. My men and I have always specialized in tearing forts down, not building them. If you have any suggestions, now's the time to make them. There's a fairly significant difference between a temple and a fort that you might want to think about. A temple says "come in," but a fort says "stay out." I think you'll see what I mean when we get there.'

'Holy Aracia is otherwise occupied right now, outlander,' the priestess Alcevan declared arrogantly.

'Listening to Bersla, you mean?' Sorgan asked. 'Has he said anything new and different today? I'm sure that Lady Aracia has heard every speech that he's cobbled together a hundred times or more. You could listen, if you'd like, and then when Lady Aracia returns you can sum them up for her.'

'Do you *really* need to have me look at this fort of yours, Sorgan?' Aracia asked.

'This is *your* temple, Lady Aracia,' Sorgan replied. 'If the bugs destroy it, your priests will have to build you a new one, and that might take them a while – quite a *long* while, I'd say, since fat people wear out in just a short time when they're doing real work. I suppose you could set up your throne in an open field somewhere, but I don't think very many of your priests would like to make speeches when it's raining on them. Let me put it to you in the simplest of terms, Lady. Come and look, or all work stops. We can't go any farther without your approval.'

Aracia's eyes went wide and she stood up. 'Let's go look, Captain Hook-Beak,' she said.

'Now that's more like it,' Sorgan said approvingly.

'It's called a catapult, Lady,' Sorgan explained. 'The Trogs invented it. Up north in your brother's Domain, it worked out quite well. It was originally invented to throw rocks at the enemy, but we used it to throw burning pitch at the bug-people. If you want to get somebody's – or some*thing's* – immediate attention, set him on fire.'

'I see that you're still putting sharp stakes in the ground,' Aracia noted.

Sorgan nodded. 'We've got gallons and gallons of the venom we leeched out of dead bugs down in Zelana's Domain. We dip the stakes in that venom before we plant them in the ground. When a bug-man steps on one of those, he dies almost immediately. It's a quick way to get rid of a *lot* of enemies.'

'Is *that* as high as you're going to make your fort, Sorgan?' Aracia asked.

'No, ma'am, that's just the base. There'll be another ten feet on top of that part of the fort.'

'Ho, Cap'n,' one of the Maags shouted. 'I think the scouts are coming back, but it looks to me like they're being chased by bug-people.'

Sorgan swore. 'I *told* those idiots to be careful!' he exclaimed. Then he took Aracia by the arm. 'Let's get up on top of the fort. It'll be safer there.'

Aracia's face had gone pale, and her eyes seemed filled with terror.

'Over that way, Cap'n,' Padan said in a fair imitation of the Maag dialect. 'There's a ladder a short way down along the wall. Once we get up on top, I'll kick the ladder away.'

'That's not a bad idea, Black-Beard,' Sorgan agreed.

'Black-Beard?' Padan muttered.

'Sorry,' Sorgan said softly. 'You've got to have a Maag kind of name, and that was about the best I could come up with.'

They reached the ladder and scrambled on up. 'Leave the ladder where it is for now, Black-Beard,' Sorgan said. 'If one of our scouts gets clear of the bug-people, we want him up here. I need to know just exactly what happened out there.'

'Aye, Cap'n,' Padan replied.

'Shouldn't I return to the main temple?' Aracia asked.

Sorgan shook his head. 'It's not safe now, Lady Aracia,' he said. 'My men and I can protect you up here on this wall, but those narrow corridors wouldn't be safe.' Then he looked out toward the west. 'There!' he said, pointing at a berm no more than a hundred feet away. 'My men are doing something right for a change. They took some high ground and it looks to me like they're holding it. There are probably a lot of dead bugs on the far side.'

'Isn't that Rabbit with the others?' Padan asked.

'That's Rabbit, all right,' Sorgan agreed. 'He's got that bow he made down in Veltan country.'

'I didn't know that he had a bow,' Padan said.

'He spent too much time with Longbow,' Sorgan declared.

'Now *that's* the one I'd like to see out there,' Padan said. 'If there's only one Longbow and a thousand bug-men, put your money on Longbow. He'll kill every one of them.'

'Our men are holding that berm,' Sorgan said then. 'The bug-people *aren't* going to get past them.'

'Those bug-things aren't very big, are they?' Aracia said then.

'You don't really see very many big ones, your Majesty,' Padan said. 'Now and then the Vlagh will *make* a big one, but most of them are what Rabbit calls "teenie-weenies."'

'The little rascal just came down off that berm,' Sorgan said, 'and he's running this way.'

'He probably wants to report, Cap'n,' Padan suggested. 'You made a big issue of that when you sent them out to scout around.

You told them all to stay alive so that they could tell you things that you needed to know.'

The little smith came scrambling up the ladder and then stood there puffing. 'We hit a snag out there, Cap'n,' he wheezed.

'Catch your breath before you report, Rabbit,' Sorgan said.

'Aye, Cap'n,' the little smith said. Then he stood breathing deeply for a few moments. 'Things went real good for a while, Cap'n,' he started again. 'Just about the only breed of bugs we saw were those little ones, but when we started back, Torl caught a few glimpses of great big ones. I ain't exaggerating one little bit, Cap'n. They stood almost ten feet tall, and they probably weighed close to a ton.'

'You're not serious!' Sorgan exclaimed.

'I'm afraid I am, Cap'n. This wall our people made here just won't work. If those big ones are as strong as the others, they'll smash down your fort here with their bare hands and then throw the bits and pieces out into the Wasteland just to get rid of them.'

'You'd better round up the men, Black-Beard,' Sorgan said to Padan. 'This wall here's going to have to be at least twice as high and three times as thick if it's going to hold off the giant bug-people.' Then he took Aracia's arm again. 'There's not much you or your people are going to be able to do to help us. Right now I'd say that blocking off most of the corridors your people included when they built the temple would be the best thing to do. You don't really want more than one hallway leading there.'

3

_—◄►—_

The men out on the berm continued to shout and to roll large rocks down the empty far side to make it appear that there were still enemies charging their position. Queen Aracia stayed very close to Sorgan, but she seemed to be growing more and more calm. 'The bug-people are truly hideous aren't they, Captain Hook-Beak?' she asked.

'Oh, yes. The first time I ever saw one of them was right after Eleria's flood had come rushing down the ravine to almost swamp the village of Lattash. That flood drowned bug-people by the hundreds, and their bodies were washed on down to the village. _That_ was when my men and I found out that those little bug-people had snake fangs and they were deadly. I almost gave your sister's gold back to her and sailed on back home at that point.'

'You were actually afraid? I didn't think you knew the meaning of the word afraid.'

'I wasn't quite ready for snake-bugs – or maybe bug-snakes – at that time. It took a while for me to get used to the notion. I have Longbow to thank for that. There's a man who isn't afraid of anything.'

'I know,' Aracia said. 'I spoke with him a few times when I was observing the war in Veltan's Domain. Is he really as good as everybody says he is?'

'Better, probably,' Sorgan replied. 'If your sister had been lucky enough to have ten men like Longbow, she wouldn't have needed me.' Sorgan shaded his eyes and peered down at the ridge lying to the west of the fort. 'My men aren't rolling rocks or throwing spears anymore, and that sort of says that they've managed to kill all of the bug-people who'd been pursuing them.'

'It's safe for me to return to the main temple, then?' Aracia asked.

'Let's hold off until morning, Lady,' Sorgan said. 'Let's not take any unnecessary chances.' Then he looked questioningly at his employer. 'Would it offend you if I had something to eat?' he asked her.

'Not in the slightest, Captain,' she replied. 'I think I'll nibble on the sunset while you have supper.'

'I'm *never* going to get used to that,' Sorgan said. 'How can *anybody* live on nothing but light?'

'It's one of our advantages,' Aracia replied. 'We don't need food, and we don't need sleep – not during our ordinary cycle, anyway. It's almost sleep-time now, though. I can feel it creeping up on me. I *wish* it would wait, though. I've got a lot of things that need to be taken care of, and I don't think I've got enough time.'

'If it's all right with you, Lady Aracia, we'll wait until the sun's up tomorrow morning before we go back to your main temple. Let's be sure that there aren't any bug-people hiding in the corridors there.'

'Whatever you think best, Captain Hook-Beak.'

Padan felt a bit puzzled. It seemed to him that once Queen Aracia had been separated from her priesthood, she was almost normal. She *also* seemed to be developing a certain attachment to

Sorgan Hook-Beak. The Maag's roughshod approach seemed to be bringing Aracia right to the brink of normalcy.

The dawn came, and Sorgan, along with Ox, Ham-Hand, Padan and Rabbit, accompanied Aracia to her throne room. They paused briefly at the door while Aracia listened. When she heard what was being said on the other side, her eyes narrowed and her face went bleak. 'Absolute scoundrels,' she said. 'Why was I ever foolish enough to believe anything they told me?'

'We all make mistakes, Lady,' Sorgan said rather placatingly.

'Well, I've made more than enough,' Aracia said. Then she looked Sorgan right in the face. 'I'm paying you to defend me, mighty Sorgan,' she said. 'You may earn some of that pay right here and now. I don't want *any* of those priests to come within ten feet of me.'

'I think we can handle that, yes,' Sorgan said. 'I take it that you're planning to hurt their feelings just a bit.'

'Watch,' she replied. 'Watch and learn.' Then she literally slammed the throne room door open.

'Clear the way!' Sorgan bellowed. 'Stand aside or die!' And he drew his sword.

It seemed to Padan that Sorgan might have taken it just a bit farther than necessary, but he drew his own sword to back Sorgan up. Then the party marched across the throne room in Aracia's wake.

'Great was our concern for you, most holy Aracia,' Bersla of the big belly declared.

'But not quite great enough to move you to come looking for me, I noticed,' Aracia replied.

'But—'

'Close your mouth!' Aracia snapped. Then she looked at Sorgan. 'If he says anything else, kill him!' she ordered.

'It will be my pleasure, most holy,' Sorgan replied with a florid bow that seemed to Padan to be totally out of character.

Aracia's face grew hard and cold. 'Much have I considered the merits – or the lack of merit – of those here in this room today,' she declared. 'I have seen greed, cowardice, indolence, o'erwhelming self-esteem, and a total lack of anything at all that even remotely resembles honor. That, however, is about to change. Hear my command, my worshipers, and obey me – lest ye die.'

'She definitely has a way with words, doesn't she?' Padan whispered to Sorgan.

'She's getting their attention, that's for sure,' Sorgan replied concealing his grin with one hand.

'Moreover,' Aracia continued, 'those who do *not* obey and escape their rightful punishment will no longer be priests and therefore no longer welcome in my temple. Hear my command and obey without question. Gather together and proceed straight forth to that part of my holy temple which lies to the west. There will you – one and all – give assistance to those who have come here to defend me. You will do what they require without hesitation or complaint, and you will continue your labor until our defenses are complete.' Then she motioned to Sorgan. 'I'm not really very good at this, am I?' she said with some shame.

'You're doing just fine, Lady,' Sorgan replied. 'You even surprised *me* just now.'

'I must have done something right then. Now, what do you think I should do to any of these halfwits who refuse?'

'I've had a fair degree of success with a whip, Lady,' Sorgan replied. 'Fifty lashes is usually about right. Then, after the others have seen a few of those floggings, I usually don't get anymore arguments.'

'I'm not sure if I could do something like that, Captain Hook-Beak.'

'That's what you're paying *me* to do, Lady. I'll take care of it for you.' Then he turned to his second mate. 'Herd them on out of here, Ham-Hand,' he said.

'Aye, Cap'n,' Ham-Hand replied with a broad grin.

Padan suddenly laughed when a peculiar thought came to him.

'What's so funny?' Sorgan asked.

'Since those priests will be working with our men, they should probably eat the same kind of food.'

'Beans?' Sorgan asked.

'It *would* be fair, Sorgan, wouldn't you say?'

Sorgan started to laugh.

ThE hORSE-SOLDIERS

1

Prince Ekial of the Land of the Malavi had been just a bit edgy about the presence of Lord Dahlaine's pet sun. She was giving them all the light they needed, and she *was* holding back the bitter chill of winter there in the far north, but the concept of using a miniature sun as a house-pet made Ekial just a bit nervous. The 'What ifs' kept nagging at him.

He'd spent some time with Longbow in Dahlaine's 'map room' carefully studying Dahlaine's miniature duplication of the rounded-down range of mountains Longbow had decided would be the best course to follow on their way on down to the upper end of Long-Pass. Ekial hadn't made a big issue of it, but he was rather looking forward to being separated from the Trogites and the Maags. They'd been very useful during the war in Crystal Gorge, but their superior attitude had rubbed Ekial the wrong way on several occasions, so he felt a certain relief when the mountain range became visible on the eastern horizon.

Longbow's friend, Red-Beard, pulled his horse, Seven, in alongside Ekial. 'How's our day gone so far?' he asked.

'*Mine* just got a bit better,' Ekial replied. 'Now we've reached the mountains, we'll be moving off in a different direction from the Trogites and the pirates. That will probably warm my heart. Don't get me wrong, Red-Beard, I *like* them, but they move so slow. I could have been here three days ago.'

'That's one of the nice things about riding a horse,' Red-Beard agreed. 'Old Seven here doesn't move very fast, but he could run circles around those foot-soldiers. Of course, he won't have to run for a while. I get to sit here until Skell delivers the archers from Chief Old-Bear's tribe. Then Seven and I'll guide them on down to the upper end of Long-Pass.'

'Longbow told me that the archers of that tribe are the best in the whole world,' Ekial said.

Red-Beard smiled. 'Every tribe believes that they're the best,' he said. 'Longbow himself *is* the best in the world, but the others in his tribe aren't nearly as good as he is.' Red-Beard hesitated slightly. 'You don't necessarily have to tell him that I said that he's the best,' he added. 'He doesn't need to know that I believe that.'

Ekial laughed. 'Your secret's safe with me, friend Red-Beard,' he said. Then he added, 'Doesn't he *ever* smile?'

'Oh – once or twice a year, I'd say. Every so often he'll even smile three times if it's a very good year.'

Longbow would be going on ahead, so getting the Tonthakans and Matans to the west end of Long-Pass would be Ekial's responsibility.

Longbow asked him if he had the route firmly in mind.

'I spent as much time looking at Dahlaine's map as *you* did, Longbow,' Ekial replied. 'Won't it be just a little dangerous for you to travel alone, though? The bug-people *will* be coming this way. That much is certain. I *could* send a party of horsemen with you.'

Longbow shook his head. 'They'd only slow me down,' he replied.

'You don't *really* believe that you can run faster than a horse, do you?' Ekial demanded.

'Not faster,' Longbow replied. 'Longer beats faster almost any time at all.'

'How long would you say that you can run?'

'Twenty hours or so, anyway, and I *can* eat while I'm running.'

'That raises another problem, friend Longbow,' Red-Beard said. 'Horses are nice enough, I suppose, but they *do* have to eat, and I don't see very much grass around here.'

'I was just about to ask you the same question,' Ekial told the archer. 'We *have* to find grass.'

Longbow shrugged. 'Tell your men to keep their eyes out for bison. They eat grass just like your horses do. When you see a bison with his head down, he's probably eating. Chase him away and you'll have happy horses in just a little while. Is there anything else?'

'Is it always *this* cold around here in the winter-time?'

'The local people have told me that it is. Be glad that it's cold now, though. If it starts to warm up, there's probably a blizzard coming your way.'

'I've heard the locals talking about blizzards a few times,' Ekial said. 'Are they *really* all that bad?'

'You might want to talk with Two-Hands about that. He was caught in one near the village of Asmie when he was very young. He had to dig a cave in the snow to survive.'

Ekial shuddered, and decided not to pursue that. 'Let's move on, shall we?' he suggested.

Since Dahlaine's little toy sun would be going with the Maags and Trogites, there wasn't too much daylight left, so they set up camp for the night before they'd gone very far to the south. Ekial was fairly sure that they should start out at first light each day. The horses could cover a fair distance in six or seven hours, but the Tonthakans and Matans couldn't move that fast, and to make things even worse, the Malavi were going to have to find grass for their horses every day, and that promised to slow things down to a crawl.

Longbow had set off the following morning.

'What's your hurry, Longbow?' Ekial asked.

'When I reach the upper end of Long-Pass, I'll need to go on down to the mouth so that I can guide the Trogites back up to the most likely places for them to build their forts.'

'You're going to wear out your shoes, Longbow. That's about four hundred miles, you know,' Ekial remarked.

Longbow shrugged. 'Whatever it takes.'

Ekial, somewhat regretfully, sent his friend Ariga and a sizeable number of other horse-soldiers off to the south to scout the eastern edge of the Wasteland to determine if the bug-people were anywhere in sight yet. He'd have much preferred to lead that scouting party himself, but he was fairly sure that wouldn't sit too well with Kathlak and Two-Hands. It was tedious – even boring – to plod along with the foot-soldiers, but it *was* sort of necessary.

There was a slight cloudiness that day, and the thin clouds made the sun look sort of pale and sickly. Winter was a very depressing time of year.

Ekial was about to call a halt for the day when Two-Hands and Longbow's Tonthakan friend, Athlan, came up through the rounded foothills to join him. 'There's company coming, Ekial,' Chief Two-Hands reported.

'Oh? Who might that be?'

'It might be almost anybody,' Athlan said. 'They're still a good ways off, but we're almost positive that they aren't people-people. They look like bug-people to me.'

'Where?' Ekial asked sharply.

'They're a few miles out in sand-country,' Two-Hands said. 'We might have missed them, but they're kicking up a lot of dust. We can't give you any kind of details, since they're still several miles away, and the dust pretty much conceals them.'

'If Long-Pass is going to be their invasion route, what are they doing a hundred and sixty miles north of that pass?' Ekial demanded.

'I haven't the foggiest idea,' Two-Hands admitted. 'I suppose that it *might* be possible that they're planning to cross over the mountains and then go south through the foothills on the other side to someplace about half-way down Long-Pass. That *would* put them behind the Trogites if the fort-builders are going to concentrate on blocking the pass on the west end.'

'How many of them would you say there are?' Ekial asked.

'It's a little hard to tell,' Athlan said. 'They're quite a ways out in that desert, and the dust pretty much conceals them. I'd say several hundred thousand at least. The dust cloud's at least ten miles wide, so we aren't talking about a couple dozen or so.'

Ekial started to swear.

2

T hey kept a close eye on the creatures out there in the desert for the next several hours, but it didn't seem to Ekial that their enemies were in any great hurry. He mentioned that to Longbow's friend Athlan when the archer returned to report that he'd just located a sizeable meadow with lots of grass just ahead.

Athlan scratched his cheek. 'From what Longbow told me a while back, this will probably be our last war with the children of the Vlagh,' he said. 'I asked him once a few weeks ago if we'd be fighting the bug-people for the rest of our lives. That's when he told me about the twin volcanos in Zelana's Domain, and the sudden flood in Veltan's part of the Land of Dhrall. Neither the bug-people or anybody else will be able to attack *those* two regions.'

'*And* that wall of blue fire in Crystal Gorge closes the only route up to Dahlaine's territory as well,' Ekial added.

'It did that, all right,' Athlan agreed. 'I go cold all over when I think about *that* disaster. I've seen blue fire before – usually in swamps, where it's just a faint flicker dancing on top of the water. The blue fire in Crystal Gorge went *way* past a flicker, though.' Athlan paused. 'He *did* tell you about that "unknown friend," didn't he?'

'Oh, yes. I wasn't sure just how much of what he said I should believe – but that was before the blue fire went roaring down Crystal Gorge. If Longbow's got a friend who can do things like *that*, why does he need to hire outlander armies?'

'It wasn't Longbow who hired you, Prince Ekial. I've heard that it was Dahlaine. Longbow himself doesn't *need* any outside help. I'm not trying to offend you, Prince Ekial, but once Longbow told me that bringing outlander armies here to the Land of Dhrall really only had one purpose. You're here to see just how terrible the people who live here can be if somebody from another part of the world decides that he wants all the gold in the Land of Dhrall. After what happened to those idiots from the Trogite Church in Veltan's Domain, I'm sure that every outlander who's here realizes what a terrible mistake it'd be to come here with some notion of getting rich. People who offend us *don't* get rich. They get dead – soon – instead.'

The weather turned bitterly cold that night, and Ekial didn't like that at all. 'Why can't it warm up just a bit?' he complained to Chief Two-Hands.

'You don't really want that to happen, Prince Ekial,' Two-Hands replied. 'A brief warm spell usually means that there's a blizzard on the way, and you *don't* want to come up against one of those. The warm spell goes away rather quickly, and it's suddenly ten times colder than it was before – at least it *seems* that way. The wind cuts into you like a knife, and the snow whirling around you blots out everything more than two or three feet away.'

'Longbow told me that you had to burrow down under the snow during a blizzard once,' Ekial said.

'Oh, *yes*!' Two-Hands said. 'I was wearing one of our bison-hide robes, and it *still* felt like I was getting frozen into a solid block of ice. I couldn't see anything beyond two feet away because the snow was so thick. I could barely see my hand in front of my face. I didn't know which way was which, and it was getting colder and colder by the minute. I knew that if I didn't get in out of that wind, I'd freeze to death. My only option at that point was to burrow down into a snow-bank. I knew that my burrow wouldn't be toasty warm, but at least it would protect me from that screaming wind. That's when I discovered that snow will pack up if you lean your back against it and push. I was finally able to open up a chamber about the same size as a small room in a very small house. There was air to breathe, and if I got thirsty, I could eat a few handfuls of snow. I happened to have a couple of slabs of smoked meat in my belt-pouch, so I had shelter, water and food. I stayed there for a few days, and then I took a look outside. It'd stopped snowing, so I made my way back to Asmie – just in time to witness my own funeral. You wouldn't *believe* how upset people become when the guest of honor at a funeral shows up and he's still breathing.' He smiled then. 'Word of what I'd done got spread around all over the village, and the young boys of Asmie thought it might be a lot of fun to make snow tunnels around the village in the dead of winter.' He shrugged. 'It gives them something to do, and it keeps them in out of the weather. Last winter eight or nine boys built what amounted to a palace under the snow on the south side of Asmie. They made miles of tunnels and they had large chambers here and there. It kept them out of mischief, so I didn't scold them or anything. I *did* order them to mark the locations of their tunnels and meeting halls, though. It's not really safe to walk over the top of a snow-tunnel. The women of the tribe mentioned that to me fifteen or twenty times a day, as I recall.'

'Are we at all likely to get hit with a blizzard like *that* one?' Ekial asked.

Two-Hands shook his head. 'Dahlaine's got a very tight grip on the weather just now. I'm not really sure exactly why, though. From what I've heard, I could go a whole lifetime without seeing that older sister of his. I guess she's gone completely crazy.'

'Oh, *that's* nice,' Ekial said. 'Why should we bother to save her? Let the bug-people eat her and have done with it.'

Two-Hands shook his head. 'If the Vlagh gets her feet into people-country – where there *is* food – she'll lay millions and millions of eggs. That's what these wars have been all about, really. The Vlagh wants the whole world, and if she wins just one war here, she'll spread out and *take* it. It won't just be Dahlaine's sister who'll be eaten, it'll be the entire world, and all the people of the world will be nothing but something to eat.'

Ekial felt a sense of horror welling up from his stomach at that point.

'There are thousands and thousands of those bug-things coming this way from that desert out there, Ekial,' Ariga reported a few days later when Ekial's horse-soldiers, the Tonthakan archers, and the Matan spear-throwers reached the narrow opening at the upper end of Long-Pass.

'Why don't you just go on out there and kill them?' Ekial asked.

'You're joking, of course,' Ariga said.

'Well, maybe,' Ekial conceded, 'but not entirely. We've got to hold those things out there back until the Trogites get here and build a fort. We have a sizeable number of Tonthakan archers here now, and Matan spear-throwers as well. We've worked with them before, and things turned out quite well.'

'I think I get your point, Ekial. See if I've got it right. The archers and spear-throwers sort of stay out of sight while *we* gallop on out there and nudge the bug-people into trying to chase us down.'

'Nudge?' Ekial asked.

'We have lances, remember? We gallop on out to where the bug-people are busy sneaking, and we skewer a few dozen with our lances. Then we gallop on back. The bug-people should be very angry because we just killed quite a few of their friends and relatives, so they try to chase after us. That's when we lead them into the range of the arrows and spears. In short, we lead them, and the archers and spear-men kill them. Isn't that sort of what you had in mind?'

'I'd say that it's worth a try, Ariga, but let's hold off until morning. The Tonthakans and Matans are probably worn down just a bit, so let's give them some time to rest before we put them to work.'

'You're getting better at this, Ekial.'

'Practice,' Ekial replied modestly.

3

—➤◆◄—

'I think we were right about why those bug-people were coming across that desert miles and miles to the north of this pass,' Kathlak the Tonthakan said the next day. 'I sent out some scouts, and they told me that there *are* enemies in the hills and along the ridges on both sides of this pass. I'd say that what happened in Crystal Gorge taught them a lesson. They learned that having enemies up above you doesn't make for very pleasant days. It looks like they learned very fast. If there *are* bug-people up above this pass when the Trogites are coming up here to build forts, life could get very exciting for them. I'd say that cleaning off those hills and ridges might be even more important than killing the ones coming toward the upper end of the pass.'

'Those bug-things seem to be more clever than everybody was telling us they are,' Two-Hands added. 'They seem to learn much faster than we'd been told they could.'

Ekial swore. 'I'm afraid that you two might be right,' he said. 'Clearing off the ridges along the sides of the pass is probably much more important than thinning out the herd coming across that Wasteland. If the Trogites are blocked off, we'll be in deep trouble.'

'A suggestion – if it's all right,' Kathlak said.

'I'll listen to almost anything right now,' Ekial admitted.

'There are trees up along those rims,' Kathlak said, 'and Tonthakans are skilled at hunting in a forest. The Matans are more accustomed to open country. If I led *my* people up into these tired, worn-out old mountains, *we* could probably deal with the bug people up there, and that would leave Two-Hands and his spear-throwers free to deal with the enemies coming in off the desert, wouldn't you say?'

'It *does* make sense, Ekial,' Two-Hands agreed. 'Throwing spears in a forest is mostly a waste of time – and spear-points. If we let the Tonthakans deal with the enemies hiding in the forest, your horse-soldiers and my spear-throwers should be able to thin out the bugs coming across the desert, don't you think?'

'I suppose we can give it a try,' Ekial agreed.

'How long would you say that it's likely to take for the Trogites to get up here?' Kathlak asked.

'I wouldn't start looking for them tomorrow,' Ekial replied. 'I think there might be some law down in Trog-land that forbids a soldier to walk more than ten miles a day.'

'That's ridiculous!' Kathlak exclaimed.

Ekial smiled faintly. 'Laws are supposed to be ridiculous, aren't they? Gunda explained it to me once. A Trogite army moves as a group, as I understood what he was saying. That means that the army can only move as fast as the slowest man can walk, and they spend a lot of their time resting.'

'If that's as fast as they can go, they don't really *need* to rest, do they?'

'I guess that it's a custom, and customs don't really *have* to make sense. It's about a hundred and twenty miles from the beach at the bottom of the pass up to here, so we're not likely to see any Trogites for twelve days or so. That gives us twelve days to clear away the bugs along the rims of the pass and thin out the ones crawling through the sand out here. We've got plenty to do, so I suppose we should get started.'

There was a mindless quality about the Creatures of the Wasteland that chilled Ekial. It appeared that they were not intelligent enough to be afraid, so they kept on trying to do what they'd been told to do despite the fact that they were running directly into the face of certain death. To some degree they *looked* like people, but they definitely didn't *think* like people. On one occasion during the war in Crystal Gorge, Longbow had told Ekial that the servants of the Vlagh were totally unaware of their mortality. 'They seem to think that they'll live forever. Of course they don't have any idea of what "forever" means. A bug lives in a world of now, and that's all that they can understand. Yesterday was too long ago for them to have any memory of it, and tomorrow will probably never arrive.'

'Idiocy!' Ekial had exclaimed.

'That's a fair description, yes,' Longbow had blandly agreed. 'Many things that work quite well when your enemies are people *won't* work when they're bugs.'

'What would you say is the best way to deal with an enemy that's too stupid to be afraid?'

'I've had a fair amount of success with killing every one I see, friend Ekial.'

'All right, then,' Ekial said to a number of his friends the next morning, 'try to remember that the enemies we'll encounter might *look* like people, but they aren't. Don't waste time trying to frighten them, because you *can't* frighten them. They have no idea of what "afraid" means.'

'They might start to understand after a lot of their friends get killed,' Skarn said.

'That's the whole point, Skarn. The bug-people don't *have* friends – at least not in the way that *we* understand the word. They don't have enough time to grow friendly with other bugs. They live for six weeks, and then they die of the bug version of "old age." They take orders from the Vlagh, and that's the only relationship they have. They'll *try* to follow the Vlagh's orders, and they won't understand what "danger" means. If we just happened to kill every bug out there but just left one of them alive, that last one would keep on trying to attack us.'

'That's stupid!' Orgal declared.

'It goes a long way *past* "stupid," Orgal. Nobody I know of has yet invented a word that describes how brainless the bug-people really are. They don't know *how* to think. They *are* poisonous, though, so don't get too close to them. Use your lances, but try not to break them. Concentrate on killing the ones that are close to the bottom of this slope. Don't go galloping out into that silly desert. All *we're* supposed to do is hold the bugs back until the Trogites get up here and build the fort. As soon as the fort's in place, we're probably going to be out of work.'

THE VIOLATION OF THE TEMPLE

1

It seemed to Ox that Captain Hook-Beak was more than a little disturbed by Lady Aracia's sudden change of position. As long as she'd been willing to sit on her throne listening to the overdone orations of praise, she hadn't caused the slightest bit of inconvenience. Now that she realized just how totally useless her priests were, Sorgan and the other Maags would have to come up with ways to step around their new – and unwanted – helpers.

'I think you'd better pass the word to the other captains, Ox,' Sorgan said when they'd returned to the *Ascension*. 'We need to talk this over and come up with some way to keep all those silly priests from finding out what we're *really* doing here.'

'I'll take care of it, Cap'n,' Ox replied. Then he went out onto the deck of the *Ascension*, lowered the skiff, and rowed back to the beach.

It took him a couple of hours to gather up most of the Maag ship-captains, and it was well past midnight before Sorgan could advise the other captains that things had radically changed.

'Everything was going just the way we wanted it to go,' he said, 'but then the lady who's paying us came to her senses and woke up. She ordered all those fat priests to go out to the west wall of that silly temple to lend us a hand.'

'Why didn't you just tell her that we don't *need* those people, Sorgan?' a captain called Squint-Eye demanded.

'She took me by surprise,' Sorgan admitted. 'That was the last thing I expected from her. She's not nearly as stupid as we all thought. She came down on those lazy priests of hers *very* hard. She threatened to kick any one of them who refused to help us out of the priesthood and banish him from her temple.'

'I wish I'd been there to see that,' a captain called Gimpy said. 'I'll bet that most of the faces of those priests fell right off.'

'They didn't seem too happy, that's for sure. Now, how are we going to get those fools out from underfoot?'

'Ah, Cap'n,' Ox said then, 'would you like to hear a suggestion?'

'I'll listen to almost anything right now, Ox.'

'We've pretty much blocked off that west side of the temple, wouldn't you say?'

'All except for adding another ten feet or so to our fake fort. Where are you going with this, Ox?'

'The west side's just about finished, Cap'n,' Ox replied, 'but the south side hasn't been touched yet, and the imitation bug-people will attack from any direction we want them to, wouldn't you say?'

Sorgan blinked.

'I'd say that solves your problem, Hook-Beak,' Squint-Eye said with a broad grin. 'You could have saved us all a lot of time if you'd learned to listen to your first mate. It sounds to me like he's about three jumps ahead of you.'

'Or maybe even four,' Gimpy added.

'I'm not really sure, Cap'n,' Ox replied when Sorgan started asking questions as soon as the other Maag ship-captains had left the *Ascension*. 'The whole idea seemed to come to me while you were telling the other captains about the problem Lady Zelana's sister dropped on us.'

'Now you're starting to sound like Longbow,' Sorgan said. 'Did you hear some lady's voice coming from no place at all?'

'It wasn't a lady's voice, Cap'n. I'm sure that I've heard it before, though. If the idea's as good as I think it is, it most likely came from somebody who knows Lady Aracia very well.'

'Veltan, maybe?'

Ox shook his head. 'No, I'm sure it wasn't Veltan. Whoever it was didn't have to say very much to me to get the point across. About all our *other* friend said to me was "Why not send those worthless priests down to the south wall of the temple and put them to work *there* instead of where the work's almost finished? Keep them busy, but out from underfoot." Then it all seemed to come together, and it made a lot of sense. I didn't mean to embarrass you or anything like that, but as soon as I thought my way through the whole notion, I just started to tell you about it without waiting until we were alone.'

'Well, *whoever* it was solved our problem for us, and I don't embarrass all that easy.' Then Sorgan scratched his cheek. 'I think we might want to take Rabbit and Torl along with us. We'll need to have them tell Lady Aracia that they saw a different group of bug-people sneaking down toward the south wall while we were holding off the west wall from the attack of their friends.'

'You might want to talk with Veltan, Cap'n,' Ox suggested. 'If we can persuade Lady Aracia to send the fat people to the south wall, a few sightings of bug-people creeping through the bushes would confirm what we tell Lady Aracia, and I'm sure that reports of those sightings will get back to her real soon.'

'Give our new friend my thanks, Ox,' Sorgan said with a broad grin. 'Whoever he is, he's doing most of the work for us in this imitation war.'

'I'll pass that on the next time he stops by, Cap'n,' Ox replied.

Then Sorgan grinned. 'Now that I've had enough time to think my way through this, I'd say that maybe Squint-Eye and Gimpy should be the ones who should oversee those modifications of the south wall. It'll give them something to do instead of dropping clever remarks on me every time I turn around.'

'I'm sure that they'll feel honored that you suggested them to Lady Aracia, Cap'n,' Ox replied with no hint of a smile.

The following morning Ox went out from the west wall of the temple to the berm where Torl and Rabbit had staged their imitation invasion. 'The Cap'n wants you two to go with him to talk with Lady Aracia,' he told them. 'He wants you to say that you saw quite a few bug-people sneaking around toward the south wall of her temple.'

'That *would* make a certain amount of sense,' Torl agreed. 'If this was *really* a war, that's the sort of thing the bug-people would do.'

'You might be right there,' Ox said, 'but that's not why he's doing it. He doesn't want all those fat priests underfoot while he's setting up his deception. There'll be things going on that ain't none of their business, and he wants to make certain sure that none of them are around when him and Veltan start playing games.'

'That's my cousin,' Torl chuckled.

2

Fat Bersla was nowhere in sight when they entered the throne room, and the snippy little priestess Alcevan seemed to have taken his place. She glared at Captain Hook-Beak when he led the Maags into the room.

'I'll get right to the point here, Lady Aracia,' Sorgan said. 'There's something we might have overlooked. It seems that the bug-people might just be getting a bit more clever. This little fellow here is known as Rabbit, the smith on the *Seagull* – my own ship – and Rabbit's much more clever than he lets on. When my scouts were holding back the new varieties of bug-people, Rabbit noticed that there were quite a few of the older ones who *weren't* trying to attack that berm. Why don't you tell her what you saw, Rabbit?'

'Aye, Cap'n,' Rabbit replied. 'What I saw didn't seem to make any sense, Lady,' Rabbit told Zelana's sister. '*Most* of them were charging toward that berm we'd raised up to hold them off, but then I caught a kind of flicker back in the bushes behind where the new bugs were charging. I looked a bit closer and saw quite a few of the little ones we've seen before sneaking down through the thick bushes. They were staying low, but I *was* able to see that there were *hundreds* of them back there, and it seemed to me that they weren't the least bit interested in the war their big brothers were fighting around our berm. They were going almost due south, and that wasn't where the war was being fought. Now, the Cap'n and his men have built a fairly good fort along that west wall of your temple, but we don't have even one single soldier on that south wall, and the construction isn't really very good. Now, *if* those other bug-people *are* planning an attack on that side of your temple, they'll probably be able to walk right in without no trouble at all.'

'I'm sure you can see where this is going, Lady Aracia,' Sorgan said. '*My* people can hold the west wall of your temple without much trouble now that we've modified it. That south wall isn't very good, and I'd say that it's not really strong enough to hold back a mosquito. I thank you for your concern and your offer of help, but I'd say that beefing up that south wall's a lot more important right now. I strongly suggest that you send your priests south instead of west.'

'I will do as you command, mighty Sorgan,' Aracia declared, 'but as soon as you and your people have beaten back the invaders, we must go forth from the temple and gather up all of my people who live beyond the temple walls and bring them *here* so that they'll be safe. We must *not* permit the servants of the Vlagh to destroy them.'

The priestess Alcevan looked sharply at Aracia. 'You can not bring all those commoners here into the holy temple. They are not sanctified, and their presence here will *defile* your holy temple!'

'The people – *my* people – are far more significant than the indigents who call themselves priests,' Aracia declared. 'If you should find their presence here offensive, feel free to go forth from the temple to seek out a different god to worship. If you would continue to worship *me*, you *will* do as I tell you to do, and *this* I say: The commons *will* join us here, and you and the other priests will see to their needs. *You* will eat only after *they* have eaten, and you will surrender your beds and your warm clothes to them without question or complaint. The *people* come first in my eyes, and you will serve *them* even as you would serve *me* – or I will send you away. You will no longer contaminate my temple.'

Alcevan's face went pale, and her expression was one of chagrin.

'Well now, Cap'n,' Ox said quietly. 'It sort of looks like maybe Zelana's sister's starting to grow up.'

'Let's not make a big issue of that just yet, Ox,' Sorgan replied. 'She *might* just change her mind again after she's gone a week or so without any adoration.'

THE GIFTED STUDENT

1

Keselo had also had some problems with Lord Dahlaine's 'toy sun.' His education at the University of Kaldacin had taught him that a sun needed a certain volume before it qualified as a true sun. Dahlaine's little toy violated almost everything Keselo had learned or worked out for himself. He knew that most of the rules didn't apply to the members of Dahlaine's family, but still—

The toy sun stayed with them all the way to the coast.

They reached the large bay where the Trogite ships Commander Narasan had hired in Castano were anchored, and Sorgan's Maags had taken about half of that fleet and sailed on south to bamboozle Lady Zelana's sister.

'I'm glad that Sorgan's the one who'll have to deal with that crazy woman,' Gunda said. 'I got more than enough of her the last time we were down here.'

'She set *my* teeth on edge just a bit, too,' Andar agreed.

'All right, gentlemen,' Commander Narasan, who'd just come up from the beach, said. 'We're not going to board *our* ships for several days. Let's give Sorgan and his men a good head start. Go tell the men to set up camp and have the cooks fix something for supper.'

'Beans?' Gunda asked with a definite note of distaste in his voice.

'What a marvelous idea, Gunda,' Commander Narasan said with mock enthusiasm. 'Beans will be just fine. I wonder why *I* didn't think of that.'

After they'd loaded about half of Commander Narasan's army on board the remaining ships, they sailed on south under a gloomy sky, and they reached the narrow bay at the mouth of the river that had carved out Long-Pass at some time in the long distant past. Just the notion of the eon after eon it must have taken that river to reach the sea made Keselo shudder. Time, it appeared, had no meaning for rivers and mountains.

They'd dropped anchor, and there on the beach – as they all probably should have expected – the archer Longbow was waiting for them.

'I will *never* understand how he can cover so much ground in so little time,' Keselo muttered to himself.

Keselo was just a bit surprised when Commander Narasan included *him* in the group of men who knew how to build forts that Longbow would lead ahead of the rest up to the top of the pass.

'How are your legs holding out, Keselo?' Narasan had asked.

'They seem all right to me, sir,' Keselo replied.

'Good. I think that maybe you should go along with the fort-builders. Gunda's just about the best fort-builder in the entire Trogite Empire. You could learn a lot by watching him.'

Keselo resented that just a bit. He *had* taken courses in architecture at the University of Kaldacin, so he already knew all about building walls.

'I'm not trying to offend you,' Narasan added. 'Gunda and Andar are sort of stuck in stone when it comes to fort-building. Their minds are locked in "the good old-fashioned way" when it comes to forts. You're intelligent enough to come up with things that won't even occur to them – *and* you can be diplomatic enough not to offend them with your shiny *new* ideas.'

'I can *try*, I suppose, sir,' Keselo agreed a bit dubiously. 'I'm not sure they'll listen, though.'

'Talk louder, then.'

When Longbow had objected to leading so many men to the head of the pass, Keselo took him aside.

'It's a precaution, Longbow,' Keselo tried to explain. 'Commander Narasan doesn't like to take chances. We've had quite a few surprises here since last spring, so the commander wants to be sure that there'll be enough men up at the head of the pass to deal with anything the Vlagh throws at us.'

'That's why we have the Malavi, Tonthakans, and Matans, Keselo,' Longbow objected.

'I mentioned that to him,' Keselo replied. Then he smiled faintly. 'The Commander has opinions, Longbow. He's not positive that our friends will do what they're supposed to do. That's why he overloaded us just a bit.'

'Ten thousand men is his idea of "just a bit"?' Longbow asked.

The protests that had arisen when Longbow abolished the traditional 'rest period' were long and loud. Keselo had long believed that those quarter-hour lounges were totally unnecessary, but the common soldiers viewed them as something on the order of a divine right. But Keselo estimated that they'd covered three times more distance than they normally would have.

'He's going too fast,' Gunda grumbled.

'This *is* sort of an emergency, sir,' Keselo suggested. 'If we don't reach the head of the pass before the bug-people do, things will probably start to get ugly. Once the fort's in place, our men should be able to rest. Up until then, we don't really *have* much time for rest, wouldn't you say?'

'You're probably right,' Gunda conceded, 'but that doesn't abolish my right to complain, does it?'

'Not at all, sir, but I wouldn't complain too much when Longbow's around. He might decide to run tomorrow instead of just walk fast. I've come to know him very well during the past three seasons, and the first rule when you're dealing with Longbow is "don't irritate him if you can possibly avoid it."'

'I think he's right, Gunda,' Andar agreed. 'We want that fort in place as soon as possible.' He paused. 'Are you open to a suggestion?'

'I'll listen,' Gunda replied.

'We've got four or five times as many men as we'll really need, right?'

'I'll know better after I've seen the ground I'll be working on,' Gunda replied, 'but I *am* just a bit overloaded with workers. Where are you going with this, Andar?'

'Why build only one fort at a time? We've got all those extra men, so why keep them all at the head of the pass? I could take maybe half of them and build a second fort a mile or so on down the pass. That should give you someplace to run to when the bug-people make your fort too hot to hold on to.'

'Thanks a lot, Andar,' Gunda said in a voice reeking with sarcasm. Then he squinted. 'You know, if we put the men to work on other forts every mile or so on down the pass, we could probably hold back the invaders until some time next summer.'

'Brilliant,' Andar said rather dryly.

'You've been thinking along the same lines, haven't you, Andar?'

'It did sort of occur to me, yes.'

'Why didn't you say something?'

'I just wanted to see how long it was going to take you to get the point, Gunda,' Andar replied with mock sincerity.

Keselo smiled. Things seemed to be going quite well.

They were three days up from the beach when the horse-soldier Ekial came riding down the pass. He reined in his horse when he reached Longbow. 'You seem to be making fairly good time, friend Longbow,' he said.

'Not *too* bad,' Longbow replied. 'Have you seen any sign that the creatures of the Wasteland are coming east yet?'

'Oh, they're coming, all right,' Ekial said. 'Ariga's got scouts out in that desert, and they've told us that there are thousands and thousands of the bug-people coming east.'

'Have your people got any kind of idea about how much longer it's going to take them to reach the head of this pass?'

'I'd say that they're still a week or ten days away. There's a bit of a diversion that's already here, though.'

'Oh? What's that?'

'When we were coming south, we saw a sizeable number of bug-people coming across the sand. Kathlak, the Chief of the Tonthakans, suggested that the bugs might have realized that things can get very unpleasant for people as well as for bugs if they've got enemies above them. When we reached the head of the pass, I sent horsemen down along the rims on both sides of this pass, and sure enough, there *were* bug-people on those rims. If we'd left them there, they'd have been dropping boulders on Narasan's army every time they got a chance. Kathlak's archers took care of that for us. The bug-men up on those rims suddenly started sprouting arrows. There may still be a few of them up there hiding in the bushes, but they aren't likely to cause any problems.'

'Have the archers of Old-Bear's tribe joined you yet?' Longbow asked.

'They're still a day or so away. Your friend Red-Beard came on ahead to let us know that they were on the way. They'll probably reach the head of the pass at about the same time your fort-builders do.'

Gunda joined them.

'You brought a lot of men with you,' Ekial noted.

'That was Narasan's idea,' Gunda told him. 'He's always believed that more is better. He might be right this time, though. I'm sure that *I* won't need all those men, so I'll hand the surplus off to Andar, and he'll be able to build *another* fort about a mile on down the pass. If the Vlagh gives us enough time, we'll have a fort standing every mile or so down the pass, and our enemy will run out of bugs before she gets half-way down.'

Then he looked at the lean, scar-faced horse-soldier. 'Have you had your supper yet?' he asked.

'I've been a little busy,' Ekial replied.

'I can't offer anything very exciting,' Gunda said, 'but you're welcome to join me if you want.'

'I could probably eat,' Ekial said.

'Let's go do it then.'

2

The river that came down through Long-Pass was somewhat wider than the one in Crystal Gorge, but not nearly as wide as the one that had been the source of the Falls of Vash. Keselo realized that the Falls of Vash weren't there anymore, and the river now rushed down to that inland sea that had drowned a generation of the children of the Vlagh *and* quite nearly all of the clergy of the Church of Amar. To Keselo's way of thinking, that particular disaster had purified the Trogite Empire to no small degree.

Despite Longbow's best efforts, it was about mid-morning on the fifth day when they reached the upper end of Long-Pass and Gunda caught his first glimpse of the projected fort site. 'It's only fifty feet across!' he exclaimed.

'About that, yes,' Longbow agreed.

'Didn't you tell Narasan how tight this is?'

'As I remember, I described it to him four or five times,' Longbow replied.

'Why in the world did he send so many men up here?'

'I think it's called "more is better," or something like that, friend Gunda.'

'You were right, Andar,' Gunda said to his friend. 'If I tried to jam ten thousand men into that skinny little opening, they'd be falling all over each other.'

'It's about fifty feet wide, I'd say,' Andar agreed.

'If that much,' Gunda replied. 'It widens out just a bit when it gets up near the rim on either side, but that won't be much of a problem.'

'How long would you say building a fort there is likely to take?' Andar asked.

Gunda shrugged. 'Three days – maybe four. There's plenty of granite lying around here. Squaring it off won't take too long.' Gunda pursed his lips. 'I think twenty feet high should do the job. When the main army gets up here, they'll have those poisoned stakes. If we plant those to the front like we've done before, I don't think very many bug-people will even reach the fort. We've got archers and spear-men – and those horse-soldiers as well. The Vlagh can send ten thousand or so bug-people here to attack the fort, but a dozen or so at most will actually reach it. Why don't you drop back a mile or so and find a good place to build that second fort you mentioned. When you find it, let me know, and I'll send you half of our men. We'll see how our first two forts turn out, and then we might want to move on to four.' He grinned. 'Give us a couple of weeks and we'll have at least a dozen forts blocking off this pass. That might just make poor old Vlagh feel sort of grouchy.'

'Poor baby,' Andar replied in mock sympathy.

'If you don't have access to mortar, you keep things in place with weight,' Gunda was explaining to Keselo the following day. 'The blocks should be squared off, of course, but it's the sheer weight that'll make your fort impregnable.'

'That's a very useful thing to know, Sub-Commander,' Keselo

replied with mock enthusiasm. Gunda was very proud of his reputation as a master fort-builder, and it didn't really cost Keselo very much to heap praise on his superior.

'Now, then,' Gunda continued. 'Every three or four layers you should connect the upper blocks to the lower ones with interlocking grooves.'

'I was wondering about that,' Keselo replied with a perfectly straight face. 'My big problem, though, is how you can lock the battlements in place.'

'That *does* get a little tricky,' Gunda replied. 'You're picking this up quite rapidly, Keselo. Give me a little time and I'll make a first-rate fort-builder out of you.'

Along with four or five professors of architecture at the University of Kaldacin, Keselo privately added.

'If you're not busy with something else,' Gunda said then, 'why don't you drop on back down the pass and see how Andar's fort is coming along. Andar and I *should* keep in touch.'

'I'll go on down there immediately, sir,' Keselo replied, snapping to attention. Right now he'd be more than happy to get away from Gunda's tedious lectures.

'I was just about to send somebody up to Gunda's fort to fetch you, Keselo,' Sub-Commander Andar said. 'A messenger just came up here from the main army. Commander Narasan wants to see you.'

'Am I in trouble?' Keselo asked.

'Not that I know of. The messenger wasn't too specific, but I think Commander Narasan wants you to go on down to that silly temple to advise Sorgan that everything up here is pretty much the way we want it to be. The forts *will* be in place when the bug-people try to attack.'

Keselo frowned. 'The commander *could* have sent somebody else down to the temple, and that messenger would have reached Sorgan long before I'll be able to.'

Andar shrugged. 'You know Sorgan much better than an ordinary messenger would have, *and* your rank would tell Sorgan that he's significant to Commander Narasan. What Sorgan's doing down there's a little silly, maybe, but it *will* keep Veltan's sister off our backs. I'm sure that the commander has things he wants Sorgan to know about, and Sorgan probably has information for the commander as well. They both trust you, Keselo, so I've got a sort of hunch that you'll be doing a lot of traveling back and forth between the pass and the temple before this is all over. I'll send word on up to Gunda to let him know that the commander's got a job for you.'

'I'd appreciate that, sir,' Keselo said. Then he considered the distance he'd be traveling for the next several weeks. 'I wonder if Ekial might lend me a horse,' he murmured to himself.

3

Commander Narasan's tent had seen better days. It had been patched so many times that there were several areas where even the patches had been patched. Near the center there was a stove that put out small amounts of heat, but quite a bit of smoke. The commander was seated at a small table carefully examining a rudimentary map. 'You made good time, Keselo,' he said when Keselo entered the tent. 'I sent the messenger up the pass only two days ago.'

'Downhill is quite a bit easier than uphill, sir,' Keselo replied.

'How's the fort coming along?'

'Which one, sir?'

Commander Narasan raised one eyebrow.

'Sub-Commanders Gunda and Andar talked things over after they'd seen how narrow the gap was at the head of the pass, sir,' Keselo explained. 'They agreed that they had far more men than they needed to build the fort that'd block off that gap, so Sub-Commander Andar took half of the men a mile or so on down the pass, and he's building a second fort. I wouldn't exactly call it a race, but there *is* a certain amount of competitiveness involved.'

The commander smiled faintly. 'That always seems to come floating to the surface when Gunda's involved,' he said.

'He *is* a soldier, Commander,' Keselo replied. 'He fights wars, and war *is* the ultimate competition, wouldn't you say?'

'You're an extremely perceptive young man, Keselo. Now, then, how well do you and Sorgan get along?'

'He thinks I'm just a little stuffy, sir. That's one of the draw-backs of an extensive education. The word "sir" seems to offend him for some reason.'

'He *does* believe you when you tell him something, doesn't he?'

'I believe so, yes, sir. I've never had any reason to lie to him.'

'I think you talked yourself into a lot of traveling, Keselo.'

'Sir?' Keselo was a bit confused.

'Sorgan and I will need to pass information back and forth to each other, and we both trust you to give us the absolute truth.'

'I'm honored that you feel that way about me, sir.'

'I've been in touch with one of the ship-captains in the bay at the mouth of this pass, and he has a small, swift sloop that's been quite useful in the past. When you reach the bay, he'll lend you the sloop and a couple of sailors who know how to use it. They'll be able to deliver you to Sorgan in about a half a day. Then, after you've spoken with old Hook-Beak, you can come back and tell *me* anything he wants me to know. When you see him, tell him that Gunda's fort – and Andar's – are nearly complete. I'm sure that he'll want to send word to me about how well his hoax is coming. Now, then, can you think of anything you might need to make these journeys a bit easier – and faster?'

'Yes, sir,' Keselo replied. 'I think I can. It might take me a while to learn how to ride one of Prince Ekial's horses, but we might want to consider that. There may be a few times when speed will be essential, and a horse is sort of a land version of that sloop, wouldn't you say?'

'I'd say that you can think about twice as fast as anybody else in the army, Keselo. I'll send word to Prince Ekial, and there *will* be a horse waiting for you on the beach when you return.'

'And a Malavi as well, sir?' Keselo added. 'I'll need somebody there to teach me how to ride a horse, because I don't really know *anything* about horses.'

The swift little sloop the captain of the *Triumph* provided for Keselo's trip down the coast to the harbor of Lady Aracia's temple made the voyage in just over a half a day, and the two skilled sailors who'd rowed her south pulled alongside the *Ascension* in the early afternoon.

Keselo climbed up the rope ladder and spoke with the extremely tall Maag known as Tree-Top. 'I've got some information for Captain Hook-Beak,' Keselo told the towering Maag. 'I think it might be best if I spoke with him here on the *Ascension* rather than in the temple. I'm fairly sure that Commander Narasan and Captain Hook-Beak would prefer to keep the priests in Lady Aracia's temple from finding out that they're in contact with each other.'

'You're probably right,' Tree-Top agreed. 'I'll get word to the Cap'n that you're here.'

'How have things been going down here?' Keselo asked.

Tree-Top laughed. 'The Cap'n seems to have got hisself on the good side of the crazy lady who owns this place. The other day she ordered all them fat priests of hers to go out to the west to lend the Cap'n and his men some help. You could hear the screaming for miles when she said that. It quieted down some after the Cap'n had several of them fat priests flogged, though.'

'Did Lady Aracia actually let him *do* that?' Keselo was more than a little startled.

'It looked to me like it made her real happy. I'll send a man ashore to let the Cap'n know that you're here, and then maybe you can tell me what's happening up there where the *real* war's going on.'

Keselo was more than a little surprised that Sorgan had somehow managed to bring Lady Aracia over to his side. Before Veltan and Lady Zelana had pulled the Trogite army out of this temple-town, it had seemed that the priests had been making all the decisions here, and Lady Aracia had been little more than a figurehead. Sorgan had somehow managed to wake her up, though, and that *might* just change a lot of things.

'It was really a mistake that turned into something very useful, Captain Sorgan,' Keselo admitted. 'None of us knew for certain just when the servants of the Vlagh would come rushing up out of the Wasteland – or how many there'd actually be. The Commander wasn't entirely sure that the Tonthakans, Matans, and the Malavi would be able to hold the bug-people off, so he sent ten thousand men up the pass with Sub-Commander Gunda – more for security than for fort-construction. When we reached the head of the pass, we saw that the opening was only fifty feet across – *and* the bug-people were still quite a long way out in the Wasteland. Sub-Commanders Gunda and Andar talked it over a bit, and they decided to build two forts instead of just one.'

'That's the sort of thing I'd expect from Gunda,' Sub-Commander Padan, who was now sporting a beard, said.

'Actually, sir, it was Sub-Commander Andar who came up with the notion. Sub-Commander Gunda was too busy inventing new swear words about then. When I left, those two forts were almost finished, and Gunda and Andar were discussing the possibility of putting the construction crews to work on *four* new forts.'

He hesitated slightly. 'When I first got here, Tree-Top was telling me that Lady Aracia might just be coming to her senses.'

'She's starting to think,' Sorgan replied. 'Her lazy priests just got themselves put to work, and they're not too happy about that.' Then Captain Hook-Beak grinned rather slyly. 'What's *really* making them unhappy is what we're feeding them. They're used to fancy food, and beans don't sit very well with them.'

'Did Lady Aracia actually accept the stories about bug-people here in the vicinity of her temple?' Keselo asked. 'Nobody's ever actually *seen* any of them, have they?'

'Veltan's been lending us a hand,' Sorgan replied. 'He's been cooking up images for the entertainment of his sister and her chubby priests. I've got men out there pretending to fight off the bugs, and those priests – and even Lady Aracia herself – have been catching very brief glimpses of those images. *That's* the thing that brought Aracia over to our side. She suddenly woke up and realized that her priests were almost totally worthless. You should have *heard* the speech she made to the priests. That lady can be a tiger when it's necessary.'

'You've done something here that nobody else has ever been able to do, Captain Hook-Beak,' Keselo noted.

'I had Veltan's help, Keselo,' Sorgan replied. 'I'm positive that it was *his* images that brought her around.'

'Tree-Top told me that you had a few of the priests flogged.'

Sorgan nodded. 'That definitely cut back all the complaining,' he said.

'Are those priests actually working alongside your men? Wouldn't that suggest to some of them that what they've been hearing about, and catching a few glimpses of, is nothing but a hoax?'

Sorgan shook his head. 'Rabbit came up with a story that sent the priests down to the south wall of the temple – bugs sneaking through the bushes and a few other all-out lies. Now the priests are tearing the southern buildings apart, and leaving my men alone here on the west side so that we can cook up more horror stories. Tell Narasan that we've got things pretty much under control down here, and you *might* want to tell him – *and* Lady Zelana and Lord Dahlaine – that Lady Aracia *seems* to be coming to her senses.'

'That *might* just be the best news they've had since last spring, Captain,' Keselo agreed.

Keselo was a bit startled when he saw that the Malavi waiting for him on the beach at the mouth of Long-Pass was Prince Ekial himself. The two of them had met during the war in Veltan's Domain the preceding summer, and they'd gotten along with each other quite well, but Keselo was quite certain that Ekial had more serious matters to attend to.

The sailors who'd been rowing the scruffy little skiff pulled the bow of the skiff up onto the sandy beach, and Keselo stepped out onto the sand. 'What are you doing down here, Prince Ekial?' Keselo asked.

Ekial shrugged. 'Friend Narasan tells me that you'd like to learn how to ride a horse,' he replied. 'I wasn't doing anything important, so I thought I might as well come on down here and teach you myself.'

'I'm honored, Prince Ekial.'

'We're friends, Keselo,' Ekial replied. 'We don't have to wave our titles in each other's faces like that. Actually, I was starting to get just a little bored up there watching Gunda and Andar building forts.'

'Have there been any signs of the Creatures of the Wasteland approaching the upper end of the pass yet?'

'A few,' Ekial replied. 'I'd say that the ones we've seen so far are just scouts. Let's get on with this, shall we? It's likely to take you a few days to get used to sitting on a horse's back, so we'd better get started.' He reached out and put his hand on the front shoulder of a rangy horse with a sabre-scar across its nose. 'This is Bent-Nose, and he's a fairly sensible animal. He doesn't bite very often, and he almost never kicks somebody who walks behind him. He's old enough not to get excited every time somebody walks by, but he's not so old that he'd rather rest than run. Now, the first thing you need to do is let the horse get to know you. I brought some apples along, and horses *love* apples. If you give a horse an apple, he'll follow you for a day or so at least. Then you want to scratch his ears and pet his nose. He needs to be able to recognize your smell.'

'I didn't realize that it was so complicated,' Keselo confessed. Then he remembered something. 'If horses like apples, isn't it possible that they'd like other sweet things as well?'

'They might, yes. What did you have in mind?'

Keselo reached into his pocket and took out several pieces of candy. 'I've always had a sort of weakness for this,' he admitted. 'It might be a sign that I never really grew up. Try one, and see what you think.'

Ekial took one of the lumps of candy and popped it into his mouth. 'Oh, my goodness,' he said with a broad grin. 'I think you might have just made a huge jump forward in the taming of horses, friend Keselo. Let's see how Bent-Nose feels about this.'

Ekial held a piece of candy out to the horse. Bent-Nose sniffed at the candy, and his ears perked up. Then he rather carefully took the candy into his mouth.

It seemed to Keselo that the horse almost shivered with delight. Then he nuzzled at Keselo's hand.

'You *do* have more, don't you?' Ekial asked.

'A couple of pounds, I think,' Keselo replied. 'I'll check my pack, but I always keep plenty of candy.'

'I think you're on to a winner, friend Keselo. If things go as fast as I think they will, you'll be riding Bent-Nose before noon tomorrow.'

It took Keselo a while the following day to learn the rudiments of mounting and dismounting, but Bent-Nose was most cooperative, and then Ekial said that they might as well ride on up the pass to report in to the commander. Bent-Nose and Ekial's horse Bright-Star moved on up the pass at a canter, and Keselo was quite pleased with how much easier it was to ride rather than walk – at least during the first morning of their journey. By the time they stopped for the night, however, Keselo realized that there were some drawbacks involved in riding.

'It takes a while for your backside to toughen up,' Ekial explained. 'Walk around a little bit, and that should ease the pain in your backside. You might want to eat standing up for a few days, though.'

'How far would you say we came today?' Keselo asked.

'Forty miles or so,' Ekial replied. 'We haven't been pushing the horses very hard. Uphill is always a bit slower than downhill.'

'We should make it up to the top of the pass in two more days, then. Have Gunda and Andar finished their forts yet?'

'As closely as *I* could determine, yes. Of course I'm not really all that familiar with forts.'

'Have the Creatures of the Wasteland made any attacks?'

'They hadn't when I left that end of the pass. The Tonthakan archers had pretty well cleared the rims on both sides of the pass, so I'm fairly sure that friend Narasan's army has reached the top by now.'

'I'd say that we're about as ready to meet the invaders as we'll ever be, then.'

'They won't get past us,' Ekial agreed. 'We might have to sit up there for a few months, but eventually that thing called the Vlagh will run out of soldiers, and that's what this is all about, wouldn't you say?'

'Sorgan seems to think that your sister's coming to her senses,' Keselo told Lady Zelana and Lord Dahlaine on the evening of the day when he and Ekial had reached the top of Long-Pass. 'She's begun to realize just how totally worthless her priests really are. Their so-called "adoration" is nothing but a ruse to make their own lives easier, and their contempt for the common people *really* angered her. Sorgan's clever mock invasion seems to have brought her face to face with reality, and she came down very hard on those who had elevated themselves to the priesthood. She ordered them to go to work helping Sorgan's men build fortifications.' Keselo grinned then. 'Quite a few of her priests refused, but after Sorgan had them flogged with whips, the refusals stopped. A good number of priests decided to run away along about then, but absurd though it might seem, that huge temple only has one door, and Sorgan put a hundred or so of his men at that door, so nobody's leaving. Like it or not, Aracia's priesthood *will* do honest work for a while.'

Lord Dahlaine laughed. 'That, all by itself, makes these attempted invasions by the servants of the Vlagh worth more than anything else that's happened in the last four or five centuries.'

Then Commander Narasan and Ekial came down from Gunda's fort at the head of the pass. 'It looks like we've got company coming,' Commander Narasan reported. 'The Wasteland off to the west isn't empty anymore.'

'How many would you say there are?' Lord Dahlaine asked.

'I wouldn't even want to try to make a guess, my Lord,' the Commander replied. 'They seem to stretch from horizon to horizon as far off to the west as I can see.'

THE DEFENDERS OF THE FAITH

1

Torl had been greatly impressed by Veltan's imaginary bug-men. The images had looked so real that several of the Maags standing on top of the berm had turned and fled when the images had briefly appeared.

Of course that had added a sense of reality to the incident, and Lady Zelana's sister now totally believed everything cousin Sorgan told her. Just hearing the word 'invasion' was one thing but actually *seeing* what had appeared to be real, live bugs was something entirely different. That single incident had turned Lady Aracia into a true believer.

That was *definitely* causing some problems for her priests. Lady Aracia's priests had scoffed at the notion that the bug-people were anything but a hoax cousin Sorgan had come up with as a way to get his hands on all the gold in the temple. But now the priests had been sent to the rudimentary south wall of the temple, where several bulky, bad-tempered Maags worked the poor fat priests as hard as they could for ten or twelve hours a day on a diet of nothing but beans. That generated a lot of sniveling, which amused Torl no end.

'Just keep an eye on them, Torl,' Sorgan instructed. 'I don't *think* they'll try anything violent. Priests aren't notorious for that sort of behavior, but desperate people do desperate things every so often.'

'I'll watch them, cousin,' Torl promised. 'It'll probably bore me to tears, but not as much as building this imitation fort does.'

'It's not *that* bad a fort, is it?' Sorgan objected.

'Watch out for mice, Sorgan,' Torl advised. 'If a mouse happened to bump your fort with his shoulder, the whole thing might tumble down around your ears.'

'Very funny, Torl. Go watch those fat priests, but stay out of sight. You're *supposed* to be fighting off the invasion of the bug-people. Let's not stir up any suspicions in Lady Aracia.'

'It shall be as thou hast commanded, mighty leader.'

'Do you really have to do that, Torl?' Sorgan asked.

'It's good for you, cousin,' Torl replied. 'I'll go watch those fat priests get skinny, and I'll keep you advised.'

'Do that.' Then cousin Sorgan went back to his imitation fort.

Torl had been exploring the somewhat makeshift temple Lady Aracia's priests (or their younger relatives) had been building (badly) for the last several centuries. As Torl had reported to Sorgan, *most* of the temple consisted of empty rooms and wandering corridors that didn't really go any place. Torl was fairly certain that Lady Aracia believed with all her heart that there were thousands of priests living here so that they could adore her in groups. As closely as Torl had been able to verify, however, there were probably no more than a couple hundred of them. The 'thousands and thousands of priests' hoax obliged the ordinary farmers of Lady Aracia's Domain to deliver enormous amounts of food to the temple. Her brave priests sacrificed themselves by eating at least ten times more food than was really good for them.

As Torl moved through the empty temple, he wondered just *who* had done all this meaningless construction. It occurred to him that in all probability assorted relatives of the established priests had realized that the life of a priest of Aracia was a life of luxury unmarred by honest work, but their relatives of high rank had most likely put a price on the aspirations of their younger relatives, and the price was most likely six or seven rooms or a hundred feet of corridor. Quite probably, Fat Bersla escorted Lady Aracia on periodic tours of these empty corridors and vacant rooms to show her how her temple was expanding. 'There's probably a lot of scrambling around by lesser priests to make all this empty space appear to be occupied.' When he got right down to it, Torl viewed the whole thing as pathetic – and Aracia herself was probably the most pathetic.

Then, from some distance off, he heard some people talking. Torl recognized the voices of Fat Bersla and the tiny priestess Alcevan. Torl moved quietly along the corridor to see if he could get close enough to hear what they were saying. Whatever it was that they were discussing didn't seem to be making them happy.

Fat Bersla was speaking in a whining kind of voice that definitely set Torl's teeth on edge. 'I have spent most of my life praising that simple-minded woman, and I'd finally reached the point where she was almost totally under my control. Then that pirate came out of nowhere with his absurd story and snatched her out of my grasp. Now she'll do almost anything he tells her to do without even consulting me.'

'We have a matter of greater concern, Takal Bersla,' the strange-sounding voice of priestess Alcevan cut in to Bersla's sniveling. 'If there's any truth to the legends of this land, ancient Aracia is right on the verge of drifting off to sleep.'

'She never sleeps!' Bersla declared.

'You mean that you've never *seen* her sleep, mighty Takal. No one living has, because she's been awake for twenty-five thousand years. There weren't even any people around when she woke up this time. The legend still tells us that she *will* sleep – soon – and she will be replaced by another divinity who goes by the name of Enalla.'

'I spoke with Holy Aracia on one occasion some years ago,' another man-priest with a rasping sort of voice declared, 'and she told me that the child-Dreamer Lillabeth is in reality this Enalla who will succeed our beloved Aracia.'

'That *can't* be true!' Bersla exclaimed. 'Child Lillabeth has no interest at all in the religion of Holy Aracia. On many occasions I have delivered masterful orations praising Holy Aracia whilst child Lillabeth was present, and she inevitably fell asleep before the end of the first hour of my praise. She has no interest in religion or priests or temples. If this Enalla is really the adult Lillabeth, she will have no need of priests or temples or hymns of praise. She will abandon the temple, and when the local people come to understand her disinterest, they will turn their backs on us, and we will surely perish.'

'That couldn't happen to a better group,' Torl muttered. Then he squinted at the ceiling. 'I wonder just how long Fat Bersla could stay alive if nobody bothered to feed him. He could probably absorb his own fat for a while, but he'd run dry eventually.'

'Holy Aracia advised me that child Lillabeth was what she called "a Dreamer,"' the raspy-voiced priest declared. 'She said that Lillabeth could cause things to happen with her Dreams that were quite beyond anything Holy Aracia or her brothers or sister could ever bring to pass. These events, as I understood what Holy Aracia told me, are what are called "natural disasters" – floods, earthquakes, volcanos – and such. Have a care when you approach child Lillabeth, for she can – most certainly – cause the sky to fall down on you.'

'That's absurd,' Alcevan scoffed.

'I wouldn't be so sure, Alcevan,' Bersla disagreed. 'Holy Aracia herself told me of several disasters other Dreamer-children had caused to happen – floods, volcanoes, and other events almost beyond human conception. It would appear that these innocent children are *not* innocent when they Dream. The gods live by a law that they will never kill anything. The Dreamers, however, have no such restriction.'

Alcevan suddenly chuckled. 'I'd say that we have a very simple solution to our problem, then. We know that there's some kind of connection between Lillabeth and Enalla. Enalla will live forever, of course, but Lillabeth? I'm not so sure about her. She eats food, and she goes to sleep. That suggests that she's *not* an immortal, and that makes things very easy for us.'

'I didn't quite follow that, Alcevan,' Bersla said.

'All we have to do is order some novice to kill her, you dunce. If Lillabeth's dead, Enalla will be dead as well. They *are* the same person, after all.'

'It wouldn't work,' Bersla declared. 'Aracia can hear our thoughts – particularly any thought that threatens the life of Lillabeth. Aracia *loves* that spoiled little brat.'

'Let *me* deal with that, Takal Bersla,' Alcevan said then. 'Since Lillabeth is *really* Enalla, she'll be the one who'll usurp Aracia's throne once Aracia goes to sleep. Aracia, however, desperately wants to retain her position as the god of the East, and she'll do *anything* to hold her throne.'

Torl turned and walked as swiftly as he dared through the dimly-lighted corridor that led to the west wall of the temple. As soon as he came out into the open area that was no longer closed in by stone blocks, he went looking for cousin Sorgan. 'I think we've got a serious problem, cousin,' he said.

'Another one?' Sorgan said. 'What's the world coming to?'

'Are you about finished with the tired old jokes, Sorgan?' Torl demanded. 'Why don't you try to laugh at this one? I just heard that priestess called Alcevan come up with a plot to kill Aracia's Dreamer.'

'You said *what*?'

'You heard me, cousin. Alcevan seems to think that if Lillabeth died, Enalla would cease to exist. Those priests desperately want to keep Aracia in charge here, since she's their only access to a life of luxury. They seem to believe that if Enalla dies – or just ceases to exist – Aracia will have to stay awake and continue providing them with everything they want.'

Cousin Sorgan's face hardened. 'I think we'd better take this to Veltan,' he said.

It didn't take them very long to find Zelana's baby brother. He was watching Sorgan's men as they continued the construction of cousin Sorgan's imitation fort, and he didn't look very impressed.

'We need to talk, Lord Veltan,' Sorgan said. 'I think we might have an emergency of sorts coming before too long.'

'Somebody's going to sneeze, and your fort will collapse?' Veltan suggested.

'The fort's not really significant,' Sorgan replied. 'It's just there to make your big sister feel more secure. It's not like there was going to be a real invasion. Cousin Torl here just overheard something that we'll have to deal with – soon. Tell him what you heard, Torl.'

'I was sort of wandering around in this badly-put-together temple a little while back, and I just happened to hear some of your sister's priests talking. They're *very* unhappy about Aracia's approaching nap time. They know that when she drifts off, your granddaughter Enalla will take charge here.'

'Granddaughter?' Veltan seemed a bit startled.

'You and the rest of your family *are* related to the younger generation, aren't you? I suppose we could call Enalla your niece, if that would be closer.'

'We *are* related, Torl,' Veltan said with a faint smile, 'but I doubt that any word you could come up with would explain the relationship.'

'Don't try to explain it to me, Lord Veltan,' Torl said. 'I probably wouldn't understand you anyway, and all it'd do would be to give me a headache. The priests I heard talking were trying to come up with some way to keep your sister awake. The little priestess Alcevan came up with a plan that the other priests seem to think might actually work.'

'Oh?'

'This gets just a little ugly, so brace yourself. Alcevan seems to have found out that the Dreamer Lillabeth is actually Enalla. Enalla, like the rest of you, doesn't need to eat or sleep, *but* Lillabeth *does*. Alcevan told the other priests that Enalla might be immortal, but Lillabeth probably isn't. Then she went on to suggest that if some novice priest just happened to murder Lillabeth, Enalla would just vanish. I don't know if it would work that way, but the other priests seemed to think it might be worth a try.'

'That's horrible!' Veltan exclaimed.

'The next question is would it work?' Sorgan said.

'I don't think so,' Veltan replied, 'but let's not take any chances.'

Then he frowned. 'I didn't know that my sister *had* any women priests,' he said.

'As far as we know, this Alcevan's the only one,' Sorgan said. 'The other priests don't seem to like her very much, but your sister spends a lot of time listening to her.' He smiled. 'I think Eleria might refer to her as one of the "teenie-weenies,"' he said. 'That particular term showed up fairly often in Zelana country. Eleria herself was a teenie-weenie, and so was Rabbit. Then, when we encountered the bug-snake-people, Eleria called *them* teenie-weenies as well.'

Veltan shrugged. 'There *are* small people here in Aracia's Domain. From what you just told me, this Alcevan priestess throws a lot of weight around – quite possibly because Aracia *told* her to. Let's go give Lillabeth some protection. We don't want to take any chances here.'

'She almost never comes here to spend any time with me,' the little girl complained. 'I think she hates me because I had that Dream.'

'No, Lillabeth,' Veltan replied. 'It's the war that's bothering Aracia so much. It'll be over soon, and then things should go back to the way they're supposed to be.'

'Do wars always take this long, uncle Veltan?'

'I really don't know, child,' Veltan replied. 'This is the first war we've ever had here in the Land of Dhrall. Torl here knows much, much more about wars than I do.'

Lillabeth looked at Torl. 'How long do the wars last in your part of the world?' she asked.

Torl shrugged. 'Sometimes they're over in about half an hour,' he replied. 'Others can go on for years and years. This one here is supposed to be over by spring-time.'

'And then everything will go back to the way it's supposed to be?' the little girl asked.

'Who knows?' Torl said. 'The world changes all the time, and that means that nothing ever really stays the same.'

'They get better, you mean?'

'Sometimes they do, but sometimes they get worse.'

Veltan winced, but he didn't say anything.

Then the door of Lillabeth's room opened, and a young priest who couldn't have been much older than fifteen or so came into the room. He was just a bit pale, and his hands were shaking. 'What are you people doing here?' he demanded.

'We just came by to visit my niece,' Veltan replied.

'Your niece?'

Veltan nodded. 'I'm Aracia's younger brother. We don't get chances to visit very often. Did someone tell you to stop by for some reason?'

'Ah – I was just supposed to look in to make sure that the little girl is all right and doesn't need anything,' the young fellow replied just a bit too quickly.

'I'm here now,' Veltan told him, 'and I'll take care of anything she needs. Was there anything else?'

'Well – no, I guess not.'

'Good. You can go now then. Tell whoever sent you that Lillabeth is just fine and that I'm here to make sure that she stays that way.'

'I'll do that,' the young fellow said, nervously backing toward the door.

Veltan smiled. 'You have a nice day,' he said blandly.

The young man fled.

'That was the one, Torl,' Veltan said. 'Alcevan promised him a quick elevation in rank if he did what she wanted him to do.'

'You can hear what people are thinking, can't you, Veltan?' Torl asked.

'Usually, yes. I don't always *want* to, but it's there if I need it. I'll stay here with Lillabeth. Why don't you follow that nervous young priest? He *might* be the only one Alcevan hired, but let's make sure, if we can.'

'I'll get right on it, Lord Veltan,' Torl replied, going to the door.

2

The pale young priest was trembling noticeably and not walking very fast as he moved along one of the dusty corridors of Aracia's temple. Torl was quite sure that he knew why the young man was reluctant to report his failure to Alcevan. The little priestess was quite obviously not the sort who'd be willing to accept failure, so the young man was almost certainly moving toward a blistering reprimand.

He finally reached one of those dusty, unoccupied rooms that didn't even have a door, but, unlike the other chambers on both sides of the corridor, there was a dim light in this one. 'I'm back, Holy Alcevan,' the young fellow said in a trembling voice. 'I wasn't able to do what you asked, though. The little girl wasn't alone. There was a stranger who called himself Veltan there, along with one of those barbarians. I think I'll have to wait a while before I try again.'

'There's no real problem, Aldas,' the priestess replied. 'We have plenty of time, so try again some other day.'

'Oh, I will, I will,' the young priest vowed. 'Believe me, the time will come – sooner or later – when I'll find the little girl alone, and then I'll do that which you want me to do.'

'Excellent, Aldas,' the little priestess said. 'I knew that I could depend on you.'

'I'll go back immediately, Holy Alcevan,' the young man promised. 'I'll watch for days and days until I can get the little girl alone, and then—' His voice abruptly stopped, and Torl heard a gurgling sound.

Torl blinked. 'She *didn't*!' he exclaimed under his breath. The stream of red blood coming through the doorway, however, said that she *had*. Alcevan quite obviously was *not* prepared to accept failure.

'I stayed back out of sight until she left the room, Veltan,' Torl said somewhat later after Lillabeth had gone to sleep. 'I'm not sure just exactly how she did it with a stone knife, but the poor boy's throat had been cut from ear to ear. First she told him that everything was all right, and then she killed him right there on the spot.'

Veltan's face hardened. 'She's even worse than I thought,' he said. 'She's after something here, and it's obvious that she'll go to any length to get it. I'm quite sure that she's *not* what she appears to be.'

Torl suddenly grinned. 'I don't really think fat old Bersla will be around very much longer, do you?'

'Interesting notion, Torl. Be very careful, but try to keep an eye on her. We *might* just be looking at extreme ambition here. If that's the case, she'll do almost anything to replace Bersla as the high priest – or Takal, as the local term has it – but it might go even further.'

'Are you saying that she wants to replace your *sister*?'

'I wouldn't rule it out, Torl. Alcevan wants *something*, but I don't think we know for sure just *what* it is. How familiar are you with all these silly corridors here in the temple?'

'I think I've got a nodding acquaintance with *most* of them, Veltan,' Torl replied. 'Of course I come across a new one every so often, but those are the ones that don't really go anywhere. I can find my way around without much trouble.'

'Good. Stay out of sight as much as possible, but do what you can to find out just exactly what Alcevan's goal *really* is.'

'I'll see what I can do, Veltan,' Torl promised, 'but I think *you* should stay close to Lillabeth. She needs protection right now.'

'I'll get right on it, Torl,' Veltan replied in an obvious imitation of something Torl had said earlier.

'Ha,' Torl replied in the same flat tone Gunda always used. 'Ha. Ha. Ha.'

Veltan burst out laughing at that point.

Torl had found an unused corridor that went past the back side of Aracia's throne room. Like most of the rest of the temple, it was not well-made, and Torl had been able to hear what was going on in the throne room. He crept through the shoddy corridor until he could hear voices. Then he put his ear to the wall.

'We don't know this Enalla person who'll replace you when you lie down to rest, Holy Aracia,' Alcevan was saying, 'but isn't it possible that she'll decide to usurp your temple and tell us that *she* is the true god of your Domain and order us to bow down and worship *her* instead of you? Of course, after a few generations, nobody will even remember that you were ever here.'

'Is there no way, Divine Aracia, that you can delay the arrival of this Enalla?' Bersla asked. 'We have the invasion by the Creatures of the Wasteland in progress right now. Could you not remain here with us until they are driven back? You are wise beyond our understanding, but this Enalla person will have only recently awakened from her long sleep, so she will be as helpless as a child. Should the Creatures of the Wasteland o'erwhelm your people, is it not possible that the Vlagh itself will assume your holy throne?'

Then Aracia's voice, colder than ice, replied. 'These matters are none of your concern – neither of your concerns. I will, before this season ends, go to my rest. Enalla *is* my alternate, and my Domain *will* be hers while I sleep. You *will* obey her in all things.' She paused and then spoke again in an icy tone. 'Why is it that you two are not at the south wall of my temple as I have commanded?'

Bersla floundered a bit. 'Most of the priesthood labors there as you commanded, Most Holy. Some few of us, however, have remained here to see to your needs.'

'I *have* no needs, Bersla. You should know that by now.' Then Aracia paused, and her voice became even more cold. 'You were fully aware of that, were you not, Takal Bersla? This "see to my needs" pose of yours is but a way to avoid strenuous labor, is it not?'

'We can *not* leave you unprotected, Divine One,' Alcevan declared.

'Brave are you indeed, small, inconsequential person,' Aracia replied in a voice dripping with sarcasm. 'First you defy *me*, and then you will attempt to hold back the servants of the Vlagh, which will most certainly kill you and then eat you. Hear me now, both of you. Proceed at once to the south wall of my temple and give aid to those who have already obeyed my commands. Should that not suit you, go from this holy temple and do not *ever* return. Know, moreover, that when you depart from here, I will mark you, and neither one of you will ever be permitted to come back to within my walls. Choose, Bersla and Alcevan, and know that which course you choose will not in any way concern me.'

Torl heard the sound of hurried footsteps, and the throne room door opened – and then closed.

Torl pressed one hand over his mouth to muffle the sound of his laughter. Then he went west again through the dusty corridor to tell cousin Sorgan and Veltan about this sudden change in Veltan's sister.

After a little while, Torl realized that he was whistling as he went.

3

---◆▶◆---

'She really came down hard on those two,' Torl reported when he rejoined Sorgan and Veltan at the west wall. 'They were trying their best to persuade her to stay awake and keep Enalla from taking over, but she told them to either go to the south wall and do what she'd told them to do, or leave the temple and never come back.'

'Well,' Veltan said with a broad smile. 'It seems that my sister has finally come to her senses.' Then he looked curiously at Torl. 'How did you manage to get into the throne room without being seen?'

'I wasn't inside,' Torl said. 'I was in one of those cobwebby corridors that just happened to have a crack in the wall. I could hear everything that was going on in there, and they didn't know that I was listening. There seem to be quite a few of those old corridors in the vicinity of the throne room.'

'They were probably put there by certain previous high priests to give them someplace where they could hear what was going on without being seen,' Veltan replied. 'They've always wanted that advantage to make sure that no other priest was getting ahead of them.'

'Are the politics here always so complicated, Veltan?' Sorgan asked.

'That sort of depends on whose territory we're talking about,' Veltan replied. 'Things in Dahlaine's Domain are a bit more formal than they are in Zelana's Domain and mine, but Aracia's Church takes politics out to the far end – or it did until just recently. Now that Aracia's come to her senses, she *might* even go so far as to abolish her Church.' Then he smiled again. 'And if Aracia doesn't, Enalla almost certainly will. The priests of her Church will probably have to go out and find honest work before spring arrives.'

'Poor babies,' Sorgan said in mock sympathy.

THE COMMANDER

1

─◆─◆─

Trenicia, the warrior queen of the Isle of Akalla, was seriously discontented with winter. The Matans had generously provided her with a double-layered bison-hide cloak, but she still spent most of her time shivering and complaining.

Her language was very colorful, Commander Narasan noted with a faint smile as his army marched up through Long-Pass. Trenicia had, in effect, joined Narasan's army when they'd both walked off and left Veltan's older sister screaming about their desertion. Aracia's arrogance knew no bounds, and the thought that they would all just walk away and leave her totally undefended sent her right up through the ceiling. 'I wonder how Sorgan's doing,' he muttered as he and Trenicia walked through a gloomy afternoon.

'I didn't quite catch that, dear Narasan,' Trenicia said in a milder tone of voice.

'Just thinking out loud, your Majesty,' Narasan replied.

'I thought that we'd discarded the "your Majesty" foolishness,' she said a bit tartly.

'Sorry,' Narasan apologized. 'Habit, probably. Down in the Empire, people are very interested in rank, so we grow accustomed to spouting terms of respectfulness. They don't really *mean* anything, but we wave them around anyhow. I'm just a bit concerned about Sorgan's scheme, is all. He's one of the few friends I have, and I don't want to lose him.'

'You have *me* as your friend, Narasan,' Trenicia said. 'That's all you really need. Someday we might want to talk about friendship. In time, friendship grows into something more interesting, and I'd say that we've almost reached that point.'

Narasan actually blushed, though he couldn't for the life of him think why.

'Is your face turning red for some reason other than the beastly chill in this region?' Trenicia asked. 'If you're having a problem, feel free to tell me all about it.'

'I'm sure it's only the weather, dear friend Trenicia.'

'Spoilsport,' she replied accusingly.

'I'm not entirely sure that Sorgan's sophisticated enough to float his scheme past Aracia – or her priests. He can *tell* them that his scouts have actually seen the bug-people invading, but I don't know if they'd accept that.'

'He has Veltan to help him, dear Narasan. That's all the help he'll probably need.' Then she paused. 'How in the world did you get so attached to a Maag pirate?' she asked. 'I thought that Maags and Trogites were supposed to be natural-born enemies.'

Narasan shrugged. 'We've been allied with each other in three wars so far, and we've learned to trust each other. If he keeps things simple, he shouldn't have many problems, but sometimes Sorgan goes to extremes. All we *really* need is for him to keep Aracia and her priests out of my hair here in Long-Pass.'

'That shouldn't be *too* hard,' Trenicia said. 'We're not talking about intelligent people here. Relax, dear Narasan. I'm sure that everything down in the temple's going exactly the way we want it to.'

It was about noon when the main army reached the back side of a fairly standard Trogite fort. Trenicia wasn't at all impressed. 'Is that the best your men can do?' she demanded.

'This is the *back* side, Trenicia dear,' Narasan explained. 'It's the *front* side that holds back the enemy. The back side is designed to make it easy for our soldiers to get inside the fort.'

'What if your enemy sneaks around behind you?'

'Would the word "how" offend you? The fort blocks off the entire pass in this spot. Believe me, dear, we Trogites have been building forts for centuries, we we've come up with answers to just about all the "what ifs" anybody can come up with. About the only one that concerns us is what's called "burrowing." That's when your enemy digs a deep hole in the ground some distance back from your fort and then starts to dig a tunnel.'

'I *knew* that there had to be a weakness!' Trenicia exclaimed triumphantly.

'Take a look around, dear,' Narasan suggested. 'You won't see very much dirt. This is a mountain pass, and that means that it's mostly rock. I guess it's theoretically possible to burrow through solid rock, but I'd say that it'd take at least ten years to get as far as the front side of the fort – and another four or five years to burrow *under* the fort to get to the back side.'

Trenicia glared at him for a moment, but then she laughed. 'I *was* being just a bit silly there, wasn't I? It's just that I *hate* forts. The notion of being locked in one place for years and years makes me want to scream.'

'You made very good time, sir,' Sub-Commander Andar said

when Narasan and Trenicia joined him at the front of the fort.

'Not as good as you and Gunda made,' Narasan replied. 'How in the world were you able to cover a hundred and twenty miles in four and a half days?

'Longbow discarded several customs, sir,' Andar replied with a faint smile. 'First he abolished the standard rest period.'

'How was he able to persuade the men to do that? That custom's been locked in stone for centuries now.'

'He used the cooks as the key to unlocking it, sir.'

'The cooks? I don't quite follow you there.'

'He put the cooks at the head of the column, sir,' Andar explained. 'He must have made a few threats, because the cooks did their best to keep up with him. That put breakfast, lunch, and supper farther and farther ahead of the men who felt the need to rest. It took the men a day or so to get his point. "Rest or eat" is a little brutal, but it *did* get his point across. Sauntering along more or less vanished along about then, and running became all the rage – particularly after that lady cook from Lord Veltan's Domain took charge of the preparation of the meals. An occasional gust of wind went down the pass, and it carried the smell of her cooking down to the men who'd been stubbornly insisting that their right to rest was more important than anything else in the whole world. The pace of the army picked up quite noticeably at that point.'

'That Longbow's an absolute genius,' Narasan declared.

'I'd say so, yes,' Andar agreed. 'It seems that when he wants something, he always comes up with a way to get it.'

'How far on up the pass is Gunda's fort?' Narasan asked then.

'Almost exactly a mile, sir,' Andar replied. 'That might vary a few times as we go on down the pass, but we'll always be quite close to a mile.'

'I suppose I'd better go on up and say some nice things about Gunda's fort,' Narasan said then.

'I'm sure he'll appreciate that, sir,' Andar said with no hint of a smile.

Since it was obviously going to take the rest of the day for the main army to get past Andar's fort, Narasan and Trenicia went on ahead to Gunda's fort. Longbow was there, of course, and Narasan had learned quite some time back that when he needed information about the Creatures of the Wasteland, Longbow was the man to speak with.

Gunda's fort went quite a ways farther than the standard Trogite one in that there were huge boulders mixed in with the standard granite blocks. 'It wasn't really my idea, Narasan,' Gunda conceded. 'Prince Ekial took a look at our rock wall and suggested that bigger rocks might add a bit. Then he had a fair number of his men start dragging those boulders here. I was more than a little surprised when I saw the size of the rocks a dozen or so horses could drag across the ground. No matter how many bug-people come charging up here, this is as far as they're going to get.'

'Have you seen any of them yet?' Narasan asked.

'Oh, yes,' Gunda replied. 'They're still about five miles away, but there are thousands of them out there. I'd say that the Vlagh's throwing everything she's got at us this time. Prince Ekial and his horse-soldiers are slowing them down quite a bit, but they *will* reach this fort before too much longer.'

'The main army's not far behind, Gunda,' Narasan assured his friend. 'They're climbing over Andar's fort right now, but I'd say that your fort will be fully manned by about noon tomorrow.'

'They *do* have those poisoned stakes with them, don't they?'

'Oh, yes. Your impregnable fort's going to be even *more* impregnable after we've planted those stakes to the front. Andar told me that there *were* quite a few bug-people up on the rims of the pass.'

'They're still there, Narasan,' Gunda replied, 'but they're dead now. Kathlak's archers went on up there and showered them with poisonous arrows. There are a lot of trees up on those rims, and once the main army gets here, I'd suggest that we send a good number of them up there with axes. Catapults are always nice to have on hand when your enemies are charging. If we do this right, this will be about as far as our enemies will get.'

'Why have you got people building more forts then?' Queen Trenicia asked.

'Just a precaution, ma'am,' Gunda replied. 'Things sometimes go wrong no matter what we do, and those extra forts will give us someplace to fall back to if it turns out to be necessary. As our mighty commander here says quite often, "Always expect the worst, and be ready for it." If it doesn't turn out that way, it's a pleasant surprise, but we don't take any chances.'

'You're a gloomy sort of fellow, aren't you, friend Narasan?' Trenicia said.

'Maybe,' Narasan conceded, 'but I *am* still alive.'

'That's all that really matters, dear one,' Trenicia said with a fond smile.

2

'Where's Prince Ekial?' Narasan asked the Malavi Ariga the following morning when they were all gathering for the customary conference.

'Ekial is giving instruction to that young Keselo on riding a horse. The two of them get along well with each other,' Ariga replied.

Narasan nodded, then looking around at everyone, he said, 'First, of course, the question is how far away from here is the enemy – and how many of them are there?'

'I drifted out over the Wasteland yesterday,' Lady Zelana said, 'and it looked to me like the Vlagh was throwing everything she's got at us this time.'

'And how many would that be, ma'am?' Gunda asked.

'A half million at least,' Zelana replied. 'Probably closer to a whole million.'

'She's definitely pushing her luck, then,' Lord Dahlaine declared. 'In the past she's always kept a great number of her children in reserve.'

'Children?' Trenicia asked in a startled voice.

'I know that it sounds very unnatural, Queen Trenicia,' Dahlaine replied, 'but the Vlagh gives birth to *all* of her servants. Of course she doesn't have children in the same way that human mothers do. She lays eggs instead. Evidently, she realizes that this will be her last chance to gain dominion of some part of the Land of Dhrall that's out beyond the Wasteland, so with the exception of the ones that take care of her in her nest, she's probably emptied the place out. If things turn out the way we want them to, she'll have very few servants left if this attack falls apart the way that the previous ones have.'

'And that would mean that she'll be out of business, doesn't it?' Andar said.

'I'm not completely positive about that,' Lady Zelana disagreed. 'It'll take her a long, long time to build the number of her children back up, but as long as she's there, she'll still be a danger for us.'

'We'll have to kill her then,' Trenicia said bluntly.

Zelana winced. 'We're not allowed to do that,' she replied.

'That's why you hired *us*, isn't it?' Trenicia suggested. 'If the best that we can do is block her off, she'll go back to her nest and lay more eggs, and next spring she'll attack again.'

'Not quite *that* soon, Queen Trenicia,' Dahlaine disagreed. 'It might take as long as another century for her to produce enough children to pose any significant threat, but—' He left it hanging there.

'Cut off her food,' Two-Hands of Matan said bluntly. 'Doesn't no food mean no new calves? You *can* play with the weather, Dahlaine. You've demonstrated that several times already this year. A drought might be the best answer.'

'Or possibly a flood,' the farmer Omago from Veltan's Domain suggested. 'That worked extremely well last summer.'

'I'd say that we can decide which way we should go *after* we've stopped the army that's coming to visit us here,' Longbow said then.

'How long would you say it's likely to take the bug-people to get into position to attack Gunda's fort, Longbow?' Narasan asked.

'A week or ten days,' Longbow replied. 'Right now I'd suggest working on catapults. They worked rather well last autumn in the north country.'

'I'll put the men to work on those,' Gunda agreed.

It was about noon on the following day when Ekial and Keselo came up to the back side of Gunda's fort. Narasan was a bit surprised by how well Keselo was riding the horse Ekial had provided. 'You two made good time,' Narasan said as they dismounted.

'That's because young Keselo here is a natural-born horseman,' Ekial declared. 'It didn't take him more than a couple hours to get old Bent-Nose there so attached to him that the silly horse wants to sleep with him now.'

'Bent-Nose?' Narasan asked. 'Isn't that an odd sort of name for a horse?'

'When he was quite a bit younger, we were fighting horsemen from a different part of our country, and one of the enemies slashed the horse across the nose with his sabre. When the cut healed, the scar changed the shape of the horse's nose. "Bent" might not be too accurate, but it sounds better than "swelled-up", wouldn't you say?'

'I see what you mean.' Then Narasan looked inquiringly at Keselo. 'How did you manage to get on the good side of the horse so fast?' he asked curiously.

Keselo smiled. 'I just happened to have some candy in my pack-sack, sir,' Keselo replied, 'and Bent-Nose seems to have a sweet-tooth. After two small pieces of candy, he was following me around like a puppy-dog.'

'Bribery, Keselo? I'm shocked.'

'I wouldn't really call it "bribery", Commander,' Keselo protested. 'I'd say that "a treat for a friend" would come closer.'

Ekial laughed. 'The young man was nice enough to give me the recipe for that candy, so if I don't eat it all myself, I'll be able to get on the good side of just about every horse in the Land of Malavi.' Then his scarred face grew more serious. 'Have the bug-people made any attacks yet?'

Narasan shook his head. 'Longbow says that they'll probably wait until all of their relatives join them. I was talking with Ariga, and he advised me that the Malavi had come up with a scheme to disrupt the advance of our enemies.'

'Lances, most likely,' Ekial said.

Then Lord Dahlaine and Lady Zelana came out of the back side of Gunda's fort and joined them. 'What did Sorgan say about our sister, Keselo?' Lady Zelana asked.

Keselo told them Aracia had finally come to her senses, thanks to Veltan's images of assorted varieties of bug-people, and then she came down on her priests – *hard* – and on the little priestess Alcevan.

'A priestess?' Narasan said in astonishment. 'I didn't even *know* that Aracia *has* female priests.'

'I gathered that Alcevan's entry into the priesthood was fairly recent. Fat Bersla orates his adoration, but tiny Alcevan *whispers* hers – continuously, even while Bersla's performing. She sounds a lot like an ordinary priest trying to get Aracia's undivided atten-tion – *but* she was recently involved in an attempt to murder Aracia's Dreamer, Lillabeth.'

'She's trying to kill Lillabeth?' Dahlaine exclaimed.

'That's what Sorgan told me, sir,' Keselo replied. 'He said that she'd already bribed a young priest to kill the little girl, but the priest showed up in Lillabeth's play-room when several other people – Sorgan included – were there. The priest reported back to Alcevan that the time wasn't right yet, but that he'd take care of it when there was nobody about. Alcevan told him that was a wonderful idea, and then she cut the young man's throat from ear to ear. Sorgan's fairly sure that she doesn't want anybody who knows what she's doing to stay alive for very long. Veltan believes that Alcevan has her eye on Aracia's throne and she'll routinely kill any accomplice after they've either done what she wanted them to do – or failed, for that matter. I'd say that the life expectancy of *anybody* who goes to work for little Alcevan will be just about one day. After that, he'll be dead meat.'

'That's terrible!'

'Look on the bright side, Lord Dahlaine. Every priest she kills now will be one less that *we'll* have to kill when this is over.' He looked over at Ekial. 'That's called "thinning the herd" down in Malavi-land, isn't it?'

It was late that afternoon when Red-Beard, riding the horse he called Seven, led the archers of Longbow's tribe – or the Old-Bear tribe – down to the upper end of Gunda's fort. Longbow, of course, went out to greet them, and Narasan, as a courtesy, went with his tall, sombre friend.

'Ho, Longbow,' a lean archer with steely eyes greeted his friend.

'Tracker,' Longbow replied with a nod. 'What took you so long?'

'We ran into some of the Creatures of the Wasteland,' the one Longbow had called Tracker replied. 'Red-Beard here told us that there had been several encounters with them along that worn-out old mountain range. I think that the Vlagh doesn't really want *too* many archers standing in the path of her children when she sends them up here. Evidently she's learned that we can eliminate her children without much difficulty, so she'd rather not have us to come up against. It took us a little while, but we cleaned them out of our way. Oh, Chief Old-Bear told us to give you his regards.'

'How's he doing?'

'The same as always, Longbow. You should know that by now. He can still bend his bow, and his arrows always go just where he wants them to go.'

'Is One-Who-Heals feeling any better?' Longbow asked. 'Word reached us that he was quite ill a month or so ago.'

'We thought that the bad news had reached you by now. We lost him, Longbow. He died a few days before the Maag called Skell sailed into our bay.'

Longbow sighed. 'We're all made less by that,' he said mournfully. 'He was one of the wisest men in all the Land of Dhrall. Was he ever able to identify the disease that took him from us?'

'I don't think it was really a disease, Longbow. Old age would probably come closer. He was at least ninety years old, and not too many people live much longer than that.'

'That's true, I suppose. I think that out of respect for him we should exterminate all the servants of the Vlagh and leave her sitting alone on that hive of hers.'

'She'll just lay more eggs, Longbow.'

'Maybe – but then again, maybe not. Oh, this is Commander Narasan of the Trogite Empire. You probably met him during the war in the Domains of Zelana and Veltan.'

Tracker nodded. 'He's been very helpful.'

'We try,' Narasan replied. 'What is it that gave you the name "Tracker"?' He asked.

'It's what he does, friend Narasan,' Longbow explained. 'Tracker can follow any animal – or man – just about any place they go. He can find tracks laid down on solid rock – or so I've been told – and I wouldn't be at all surprised to find out that he can track fish as well.'

'Only if the water isn't too deep, friend Longbow,' Tracker said. 'I don't really swim very well, so fish can usually get away from me. The little rascals can move very fast when they need to.'

'Let's go on back to Gunda's fort, gentlemen,' Narasan suggested. 'It's a bit chilly out here, and I'm sure your men would be very happy to get something to eat along about now.'

'What a great idea,' Longbow said without cracking a smile.

The arrival of the members of Longbow's tribe seemed to have changed their friend quite a bit. Longbow had always seemed to be a solitary sort of man, but now that he had his friends here, he even smiled on occasion.

The next morning, just after sunrise, the bug-people began a steady march toward the steep slope that led up to Gunda's fort at the upper end of Long-Pass.

Ekial's horsemen savaged them as they advanced, but it didn't seem to Narasan that the bug-people were slowing their pace very much.

During the previous night, however, the men from the main army had reached Gunda's fort and had delivered the barrels of naphtha, pitch, and tar. Gunda had then moved his catapults into position and the catapult crews were carefully mixing the three elements in preparation for launching fire missiles.

'Did you speak with Ekial, Gunda?' Narasan asked. 'We don't want to start throwing fire at our friends, you know.'

'We've got it all worked out, Narasan,' Gunda replied. 'We're falling back on toots. When Ekial and his men hear the horns blowing, they'll get clear. Then the catapult crews will set fire to enough bug-people to persuade the other ones to go play somewhere else.'

'That's the most brutal way to make war on somebody that I've ever heard of,' Trenicia said.

'In the long run, it probably saves a lot of their lives, dear,' Narasan told her. 'Even the stupidest enemy in the world will turn and run when he sees his friends engulfed in fire. The bug-people aren't any too bright, but even *they* will probably turn and run when it starts raining fire.'

'Then we've just won another war, wouldn't you say?'

'I'm not at all that certain, dear,' Narasan replied, looking out at the massed Creatures of the Wasteland marching up the slope. 'We don't have an unlimited supply of fuel for our fire missiles, and when we run out, the enemies will most probably resume their advance.'

'Right up until they reach the poisoned stakes,' Gunda added. 'Then after they come through the stakes, the archers from Longbow's tribe and Kathlak's Tonthakan archers will shower them with poisoned arrows. If any of the bug-people get past *that*, the Matan spear-throwers will greet them. I'd say that dear old Vlagh's going to lose about half of her army on that slope, and then they'll come face to face with this fort. They're *not* going to get past us, but even if they do, they'll come up against Andar's fort a mile or so down the pass – and more forts farther on down the pass. The Vlagh may have started out with a million or so soldiers, but she'll be lucky if she's got even a dozen left after a week or so.'

CONFUSION

1

Rabbit was fairly sure that Fat Bersla and tiny Alcevan would be nowhere near any place along the rickety southern wall of the temple where *most* of Aracia's priests were engaged in honest work and endless complaints about it – *and* about the steady diet of beans. Gimpy and Squint-Eye were Maag ship-captains, but they'd been put in charge of the construction of what passed for the south wall more because they'd irritated Sorgan than because they were good builders. Rabbit was quite sure that the two of them weren't certain just how many of Aracia's lazy priests were supposed to be working on that wall. That should have made it quite easy for Bersla and Alcevan to slip away. 'Except that there won't be much for Bersla to eat – except maybe for cobwebs,' Rabbit muttered. 'I think I'd better go see if I can find those two,' he decided. 'If they're still trying to come up with a way to kill Aracia's little Dreamer, I'd better stay right on top of them.'

Given Bersla's need for *lots* of food, Rabbit was quite sure that they wouldn't be too far from the nearest kitchen.

He roamed around in the dark, dusty corridors near the rickety south wall of the temple, searching more with his ears than his eyes, and as luck had it – or possibly destiny – he heard the priestess

Alcevan talking in her peculiar voice. 'Stay calm, Takal Bersla,' she was saying. 'I still have my hands on a fair number of novice priests. In the light of all this chaos, nobody's really paying much attention to the various corridors leading from here to the central temple, so sooner or later one of my agents *will* get through and kill the spoiled brat Lillabeth, and that should put Aracia back under our control.'

'I'm not sure that you're right, Alcevan,' Bersla disagreed. 'I know Aracia much better than you do, and she's totally independent now. The old Aracia would *never* have dismissed me the way this new one did. She's not at all the same as she was before that cursed pirate Sorgan arrived. She *used* to rely on me for all things, but now she turns to Sorgan instead.'

'That's the work of the younger goddess Enalla, you fool,' Alcevan declared. 'Once Enalla's gone, Aracia will be ours again. That's why we *must* kill the child Lillabeth. She's Enalla in disguise. When *she* dies, Enalla also dies.'

'You could be right, I suppose,' Bersla admitted dubiously.

That struck Rabbit as more than just a little bit peculiar. Bersla was the highest-ranking priest in Aracia's temple, but it seemed to Rabbit that the Fat Man was falling in line with the recently arrived Alcevan every time she opened her mouth. She seemed to have some kind of overpowering grip on the head of the Church of Aracia. 'I think that maybe I'd better go warn Veltan that these two *still* want to kill that little girl,' he muttered.

'She's still sending those low-rank young priests through the corridors to come here and try to kill Lillabeth, Veltan,' Rabbit advised Zelana's younger brother when they met in the cabin of the *Ascension* later that day. 'She's absolutely certain that Lillabeth is really Enalla in disguise, and that if Lillabeth is killed, Enalla will die as well.'

'She doesn't fully understand what's happening, Rabbit,' Veltan replied, leaning back in the bulky chair near the broad window on the stern side of the cabin. Then a rueful sort of expression came over his face. 'Of course, I'm not all that sure that *I* do either. When Eleria started to refer to Balacenia as "Big-Me," it startled me more than a little. The Dreamers and the younger gods *are* connected in ways that Dahlaine didn't anticipate when he came up with his scheme, and they're connected with each other in ways that none of us could have imagined.'

'They share their dreams with each other, you mean?'

'Exactly. We weren't ready for that. *We* tend to avoid each other as much as possible, but our younger counterparts are much more closely linked.'

'You know that you *could* take Lillabeth over to the cap'n's fort on the west wall. If he put out the word that *no* priest will be permitted to go there, Alcevan's scheme would go to pieces, wouldn't you say?'

'It probably would, Rabbit,' Veltan agreed, 'but I think I'd better keep her right here. I can protect her here, and I've got a strong feeling that I should stay very close to my big sister. Aracia's more or less come to her senses, but she might start veering off again. That priestess Alcevan is about ten times more clever than Fat Bersla will ever be, and if she wheedles her way back into Aracia's presence, she'll probably start pushing big sister off balance again.'

'You could be right, I guess,' Rabbit agreed. 'When we first got here, we were all sure that Fat Bersla was the main one in your sister's priesthood, but when I heard the Fat Man talking with Teenie-Weenie, she was calling all the shots. There's something very strange about her, and I think maybe we should all do what we can to find out just what that is. Fat Bersla makes speeches, but "Teenie" spends all of her time whispering to your big sister.' Then Rabbit stopped, and he felt just a bit foolish. '*You* could listen to those whispers, couldn't you?'

'Probably, yes.'

'*And* neither Alcevan or your big sister would know that you're listening, would they?'

'Aracia *might* sense my presence, but I think I could conceal it from her.'

Rabbit shook his head. 'Bad idea, I think. If you're busy eavesdropping who's going to look out for Lillabeth?'

Veltan's expression became a bit sheepish. 'I seem to have overlooked that,' he admitted. 'Why don't I have a talk with Zelana instead? She can either protect Lillabeth, or do our eavesdropping for us.'

'That's probably the best idea right there,' Rabbit agreed. Then he remembered something from the previous summer. 'I think I know of a way to stop those novice priests from coming here,' he said.

'Oh?'

'I'll need a lot of spider-webs that are quite a bit thicker than the ones the local spiders have been spinning in the hallways here in your sister's temple. You *do* remember what happened to Jalkan and that churchman from the Trogite Empire, don't you?'

Veltan shuddered. 'I don't think I'll *ever* forget that.'

'If I gather those beginner priests together and warn them that there are spiders in those hallways that are almost as big as horses and then describe what happened to Jalkan and the Trogite priest down in your territory, Alcevan's going to have a lot of trouble hiring killers, I think.' Then Rabbit squinted at Zelana's younger brother. 'You can make just about anything you want to, can't you, Veltan?' he asked.

'What exactly do you think you'll need?'

'Bones, mostly – but not just random bones scattered around. I think complete skeletons would be best. That way anybody who comes across one of them will know that he's looking at a dead person rather than a fox or a cow, and it might be useful if the skeleton has a few rags attached as well – rags that look like they used to be those robes all of Aracia's priests wear.'

'And maybe a brief image of a very large spider – or ten – scampering around in those corridors?' Veltan suggested.

'You *can* do that, can't you?' Rabbit said. 'I'd forgotten about that. If we have a few sightings of spiders that are ten feet across, human skeletons wearing bits and pieces of priest robes, and spiderwebs as thick as anchor ropes, *nobody* with his head on straight will go anywhere near those corridors.'

'I like it!' Veltan declared with a wicked grin. 'Go back to the south side of the temple and start telling stories, Rabbit. I'll make sure that anybody who ventures into one of those corridors sees things so terrible that he'll *never* go back again.'

'I think we just sank Alcevan's boat,' Rabbit said with a broad grin.

'I'm fairly sure that she'll never be able to give those halfwit young priests what she's promising,' Rabbit told the two Maags, Gimpy and Squint-Eye, 'but around here, a promotion is worth more than gold. I'm going to need some verification, though. If it's not too much trouble, put on long, worried faces and talk about some of your sailors who went along one of those corridors and never came back.'

'You're a nasty little fellow, Rabbit,' Captain Squint-Eye said. Then he assumed the facial expression that had given him his name. 'Maybe if we had one of those imitation skeletons you were telling us about dressed in Maag clothes and armed with Maag weapons, the limp-brained priests will get your point.'

'And maybe put up some danger signs at this end of those hall-ways,' Captain Gimpy added. 'You know, a red sign with a big picture of a spider painted on it. If we pile up enough awfuls for those halfwits to see, not one of them will even consider going back to the main temple, no matter *what* the little lady priest offers them. It's a lot like that old Maag saying that has to do with gold, wouldn't you say? "You've got to be alive to spend it" gets right to the point, doesn't it?'

'And Gimpy and I'll announce that we want all those priests to come to an "emergency conference," and then you can dump awful-awful all over them,' Captain Squint-Eye added. Then he laughed. 'You know, something like this is even more fun than a war.'

'Of course,' Rabbit agreed. 'Deception is always more fun than war, and, if you do it right, you don't even have to bleed.'

2

'No, Rabbit,' Captain Hook-Beak said. 'I think *you'd* better do it. You and Torl and several others have been passing on stories about your encounters with imaginary bug-people ever since we first got here. I'll back you up, of course, but the lazy priests would believe *you* a lot sooner than they'd ever believe me.' He paused, staring out across the berm his men had built out to the front of the west wall. 'Don't go *too* far, though. When you get right down to it, all you're really going to do down by the south wall is set things up for the appearance of those imitation skeletons wearing priest robes that Veltan's going to conjure up. Keep your description of what the spider-bugs have been doing to the local priests those imitation skeletons are going to represent pretty much accurate. Don't get too creative. The real thing down in Veltan's Domain was awful enough, so you won't have to take it much farther.'

'That's the way we'll do 'er, Cap'n,' Rabbit agreed. 'I'll start out by telling them that the spider-bugs slipped past us before we even started building walls and that they're hiding in *most* of those hallways. Then I'll move on into a description of what happened to Jalkan and Adnari Estarg. That should set things up for Cap'n Gimpy to uncover those imitation skeletons.

'You're *very* good at this sort of thing, Rabbit,' Sorgan said admiringly.

'I've had lots of practice, Cap'n,' Rabbit replied with a broad grin. 'All I had to do to keep Ox and Ham-Hand from putting me to doing *real* work was to stand there tapping on my anvil with a hammer. I'm a natural-born expert when it comes to deception.'

'Except that Longbow saw right through you the first time he ever met you,' Sorgan added with a broad grin.

'Longbow don't count, Cap'n,' Rabbit replied. 'He sees through everything.'

Rabbit was almost certain that Takal Bersla would *not* be present during Captain Squint-Eye's 'emergency conference.' He was too well-known, for one thing, and, since he'd gained his position in the temple by making speeches, he probably wouldn't care to listen to speeches delivered by someone else. The priestess Alcevan would almost certainly want to be present, though, since the term 'emergency' strongly suggested that something had come up that would make her hired assassins very reluctant to do what she wanted them to do. Rabbit was very well acquainted with all the tricks a small person could use to watch and listen without being seen, so he ran his eyes carefully over the gathered crowd of priests to see if he could locate her.

Then a brief flicker of movement caught his eye, and there was Alcevan, crouched low among the ruins of the poorly-constructed wall along the south side of the temple. She was in the shadows, so nobody would even know that she was there – *if* she stayed still and didn't move. Either she didn't know that, or she was positive that nobody would be looking for her. Rabbit, however, *had* been searching, and he'd just found what he wanted. 'I don't think she's going to like this very much,' he murmured to himself as Captain Gimpy climbed up onto a large stone block to speak to the gathered priests.

'Captain Squint-Eye and me decided that there's something you priests really ought to know about, since your lives could very well depend on your knowing what it is,' Gimpy declared. 'To keep it short, our scouts saw quite a few bug-people sneaking through the bushes toward this south wall, and that's why you're here to lend us a hand. There was something that'd happened earlier, though, that our scouts didn't know about.' He put his hand on Rabbit's shoulder. 'This little fellow has actually *seen* a certain variety of bugs in the corridors that lead to the main temple, so he can tell you what they look like and just how dangerous they are.'

'I'll do my best, Cap'n Gimpy,' Rabbit said. Then he looked out at the not really too interested priests. 'This will be the fourth war we've had with the bug-people since last spring, and I've managed to live through all four of them – so far, anyway. There are dozens and dozens of different kinds of bug-people. Most of them are fairly stupid, so we've been able to outsmart them three times already. An entirely different kind of bug showed up in the second war last summer, and that's the bug that somehow got into these corridors. Most bugs have six legs, but these ones we've seen in these corridors have eight. Now, *most* bugs chase things – or people – that they want to eat. The eight-legged ones set traps, though.'

'That's absurd,' one of the priests declared.

'Not really,' Rabbit disagreed. 'Most of the corridors here in the temple have spider-webs all over the walls and hanging down from the ceiling. The spider-bug we encountered last summer was fifty or a hundred times bigger than any other spider I've ever seen. We had two different enemies in that war off to the south. One of the enemies was the bug-people, of course, but the other one came from Trog-land, and *they* came here to look for gold, and they thought that they saw more gold than they'd ever seen before lying out there in the Wasteland.'

Rabbit smiled then. 'We had two enemies, and they were running toward each other. It wouldn't have been very polite to interfere with either one of them, so we just got out of the way. The Trog-landers encountered bug-people with poisonous fangs, and that eliminated quite a few of them. But then the Trogs came up against the spider-bugs we've been talking about here. The huge spider-bugs had spun out their webs, and a fair number of Trogs got snared in those webs. Then the spider-bugs came out of their hiding places and bit the snared up Trogs. The venom of the ordinary bug-people is so poisonous that it kills people instantly. The venom of the spider-bug works differently, though. It dissolves the innards – hearts, livers, lungs, and so on – so the person caught in the web has had most of his insides turned into a liquid. A spider doesn't have to chew its food. It drinks it instead. The Trogs were snared in those webs, so they couldn't move. Then, any time the spider got hungry again, it'd just tiptoe along the web, bite a hole in one of the Trogs, and then drink a gallon or so of the liquid that used to be the insides of the trapped Trog. The screaming when that happened isn't the kind of screaming you really want to hear.'

'Are you saying that those men were still alive after their insides were dissolved?' an older, chubby priest demanded skeptically.

'I've never heard a dead man scream,' Rabbit replied. 'I'd guess that the spider wants fresh food, so its venom dissolves things, but doesn't kill. *That's* what you'll be coming up against if you try to go back through those corridors to the main temple.'

'We *have* managed to recover what was left of several of the victims of those overgrown spiders,' Captain Gimpy smoothly stepped in. 'There wasn't really very much of them left – except for their bones. It looks to me like spider venom doesn't dissolve bones, so we can show you what condition you're likely to be in after one of the spiders eats most of you.' Then he pulled back a tarp to reveal four skeletons. Gimpy tapped one of the skeletons with his foot. '*This* one was probably a Maag before the spider ate most of him. He was wearing fairly standard Maag clothes, though, so that sort of identifies him. The other three . . . ?' Gimpy shrugged. 'Maybe one of you can identify the clothing on those others. Clothes are about all we've got to work with. Bones are bones, and they all look pretty much the same.'

The priests all shrank back from Gimpy's suggestion. Rabbit was fairly sure that none of them had ever *seen* a human skeleton before. Finally, one of the older priests ordered a novice to go look. The young man turned pale and hesitantly approached Veltan's recently manufactured skeletons. 'It's sort of hard to tell, your reverence,' he said in a trembling voice. 'There are only a few rags attached to any one of these three.'

'What color are the rags?' the old man demanded.

'Black, your reverence.'

'I'd say that sort of answers the question,' Gimpy declared. 'Maags don't wear black clothes. It's considered to be unlucky. You priests here *all* wear black robes, though, so those three skeletons are – or were – almost certainly priests who served Lady Aracia. I want all of you to take a good hard look at those three skeletons. If you happen to get some kind of urge to go back to the main temple, you'll almost certainly end up looking exactly like these three do. Of course, dead people don't really care what they look like, do they? They're too busy being dead to worry about their appearance. It's entirely up to you men, though. I'm not going to make staying out of those hallways an order. You might have very important things to do back in the main temple, but your chances of actually *reaching* the main temple aren't very good, but that's up to you. I won't interfere with anybody's religious obligations.'

Rabbit rather casually looked at the tumbled-down wall where Alcevan had been hiding, and he saw that the look she was giving Cap'n Gimpy was filled with frustration and hatred.

'I'd say that poor "Teenie-Weenie" just got cut off at the pockets,' Rabbit murmured, doing his very best to avoid laughing out loud.

THE TRIBE OF OLD-BEAR

1

The weather had turned bitterly cold as Red-Beard, mounted on the horse he called 'Seven,' led Skell and the archers of Old-Bear's tribe south along a worn-down mountain range toward the upper end of Long-Pass. The Matans of Tlantar Two-Hands *had* given Skell and the other Maag seamen those densely furred bison-hide cloaks, but the chill was still brutal.

The archers of Old-Bear's tribe were very interested in Red-Beard's horse, and Longbow's friend described the 'slash and run' tactics of the Malavi in some detail.

'That might be all right in open country,' an archer called Sleeps-With-Dogs said, 'but I don't think it'd work out too well in the forest.'

'You're probably right,' Red-Beard admitted, 'but most of the country here in the North or off to the East is open. If I remember right, you were with us down in Veltan's Domain, and the country above the Falls of Vash didn't have very many trees. A forest is good for hunting, but when you get into open country, the distance between here and there seems to go on forever. That's when a horse becomes *very* useful. You don't have to do your own walking – or running – if you've got a horse.' Then he gave the archer from

Longbow's tribe a curious look. 'How in the world did you come up with a name like "Sleeps-With-Dogs"?' he asked.

The archer shrugged. 'I found out quite some time ago that having dogs in your lodge in the winter-time means that you're not going to need very much firewood. If you bed down with three or four dogs, you'll stay nice and warm. The fleas are sort of troublesome, but not as much as ice is.'

'I might give that a try myself,' Red-Beard said. 'I'm sure that Seven here gives off heat when he sleeps, but he sleeps standing up.'

'What made you decide to call him "Seven"?' the archer asked.

Red-Beard laughed. 'That wasn't my idea at all. His original owner was a gambler, and he just *loved* to play dice-games. As I understand it, Seven's a very important number when you're playing dice-games. When the Malavi were sailing north on board quite a few Trogite ships, they didn't really have much to do, so they gambled, just to pass the time. I've heard that Seven's original owner won a lot of money in those dice-games – right up until the other Malavi found out that he'd been cheating. They threw him off the ship into deep water, and since he'd never learned how to swim, he sank like a rock.'

'Drowned?'

'You couldn't prove that by me, Sleeps-With-Dogs,' Red-Beard replied, 'but after he'd been under water for an hour or so the other Malavi divided up what he'd left behind, and they gave *me* old Seven here. He's a sensible old horse, and he and I get along very well. I don't have to walk much now, and I don't force him to run. It works out fairly well for the both of us.'

'How much farther would you say it is to this Long-Pass place?' Skell asked Red-Beard.

'Dahlaine's map said that it's about a hundred and sixty miles from where we started down along this mountain range,' Red-Beard replied. 'I'd say that we're about half-way there, Captain Skell. Since it took us four days to get *this* far, it'll probably take us another four days to get to where we're going.'

'I was sort of afraid that it might take that long,' Skell said sourly.

'Have you heard anything at all about what cousin Sorgan's up to down in Lady Aracia's temple?' Skell asked Red-Beard as they set out the next morning.

'Deception for the most part, I've been told,' Red-Beard replied. 'Zelana's big sister wants everybody in the world who owns a sword to run down there and defend her. I've heard that Sorgan told her that he could hold off the bug-people *if* she'd pay him a lot of gold.'

'That's Sorgan, all right,' Skell said with a faint smile. 'My cousin is probably the greatest cheater in the world. Before I left to go fetch the archers from Old-Bear's tribe, people were saying that the bugs would attack through Long-Pass, and that Aracia's temple wasn't in any danger at all, and that Aracia herself wasn't either. How in the world did cousin Sorgan manage to squeeze any gold at all out of her?'

'He lied, of course. You know how Sorgan is. From what I've heard, his plan was to send people who can lie with a straight face out into the farm-land and come back with all kinds of horror stories about bug-people living on a steady diet of people-people. That's supposed to keep Aracia's holy-holies penned up inside the temple while the *real* warriors are fighting off the bugs in Long-Pass.' Then Red-Beard tugged at his whiskers. 'If what I've heard about Zelana's sister comes anywhere close to being true, she wants

– even *needs* – to have the bug-people attack her holy temple. If they don't bother to attack her, it would sort of mean that she's not very important to them, wouldn't it? She just couldn't stand that, you know. She *has* to be important, and if the bugs just ignored her, she'd shrivel up and blow away. I think *that's* what your cousin is counting on. Aracia will believe any lie he – or one of his paid liars – tells her, because she *has* to believe.'

'That's the saddest thing I've ever heard,' Skell declared. 'She'd rather die than be ignored.'

'Except that she *can't* die,' Red-Beard said. 'In some ways that makes it even sadder, wouldn't you say? She'll live forever, but nobody's ever going to pay any attention to her.'

Skell shuddered and changed the subject. 'Sorgan always manages to have all the fun,' he said sourly. 'A war against an enemy who isn't really there would be a lot easier than a real war.'

'He took your brother Torl with him,' Red-Beard said. 'From what I've heard, Torl's probably one of the greatest liars in the whole world.'

'He's good at that, all right,' Skell agreed. 'Have any new varieties of bug-people shown up yet?'

'I wouldn't know for sure,' Red-Beard replied. 'I've been riding poor old Seven here back and forth across this part of the Land of Dhrall since late last fall, so I haven't been anywhere near the Wasteland.'

'Is learning how to ride a horse very difficult?' Skell asked curiously.

'That sort of depends on the horse. Old Seven here is fairly placid and easy to get along with. Most of the Malavi horses are much more frisky than Seven, and that doesn't hurt my feelings one little bit. Seven can't run as fast as most of the other Malavi horses, but I'm not in *that* big a hurry to get from here to there.'

'I'll go along with you there, Red-Beard,' Skell agreed.

A fair number of Old-Bear's archers had gone on ahead that afternoon, and along about sunset the main party reached the camp site on the bank of a wide river that flowed down out of the mountain range. Somewhat to Skell's surprise, the archers had managed to kill several of the bison that grazed nearby. 'I've been told that it's very difficult to kill those bison with arrows,' Skell said to the archer called Tracker.

'Not if you've got metal arrowheads,' Tracker replied. 'Stone arrowheads aren't as sharp, and metal cuts through much easier. We'll have fresh meat for supper tonight. Your cousin Sorgan gave us exactly what we needed to make our lives more pleasant.'

'I'm sure that he'll be glad to hear that. Did you happen to encounter any bug-people?'

'We saw a few of them, but they were holding back for some reason.'

'I've been meaning to ask one of you people a question,' Skell said then.

'I'll answer it if I can,' Tracker said.

'Over in the Land of Maag, we almost never see a bug roaming around in the winter-time, but the bugs out in the Wasteland don't seem to pay any attention to the fact that it's turned very cold.'

Tracker shrugged. 'The Vlagh does all sorts of things that other bugs don't,' he replied. 'Our shaman, One-Who-Heals, told us that the Vlagh wants the Wasteland all to herself. The other bugs hole up in the winter-time, but the Vlagh's children don't. They break into the nests of the other bugs, kill them all, and then run back to the Vlagh's nest with all the food the other bugs had stored up for the winter.'

'That's terrible!' Skell exclaimed.

'"Terrible" pretty much describes the Vlagh, yes,' Tracker replied with a faint smile. 'If I understand it right, she wants the whole world, and she wants her children to eat everything – and everybody – who lives there. For her, more food means more children.'

'We've got to get rid of that monster!' Skell declared.

'You should take that up with Longbow, Skell. That's his life-long goal. After one of the Vlagh's children killed Misty-Water, Longbow set out to kill the Vlagh, and sooner or later, he'll probably do just that.'

'Who was Misty-Water?' Skell asked.

Tracker sighed. 'She was the daughter of Chief Old-Bear, and she and Longbow were right on the verge of mating. One of the servants of the Vlagh killed her, though, and now killing the Vlagh is Longbow's only real goal in life.'

'That explains a lot of the things about Longbow that I didn't really understand,' Skell said. 'I'm glad that he's on *our* side. Having Longbow for an enemy would cut back a man's life-expectancy by quite a bit, wouldn't you say?'

'Almost back to nothing at all,' Tracker agreed.

2

It was about noon on a cloudy day when they reached the upper end of Long-Pass, and Skell was forced to concede that Gunda's fort was very impressive.

'I can't really take credit for all those boulders in the front wall,' Gunda said. 'Ekial and the Malavi hitched their horses to rocks almost as big as houses and dragged them here. I don't think the bug-people will have much fun trying to climb that wall, particularly now that we've got all those archers you just brought here.'

Then Longbow and the Trogite army-commander Narasan came out to greet Longbow's friends.

'Ho, Longbow,' Tracker called.

'What took you so long?' Longbow asked with a faint smile.

'We ran into some of the Creatures of the Wasteland. Red-Beard said that they've been sneaking around quite a bit. I don't think the Vlagh's too happy about all the archers her people are going to come up against. They didn't rush us or anything, but they *were* watching. Oh, Chief Old-Bear told us to give you his regards.'

'How's he doing?'

'The same as always. He can still put arrows where he wants them.'

Skell went over to the south side of Gunda's fort to speak with the other Maag sailors who'd come along with Longbow's friends. 'I want you men to behave yourselves,' he told them. 'Don't insult the Trogites or the natives. They're on *our* side in this war, so don't make fun of them.'

'We've heard all this before, Skell,' a bearded sailor said.

'Good. Now you've heard it again. Maybe if you hear it often enough, it'll start to seep through into your mind.'

'We've been using Keselo as our go-between, Skell,' Commander Narasan said the following morning. 'He has access to a fast sloop that can take him down to the temple-town in about half a day, so your cousin can keep him up to date on what's happening down there.' Narasan smiled then. 'Keselo came up with another idea as well. Prince Ekial gave him a horse called Bent-Nose, and Keselo tamed the horse in about a half a day.'

'With a whip?'

Narasan laughed. 'No, not really. He even startled Ekial when he used candy instead. It seems that a horse will do almost anything for candy. That means that Keselo can reach your cousin in about a day and a half, and he can bring information back to us in about the same amount of time.'

'I'd start watching my tail feathers very close, Commander,' Skell said. 'A young fellow as clever as Keselo might start to have ambitions, and he *might* just decide that he'd be a better commander than even you are.'

'He *does* show quite a bit of promise,' Narasan agreed. 'Anyway, your cousin has persuaded Queen Aracia that the bug-people are running all over her Domain, and she's even gone so far as to order all those fat, lazy priests of hers to go help your cousin build forts to hold back the creatures of the Wasteland. The priests aren't very happy about that, but they're even *un*happier about the steady diet of beans Sorgan offers them three times a day.'

Skell laughed. 'Sorgan's very good at things like that,' he said.

'Indeed he is, and he's keeping Aracia and all of her priesthood so frightened that they don't even know that we're fighting the *real* war up here in Long-Pass.'

'That's all that really matters, I guess,' Skell replied.

A REPORT FROM THE NORTH

1

'She moves right along, that's for sure,' Red-Beard said to Keselo as the sloop cut through the waters of Long-Pass bay.

'When you add oarsmen to a good following wind, you're not going to stay in one place for very long,' Keselo agreed.

'How did you get stuck with being the messenger boy between Narasan and Sorgan?' Red-Beard asked the young Trogite.

Keselo shrugged. 'I spent a lot of time with Sorgan during the war in Lady Zelana's Domain, and we got to know each other quite well. Commander Narasan felt that using somebody Sorgan knew and trusted as the messenger would work out better for all of us. Sorgan will tell *me* things he wouldn't mention to a stranger or some low-ranking soldier who doesn't know what's really going on.' Then he smiled. 'I'm not really complaining about it, Red-Beard. Prince Ekial gave me Bent-Nose, so I don't have to walk very much.'

'Horses *are* sort of fun, aren't they?' Red-Beard said, 'and they *do* move a lot faster than we can.'

'That's the *good* part of the task Commander Narasan dropped on me. Bent-Nose does all the running and these two sailors do the rowing. All I have to do is sit.'

Red-Beard smirked. 'I wouldn't spread that around too much, Keselo,' he said. 'If other men find out how easy life becomes when you've got a horse, they might decide to poach old Bent-Nose from you, and you'll go back to walking.' He looked across the bay at the shoreline. 'I sort of hate to admit this,' he admitted, 'but this sloop moves *almost* as fast as my canoe.'

'I saw you and Longbow moving back and forth out in the bay of Lattash,' Keselo replied. 'You were both going very fast, but I'm not sure I'd care to ride in a boat made of tree-bark.'

'The tribes of Zelana's Domain have been using tree-bark canoes for a long, long time, Keselo. You wouldn't want to drop a heavy rock into one of them, but they move very fast and very quiet. That's important when you're hunting. Where do you usually have your conferences with old Hook-Beak when you get down to temple bay?'

'Sorgan kept one of the ships that carried his army on down to the temple harbor,' Keselo replied. 'She's named the *Ascension*, and she serves Sorgan's purposes very well. She gives him a private place to confer with his men without worrying about being overheard, and since there's quite a bit of trickery involved in what he's doing there, privacy's fairly important. It also gives *me* a place to speak with him without being seen by any of Lady Aracia's priests. Of course, we don't really have to worry about that now, since Sorgan tricked her into sending *all* of her priests on down to the south wall of the temple to help the Maags build defenses to hold off their imaginary enemies – maybe not quite all *that* imaginary now, though. Veltan's been able to conjure up images of bug-things so awful that even the Maags are about half afraid of them.'

The sloop heeled over sharply when they reached open water and the two sailors who'd been manning the oars stood up and re-set the sails.

'Sorgan thinks of everything, doesn't he?' Red-Beard suggested.

'Actually, he listens well. *Most* of these deceptions come from men like Rabbit or Torl. Sorgan polishes them a bit and then waves them in Aracia's face.'

Red-Beard was staring at the shoreline. 'This baby *really* moves,' he said. 'Trying to keep up with her would probably sprain my shoulders if I was in my canoe.'

'It's the sail, Red-Beard,' Keselo explained. 'Why strain yourself if the wind's doing all the work?'

It was about mid-afternoon on a cold, cloudy day when the sloop hauled into the harbor of what Keselo called temple-town, and the two skilled sailors rowed the sloop up alongside a large, squared-off Trogite ship anchored alone in the harbor. As Red-Beard probably should have anticipated, Sorgan and Veltan were standing at the rail of the *Ascension* watching. Red-Beard straightened and looked up at the two friends. 'Zelana and Dahlaine sent me down here to advise you two that the archers of Old-Bear's tribe are in place at the upper end of Long-Pass,' he called up to them.

'Come on board, Red-Beard – and you too, Keselo,' Sorgan told them. 'Let's avoid all this shouting back and forth. Aracia *seems* to be improving, but let's not get her started again.'

Red-Beard and Keselo climbed up the rope ladder and joined Sorgan and Veltan on the deck of *the Ascension*. Then Sorgan led them all into the oversized cabin at the stern, where Rabbit and Torl were waiting.

'Will I get to see these imaginary bugs you've been showing Aracia?' Red-Beard asked Veltan.

'They couldn't *be* much better,' Veltan replied with a broad grin.

'My big sister's finally come to her senses, and she ordered all her priests to go help the Maags.'

'They're in the way, naturally,' Rabbit said, 'but at least they're out of the throne room, so Queen Aracia doesn't have to listen to them all day every day.'

'Is she really buying that story about invading bugs?' Red-Beard asked.

'Veltan's images look pretty real – out in the open where everybody can see them – for like maybe a half a minute or so,' Sorgan's cousin Torl replied.

'I don't *really* want them to be in sight for very long,' Veltan explained with a big grin. 'My sister's chubby priests wouldn't know a bug from a cow, but we *don't* want Aracia herself to look at them too closely or too long. Aracia's starting to come to her senses, and *she* knows what the bug-people *really* look like. If she smells this hoax of ours, her head might start to come apart, and she'll go back to being adored. That's the *last* thing we want. She's finally come to realize that her priests are totally worthless, and we want to keep it that way. We'll let her catch brief glimpses of our imaginary bug-people, but "brief" is the important word right now.'

Then Keselo looked at Red-Beard. 'I haven't been that far up the pass for quite a while now,' he said. 'You just came down the pass, friend Red-Beard. How many forts are in place now?'

'Eight, if I counted right,' Red-Beard replied, 'and there are several others being constructed right now. I'd say that poor old Mama Vlagh's going to lose a lot of puppies this time out.'

'What a shame,' Sorgan replied sardonically.

'We *could* send her a note of sympathy, Captain Hook-Beak,' Keselo suggested, 'but I don't think she knows how to read – or just exactly what a note is. She might just crumple it up and eat it.'

Sorgan squinted. 'I don't suppose that anybody happened to bring any poison with him,' he said.

'We *should* be able to come up with *something* that'll kill her – or at least make her terribly sick,' Red-Beard added.

'Don't rush me,' Sorgan said. 'I'm working on it.'

'Squint-Eye and Gimpy weren't keeping very close track of all the priests Aracia sent down to the south wall to help them,' Sorgan was saying the following morning after breakfast on board the *Ascension*, 'so there was quite a bit of sneaking back to the main temple going on. The ordinary priests were more interested in getting something to eat beside beans, but the priestess Alcevan was still trying to send young priests there to kill Lillabeth.'

'You said *what*?' Red-Beard demanded.

'We've got it all under control, Red-Beard,' Rabbit said. 'There are several priests who are terrified by the coming change-over. They know that Aracia will be going off to sleep before long, and then Enalla will take over. They're quite sure that Enalla will abolish the priesthood and order them to tear down the temple. This Alcevan priestess is a newcomer, and she's positive that if Lillabeth dies, so will Enalla, and Aracia will *have* to stay awake. There were a few attempts before Aracia sent *all* of her priests off to the south wall to help build the fort. Alcevan was sending novice priests back to the main temple to kill Aracia's Dreamer every chance she had, but we put a stop to that.'

'How?' Red-Beard asked.

'More imitation bugs,' Sorgan chuckled. 'Rabbit remembered what had happened to Jalkan and Adnari Estarg back in Veltan country. He spoke with Veltan about it, and now there are cobwebs that look like anchor ropes in every corridor leading back to the main temple, and every so often a spider that's about ten feet across skitters through the shadows. Squint-Eye and Gimpy described what happened to Jalkan and that Trogite Adnari several times, and then Veltan made several skeletons that were wearing scraps of what *looked* like the material of those priestly robes. The apprentice priests stopped paying attention to Alcevan about then. The notion of being dissolved and then slurped up by a ten-foot spider had terrified them to the point that *nothing* Alcevan offered even interested them one little bit. All those priests are bunched up by the south wall, and they won't go *near* any of those hallways.'

Red-Beard laughed. 'These hoaxes seem to be getting better and better,' he noted. 'Who's guarding the little girl, though?'

'Torl's got a hundred men stationed all around Lillabeth's room,' Sorgan replied. 'They're some of the biggest men in our whole army, and they've got some *very* ugly weapons. *Nobody's* going to get anywhere *near* that little girl, we'll see to that. Most of those priests aren't at all interested in Alcevan's scheme, though. They're all terribly disappointed by the food Squint-Eye and Gimpy are offering. They're used to eating very fancy food, and a steady diet of beans doesn't sit too well with them. Gimpy told them that they had a choice, but when he said, "You can eat beans, or you can eat dirt," it didn't sit at all well with them.'

the plea of alcevan

1

❖

Balacenia was floating in the air above the temple of Aracia to keep an eye on things. Since she would be the dominant god during the next cycle, Balacenia felt a certain responsibility, even though she wasn't supposed to wake up yet. Dahlaine's 'grand plan' had in effect split each one of the younger gods right down the middle. From what she'd seen during several brief encounters with the other younger gods, their Dreamer alternates were pretty much the same as their real personalities. Eleria, however, seemed almost to be a total stranger. She *definitely* had her own personality, and it did not even remotely resemble Balacenia's. They were now so far apart, that Balacenia was almost positive that they'd never be able to completely unite again. Balacenia sighed. 'At least I'll have somebody to talk with when I'm lonesome.'

Balacenia had some very serious doubts about Sorgan's declaration that Aracia had returned to sanity. Zelana's older sister had always been a towering egomaniac, totally convinced that she was the most important being in the entire universe. That, of course, had opened the door for a number of self-appointed 'priests' who'd found their way to lives of luxury over the past several eons. They'd made lifelong careers of piling counterfeit adoration on Aracia, and she'd wiggled like a puppy and begged for more.

Over the countless centuries, Aracia's priests had spread the word that she'd *really* like to have a glorious temple built for her, and they'd managed to persuade the common citizens that it was *their* duty to construct it. Unfortunately, nobody had bothered to draw up an overall plan, so Aracia's 'glorious temple' was a hodge-podge of corridors that didn't go anywhere, chambers without doorways, and extensive unroofed areas.

Aracia spent most – if not all – of her time in her throne room, so she had no real awareness of how ridiculous her glorious temple really was. It was a mile square, though, and the word 'mile' seemed to thrill Aracia right down to her bones, and she sat contented in her glorious throne room on her glorious throne, accepting the glorious adoration of generation after generation of lazy priests.

Then, quite suddenly during Sorgan's imitation invasion hoax, Aracia had changed direction – to the horror of her priests. Her voice suddenly became steel-hard, and she commanded her priests to go out and do some honest work for a change.

'It just doesn't fit,' Balacenia complained. She was catching a strong odor of tampering here, but she had no idea of who might be trying to change things.

Then her eye caught a flicker of movement outside the unstable east wall of Aracia's temple. Rabbit's 'spider hoax' had terrified everybody in Aracia's Domain, and terrified people don't wander around alone – particularly not after the sun goes down.

Curious, Balacenia drifted lower and saw a small person wearing a priest robe scurrying along outside the rickety temple wall. 'That almost *has* to be that self-appointed priestess called Alcevan,' Balacenia murmured. 'What's she up to now?' Then she remembered Veltan's imitation spiders, and that explained just *why* Alcevan was staying outside the temple, and it also suggested that Alcevan desperately needed to talk with Aracia.

Then Balacenia remembered Torl's description of an unused corridor that just happened to have a crack in the wall where he'd been able to listen to what was happening without being seen. 'I'd say that "sneak around" time just got here,' she murmured to herself.

She drifted down through the poorly constructed roof of Aracia's temple and settled in Torl's dusty corridor. She could even see Torl's footprints in the dust, and that made things very simple.

'Please don't leave us, dear one!' Balacenia heard Alcevan's peculiar-sounding voice coming through the crack Torl had found. There was a desperation in the voice, but also just a hint of insincerity.

'You're just wasting your time – and mine – Alcevan,' Aracia's cold voice declared. 'I have no choice. My cycle nears its end. I *must* sleep, and soon. I cannot remain awake when my cycle ends.'

'You must *try*, dear one!' Alcevan's voice was almost shrill. 'We do not know this Enalla creature, but I am almost positive that she'll abolish your Church – or even worse, change it so that the people – and priests – of your Domain will worship *her* instead of you.'

Balacenia caught a brief smell of a very peculiar odor. Then Aracia's attitude – and even her voice – changed. 'I will *not* permit that! The Church is *mine*!'

'Could you not delay her awakening, dear one?' Alcevan asked. 'Surely you can stay with us for just a few more years.'

Aracia, it seemed, even considered that. Then she spoke in an ominous tone. 'Maybe I can at that,' she said. 'And I think I know of a way to keep Enalla from *ever* usurping this throne that is right-fully mine.'

'And which way is that, dear one?' Alcevan asked, though it was obvious to Balacenia that the small priestess already knew.

'You don't need to know that just yet, Alcevan,' Aracia declared.

Balacenia could catch bits and pieces of Aracia's thoughts. Her brain was fairly scrambled, but the word 'kill' kept cropping up.

'I think I'd better warn Veltan about this. His big sister isn't quite as sane as Sorgan seems to think she is.'

The Trogite ship called the *Ascension* that Narasan had given to Sorgan was anchored in the harbor, and Balacenia sensed Veltan's presence in the large cabin at the ship's stern. Fortunately, he was alone, and Balacenia was certain that the two of them needed to talk privately. She could have just drifted down to the deck of the *Ascension* and then knocked on the cabin door, but she chose at the last minute to just suddenly appear in Veltan's presence with no warning.

Veltan visibly flinched when she dropped into the cabin. 'What are you *doing*?' he demanded.

'I just thought I'd drop by and warn you that there's a great deal of trouble coming your way, uncle Veltan,' Balacenia replied. 'I was sort of keeping an eye on things in your big sister's temple, and I saw that little priestess Alcevan sneaking along the east wall. She went on inside, and I used that corridor Sorgan's cousin found to get close enough to the throne room to eavesdrop. I hate to tell you this, uncle Veltan, but that little priestess Alcevan just put a stop to your sister's journey into the land of people who aren't crazy.'

'You aren't supposed to be doing that sort of thing yet,' Veltan protested.

'Don't worry so much about "supposed to", uncle. I just discovered that Alcevan isn't at all what everybody seems to think she is. Actually, she's a bug.'

Veltan's head came up sharply. 'What are you talking about?' he demanded.

'I was talking about Alcevan the bug. Weren't you listening? This *has* happened before. If you think back, you'll remember that tribe in Tonthakan who were positive that they'd been terribly insulted – right up until the Maag called Ox brained a couple of men – who turned out *not* to be men. Alcevan's of that same variety of bug.'

'How do you know that?'

'I could smell her. She's emitting the same kind of odor the ones in Tonthakan were, so Aracia believes everything Alcevan tells her, and she's coming very close to trying to keep Enalla from taking over here by killing Lillabeth.'

'She wouldn't *do* that. It's totally forbidden.'

'"Forbid" just blew out of the window. Aracia is all wound up, and the word "kill" keeps coming into her mind. I'm almost positive that Aracia believes that if she kills Lillabeth, it'll almost certainly kill Enalla as well. I think it's time for a conference, Veltan. Why don't you go speak with Dahlaine and Zelana? The other Dreamers are with them. I'll snatch Lillabeth out of Aracia's temple.'

'That might be just a bit tricky, Balacenia,' Veltan said. 'Sorgan's cousin Torl has a hundred oversized Maags there guarding her.'

'So?'

Veltan blinked. Then he laughed a bit ruefully. 'I keep forgetting who you really are, Balacenia. You're not at all like Eleria, are you?'

Balacenia sighed. 'Not really. I love her, but she goes her own way. I don't think we'll be able to merge when this is all over, but we can worry about that later. Right now, getting Lillabeth to safety is more important than anything else. Where do you think we should meet?'

Veltan frowned. 'I'd say Mount Shrak. It's the most secure place. The snow's probably ten feet deep up there, and that should definitely keep the bugs from getting close enough to hear what we're saying.'

'Good idea. We need to make some decisions. If necessary, we might *all* have to come down on Aracia with both feet. Let's get started, uncle. We've got a long way to go, and not very much time.'

It wasn't particularly difficult for Balacenia to take Lillabeth right out from under the noses of Torl and the hundred massive sailors Sorgan had sent to guard her. The Maags guarded doors and hallways, but they didn't guard the roof. Many things were coming back to Balacenia now, and she had no difficulty passing down through the roof to join the little girl who was *really* Balacenia's sister Enalla. 'We've got an emergency, Lillabeth,' Balacenia declared, 'and we're all supposed to meet with the elders up at Mount Shrak.'

'Why didn't Aracia come here and take me there?' Lillabeth demanded.

'There's a war out there, Lillabeth,' Balacenia reminded her sister. 'Aracia's very busy right now.' She paused. 'I don't suppose you remember how to fly,' she said.

'I've never tried,' Lillabeth said. 'I'm sure that Aracia would be terribly upset if I suddenly sprouted wings.'

'We don't use wings, Lillabeth. There's a much easier way to do it. I'll carry you. You're not really all that heavy.'

'You're the grown-up Eleria, aren't you?'

'Well – sort of. Eleria and I are much further apart than you and Enalla are.'

'When the time comes, will I have to grow up before I become Enalla? Or will there just be a poof, and I'll be all grown up?'

'We've never done this before, Lillabeth,' Balacenia replied. 'I think each one of us will have to make it up when the time comes.' She held out her hand. 'Shall we go?' she said.

Lillabeth's eyes went very wide when the two of them passed up through the roof of Aracia's temple. 'How can you *do* that?' she said in a trembling voice.

'It has to do with thought, little sister,' Balacenia replied. 'Aracia could do it, if she ever left her throne room. There are all sorts of things we can do that ordinary people don't even think about. Just look at the scenery, Lillabeth. I'll take care of this.'

'Where are we going?'

'I told you, Mount Shrak. You've been there, so it shouldn't bother you.'

They rose up through the chill winter air until Balacenia located a wind coming out of the southeast. She latched onto it, and it carried them in a generally northwesterly direction. Balacenia had always enjoyed riding the wind. It was an easy way to go from here to there, since the wind did all the work.

'How high up in the air are we?' Lillabeth asked in a trembling sort of voice.

'That doesn't really matter, child,' Balacenia replied. 'Don't let the height bother you. I won't let you fall.'

'I've never been up this high in the air before,' Lillabeth said. 'The world's a lot bigger than I thought it is. How far is it from one side to the other?'

'The world doesn't *have* sides, child. It's round – almost like a ball, but it's much larger than an ordinary ball. There are thousands of miles between one side of the world and the other.'

Lillabeth peered down at the earth far below. 'Why is it all white like that?'

'It's covered with snow, Lillabeth.'

'Like that snow we saw back in Lattash last spring?'

'I'd almost forgotten that you were there with the rest of us,' Balacenia admitted. Then she pointed on ahead. 'That's Mount Shrak there. The rest of the family should be there by now. I'd say that you should listen, but don't say very much. They're likely to say things about Aracia that you won't like, but just keep your feelings to yourself. The whole purpose of this meeting is to come up with a way to keep Aracia from hurting you.'

'She wouldn't do that!' Lillabeth protested.

'I wouldn't be too sure, Lillabeth. Aracia's mind isn't working the way it's supposed to right now. That's what this meeting's all about. If we don't get her mind to working right, we could lose her.'

Balacenia began their descent, and they came down just outside the entrance to Dahlaine's cave. She was just a bit out of practice, but things seemed to be returning to normal.

The two of them went on inside, and they soon reached the part of the cave Dahlaine used for living quarters.

'Did you have any problems?' Veltan asked.

'I don't *have* problems, uncle,' Balacenia teased him. 'You should know that by now. Torl's men were guarding the doors, but I went into Lillabeth's room through the ceiling. Then we came out the same way. It'll probably be three or four days before anybody in the temple discovers that Lillabeth isn't there anymore.'

'Let's get on with this,' Dahlaine said. 'Veltan told us that you've discovered that one of sister Aracia's priests is a disguised servant of the Vlagh.'

'Priestess, uncle,' Balacenia corrected. 'I can't be sure just how she managed to persuade Fat Bersla and the others that women can be priests just like men can. She *might* have used that odor you encountered in Tonthakan, but that's not really important. She's got your sister completely under her control now, and she's doing her best to drive Aracia into killing Lillabeth here.'

'She can't *do* that!' Dahlaine exclaimed.

'Not since I grabbed Lillabeth and brought her here, she can't,' Balacenia reminded him. 'Our problem now is how are we going to deal with that smelly bug.'

'Kill it,' Yaltar, the childish form of Vash said bluntly.

'Didn't you tell him that we're not permitted to do that, uncle Veltan?' Balacenia asked.

'I didn't get into too many details,' Veltan admitted.

'We could always send for Longbow,' Eleria said. 'He kills bugs all the time.'

'Or maybe Ox,' Dahlaine's Dreamer Ashad said.

Then there came a glow of light out of the passage that led to the outside of Mount Shrak, and Ara was there. 'What seems to be the problem, children?' she asked.

'One of the bug people has stolen the Beloved's big sister,' Eleria replied. 'We'd like to get her back, but we don't know exactly how.'

'Which one of you discovered that?' Ara asked.

'It was Big-Me,' Eleria replied. 'You know how clever Big-Me can be.'

Ara frowned slightly. 'Who's she talking about?'

'That would be me,' Balacenia said. 'She's had a peculiar way of talking ever since she started playing with the dolphins. There's a woman called Alcevan down in Aracia's temple who pretends that she's a priestess. I overheard her talking with Aracia and she was letting out that peculiar odor the servants of the Vlagh use to confuse people. She's come very close to persuading Aracia that when Enalla takes charge in the East, she'll usurp the temple and the priesthood and make everybody in Aracia's Domain worship *her*. Aracia accepted that absurdity, and she was getting very close to murdering Lillabeth here as a way to destroy Enalla. Just to be safe, I snatched Lillabeth and brought her here.'

Ara's face went cold. 'Aracia should know that she's not permitted to kill *anything*.'

'I'm sure that she knows that,' Dahlaine said, 'but we've seen this sort of thing before. Once one of the bug-people unleashes that odor, people lose their grip on reality. We've been trying to come up with an answer, but we haven't got very far yet. We're working on it, though. We'd be more than happy if you can give us a solution.'

Ara squinted at him. 'First off, you can't send Lillabeth back to that silly temple. She's too innocent to protect herself, but Enalla can. I'll help her a bit, and she'll look exactly like Lillabeth. Then, when Aracia commands her to die, Enalla can block that command with no trouble and – we can all hope – she'll prevent Aracia from going *too* far. If she goes over the forbidden line, she'll cease to exist.'

'Die, you mean?' Ashad asked.

'Not exactly. She just won't be there anymore. She'll simply vanish.'

'That's the last thing we want,' Dahlaine said. 'Aracia's never really been very stable. She's obsessed with her divinity, and sooner or later she's almost certain to step over that forbidden line. I think it's altogether possible that we'll lose her, no matter what we do. Then we'll have to replace her.'

'Make a new person, you mean?' Ashad asked.

'Maybe. We'll see.'

Balacenia saw the perfect answer standing right there, but she was fairly sure she'd have trouble convincing Dahlaine, so she kept it to herself for now.

THE DREAM OF OMAGO

1

Ara was humming softly to herself as she prepared a breakfast for the Trogites who were manning Gunda's fort at the head of Long-Pass. The weather had turned bitterly cold, but Ara's kitchen was pleasantly warm. The Trogite army cooks used stoves made of iron, but that didn't suit Ara one little bit. Iron stoves didn't produce constant temperatures, and constant temperature was the key to good cooking. She'd tried one of the iron stoves when she and Omago had first reached Gunda's fort, and the results had been disastrous. Omago was almost immediately aware of her dissatisfaction, and he had built her a stove much like the one back in their kitchen near Veltan's house, and Ara had always been more comfortable with a stove made of fired bricks. Her ovens were exactly where they were supposed to be. Different foods needed different heats, and Ara had always depended on distance from the fire to precisely control the heat in each oven. The Trogite army cooks could prepare large amounts of food, but quite a bit of it was overcooked – almost burned – and much of it was still half-raw. The Trogite soldiers were very brave, so they didn't complain when half of their food was partially burned and the other half was not even very warm.

Ara was still very concerned by child Balacenia's discovery that Aracia was almost totally under the control of one of the servants of the Vlagh. Lillabeth would be safe, though, and that was all that really mattered. Ara smiled faintly. Aracia – and her buggish priestess – were likely to be very surprised when they encountered what *appeared* to be the child Lillabeth, but in reality was the younger goddess Enalla. With Enalla and Balacenia there to block them, Aracia and Alcevan wouldn't have any chance at all of achieving their goal. Dahlaine had been more than a little reluctant to admit that Aracia wouldn't be around much longer, but his sister was quite obviously out of her mind, and very soon she would almost certainly cease to exist.

'Good morning, Dear Heart,' Omago said as he came into the kitchen.

'You finally woke up, I see,' Ara said. 'Here it is almost daylight, and you're only now getting out of bed. Aren't you feeling well?'

'Not really, dear,' Omago replied. 'I had a very peculiar dream last night.'

'Oh?'

'You and I were drifting in a strange place where there wasn't much light at all.'

'What exactly do you mean by "drifting"?' Ara asked.

'We seemed to be just floating up in the air,' Omago replied, 'except that there wasn't any air.'

Ara put down her large spoon. 'I think that maybe everybody has one of those "floating" dreams every now and then.' She smiled. 'I suppose that it might mean that we're all secretly envious of birds. They can fly, but we can't.'

'I wasn't really thinking about birds, Ara, and I've never had a "floating dream" before. Anyway, everything around us seemed to be moving toward an extremely bright light – so bright that it hurt my eyes just to look at it.'

'It must have been the sun, then.'

Omago shook his head. 'It was even brighter than the sun, Ara – much, much brighter. Anyway, everything kept moving faster and faster as it rushed toward that bright light. Then the light started to shrink down, growing smaller and smaller until it wasn't any bigger than my thumbnail, but it was still growing brighter. Then everything went darker than night, and for some reason that I couldn't understand at all, you and I both said "*Now!*" and the light was there again, but it definitely wasn't shrinking anymore. It was growing larger and larger so fast that I couldn't even keep track of it. The light almost seemed to be exploding and spreading out, shoving the darkness aside as it went.'

Ara was suddenly cold all over. This wasn't supposed to be happening. 'Just how long did that last, Dear Heart?' she asked, trying to keep her voice calm and ordinary.

'I couldn't really say, Ara. It was still expanding – or growing, maybe – when I suddenly woke up. Something very strange was going on. It's very, very cold in the sleep chambers of this fort, but I was covered with sweat as if I'd been out in my fields in the middle of summer.'

Ara smiled. 'I'd say that your dream was very useful, then, dear, dear Omago. You were feeling cold, and your dream warmed things up for you.'

'It definitely made me feel warmer. Anyway, before I woke up, that immense light had started to spin off bits and pieces that whirled out in bright little chunks, spinning and flying. They seemed to remind me of stars, for some reason.'

'Maybe you should talk with Dahlaine, dear Omago. He might

be willing to pay a lot for a dream like the one you just had.'

Omago smiled faintly. 'Will it be long before breakfast?' he asked. 'I think I should walk around just a bit and see if I can shake off what's left of that dream.'

'You have about a half-hour, Dear Heart,' Ara replied. 'Go out in the open and throw the dream away. Don't forget to put on your fur cape, though.'

Omago nodded and went out of Ara's kitchen.

'How did he *do* that?' Ara demanded out loud. 'We agreed that he wouldn't remember any of this for years and years. He's supposed to be an ordinary man, but no ordinary man is going to have dreams about something that happened millions of years ago.'

There had been a certain practicality in Omago's decision to transform himself into an ordinary human with no memories at all of his real identity. The man-creatures were a recent development, and, unlike most other creatures, it appeared that they were able to think at a much more complex level than the other living creatures on this particular world. Omago had decided that the best way to understand the man-creatures would be to duplicate their experiences and abilities by living out the life of an ordinary human here in the Land of Dhrall. He might have been able to try it elsewhere, but this world and this particular region were most important right now.

Omago's description of his dream had raised certain memories for Ara. Her mind went back to the time before time when she'd been awareness only, with no body. Her awareness had moved about the universe through endless eons, searching, searching for something – anything – that might dispel her dreadful loneliness.

And then Omago's awareness had reached out to her, and she'd no longer been alone.

For eons uncountable they had drifted together, growing more attached to each other as they searched for other awarenesses. But as far as they'd been able to determine, there were none.

And then, with no warning whatsoever, there was light – a light so intense that Ara could not bear to look at it. 'What *is* that thing?' she demanded.

'I couldn't really say, Dear Heart,' Omago's awareness replied. 'I've never seen anything like it before.'

'Make it go away.'

'How? It's millions of times larger than anything I've ever seen before, and other things that are also bright seem to be joining it. I think that something very important is about to happen.'

'Why now, and not before?'

'I'm not sure that there's a difference between now and before, Ara.'

'That just changed, Dear Omago. That bright thing makes "now" very important.'

'I think you might be right, Dear Ara. Something just started that didn't exist before.'

'Is it my imagination, or is the bright thing growing smaller – and even brighter?'

Omago gasped. 'Come away!' he shouted in the silence of her mind. 'We can't stay here! We'll be destroyed if we do!'

'We'll be *what*?'

'We'll cease to exist. Come with me – *now*!'

And quite suddenly, Ara was no longer only thought. She had a tangible body, and Omago had one as well. He reached out and took her hand in his, and they turned and fled from the now tiny bright light.

And then, for some reason neither of them understood, they both said, '*Now*.'

And time began as the tiny light stopped being tiny and suddenly flared out to enormity, engulfing the darkness as it went.

Then Omago seized Ara's new form and carried her away, and she suddenly realized that they were moving even faster than the light.

In time – now that time existed – the light slowed, and the vast light began to break into smaller pieces Omago called 'suns,' but Ara called them 'the children of the light.' That seemed nicer than 'suns' to Ara, but she chose not to make an issue of it with Omago. Then, in the endless eons that plodded along in time, the various suns *also* bore children that Omago called 'worlds.' Eventually, of course, the worlds *also* had children. Trees and grass came first, but then other living things began to appear, primarily in the oceans of the various worlds. Life, as Ara understood it to be, began in worlds uncountable in the vastness of the universe.

The universe continued to expand, but Ara and Omago concentrated their attention on a specific world *and* on what appeared to be a sub-continent that Ara named 'Dhrall.' It was a nice-sounding name that didn't really mean anything. 'I think that might be a perfect place for a bit of experimentation, Dear Heart,' she said to Omago. 'This form you've given us seems to be most practical. Creatures that resemble us would probably be able to do many things that other creatures would find quite impossible.' She held up one of her hands. 'This alone would give our creatures an enormous advantage over creatures that only have feet. How were you able to invent hands when the time came for us to have bodies as well as awareness?'

Omago smiled. 'Think back, Dear Heart,' he told her. 'We were in a very dangerous place, and we needed to leave – in a hurry. I wanted something that I could use to grab hold of you and pull you off to safety. If you'd like, we could call them "Ara-grabbers," I suppose.'

'Not if you want me to say anything to you for the next million years, you won't,' Ara replied tartly.

'I was only teasing, dear,' Omago replied. He looked down at the land they called Dhrall. 'I think it might be quite a long time before we'll be able to experiment, though. That land below is still at a very primitive level of development. I don't think *any* life-forms will appear on this world until the fire-mountains go to sleep.'

'You're probably right, Dear Heart,' Ara agreed. 'This might be a good time for some exploration. This particular part of the world might be very nice after it cools down, but I think it might be a good time for us to find out what the rest of this world looks like, don't you?'

'That might take a long time, my love,' Omago replied a bit dubiously.

'Not if I fly, it won't.'

'You're going to sprout wings?'

'Why would I want to bother doing that? I'll just set my body aside and go exploring with my awareness.'

Omago blinked. 'I never thought of that,' he admitted. 'Are you sure that you can separate yourself from your body, though?'

'We'll find out in just a moment or two. I won't be long, Dear Heart. I don't think I'll really need to count pebbles or anything like that. All we need right now is a general idea of the shape of the various other bits and pieces of land here on this world. Take a nap or something. I'll be back in a day or so.'

Ara felt a tremendous sense of freedom when she separated her awareness from her body. It was a nice enough body, but the limitations it imposed on her mind had been almost intolerable. Now she was free again, and she soared off into the sky.

The sea that lay to the west of the Land of Dhrall was extensive, but Ara's awareness found no signs of life there. 'Ah, well,' she sighed. 'It looks as if we'll have to start from the beginning.'

That took some of the joy away. It appeared that this particular world was barren, totally devoid of any form of life.

When she reached the land mass on the western side of the empty sea, she saw no signs of plants of any kind. There *were* mountains, however, but many of them were spouting fire miles and miles into the air.

'Oh, stop that,' she told the mountains irritably.

And they did.

That startled Ara more than a little. 'Good babies,' she told them and then turned toward the south. *If* she could stop these eruptions with just a word, this plan she and Omago had devised *might* not be as difficult as it had previously seemed.

The land to the south was far less rugged than the land to the west had been, and Ara saw no tell-tale columns of smoke rising into the air. Evidently there *were* no fire-mountains down here – or if there were, they had exhausted their supply of molten rock.

'That's more like it,' Ara said with a certain satisfaction.

She roamed about in the sky for several days and found even more regions with no fire-mountains. After another few days, she turned north to return to the Land of Dhrall. Omago was probably starting to worry, so it was time to go home.

2

'Where have you *been*?' Omago demanded when Ara's awareness returned to the Land of Dhrall and rejoined her body. 'I was starting to think that I'd lost you forever.'

'You're not going to get away from me *that* easy, Dear Heart,' she replied. 'Actually, you'll never get away from me at all, so don't even think about it. We'll still be locked together when the universe is old and grey. I more or less found out what we needed to know. There *are* fire-mountains in other parts of this world, but not as many, and they aren't spitting fire nearly as far up into the air as the ones here in the Land of Dhrall are. I'd say that this is the newest part of this world.'

'Did you encounter any life-forms at all?'

'Not on dry land. I sensed a few very primitive forms of life in the seas, but they've got a long way to go before they'll start coming up on dry land.'

Omago looked out across the rolling sea. 'We seem to have come here at the right time, then. We might want to experiment just a bit. We've seen many forms of life on other worlds, and they have characteristics that might be very useful. If we really *want* to, I'm sure that we could create a creature with wings *and* a level of intelligence that no bird-thing will ever have. Then we could *also* create an intelligent creature with gills, and that one could live out its life in the sea.'

Ara shook her head. 'No, Dear Heart,' she said. 'We *know* exactly what kind of creature we want here, and wings or gills wouldn't fit, and they could cause problems later on. *Our* creatures should resemble *us*. Our body-forms will prove to be the best, I think, so let's not start tampering.'

'Oh,' Omago said then, 'this part of the world already has a life-form much like some of those we've encountered on other worlds.'

'Could you be just a bit more specific, Dear Heart?' Ara asked. 'Exactly what *is* this creature?'

'It's primarily a bug, dear,' Omago replied. 'It has six legs, a sort of shell to keep other creatures from eating it, and a tendency to live in caves. I very briefly touched what passes for a mind, and this bug-creature is very ambitious. It wants this entire world, and it's creating children by the thousands to take this world for it. It calls itself "the Vlagh," which most probably means "mother." I'm quite sure that any creatures *we* make will have to deal with it.'

'I've been considering this for quite some time now, Dear Heart,' Ara said to Omago some time later. 'You and I aren't limited to this particular world. Things have a way of popping out when we least expect them, and if some emergency breaks out on another world, we could very well have to go deal with it no matter what's in the wind here.'

'It's possible, I suppose,' Omago conceded. 'I take it that you've come up with an answer?'

'I think we need children, Dear Heart,' Ara replied.

Omago's face suddenly turned bright red.

'Is there some sort of problem with that?' Ara asked with wide-eyed innocence.

Omago blushed even more, and Ara laughed with pure delight. 'Are we having some problems with the idea, dear, dear Omago?' Then she fondly touched his face. 'We don't necessarily have to do it that way, you know. We have alternatives available to us. I can call them up with a snap of my fingers – and they wouldn't be of much use if they were infants anyway. Once they're in place, you and I can sort of fade back and let *them* deal with any ordinary problems while you and I take care of more extraordinary ones.'

'I don't know, Dear Heart,' Omago said a bit dubiously. 'If we give them absolute power, they could make some disastrous mistakes.'

'Not if we put some limitations on them, they won't. "No killing" should probably be at the top of the list, wouldn't you say?'

'Definitely.'

'Of course, if we don't permit them to kill, that would mean that they won't eat.'

'We can get around that if we have to,' Omago said. 'They can absorb light instead of food.'

'Very good,' Ara agreed. 'Then too, they'll need to be awake all the time as well. Emergencies crop up without much warning, so I don't think they should need sleep.'

'No creature stays awake eternally, Ara.'

'I'll work on that and see what I can come up with.'

'It won't work, Dear Heart,' Omago said when Ara described her concept of the god creatures who would rule the Land of Dhrall.

'What's the matter with it?' Ara demanded.

'Females are very pretty, but I think we'll need males as well.'

'What for? They aren't going to have children.'

'Would you be contented if *I* wasn't around?'

'Bite your tongue!' Then Ara felt just a little foolish. 'For some reason it just never occurred to me that we'd need males as well as females.'

'Something else too, dear,' Omago continued. 'I think we should give some serious thought to producing ordinary creatures who'll closely resemble these gods. We want the gods to have a sense of responsibility. That in itself will keep them from wandering off.'

'Now *that's* a very good idea, Omago,' Ara agreed. Then something came to her. 'You *do* realize that we'll be creating an entirely new species, don't you?'

'So?' Omago replied blandly.

'You're making this very complicated, Dear Heart,' Ara complained.

'That's all right, Ara. Complications make things much more interesting, don't they?'

Ara glared at him for a moment, but then she laughed.

3

Ara was quite sure that Omago's form and hers should also be the forms of the gods of the Land of Dhrall. 'The time may come when we'll need to speak with them, Dear Heart,' she told her mate, 'and they won't be disturbed if we resemble them to some degree. Then, when we create their worshipers, they should also resemble their gods – and us as well.'

'Not a bad idea at all,' Omago agreed. 'The time may come some day off in the future when we'll need to blend in with the worshipers and their gods, and it'll be much easier if we all have the same number of arms and legs. Shall we begin?'

'Why don't you make the bodies, dear? Just the general shape. I'll build their faces, and then we can both work on their characteristics. We'll want them to have individual identities and personalities, wouldn't you say?'

'You're very creative, Ara,' Omago observed.

'Details, Dear Heart. Fine art grows out of details. In a certain sense what we're about to conjure up *will* be fine art. They'll need awareness as well as bodies, and we'll want them to think like we do as well as resemble us.'

'A thought before we begin,' Omago said then. 'They should

probably have memories when they become conscious. I think they should believe that they've always been here, and that this day is just an ordinary day like one of several million others.' Then he frowned. 'They may *think* that they've lived for thousands of years, but you and I will both know better. They *will* live for a long, long time, but eventually the years will catch up with them, and they'll need to sleep for quite some time to refresh their minds.'

'Who's going to mind the Land of Dhrall when they drift off to sleep, Dear One?' Ara protested.

Omago scratched his cheek. 'If we do this right and don't permit any weaknesses to crop up, I'd say that they'll be good for about twenty-five eons, and then they'll *have* to sleep for the same amount of time.'

'There goes our grand plan,' Ara observed.

'Not really, Dear One,' Omago said with a sly grin. 'All we'll need is a second generation to take over when the elders start to snore. We decided that four gods would be sufficient, but it seems that we were wrong. We'll need eight instead. The first four will tend to things for about twenty-five eons. Then *they'll* go to sleep, and the second four will take over. If they pass it back and forth like that, they should all survive for a long, long time, and that's what this has been all about. You and I must *not* be tied down here. We have other responsibilities as well as this one. Let's get started, Dear Heart. This might take a while.'

Omago was nice enough not to protest when Ara declared that *she* would name the gods – both the elders and the youngsters. Omago was not particularly poetic, but Ara could weave names by the dozens. After much thought, she named the elder gods Dahlaine, Zelana, Veltan, and Aracia. There was a musical quality about those names that Ara found very attractive. The younger gods – when the time came for them to wake up – would be Balacenia, Vash, Enalla, and Dakas.

Omago carefully planted those names in the minds – and false memories – of the assorted gods, and then he stepped out of sight and stirred the awareness of the four elders.

'What's going on here?' the grey-bearded, but still only three or four minutes old, Dahlaine demanded.

'I was just about to ask you that same question, big brother,' the goddess Zelana declared. 'As I remember, I was looking at a range of mountains, but they're not there anymore.'

'I'm not sure that I'm right, Dahlaine,' the youthful Veltan declared, 'but it seems to me that you called us together to warn us about something you called the Vlagh.'

'Ah,' Dahlaine replied, 'now it comes back to me. I've spent many, many eons watching insects. I pretty much understand the ones that have been around for a long, long time, but this Vlagh insect seems to have a number of troublesome ambitions.'

'That's absurd, Dahlaine,' the goddess Aracia declared. 'Bugs can't think coherently enough to have anything even remotely resembling ambition. All *she* wants to do is lay eggs – by the thousands.'

'Exactly,' Dahlaine replied. 'The Vlagh seems to think that if she lays enough eggs, her children will run out and steal the world from us. She seems to think that the whole world rightfully belongs to *her*.'

'Not while *I'm* around, she won't,' Veltan declared. 'If she even tries to usurp any part of my domain, I'll tie all six of her legs into a knot so tight that it'll take her years to get unraveled.'

'Can we watch, baby brother?' Zelana asked with some show of enthusiasm.

'Feel free, big sister,' Veltan replied. 'If the Vlagh comes south, I'll climb all over her.'

Ara smiled. The memories Omago had planted in the minds of these newly-created godlings had convinced them that they'd been around for eons and eons instead of just the few minutes that they'd *really* been here. 'Everything seems to be working the way we want it to, Dear Heart,' she sent her thought to her mate. 'The false memories you gave them are firmly in place. Do you think we should make the younger ones as well right now?'

'We don't really need them right now, Ara,' Omago replied.

'When do you think we should start making their worshipers?'

'Let's hold off on that for a while,' Omago said. 'I think these elders will need some time to adjust before we make the ordinaries who'll worship them. There are enough animals here to make these elders know that they aren't the only life-form in this world.'

'Are we pretty much finished here?' Ara asked.

'I think so, yes.'

'Maybe we should drift around and have a look at the other lands on this world,' Ara suggested. 'If there are people in *those* lands, we might need people here as well.'

'Let's go look then,' Omago agreed.

Omago was more than a little reluctant to set his body aside and revert to awareness only when they left the Land of Dhrall to look at the other lands.

'It's much, much faster, Dear Heart,' Ara advised. 'There are several limits involved if you drag your body along. All we need to do is look, and our awareness can take care of that.'

'It just seems so unnatural to do it that way,' Omago complained.

'What's "natural" got to do with anything?' Ara demanded. 'You and I are from another time and place, so the rules of *this* time and place don't apply to us. Just try it, Omago. I've done this before, remember? There are – or may be – things we need to know before we make any decisions, so let's get on with it.'

'All right,' Omago surrendered.

Ara smiled. 'See? That wasn't too hard at all, was it?'

They separated their awareness from their bodies and crossed the rolling sea lying to the west of the Land of Dhrall.

'Is that what I think it is?' Omago's thought silently asked.

'Where?' Ara asked.

'Right at the edge of the water,' Omago replied. 'I don't think it's an animal of any kind.'

'It's standing on its hind legs,' Ara agreed, 'and it *does* have hands. I don't think any animals have hands. What's it doing down there?'

'I think it might be trying to kill a fish-creature,' Omago replied. 'That's probably why it's carrying that long, pointed stick. It's probably hungry, but very primitive. Let's move on, Dear Heart. There might be more advanced people in other lands. If they're all as primitive as this one, I think we can hold off on providing the gods of the Land of Dhrall with worshipers.'

They drifted on down toward the south, and when they reached the land beyond the sea, they saw a fair number of collections of what appeared to be rude huts.

'Shelters,' Omago surmised. 'Protection from bad weather. If they're intelligent enough to build things like that, they almost have to be people.'

'And that smoke says that they've discovered fire,' Ara added. 'They may have found out that fire will protect them from cold weather.' Then she peered down at a fair-sized collection of huts. 'What in the world is *that* one doing?' she demanded. 'It appears to be a female, and it's got part of some other animal propped up over an open fire.'

'It smells quite interesting,' Omago added. 'I'd say that the she-thing had found a way to make animal flesh taste better.'

'Now *that's* something that never occurred to me,' Ara said. 'Raw meat would probably taste a lot like blood.' She considered the notion and decided to try it when they returned to the Land of Dhrall. 'I know that you'd rather wait a while before we made worshipers for the gods we've already created, but if the Vlagh tries to usurp the Land of Dhrall, we're going to need people. The gods we just created aren't permitted to kill, but it seems that people don't have that kind of restriction. They might not want to *eat* the children of the Vlagh, but killing doesn't *always* involve eating.'

'I think you're right, Dear Heart,' Omago agreed. 'I thought it might be best to wait a while before we introduced worshipers, but that might have been a serious mistake.'

They drifted on farther to the south and saw that the people of that area ate roots and berries and other forms of plant life as well as animal flesh.

Ara was quite certain that they should create man-things as well as gods to inhabit the Land of Dhrall, and, unlike the gods, the man-things would need food. Raw food would keep the man-things alive, but food that had been placed in the vicinity of fire would almost certainly taste better.

That thought alone opened all kinds of doors for Ara.

THE VISITOR

It was bitterly cold at the head of Long-Pass, and even the shaggy bison-hide robes Chief Tlantar Two-Hands of the Matan Nation had provided us didn't entirely keep the chill away. I'd found a fairly well protected place in Gunda's fort, and after the sun had gone down and I'd finished eating supper, I decided that it might not be a bad time to catch up on my sleep. The Malavi had held back the Creatures of the Wasteland, so there was nothing much for me to do, and, though I wouldn't admit it to my outlander friends, the days and days of running down along that tired old mountain range and through Long-Pass itself had taken a lot out of me. Evidently, the years were catching up with me.

I drifted off to sleep, and, as had been happening more and more frequently here lately, I had a dream of the time when I was very young and I was living in the lodge of Chief Old-Bear. In those days the only thing on my mind had been Misty-Water, Old-Bear's beautiful daughter, and in my dreams I saw her again and again, and just the sight of her made me go weak all over. Even when I was asleep and dreaming, I knew that one day something would happen that would come very close to destroying me. I always pushed that aside, though, and fixed my attention entirely on my vision of she who would one day be my mate.

'Wilt thou hear me, brave warrior?' the now familiar voice of my 'unknown friend' reached out to me. I knew who she really was now, but just her interruption of my dream irritated me.

'Now what?' I demanded harshly.

'Be nice,' she scolded me.

'I'm sorry,' I apologized. 'I had something else on my mind just now. Was there something you wanted to tell me?'

'Nay,' she replied. 'I come to thee to ask, not to tell.'

'That's unusual. Is there a problem of some kind?'

'One whom thou dost know quite well hath done that he was not supposed to do as yet.'

'I suppose you could spank him and send him to bed without any supper,' I suggested. She still had me a bit irritated.

'I don't find that particularly amusing, Longbow,' she told me, lapsing out of her antique formality. Her familiar voice confirmed what I had come to realize back at Mount Shrak.

'I'm sorry,' I apologized. 'Just exactly was it that this friend of ours did that he was not supposed to do?'

'He dreamed,' she retorted, and her irritation was fairly obvious.

'One of *those* dreams?'

'Not exactly, no. He didn't cause a flood or set fire to a mountain as the children do. He reached back instead and discovered his *true* identity. He's not supposed to do that yet.'

'And why is that?'

'You don't need to know that, Longbow.'

I shrugged. 'Then I guess I won't need to talk with him. Those are the rules, unknown friend. If you don't talk to me, I won't talk to Omago.'

'How did you know—' She left it hanging.

'You're fairly obvious, Ara. Omago's your mate, and that's why you're so upset. Why is it that Omago's not supposed to know who he really is?' Then something came to me. 'You two have been mated since the beginning of time, haven't you?'

'*Before* the beginning of time, actually,' she replied. 'Time began when we both said "now" at the same moment. That's when everything started – and *that* lay at the core of Omago's dream, and he's not supposed to know about it yet. That was the whole idea behind what he was trying to accomplish. We needed to know about the *true* nature of you man-things, so Omago blotted out all his memories of the past so that he could live the life of an ordinary man-thing. But now he's sneaking around things he's not supposed to know about. Curiosity is one of his great failings.'

'Just exactly when was it when you two ordered time to begin? I mean, how many years?'

'There's no word for that number, Longbow. A million millions doesn't even come close.'

'Just exactly what was happening back then that you two found so important?'

'It was when the universe began.'

'The universe has always been there, hasn't it?'

She shook her head. 'There wasn't *anything* back then. Not even Omago and I existed in our present forms. We were awareness only, and it took us a long, long time to even find each other. We can talk about that some other day. The important thing right now is that one of our children will try to do something that's forbidden, and she will cease to exist when she does that. I fear that Omago will not be able to bear her obliteration.'

'We're talking about Aracia here, aren't we?'

'I did not say that.'

'You didn't have to. It *is* fairly obvious, you know.' Then I suddenly saw where this was going. 'She's going to try to kill the little girl named Lillabeth, isn't she?'

'I do fear me that thou are correct.'

'She can't *do* that!'

'I know, and her attempt will obliterate her.' There was a kind of agony in her voice.

'Can't you stop her? As far as I can determine, there's nothing that you *can't* do.'

'That's in the world of things, dear Longbow. I can't do that in the world of thought. When Aracia tries to destroy Lillabeth – or Enalla, actually – she'll step over the forbidden line.'

'And she'll die?'

'She *can't* die, Longbow. She'll just cease to exist.'

'Isn't that what dying means?'

'No. It goes quite a bit farther.'

'And it's *that* you're afraid of, isn't it, Ara?'

'How did *you* come to know who I am?'

'You're extremely upset, so you've been letting some things slip. I probably should have realized that from the very beginning. You *are* Aracia's mother, after all, and just the thought of her obliteration is tearing pieces out of your heart.'

'I think that maybe it's *Dahlaine* who needs a good spanking. His "Dream" idea seems to be working quite well, but it appears that it's setting off some other Dreams that aren't supposed to happen just yet.'

'Such as the one *I'm* having right now?'

'This one's altogether different, my son.'

'Maybe some day you'll get around to telling me just exactly *how* it's different, Mother.'

All right, it was a silly thing to say, but it was just too good an opportunity to let slip by. 'Am I supposed to go to my room now?' I asked her.

'No. You're supposed to go to the place where Omago's sleeping and try to keep him from going all to pieces.'

'I'll get right on it, Mother.'

'Will you *stop* that?' she flared.

'Anything you say, Ara.'

BE NO MORE

1

—◄─►—

'Your presence there should conceal Enalla and me from Aracia, Little-Me,' Balacenia told me while we drifted through the chill air above Aracia's silly temple.

'I'm not sure that I follow you, Big-Me,' I told her. 'If everybody's right, the Beloved's older sister has had her mind turned off by the bug-woman they call Alcevan. If her mind isn't there anymore, she won't recognize anybody, will she?'

'That's one of the things we need to find out, Eleria,' Big-Me replied. 'If Aracia's mind is still working to some degree, we *might* be able to pull her out of Alcevan's grasp.'

'I wouldn't get my hopes up too much, Big-Me,' I told her. 'That stink Alcevan's using on Aracia is probably about the same as the one that showed up in Tonthakan in Dahlaine's part of the world. If we had Ox and his war-axe here, he could probably solve the problem for us.'

Big-Me shook her head. 'The others and I have talked it over already,' she said. 'Alcevan could very well turn out to be the key that'll lock the Vlagh away permanently, so we don't want anybody to kill her just yet.'

'Why not just send for Veltan?' I asked. 'If he took the Vlagh to the moon and left her there, she'd never be able to come back, could she?'

'I'm not sure that Veltan could do that, Eleria. That might step over the line that we don't want Aracia to cross. We all love Veltan too much to take any chances.'

'Just what do you want me to do, Balacenia?' I asked her.

'What happened to "Big-Me",' she asked with a faint smile.

'There's nothing wrong with "Balacenia",' I told her. 'It's a very pretty name, and I like to use it every now and then when I'm talking with you. Just what do you want me to do?'

'Why don't you just tell Enalla – who'll appear to be Lillabeth – the stories about the pink dolphins you played with when you were younger?' She paused. 'You *do* know that it was the time you spent with those dolphins that separated us so much that we'll probably never be able to merge again, don't you?'

'The Beloved didn't mention it,' I replied, 'but I'd more or less come to realize it myself. Don't worry about it so much, Big-Me. We might not be such a bad thing, you know. There will be two of us during the next cycle, so we'll be able to get a lot more done. Don't forget that Longbow's *mine*, though.'

'You love him, don't you?'

'Of course. I think we all love Longbow, don't we?'

Balacenia sighed. 'We may all love him, but *you're* the one who owns him.'

'I wouldn't say "owns." Nobody owns Longbow. I think that if we got right down to it, we'd find that *he* owns *us*. I wouldn't let my hope of pulling Aracia back to normal build up too much, Big-Me. You don't have to mention this to the others, but I'm almost positive that we've lost Aracia permanently. Little Stinky has her pretty much tied down.'

'Stinky?' Big-Me said with a little laugh. 'That *does* identify Alcevan, doesn't it? You're absolutely perfect, Little-Me.'

'I don't know about "perfect," Big-Me. I *do* have my share of faults, you know. Anyway, "Stinky" sort of came to me from nowhere, and I scraped it off the wall. Sometimes I have trouble finding the right word when I'm using people-talk. I still speak – and think – in the language of the pink dolphins.' Then I paused, as I almost always do. Then I said, 'Isn't that neat?'

And Big-Me broke down and laughed.

Balacenia sort of faded out of sight as we drifted down through the shabby roof of Aracia's poorly constructed temple. I could still sense her presence, but she wasn't visible anymore. Enalla was sitting in Lillabeth's ornate room, and she looked so much like Lillabeth that she even startled me. I had met Lillabeth during the war in the Beloved's Domain last spring, and I'd joined her during our joint recitation of her Dream – to the great chagrin of Aracia, who'd been desperately trying to hide that Dream – so even though I knew that she was really Enalla, I felt quite comfortable with her.

'We *are* the same person, Eleria,' Lillabeth's other personality reminded me in a voice that was a bit more mature than Lillabeth's. 'We're much the same as you and Balacenia are.'

'Not entirely, sister,' Balacenia's voice told her. 'Eleria here spent most of her time with the pink dolphins during her early child-hood, and I'm afraid that the dolphins permanently separated us.'

'Why did Zelana permit that?' Enalla demanded.

'The Beloved had her mind on music and poetry,' I explained. 'She was very fond of the pink dolphins, and after Dahlaine dropped me in her lap, she knew that somebody – or some *thing* – would have to nurse me. That's when she turned to Meeleamee.'

'Dolphins have names?' Enalla asked, sounding a bit startled.

'Oh, yes,' I replied, 'and they also have a language. The Beloved speaks their language, so she could call out to Meeleamee when she discovered that I couldn't live on just light the way she does. Meeleamee nursed me, and in some sense she was the mother I never had.'

'Aracia just handed me off to a fair number of local women to nurse me,' Enalla said. 'I never grew as close to any of them as you did to Meeleamee. They nursed me, but I never grew attached to any of them.'

'That's probably what kept you from having any fun when you were a baby. The pink dolphins seemed to think that teaching me how to swim was almost as important as nursing me was. I could swim like a fish long before I learned how to walk.'

'Why don't you tell me all kinds of stories about your pink dolphins, Eleria?' Enalla whispered. 'Balacenia and I are fairly sure that might persuade Aracia that we're just an empty-headed pair of little girls.' Then she spoke louder. 'How in the world could a baby possibly learn how to swim?' she asked as if she was terribly interested.

'It's not really all that difficult, Lillabeth,' I replied. 'Meeleamee wasn't the only female dolphin who was nursing me. There were many others as well, and more of them turned up in that pond inside the grotto when they heard that I was rewarding the ones that nursed me with kisses.'

'So *that's* where you picked up your kiss-kiss habit,' Enalla said. 'I've always wondered about that.'

'I found out early that kisses and hugs will get you almost anything you want, Lillabeth,' I told her. 'I kissed Longbow into submission in about five minutes. Anyway, the pink dolphins began to herd fish into the grotto so that I could learn how to feed myself. Once a baby starts to grow teeth, nursing the child can start to be quite painful. Dolphins are sea-animals, so they live on a steady diet of fish. They started to give me bits and pieces of fish, and after a while they decided to teach me how to catch fish by myself. They were all very pleased when I caught and ate my very first fish.'

'I've noticed that there aren't any fires in Zelana's grotto. How were you able to cook the fish you were eating?'

I shrugged. 'I didn't cook them. It might be a little hard to keep a fire burning if it's under water.'

'Are you saying that you ate those fish *raw*?'

'Of course. That's one of the reasons Meeleamee and the others gave me pieces of raw fish when they were weaning me off a steady diet of dolphin milk. I was *so* proud when I caught and ate my first fish in the little shallow pool at the mouth of the grotto. The fishing was much better out in deep water, though, so I didn't miss too many meals.'

'Are you saying that Zelana approved?'

'The Beloved doesn't eat anything at all – except for light, of course, so she turned the feeding over to the dolphins.'

'I've always been curious about just why you always call her "the Beloved.'

'That's what the dolphins called her. I picked it up from them, but I used *her* language instead of theirs. Of course that's fairly recent. I spoke "dolphin" long before I learned how to speak in "people." I didn't care *too* much for the name they gave me, though. They called me "Beeweeabee", which translates into "Short-Fin-With-No-Tail." I was much happier when the Beloved named me Eleria. I still swam with the dolphins when I got hungry. And then one day Meeleamee introduced me to an old cow-whale – who probably wasn't a whale at all – and she led me on down to the bottom of the sea where an oyster opened its shell and gave me the pink pearl that started to give me Dreams as soon as I rejoined the Beloved in her pink grotto.'

'Zelana mentioned that,' Enalla-Lillabeth said. 'Did that first Dream you had go all the way back to the beginning of the world?'

'That's what the Beloved told me,' I said. 'From what I saw in the Dream, the whole world was on fire.'

'I wouldn't take it any further back, Little-Me,' Balacenia's voice came silently to me. 'If Aracia happens to still be listening, we don't want her to know where – and when – your Dream *really* began.'

'How did *you* know about that?' I demanded.

'Eleria,' Balacenia's silent voice came to me again, 'we *are* the same person, you know, so *I* can remember your Dream as well as you can. I remember that when your Dream began, the universe wasn't there, and neither was time.'

'Then you saw Mother and Father too?'

'Of course I did, Little-Me.'

I felt just a little pouty about that. I'd always believed that the earliest part of the Dream was mine alone – something on the order of a gift from Mother and Father because I was their favorite child. Big-Me had just filched my gift, and I didn't like that one little bit.

'We'll talk about that some other time, Little-Me,' Balacenia said. 'We *don't* want Aracia to find out about it. She'll do some-thing even *more* stupid if she knows the whole story of the Dream. Let Lillabeth-Enalla talk for a while now. Ask them about life here in this silly temple. That should draw Aracia's attention away from *your* Dream. Let's stay on the safe side.'

*　　*　　*

'Sometimes it almost made me want to throw up,' Lillabeth told me. 'Fat Bersla could go on for hours and hours telling Aracia how wonderful she is. It made me sick to my stomach, but Aracia just couldn't get enough of it. She adores being adored, so those speeches were meat and drink. She didn't seem to realize that he was waving what he called his adoration in her face every chance he got for one reason and one only. As long as she hungered for what he called his adoration, he didn't have to any honest work, and not working has always been Fat Bersla's main goal in life.'

Then Big-Me spoke silently to Enalla. 'Don't get *too* specific, dear sister,' she said. 'Alcevan the bug might be listening, and her purpose right now is persuading Aracia to kill Lillabeth – and you, of course. The bug-people *really* want Aracia to live – or stay awake – for a while longer, because they can control her. I'm quite sure that they know that they won't have that kind of control of you, and that's why they want Aracia to kill you.'

'Then they don't know about what will happen to Aracia if she even tries to do that, do they?'

'It's not one of those things we mention very often,' Big-Me replied.

'There is *one* thing that I don't quite understand,' Enalla admitted. 'So far as I can determine, Alcevan is the only female priest in Aracia's Domain. How did she manage to foist that off on dear old Bersla?'

'Dear old "Stinky" probably used her gift to pull it off,' Big-Me replied.

'Stinky?' Enalla silently asked, trying quite hard to keep from laughing.

'That's what Little-Me calls her,' Balacenia replied. 'She *does* use an odor to control people, and that's probably how she pulled Fat

Bersla into line.' Then she paused. 'I'm not entirely positive that she actually stinks terribly, but just that name alone takes her down a peg or two, wouldn't you say?'

'I think I'll keep that name tucked under my arm,' Enalla said. 'It might be very useful at some time in the not-too-distant future.' Then she sighed. 'I was fairly sure that Sorgan Hook-Beak's deception had brought Aracia to her senses. You wouldn't *believe* the look of pure horror on Bersla's face when Aracia ordered him – and all the other priests – to go on down to the south wall of the temple to help construct the stronger defenses. How did Stinky manage to escape and come back here and steal Aracia from us again?'

'She went out over the wall and came back here out on open ground,' Big-Me replied. 'She'd been trying to send novice priests back here to murder Lillabeth – in much the same way she tried before Aracia ordered her to go down to the south wall.'

'Are you saying that there are novices out there so stupid that they'd believe her after she cut the throat of the first assassin she sent here to murder Lillabeth – or me?' Enalla demanded.

'I'd imagine that news of that killing didn't get around very much,' Big-Me replied. 'It wasn't as if Alcevan had left the body lying in the throne room or anything like that. Anyway, her plan fell apart after that clever little Maag called Rabbit came up with a way to make just about everybody too terrified to even *think* about coming back here through the corridors.'

'Oh?'

'He managed to make everybody believe that there were giant spiders creeping around in the corridors, and that being killed – and eaten – by a spider is the most hideous fate in all the world.'

'Even worse than snake-bites?'

'Much, much worse, dear sister,' Big-Me declared. 'Nobody –

and I *do* mean *nobody* – would even consider taking that kind of a chance, no matter what kind of reward has been offered.'

'Why don't we just send for Longbow, Big-Me?' I suggested. 'He could kill Stinky from so far away that her odor wouldn't reach him.'

'That might just be the best idea of all, Balacenia,' Enalla said. 'Once we get rid of Stinky, Aracia should return to good sense.'

'Except that Longbow's involved in the war up in Long-Pass,' Big-Me replied. 'I'm afraid that Stinky is *our* problem, and we'd better solve it very soon.'

2

---◆---◆---

'I think it's time for you to go to sleep, child Eleria,' Mother's voice came to me.

'You said *what*?' I demanded.

'You're going to have to Dream, Eleria. That's probably the only way we'll be able to prevent Aracia from destroying herself – and I'm not sure that even *that* will be enough. Alcevan has warped Aracia's mind to the point that she thinks that she's immune to what's almost certain to be the result of her attempt to obliterate Lillabeth. I'm hoping that your Dream will bring her back to her senses.'

'You want me to pretend that I'm asleep and then tell her a story so awful that she won't *dare* to try to kill Lillabeth?'

'Drop "pretend", Eleria,' Mother told me. 'You *will* be asleep, and you *will* have a Dream. Then you and Enalla – who *appears* to be Lillabeth – will recite the Dream in unison, in the same way that you and Lillabeth did last autumn. Aracia *knows* that the Dreams have power far beyond anything she can do, and your Dream *should* frighten her enough to make her reconsider Alcevan's suggestion.'

'What if it doesn't?'

'We'll lose Aracia,' Mother bluntly replied, 'and I'm not sure what the result will be.'

I knew that I was asleep. That's one of the things that separates 'those' Dreams from ordinary ones. The Dream that Mother provided was moderately terrible, and I was fairly sure that it would give Aracia some second thoughts.

But it didn't turn out that way. Aracia – or Alcevan, the bug – was already ahead of us. The door to Lillabeth's nursery banged open, and Aracia, wild-eyed with fury and with her hair tangled and sticking out in all directions, burst into the room. She was screaming what sounded much like curses in a hoarse voice. Little Stinky was right behind her with an expression of victory on her face.

'I have Dreamed.' Lillabeth, who was really Enalla, and I began to recite the content of the Dream Mother had given me, but I saw almost immediately that Aracia wasn't even listening. I suppose that it's possible that Alcevan the bug had turned her ears off.

'Foul usurper!' Aracia screamed at the child she thought was Lillabeth. 'Violator of my temple! I have cared for thee with all my heart, but thy first act when I have gone to my sleep will be to betray me. Know ye that thou shall *not* have this temple, nor the worship of those who serve me, for I must banish thee now and forever from the world of the living, wicked child. Be no more, wicked Lillabeth!' Aracia screamed. 'Exist no longer!'

For about a moment she stood in one place as if she had just been frozen, and then, as my Dream had predicted, she gradually began to change from what appeared to be human into tiny speckles of light – even as she had in my Dream. Her outward shape didn't seem to change, but it now consisted of those specks of light. I was quite sure that Big-Me and Enalla had simply turned her command around and thrown it back at her, but the more I thought about it, the more I realized that her command had turned on her all by itself. Had Enalla and I been allowed to describe my Dream, would that have saved Aracia? I do not know. If killing is forbidden, telling someone – or something – to die, *might* just destroy the speaker rather than the intended victim. From what I could make out of Aracia's face, she had an expression of sheer horror on what passed for her face. Then her face was gone, and the specks of light grew brighter and brighter. Then there was an enormous burst of pure light, and Aracia wasn't there anymore.

Alcevan howled in frustration, and then she fled as Lillabeth began to weep and moan in her grief. Enalla was standing with Big-Me near the door, so poor Lillabeth was suffering her grief all by herself. I took her in my arms and held her. It wasn't really all that much in the way of comforting her in her time of sorrow, but it was the best I could come up with.

Lillabeth was still weeping when Veltan came rushing into the room. 'What was that awful noise just now?' he demanded.

I wasn't feeling very kindly toward *anybody* just then, so I answered Veltan's stupid question in a cold, blunt tone of voice. 'Your sister just destroyed herself. She came in raving and with Stinky right behind her. Then she commanded Lillabeth to be no more. Since that's forbidden, her curse – or whatever you want to call it – turned and flew right back into her face, and she suddenly turned into little speckles of very bright light. The speckles grew brighter and brighter, and then there was a huge burst of pure light, and your sister wasn't there anymore.' I had decided *not* reveal my involvement to any members of the family. If Mother wanted to tell them, that was up to her, but I chose to keep my mouth shut.

Veltan went suddenly very pale, and then he also began to weep as his sorrow overwhelmed him.

Then Mother suddenly appeared. 'What's going on here?' she demanded – as if she didn't know.

'Aracia came here with that bug-thing that calls herself Alcevan right behind her,' I replied. 'I'd say that Alcevan turned her odor loose and persuaded Aracia to try to destroy Lillabeth. I couldn't prove that Alcevan was responsible, but she *was* there, and Aracia ignored a very important rule and ordered Lillabeth to dissolve – or something like that – but her order turned around and dissolved her instead. I'm afraid you just lost one of your babies, Mother, and there isn't enough of Aracia left to even try to bury.'

Mother touched her finger to her lips and then gave me a very stern look to keep Veltan and the others in the room from finding out what had *really* happened. Then she spoke in that voice she uses to reach out to her assorted children. 'Dahlaine,' she said, 'and Zelana. We've got a crisis here in Aracia's silly temple. You'd better come here as fast as you can, and bring the children.'

Lillabeth was still weeping when the others joined us in her room, and I was still doing my best to comfort her. But then, at Mother's suggestion, I'm sure, Enalla took Lillabeth into *her* arms, and Mother told me to repeat the story of Aracia's self-destruction for the others.

'It's better without her,' Vash of Veltan's Domain declared.

'No, Vash,' Big-Me disagreed. 'Actually, it's worse. We're one god light now, and that throws everything out of balance. If we don't do something to correct that, it won't be long, I'm afraid, before we'll all be joining her.'

'Don't be absurd, Balacenia,' Mother told Big-Me. 'All you have to do is replace her.'

'With who?' Enalla, still holding Lillabeth in her arms, demanded. Then she turned to speak to Dahlaine. 'You'd better come up with something very soon, big brother, or we'll *all* be turning into gleaming dust.'

Mother, quite naturally, was about three jumps ahead of Enalla – and all the rest of us as well. 'The answer is really very simple, dear Enalla,' she said. Then she smiled at me. 'You'll have plenty of time to get used to the idea, Eleria,' she told me. 'It's going to be twenty-five eons before you'll have to take Aracia's place as the goddess of the East. Your childhood with the pink dolphins has separated you from Balacenia – or "Big-Me" – so much that you aren't the same anymore. That leaves you floating around with nothing to do, so *you'll* replace poor Aracia.' She paused a moment and then threw my own favorite remark right back in my face. 'Won't that be neat?' she demanded.

the decline of the temple

1

Sorgan Hook-Beak of the Land of Maag was sleeping in his imitation fort that night. He'd have much preferred sleeping on
the *Ascension* out in the harbor, but it *was* fairly essential for him
to keep up the pretense of the mock invasion of the bug-people,
and sleeping on board a ship out in the harbor *might* just make
Lady Aracia more than a little suspicious. Now that she'd come to
her senses and ordered all of her fat, lazy priests to help build the
defensive walls around her temple, staying on the good side of her
was fairly important.

It was just after midnight, as closely as Sorgan could determine,
when cousin Torl came into Sorgan's room, accompanied by Lady
Zelana's Dreamer, Eleria.

'What are you two doing running around at night like this?'
Sorgan demanded.

'Lady Zelana told me to bring the little girl here so that she can
tell you something that *might* be fairly important, cousin,' Torl replied.

'What is it now?' Sorgan grumbled.

Eleria gave him a little smirk. 'The Beloved thought that you
ought to know that the lady who hired you isn't around anymore.'

'Where did she go?'

'That's a little hard to say, Captain Hook-Big,' Eleria replied. 'She broke one of the rules, and she went poof.'

'Poof?'

'That's about as close as I can come to describing what happened. She came into Lillabeth's room and commanded her to "be-no-more," but now *she's* the one who no longer exists.'

'Who did it? I mean, who ordered her to stop being alive?'

'She did – all by herself. I think it's built into the gods. They're not allowed to kill things, so when one of them tries to do that, it comes back and hits them right in the face. Didn't the Beloved explain that to you when you first came here to work for her?'

Sorgan blinked as a horrid possibility crashed in on him. 'My gold!' he exclaimed. 'Did *that* all go "poof" when she did?'

'I sort of doubt that, Hook-Big,' Eleria replied. 'The temple's still there, so the gold probably is as well. You could go look, I suppose, but we've got something else to worry about now.'

'What's happening?' Sorgan demanded.

'There are a lot of people in the temple who just lost their god. I don't think it's going to be much longer before a war breaks out. Now that Aracia isn't around to tell them to behave, things are probably going to get a little messy in the temple. I think you'd better send somebody down there to keep an eye on things.'

'And to find the store-room where Aracia kept all her gold,' Sorgan muttered to himself. That could wait, though. He turned to look at cousin Torl. 'Did that young Trogite Keselo leave the harbor yet?' he asked.

'I doubt it,' Torl replied. 'It was almost dark when he went out to the *Ascension*. He'll probably go north again when daylight comes along.'

'Good,' Sorgan said with a certain relief. 'Go on out to the

Ascension and tell Keselo what just happened here. We *definitely* want Narasan to know about it, so as soon as Keselo reaches Long-Pass, he'd better climb upon his horse and go up the pass to whatever fort Narasan's holed up in and tell him that Lady Zelana's sister isn't around anymore.'

'Sound thinking, cousin,' Torl agreed.

'I'm glad you liked it. Then I want you to nose around in the temple and see what's going on there – and see if you can locate the strong-room where Aracia kept all of her gold. She doesn't need it anymore, but *we* do.'

'I'll see what I can find, cousin,' Torl replied. Then he took Eleria by the hand, and the two of them went back toward the main temple.

Sorgan gave some thought to Eleria's warning. The priests of the temple didn't really pose much of a threat, but there was no point in taking any chances. He went to the chamber where Ox and Ham-Hand slept and woke them up.

'What's afoot, Cap'n?' Ox asked.

'We just got a nasty surprise,' Sorgan told him. 'It seems that Lady Aracia lost her grip on things again – probably because that little priestess – who's really a bug – turned that smell loose on her the way she did before, and Lady Aracia went crazy. She rushed into the room where her Dreamer lived and ordered her to stop living. I guess that's against all the rules, so Aracia's not around anymore.'

'She just fell over dead?' Ham-Hand asked.

'From what Eleria said – and she was there – there wasn't enough of Aracia left to fall over. Eleria used the word "poof" to describe what happened. I guess Aracia's body just faded away, and it was replaced by little speckles of light. Then the light went out, and there wasn't anything called Aracia anymore. That probably sent all those fat, lazy priests right straight up the wall. When they come down, they'll start scheming against each other, and the "holy temple" is very likely to be ankle-deep in blood.'

'What a shame,' Ox said with a broad grin.

'Isn't it, though?' Sorgan agreed. 'We don't want them out here, though, so take some sizeable parties of men along the corridors that lead to the main temple and block them off.'

'We've already been paid, Cap'n,' Ham-Hand said. 'Why don't we just take that money and run?'

'Because there's probably a lot *more* money piled up somewhere in the main temple. I'm not about to just walk away and leave it behind. My cousin Torl's in the main temple right now to see what's *really* happening there, and in his spare time, he's checking every room in that part of the temple for gold. Once he finds it, we're all going to become very, very rich.'

Torl came back out to the fort a couple days later, and he had a peculiar expression on his face when he entered Sorgan's chamber.

'Are we having a problem, cousin?' Sorgan asked him.

'You wouldn't *believe* what's going on in that main temple, cousin,' Torl replied. 'Those people have all gone crazy.'

'Exactly what do you mean by "crazy", cousin?' Sorgan asked.

'Right at first they were falling back on simple murders – all the usual ones like knife in the back, cutting throats, and bashing out brains with clubs or big rocks. They've been killing each other by the dozens. I'd say give it another day or so and there'll be open war over there. There's already a lot of blood splashed on the walls, but there'll probably be an ocean of blood when they move on to a full-scale war.'

'Were you able to locate Aracia's gold-room?'

'Not yet. I came back out here to warn you that things are very dangerous in that part of the temple.'

'I appreciate that, Torl. I've already got men blocking off every corridor that leads to the main temple.'

'Good thinking, Sorgan. Have you heard anything from Veltan yet?'

'Not a word. I'd say that he's got a family emergency on his hands right now. His older sister just vanished – or just stopped being any place anymore, and that might bring down a whole lot of trouble. Get on back to the main temple, cousin, but watch your back. We *really* want to find that gold store-room. We're nailed down here until we locate it.'

2

It was about mid-morning on the following day when the fat priest called Bersla came around the outer wall of the temple to Sorgan's makeshift fort. Sorgan was just a bit surprised by the fact that Bersla was traveling alone. If the oarsman Platch had been right, Bersla never went anywhere all by himself.

'Well, now,' Sorgan called from the outer wall of his makeshift fort, 'if it isn't Holy Takal Bersla. Does Lady Aracia want to talk with me about something?' He watched the Fat Man closely, and, as he'd more or less anticipated, Bersla's face suddenly went very pale. Then he pulled himself together. 'I speak for Holy Aracia in a matter of some urgency, mighty Sorgan. It would appear that the foul servants of That-Called-the-Vlagh have infiltrated the Holy Temple, and even as we speak, they are creeping about with murder only on their minds. Now I, of course, would be more than willing to face the foul servants of the Vlagh alone, but Holy Aracia has commanded me to speak with you.'

'I'll be more than willing to listen, Takal Bersla,' Sorgan declared. 'Let's keep this sort of to ourselves, though. One of my men at the gate will show you the way to my quarters, and I'll meet you there.'

Sorgan was rubbing his hands together as he went down the

narrow flight of stairs toward the central yard of his fort. If anybody in the whole temple would know exactly where Aracia's gold was hidden, it would be Fat Bersla.

He went into the room where he usually slept, and a few minutes later a burly Maag escorted the priest into Sorgan's room. After the sailor had left, Sorgan squinted at the priest. 'I hadn't heard that the bug-people had managed to get inside the temple, and I've got men watching just about every square foot of the place. How did they manage to get past my people?'

Bersla floundered for a moment, and then he said, 'Tunnels, I've been told. As I understand it, these creatures can chew their way through solid rock.'

'Indeed they can, Takal,' Sorgan replied. 'During the first war off to the west in Lady Zelana's Domain, thousands of bug-people came swarming up out of tunnels that'd taken them centuries to chew through solid rock. Tunnels are the most effective way to get under walls and buildings without being seen. Now then, let's get something out of the way right now. These sneaking bugs aren't spiders, are they? If I even mention the word "spider," I'll be lucky to have a dozen men left by morning.'

Bersla looked a bit startled. 'I'm sure they aren't spider-bugs. Spiders have eight legs, don't they?'

'That's what I've been told,' Sorgan replied.

'We're safe, then. The bugs crawling through the tunnels under the temple have six legs, not eight.'

'That's a relief. Now then, how are we going to go about this? If I put several thousand men in the temple hallways, they should be able to push the bugs off balance.'

'You are the warrior, mighty Sorgan,' Bersla replied. 'I know little or nothing of such things.'

'All right, then,' Sorgan said. 'How much will you pay me to keep you alive?'

'I know very little about money, brave Sorgan,' Bersla admitted. 'I do, however, have access to many blocks of the yellow metal your people call gold.'

'There's the answer right there, Takal Bersla,' Sorgan said with a broad grin. 'Each evening when you're still alive, give one of those blocks to my cousin Torl. One is an easy number to remember, so neither one of us will be confused. Let's start with a couple dozen of my men. If Torl thinks that won't be enough, I'll send more to guard you.'

Bersla heaved a huge sigh of relief, and his hands almost stopped trembling.

'I'll send an escort with you back to the main temple, Takal,' Sorgan said. 'You won't have to go back outside the walls now. I've got men blocking off the corridors, but they'll let you pass. After all, you and I are friends now, aren't we?'

'Indeed we are, mighty warrior,' Bersla declared. 'Indeed we are.'

Sorgan probably should not have been particularly surprised the next morning when the tiny priestess Alcevan came out to the fort with a request that was almost identical to the one Takal Bersla had made the previous afternoon. At least, unlike Bersla, she didn't try to foist on Sorgan an absurdity about bug-people creeping through tunnels as Bersla had. 'The Church of Divine Aracia is now divided, Captain Hook-Beak,' she declared. 'The one who elevated himself to "High Priest" believes that he alone can speak for Holy Aracia, and he has dispatched assassins to murder those of us who know full-well that his self-aggrandizement did *not* come from Holy Aracia. Since I live only to serve her, Bersla has commanded his henchmen to concentrate on *me* in advance of all others, for I am the *true* leader of the clergy in Aracia's holy temple. I can *not* permit him to usurp my position. So I must be protected from Bersla's villains. I will pay you much to defend me. Name your price, and gladly will I pay.'

'Oh, I don't know,' Sorgan said. 'How does one gold block a day sound to you?'

'Most reasonable, Captain Hook-Beak. Should I send the gold here?'

'Those corridors aren't really safe, priestess,' Sorgan replied. 'My cousin Torl will be right there in the temple. Why don't you just give him one of those gold blocks every morning? Torl *loves* gold, so he won't let anything happen to the lady who gives him a gold block every morning at breakfast time.'

'It shall be as you have requested, mighty Sorgan,' the tiny priestess agreed.

It was all Sorgan could do to keep from laughing out loud. There were two people in the temple who hated each other with a passion, and now they were *both* paying Sorgan a block of gold every day to protect them from each other.

It was about noon two days later when Torl came back out to Sorgan's imitation fort with four blocks of gold. 'I can't for the life of me find out where the treasure-room is located, cousin,' he declared. 'Bersla and Alcevan never leave that throne room but morning and evening, one of them hands me one of these gold blocks.'

'The pay's very good, cousin,' Sorgan said with a broad grin, 'and the work's not really very hard.' Then he frowned. 'The only drawback is how long it's likely to take us to empty out the treasure-rooms – assuming, of course, that they're each filching these blocks from a different room. For all we know, they could both be taking the blocks out of the same room.'

'If that's the case, that room *will* get emptied eventually.'

'That's all right with me, Torl,' Sorgan said. 'One day with no pay, and we're out of here.'

'They probably *will* kill each other as soon as we're gone, cousin,' Torl said.

'And we'll both be terribly sad when that happens, won't we?' Sorgan suggested with a wicked grin.

'I don't really think that's going to break my heart, cousin,' Torl replied. 'It might bend it just a little, but I'm fairly sure it won't break.'

'You *do* have a fairly strong heart, cousin,' Sorgan agreed.

Then they both laughed.

3

It was later that same day when Veltan came crashing in on his pet thunderbolt. As usual, the loud crash shook Sorgan right down to his toenails. 'Where have you been?' he demanded of Lady Zelana's younger brother.

'We *did* have a family emergency, Sorgan,' Veltan replied.

'I know,' Sorgan said. 'What are you doing about it?'

'We haven't really decided yet. Is anything unusual going on down here?'

'I think it's called "church politics," Veltan,' Sorgan replied, 'which is a polite way of saying "open war." Takal Bersla and tiny little Alcevan are right on the verge of going all out. So far, all they've been doing is sending out murderers to kill off various members of the opposing side. Bersla and Alcevan both know that they're in mortal danger, so they've both hired *me* to protect them. I've got men over in the main church keeping the churchies apart.' Then he grinned. 'Actually, this upcoming war has turned into a golden – and I *do* mean "golden" – opportunity for me. A while back Takal Bersla hired me to protect him, and the next morning teenie-weenie Alcevan came by, and she *also* hired me. Each one of them pays me a gold block every day to keep them alive, so this is turning into a profitable little war for me. They hate each other all the way down to the ground, and I'm fairly sure that there are a couple of *other* things they'd like for me to do, and they are almost certain to make me even more interesting offers before too many days go by.'

'You're not *really* going to get involved at that level, are you?'

'Of course not, Veltan. I will take the gold, though. Then I'll just take the money and run.'

'That's terrible!' Veltan exclaimed.

'I know,' Sorgan admitted. 'Fun, though.'

Torl came out to the fort a few days later to bring the loot to Sorgan. 'I think you might want to take a fairly close look at these blocks, cousin,' he said. 'I *think* I've found the gold-block warehouse. If you look at the blocks, you'll see that each one of them has quite a bit of sand ground in along one side.'

'Why would anybody do *that*?' Sorgan demanded.

'It's a way to hide the gold, cousin. That coat of sand makes these gold blocks look like ordinary building blocks.'

'Well, sort of, I suppose. What's the point of doing that, though?'

'It's a way to hide the gold. I *have* found the place where Aracia kept all her gold.'

'Well, *finally*!' Sorgan said. 'Where is it?'

'In her throne room, cousin. Actually, Holy Aracia's throne room is walled in with solid gold that's been disguised to make it look like ordinary bricks. I scraped a few places with my knife when nobody was watching, and sure enough, every brick I scraped was actually a gold block.'

'That throne room is enormous!' Sorgan exclaimed.

'It is indeed, cousin, and it's walled in with solid gold. I'd say that *one* of Aracia's priests – possibly Takal Bersla – came up with the idea even before Narasan's Trogite army arrived here last autumn. We've spent days and days looking for the gold warehouse, and it's been right there in front of us every time we went into the throne room. We're going to need a *lot* of ships to carry our gold when we leave this place.'

Sorgan began to tremble violently. 'I think I'd better go over there and have a close look,' he said. 'I don't think we've got enough ships in the whole Land of Dhrall to carry *that* much gold, and I'm *not* going to just sail away and leave most of it behind.'

'It's safer here, cousin,' Torl declared. 'They won't know that we're in this hidden corridor, and quite some time ago I pried out a couple of ordinary stone blocks so that I could *see* what they were doing in that silly throne room, as well as hear what they were saying to each other.' He paused for a moment. 'If I'd just reached in through the holes I'd made in this wall, I could have gathered up several dozen of those gold bricks.'

'You missed your chance, Torl,' Sorgan said with a faint smile. Then he peered through Torl's small opening. He was just a bit startled when he saw fat Takal Bersla sitting on Aracia's gold throne. 'Isn't that pushing things just a bit?' he asked Torl. 'Aracia's only been gone for a week or so, and now the Fat Man has sort of usurped her throne.'

Torl shrugged. 'At least it protects his back if somebody tries to kill him. Then, too, he almost certainly believes that he's going to come out the winner in this skirmish he's having with Alcevan.'

'My fellow priests,' Bersla declared in his oratorical voice, 'dear Holy Aracia has gone forth to look upon the creatures who are currently invading this most holy of the four Domains of the Land of Dhrall. It is by her command that I have taken her place here. She has spoken to me, and only *I* know what she wants.'

'Over there, Sorgan,' Torl whispered, pointing toward the far side of the throne room.

Sorgan peered across the room and saw a sizeable party of hooded priests coming through the main door of Aracia's throne room. They crossed the oversized room to the throne Bersla had usurped, and then they knelt down in seeming adoration – all of them except one. That one came forward with a tray heaped with exotic food.

'That's *one* way to get the Fat Man's attention,' Torl whispered.

'The *best* way,' Sorgan agreed softly.

Takal Bersla looked very pleased, and he eagerly reached out to take the overloaded tray. Then he began to take large bites of the assorted food heaped on the tray, and he wasn't paying much attention to the hooded ones kneeling before him.

Then the one who had given Bersla the tray pushed back the hood, and Sorgan was startled to see the small priestess Alcevan. With a look of triumph she opened her robe and pulled a broad dagger that was obviously of Maag origin out of her waist sash.

'Where did she get one of our daggers?' Torl exclaimed.

'Stole it, most likely,' Sorgan replied. 'She *is* a bug, after all, and the bugs steal everything they can put their claws on.'

Then Alcevan stood up and lunged directly at fat Bersla, driving the dagger all the way to the hilt into the Fat Man's belly.

Bersla dropped the food he'd been wolfing down and screamed as he tried to wrest the dagger from the little priestess. Alcevan was obviously much stronger than she appeared to be. She pushed Bersla's hands out of her way and slowly ripped him up the middle with that very sharp dagger.

Bersla screamed, trying to hold in his intestines, which were spilling out of Alcevan's gash.

Several dozen of Bersla's followers rushed toward the throne, but the hooded ones who'd accompanied Alcevan met them with swords and spears. The followers of Bersla died by the dozens as Bersla, still screaming, clutched at his surging-out innards.

Alcevan had already moved on, however. She seized Bersla by the hair at the back of his head, pulled it and then began to saw at his throat with the sharp dagger.

Bersla's screams suddenly stopped and huge amounts of blood came squirting out of the gash in his throat.

That *should* have finished it, Sorgan believed, but Alcevan wasn't through yet. She continued to slash and saw at Bersla's neck until his head finally came free. Then Alcevan lifted Bersla's detached head by the hair. 'Behold Divine Bersla!' she shouted. 'Follow him if you choose, and you shall soon go with him to the house of the dead! Truly I say to you, *I* now rule here in the holy temple.'

'Now *that's* something I never expected,' Torl declared. 'That little one's a savage, isn't she?'

'No, cousin,' Sorgan disagreed. 'Actually, she's a bug, and I wouldn't be at all surprised if she ate all the remains of poor old Bersla.'

'That might take her quite a while,' Torl observed. 'She's not very big, and there's a whole lot of Bersla sprawled out on that throne.'

Sorgan shrugged. 'Maybe she'll just have a banquet for all the assorted priests who supported her.'

'And kill any of them who refuse to eat their share?'

'That's possible, I suppose,' Sorgan said. 'Right now, though, you and I had better come up with some way to get all the gold building blocks out of this throne room and then haul them down to the harbor. I've got a hunch that "take the money and run" might just go on for quite a long time.'

THE BLIZZARD

1

$\rightarrow\!\!\!\rightarrow\!\!\!+\!\!\leftarrow$

Tlantar Two-Hands wasn't particularly surprised when a sudden blizzard came sweeping in out of the north. Dahlaine had held the normal snowstorms back while the various armies had come down along the mountain range to the mouth of Long-Pass, but now that they were all in place, that was no longer necessary. It appeared that winter had much resented being cut off from her normal entertainments, and now that she was free, she seemed to want to unleash at the same time all the previous storms that Dahlaine had prohibited before.

Tlantar had no problems with that. He and his friends had the fort of Gunda the Trogite for shelter, but the Creatures of the Wasteland were all right out in the open where winter could bury them all under twenty-foot snowdrifts.

On about the third day of the screaming blizzard, Longbow the archer suggested that a few of them should probably go up to the top of Gunda's wall and see just exactly what was going on down on the slope leading up from the Wasteland to the mouth of Long-Pass.

'How long would you say this is likely to continue?' Gunda asked Tlantar after Longbow had led them to the top.

Two-Hands shrugged. 'A week or so at least,' he replied.

'Dahlaine has held winter back for quite some time, so it's likely to take her a while to get over her frustration. I've noticed that winter is like that. She hates it when she's not permitted to play with her toys. I wouldn't say that *we've* got much to worry about. Your fort here will give us all the protection we're likely to need. The bug-people are right out in the open, though, so this won't be a very pleasant time for them.'

'Oh, the poor, poor babies,' Gunda said with a wicked sort of grin. 'Dear old Mama Vlagh will probably lose a lot of her children before this snowstorm goes away.'

'It's not impossible,' Two-Hands agreed. 'They won't be able to see for more than a few feet, and there's nothing on that slope for them to see anyway, and nothing to shelter them. Most of them will probably be frozen solid by the time spring arrives.'

Gunda pulled his bison-hide cloak tighter about him. 'Have you seen all that you need to see, Longbow?' he asked the tall archer. 'I'd really like to get back inside where it's warm. My feet are starting to get very cold.'

'Let's go back inside, then,' Longbow agreed.

They went on back down the narrow stairway to the lower part of the fort and rejoined Sleeps-With-Dogs and the farmer Omago from Veltan's Domain in a sizeable room with a solid stove standing against one of the rock walls. Two-Hands had noticed that the Trogites were very fond of stoves, in spite of the fact that their homeland almost never received much snow.

'Is that snowstorm out there letting up at all?' Sleeps-With-Dogs asked.

'I'd say that it's getting worse,' Longbow told his friend.

'Ah, well,' Sleeps-With-Dogs said, 'this lodge made of stone should hold it off. Are the bug-people up to anything?'

'That's just a bit hard to say,' Longbow replied. 'The snow's so thick that we couldn't see more than a few feet.'

'How cold would you say it is out there?' Omago asked.

Gunda laughed. 'I didn't try it, but I'd say that if a man happened to spit any place out there, the spit would turn into ice before it hit the ground.' He looked around. 'This is a very good fort, I guess, but if it keeps snowing and getting colder every minute, we might not need it at all. The bug-people will all freeze to death before they even get up here.' He gave Tlantar a speculative look. 'This blizzard is Lord Dahlaine's way to stop the bug-people right in their tracks, isn't it? I mean, he *can* do that, can't he?'

Two-Hands shook his head. 'Dahlaine's not permitted to kill things. *We* can kill them, but *he* can't. I'd say that this blizzard is just a natural reaction of winter to Dahlaine's decision to hold the weather back until *we* all got here. As soon as Dahlaine loosened his grip on her, she threw all the storms down this way at the same time. The seasons get very cranky when somebody interferes with their personal entertainment.'

'Are you saying that the seasons can actually think?'

'I wouldn't call it thinking, friend Gunda,' Longbow stepped in. 'Things build up as time passes, and winter things build up more than things in the other seasons. This particular storm probably didn't originate in winter, though. I took a quick look down Long-Pass when we started to come back down from the top of the wall. It's snowing very hard on the slope that comes up out of the Wasteland, but it's hardly snowing at all down in Long-Pass. I'd say that *somebody's* tampering.'

'Your "unknown friend" maybe?' Gunda asked.

'It's altogether possible, wouldn't you say? She *is* on our side, after all, and every bug the blizzard kills is one less that *we'll* have to kill.'

'That takes a lot of the fun out of *this* war, Longbow,' Gunda complained.

'I suppose you could scold her if you're feeling cheated,' Longbow replied mildly.

'Ah – no, I don't think I'll do that,' Gunda said. 'I *definitely* don't want to irritate *that* one.'

'Sound thinking,' Two-Hands noted.

Narasan, the chief of the Trogites, had been conferring with Gunda's friend Andar in the fort that was about a mile down the pass from this one, and he came up to Gunda's fort the next morning with his constant companion, the warrior queen Trenicia. 'Is somebody tampering again?' he asked when he joined Gunda and his friends in the central room of the fort. 'All we were getting down in Andar's fort were a few random snowflakes, but that's a serious snowstorm off to the west.'

'Longbow here thinks that it might be his unknown friend again,' Gunda replied. 'After some of the things she did down in Veltan-land last summer and what she did a month or so ago in Dahlaine-land, this snowstorm is the sort of thing she seems to like. She's got the bug-people all pinned down on that slope that comes up out of the Wasteland, and they're probably all very busy freezing to death.'

'I just wish that our friend out there could come up with a way to eliminate the Vlagh,' Narasan said. 'Once the Vlagh is gone, we'll all be able to go back home.'

The farmer Omago smiled. 'We'll miss you terribly, Commander,' he said, 'but you have things that need to be done when you return to your homeland, don't you?'

'I'm sure that we do,' Narasan replied. 'I think I'd like to get to know our new emperor a little better. He's pretty much destroyed the Trogite Church, but there are some other things he might want to consider. Selling the higher-ranking members of the clergy as slaves was most appropriate, but I think it's about time to take a hard look at the whole idea of slavery.'

'I don't know about that,' Gunda said. 'If he tries to abolish slavery, the people who own slaves and the rascals who sell them will put a sizeable price on his head.'

'Now *there's* a thought,' Narasan said. 'If we hired on to protect him, we could ask just about any price, wouldn't you say?'

'The Palvanum would come unraveled if we stuck our hands *that* deep into the imperial treasury,' Gunda replied.

'Maybe it's time to take a hard look at the Palvanum as well, Gunda,' Narasan suggested. Then he looked around at the others in the room. 'This is an internal matter in the Empire, and I don't think our friends here would be very interested. Right now we'll need to concentrate on what we'll need to do here when it stops snowing.'

Two-Hands was catching a strong odor of ambition. When Narasan returned to his homeland again, he'd probably become extremely important in the Trogite Empire, and sooner or later he could very well take the imperial throne for himself. Two-Hands smiled. If that *did* happen, he was fairly sure that he knew exactly who would be the Empress in the Land of Trog.

It was about mid-morning on the following day when the young Trogite soldier Keselo rode up to the back of Gunda's fort. The blizzard had subsided a bit during the night, but the snow was still piling up on the slope below the fort.

Keselo climbed down off his horse and came on into the fort. He touched one hand to his forehead in what the Trogites called a salute when Narasan joined him.

'Is there a problem of some kind?' Narasan asked him.

'There's no easy way to say this, sir,' Keselo replied. 'It seems that Lady Zelana's sister doesn't exist anymore.'

'You said *what*?' Narasan exclaimed.

'I didn't see it personally, sir, but Captain Sorgan told me to get up here as fast as I could and let you know what happened. If I understood him correctly, Lady Aracia ordered the little Dreamer Lillabeth to vanish – or die – or something like that.'

'She killed that baby?' Narasan exclaimed.

'She might have been trying, sir,' Keselo replied, 'but that's not what happened. As soon as she said it, she just disintegrated. At least that's what Eleria told Sorgan. Her body turned into little speckles of light. Then the lights all faded, and Lady Aracia wasn't there anymore. Captain Sorgan had spoken with Veltan, and Veltan told him that his sister had tried to do something that's prohibited, and when she attempted to do that, she was obliterated.'

'Dear Gods!' Narasan exclaimed. 'Who's in charge down there now?'

'I suppose you could say that it's the child Lillabeth, sir,' Keselo replied, 'but Captain Sorgan has seen her a time or two, and she's no longer a child, and her name is Enalla now.'

'Are all those fat priests worshiping this Enalla now?' Gunda asked.

Keselo shook his head. 'Captain Hook-Beak told me that she ordered them not to, and then she sent word out to the local farmers that they didn't need to deliver food to the temple anymore.'

'My goodness,' Narasan said mildly. 'What are the priests supposed to eat now?'

'Their shoes, probably, sir.'

'What moved Lady Aracia to try to do something that's absolutely forbidden?' Gunda demanded.

'Captain Sorgan told me that it was the same thing that caused those problems in the Tonthakan Nation in Lord Dahlaine's part of the Land of Dhrall, sir. There was a tiny little priestess called Alcevan who was able to control Lady Aracia with an odor – in much the same way that those two controlled the chief up in Tonthakan – up until the Maag called Ox brained the both of them with his axe.'

'It would seem that the Vlagh is playing games again,' Gunda growled.

'So it would seem, sir,' Keselo agreed. 'Oh, one other thing. Captain Hook-Beak asked me to advise you that his men are going to take all the gold they can get their hands on down there, and then they'll come on up here to lend us a hand – *and* to share the gold with us.'

Narasan blinked in astonishment, and then he started to laugh.

2

It took several more days for the lopsided blizzard to move off to the south, and when the pale winter sun returned, it more or less confirmed Longbow's assessment of the storm. The slope leading up from the Wasteland was covered with deep snow, but it appeared that very little snow had fallen into Long-Pass. Two-Hands now agreed that something very unusual had conjured up this particular blizzard.

As soon as the weather cleared, Gunda put most of his men to work clearing the snow off the top of the wall while the young Trogite called Keselo gathered the catapult crews near the back side of the fort where they all carefully mixed several liquids together to produce the fire-missiles that had proved to be extremely useful during the war in Crystal Gorge.

That might have disturbed Two-Hands more than just a little. Arrows and spears were one thing, but balls of liquid fire were quite another. Had their enemies in this war and the previous one been people-people, Two-Hands would have protested quite extensively. But bug-people were quite a different matter. Setting fire to bugs didn't bother Two-Hands at all.

The Trogite soldiers were still busily clearing away the snow piled high on the top of the wall when Longbow's friend, Sleeps-With-Dogs, came up to join them. He peered down the slope for a few moments, and then pointed out a sizeable number of snow-piles down there. 'Shouldn't the wind have blown those away?'

'That would sort of depend upon how tightly those snow-piles are packed,' Two-Hands replied. Then he gave it some thought. 'Now that you mention it, though, those piles shouldn't really be there. The wind should have carried them away quite some time ago.'

'Doesn't that sort of suggest that those piles aren't natural?' Sleeps-With-Dogs suggested.

'Indeed it does,' Two-Hands agreed. 'I'd say that the bug-people sort of improvised shelters to protect themselves from the weather, and we weren't able to see what they were doing because the blizzard was hiding everything down there. It's a good thing that *one* of us still had his eyes open.'

'If we're at all close to being right, before too much longer a bug will show up down there – unless they're going to try to burrow their way up here under the snow,' Sleeps-With-Dogs said.

'If any of them try that, they won't live very long,' Gunda declared. 'There are a thousand or so poisoned stakes down under all that snow, and one little scratch from one of those stakes will kill anything that tries to come up here – either on top of the snow or down underneath. One-Who-Heals gave us that idea, and those stakes have probably killed more bug-people than all the rest of us put together have.'

'One-Who-Heals was probably the wisest man in all the Land of Dhrall,' Sleeps-With-Dogs said proudly.

'We heard that he'd died not too long ago,' Gunda said. 'What killed him, anyway?'

'Old age,' Sleeps-With-Dogs replied. 'No matter how many wars we win, old age will end up killing us all.'

'That's a gloomy way of looking at things,' Gunda said in a sour tone of voice.

'Always look on the dark side, friend Gunda,' Sleeps-With-Dogs replied. 'Then, if you get killed with an arrow or a spear, it brightens things up, wouldn't you say?'

Two-Hands covered his mouth so that Gunda couldn't see his broad grin.

It was not much later when the side of one of the snow-heaps down on the slope buckled outward and a somewhat larger than usual bug-man kicked its way out into the open.

'Am I seeing things right?' Gunda asked. 'It looks to me like that overgrown bug is wearing one of the bison-hide cloaks that the Matans gave us to keep us from freezing to death.'

'It's possible, I suppose,' Longbow agreed. 'I'd say that it's much more likely that the Vlagh saw how useful they are, and she modified a new hatch to add those cloaks.'

'He's carrying a spear as well,' Two-Hands noted. 'Can the Vlagh take things *that* far?'

'The bugs have been stealing those spears for a long time now,' Gunda said. 'They pillage battlefields to steal weapons from dead men.'

'I wouldn't worry too much about that, Gunda,' Longbow said. 'Spears will reach out quite some distance, but arrows reach farther, and we have a lot of archers here – and fire-missiles as well. I've noticed that the Vlagh usually depends on numbers when she goes to war, but numbers don't mean much when the bug-people come up against arrows and fire-missiles.'

'You know,' Kathlak, Longbow's Tonthakan friend said, 'I noticed the same thing during the Crystal Gorge war. What do you think, Longbow? Should we start picking them off as soon as they come out of those snow-piles, or should we wait until most of them are out in the open?'

'Let's hold off until they get closer,' Longbow replied. 'Let's not waste arrows trying to hit them at long range. Then too, the snow's quite shallow up here at the top of the slope, and Ekial has horse-soldiers more or less hidden near the upper end of Long-Pass. We should be able to drop thousands of bug-people with our arrows, and then the horse-soldiers will be able to kill many, many more.'

Two-Hands saw that the bug-people weren't able to move very fast as they came by the thousands up the slope. It was quite obvious that they weren't at all familiar with snow and its drawbacks. After a few hundred of the bug-people had waded through the snow, they'd packed it down to the point that it was very nearly solid ice, and nobody – man or bug – can move very fast when walking on ice.

'What do you think, Longbow?' Kathlak asked.

'They're probably close enough now,' Longbow agreed. 'Do you want to give the order?'

'Why don't *you* do it?' Kathlak suggested. '*Nobody* argues with *you* when you give orders.'

'All right,' Longbow agreed. Then he took a long breath and shouted, 'Shoot!'

The arrows swept out in a vast wave from the top of Gunda's fort, and the front ranks of the advancing enemies toppled like fresh-cut wheat. The piles of dead bug-men were almost like a wall that blocked off the advance of the ones coming up the slope behind those first ranks. Then the horse-soldier Ekial shouted, 'Charge!' and his men galloped across the upper end of the slope, killing thousands more of their enemies.

Then there came the sound of a trumpet, and the horse-soldiers pulled back. Two-Hands was just a bit awed by how smoothly things had gone for them. Then the young Trogite called Keselo shouted 'Shoot!', but he wasn't talking about arrows. Great gobs of burning pitch came over the front wall of Gunda's fort, and absolute chaos brought the charge of the bug-men to a dead stop as burning bugs ran this way and that through the snow.

'Don't they know that all they have to do to put out those fires is roll around in the snow?' Two-Hands asked Longbow.

'Not really,' Longbow replied. 'These particular bugs come from a desert, so they probably don't know that snow is just another form of water.'

The winter sun was going down off to the west, and it touched the clouds of smoke with light that the smoke made bright red.

'I've always sort of liked sunsets,' Gunda said. 'The best thing about a sunset is that it means supper-time, and I'm starting to get very hungry.'

the alternate

1

—•——•——

Omago's Dream had released his memories of times long past, and now he knew just who – and what – he really was, and that knowledge had shaken him down to his very core.

Now that things were quieter, he felt that the time had come for him to get a better grip on that stunning reality, but he needed to be alone for that. And so, as midnight approached, he went up to the top of the main wall of Gunda's fort at the head of Long-Pass.

The weather was bitterly cold, but it came to Omago from out of the distant past that he was immune to weather – cold or hot – and he had no real need of air to breathe or food to eat. He sent his memory back to the time some thirty years ago when he'd first revealed his plan to Ara.

'It's something we need to know, Dear Heart,' he'd explained. 'The minds of the man-things here in the Land of Dhrall are unlike the minds of any of the other creatures here, and I think the best way to find out just why would be to erase all previous memories and live out the life of an ordinary man-thing.'

'I don't see any particular value in your plan, Omago,' Ara had replied. 'A prince or a chieftain might have *some* knowledge you'd find useful, but the ordinaries have trouble distinguishing night from day.'

'They're not really *that* bad, Ara. Princes and chieftains have very little contact with reality. They spend most of their time trying to *avoid* reality. I've been considering the life of an ordinary farmer – most probably in the Domain of Veltan of the South.'

'Why there, Dear Heart?'

'Apple-blossoms, Ara,' he'd replied with a sudden grin. 'I think they're the most beautiful flowers I've ever encountered in this world – or any others in this part of the universe. I *need* beauty, Ara. That's why we've been together for so long. Your beauty has held me captive since the beginning of time when we first added forms to our awareness.'

'Flattery won't get you very far, Omago.'

'Oh, I'm not so sure about that, Dear Heart,' Omago had replied with a sudden smile. Then he'd grown more serious. 'There's another reason that I think I should stay close to Veltan. As far as I can determine, he's the best teacher of all the gods. Dahlaine's too busy being important, and Vash and Dakas are just a bit abrupt and not really very bright.'

'What's wrong with the females?'

'Males and females don't think alike, Ara. Haven't you ever noticed that?' Then he'd grown more serious. 'I have a strong feeling that something very important will happen in the Land of Dhrall. The man-things of this world will continue to exist, or will become extinct, because of something that will take place in that obscure part of this world. There's a creature there that wants to obliterate them, and if the man-things are obliterated there, they'll also be eliminated in *all* parts of this world. I need to find out what that thing is and stop it – or even destroy it, if I have to.'

Ara had sighed. 'You aren't giving me too much room here, Dear Heart,' she'd accused him. 'Go ahead with this game of yours, but I'm *not* going to let you play alone. I'll be with you, like it or not, and I know who you *really* are. If you make any serious mistakes, I'll be there, and I'll be able to step in if it's necessary.'

'I *would* miss you, Dear Heart,' Omago confessed.

'Don't worry, Omago. I'll see to it that you don't.'

Omago clearly remembered the early years of his alternate identity when Veltan had given the young man a surprisingly complete education. As the young man had grown older, the other farmers of the region had taken to using him as a 'messenger-boy' of sorts to convey information to Veltan rather than going up the hill to Veltan's massive house on their own. It wasn't that they were actually afraid of Veltan, but he *was* a god, after all. The farmer version of Omago had dutifully carried that information up to Veltan's house, and as time went on, he'd added his own assessment of the various farmers of the region. For example, he'd told Veltan that the little farmer called Selga was much more interested in gaining Veltan's respect than he was in passing warnings and the like to the local god.

The farmer version of Omago hadn't had much interest in women during his early years, and the elder version knew exactly why. Ara had quite obviously been tampering. Omago actually laughed when he realized that.

'What's so funny?' Ara's voice came out of nowhere along about then.

'Nothing, Dear Heart,' Omago lied. 'I just remembered something that was sort of amusing, is all.'

Then Omago the elder quite vividly remembered Ara's rather

blunt proposal. Her words still jumped out at him. 'My name is Ara,' she'd begun. 'I'm sixteen years old, and I *want* you.'

'It *did* get right to the point,' the elder conceded, 'but it might have been just a little too specific to drop on someone as innocent as my alternate was.'

The more Omago considered things, though, it came to him that his true identity had unobtrusively stepped in on several occasions. When Veltan had given the young farmer version of Omago the iron knife, it had been the eternal version that had guided the younger one through the invention of the spear.

The older version had also nudged the younger into the notion of what Keselo had called 'The Phalanx.' The younger Omago was not as totally innocent as he'd appeared right at first – largely because the elder Omago had been tampering for all he was worth. The grand plan of the original Omago seemed to have had quite a few holes in it.

When the foul-mouthed Jalkan had insulted Ara, however, young Omago had punched him squarely in the face without any help at all from eternal Omago, and he'd done it so fast that it had actually startled his eternal awareness.

'He *did* show some promise there,' eternal Omago murmured with a faint smile.

He spent the next hour or so remembering the experiences of his alternate personality. Despite his lack of training, younger Omago had been clever and resourceful during the war in Veltan's Domain, and even more so during the war in the north.

'Enough of that,' he murmured. He and his mate had been drawn to the Land of Dhrall by their certainty that *something* would happen here that would prevent the extermination of the man-things here on this world. The events here during the past three seasons had made it abundantly clear that That-Called-the-Vlagh would be the exterminator. If she succeeded *here*, she would move on to the other parts of this world and delete the man-things in each of those as well. Given a few years, there would no longer *be* man-things anywhere on this world, and then the Vlagh would produce offspring by the millions, and they would spread out and kill off all other living creatures. 'Not as long as I'm around, they won't,' Omago vowed to himself. The more he thought about it, the more certain he became that the Alcevan creature would be the key to the obliteration of the man-things, and if they stopped Alcevan, they could surely stop the Vlagh as well.

But how?

'Have we turned into night-creatures now, Omago?' the sombre-faced archer Longbow asked.

Omago was startled. 'Can't you make a little noise before you do that, Longbow?' he demanded.

'That might be just a little difficult, friend Omago,' Longbow replied, holding up one of his feet and pointing at the soft leather shoe he wore.

'You could always cough, or something,' Omago said sourly.

'Is there some reason why you're still awake in the middle of the night?' Longbow asked.

'Something that might turn out to be very important,' Omago replied. 'It's important enough anyway that I don't think I'll sleep very much until I find some way to deal with it.'

'Oh?'

'The Vlagh has many servants – or children, actually – but most of them are as stupid as rocks. If what I've heard actually happened, the Alcevan creature is far, far more intelligent. If that's true, the children of the Vlagh will quite probably defeat us. I *think*, however, that I've come up with a way to defeat *her* instead. What I really need right now is more information about the nature of her servants.'

Longbow's expression changed slightly at that point. 'You're not *really* just an ordinary farmer, are you, Omago?' he asked.

'Well—' Omago left it sort of up in the air.

'I didn't really think so. I don't think your mate would have been very interested in somebody whose main purpose in life was picking apples or growing beans.'

Omago felt just a bit crestfallen about then. 'Have I been *that* obvious?'

Longbow smiled. 'I've come to know Ara very well since the war in Veltan's Domain. You two have been here for a long, long time, haven't you?'

'From even before the beginning, yes.'

'But you weren't aware of that until just recently, right?'

'How did you know *that*?' Omago demanded.

'You probably shouldn't have told your mate about that dream you'd had. She was *very* upset when you told her about it. She wanted *me* to do something about it. I'm not sure just *what* she wanted me to do, but she laid it in my lap. That's why we're having this present conversation. What made you think that it was time to shed that farmer pose and become the *real* eternal Omago?'

Omago smiled. 'Ara does that every so often,' he said. 'She didn't really like the idea of a simple-minded Omago, but now she wants to defend him – even though he's not particularly useful now. My original intention was to be just an ordinary farmer so that I'd understand the man-things here in the Land of Dhrall. You people here do things that nobody else in this whole world would ever do. I wanted to see things the way that the native people of the

Land of Dhrall see them, but evidently my mind has ways to step around any restrictions I've laid upon it – probably when an emergency pops up.'

'Omago,' Longbow asserted then, 'we've been neck-deep in emergency since last spring. Did your mind just now wake up to that?'

'I think it might have been the Alcevan creature that shook it awake. The Vlagh – or her children – have come up with a way to eliminate people – *all* people, I think. That odor they use makes people believe whatever the Vlagh *wants* them to believe. It was fairly crude over in Tonthakan, but the Alcevan creature took it much, much farther, and eliminated Aracia in the process. I'll get to Alcevan in good time, but right now I think I need to know more about the Vlagh creature herself.'

'I've seen her servants many times,' Longbow replied, 'but the only time I've ever seen *her* was back in Veltan's Domain when her servants were carrying her back out into the Wasteland. What is it that you want to know about her?'

'I need to know where she lives, and just who takes care of her.'

'You might want to speak with Dahlaine,' Longbow suggested. 'He's fairly busy right now, though. I think that Keselo might be able to tell us quite a lot about the world of bugs. He told me once that he used study as an excuse to avoid doing honest work, and he spent a lot of time studying the world of fishes and birds – maybe he studied bugs as well. Why don't we go wake him up? As long as you and *I* are awake, we might as well rouse him too, wouldn't you say?'

'My teachers at the University of Kaldacin weren't really all that interested in insects,' Keselo told them when they asked him about the world of bugs. 'They had a fair grasp of the nature of bees, of course, since honey can be quite valuable. They also warned us about locusts and ants, but that was about as far as it went. I *have* picked up quite a bit of information about the Vlagh from Dahlaine, though. Maybe you should ask *him*. When you get right down to it, though, I've picked up just about everything I know about bugs from *you* Longbow – and from your Shaman, One-Who-Heals. Is it at all possible that the Vlagh had your shaman killed because he knew too much about her and her children?'

'That gives me another good reason to kill her,' Longbow said. Then he paused. 'Male bugs aren't really very important, are they?'

'Only at breeding time,' Keselo replied. 'There's no such thing as a king bee – or a king ant.'

'Has Dahlaine ever found the exact location of the nest of the Vlagh?' Omago asked.

'Oh, yes,' Keselo replied. 'He knows *exactly* where she is. If it was permitted, he could probably obliterate her and all of her children.' The young Trogite frowned. 'That's one thing I've never understood. Dahlaine is a god, and he can do almost anything – except kill any living creature. I wouldn't be at all surprised if chopping down a tree would obliterate *him*.'

'It worked quite well recently,' Longbow said. 'Aracia *really* wanted to obliterate Enalla. Wars between various people aren't really all that significant, but a war between gods might just set the world on fire.'

'Has Dahlaine ever described the servants of the Vlagh?' Omago asked. 'I mean just exactly what are they supposed to do?'

'They feed mother,' Keselo replied, 'and keep her warm, of course. I'm just guessing here, but I'd say that if there wasn't anything for the Vlagh to eat, her servants would offer her themselves, and they'd set themselves on fire if she started to shiver. Self-sacrifice seems to show up quite often in the nest of the Vlagh.'

'I think we might be getting somewhere now,' Omago said. 'The Vlagh has been modifying her children since last spring. She's been turning them into imitation people – except that they have no sense at all of self. If there was some way that we could give them a sense of personal identity, they might not be so eager to sacrifice themselves.'

'Persuade one of the others to do it instead, maybe?' Keselo suggested.

'That would probably be the first step,' Omago agreed.

'They'd have to have names then,' Keselo added. 'The name lies at the very core of personal identity.' He hesitated slightly. 'I didn't come up with that all by myself,' he admitted. 'One of my teachers at the university dropped it on us. He made quite an issue of it when he told us that a man without a name is not a man. He never got around to telling us just exactly what a man without a name really was, though.'

'We'll have to pick up Rabbit before we go out into the Wasteland,' Longbow reminded them.

Omago blinked, and then he felt a bit embarrassed. 'We *will*, won't we?' he said. 'I should have thought of that myself.'

'And now we are – or will be – four,' Keselo declared quite formally. Then he laughed. 'Sorry,' he apologized. 'It was just too good an opportunity to let slide by.'

2

'**A**re you certain that we're really going to need that Maag called Rabbit?' Omago asked Longbow and Keselo a bit later.

'He's very clever,' Keselo replied, 'and on several occasions he's come up with ways to accomplish things that never would have even occurred to me.' The young Trogite smiled. 'It just wouldn't be the same without him,' he added.

'Do either of you have any idea of exactly where I might be able to locate him?'

'Sorgan Hook-Beak would know,' Longbow replied, 'and Sorgan's almost certainly in Aracia's temple – stealing everything of value in that oversized building. I can go down there and find him, if you like.'

'I'll take care of it, Longbow,' Omago replied. 'I have certain advantages that aren't available to you.'

'You're going to fly, I take it.'

'Well – sort of,' Omago said. 'I can go from here to there very fast when it's necessary.'

'You have a tame thunderbolt the same as Dahlaine has?' Keselo asked.

Omago smiled. 'Not exactly,' he said. 'Why don't we just leave it there? It's one of those things you *really* don't want to know about. Rabbit and I should be here in a day or so. Then we can go to the nest of the Vlagh and see what we can do to disrupt things for her.'

Omago went down the stone staircase to the center of Gunda's fort, and when he was out of the sight of Longbow and Keselo, he rose rapidly up into the still, night-dark air and willed himself to the shabby stone building Aracia's overweight priests had constructed to make their owner happy.

He sent out his thought in search of Rabbit, but the little smith wasn't there. He *did* sense the presence of Sorgan's cousin Torl, however, and he dropped down into the temple to have a few words with the clever Maag. 'I've been looking for Rabbit,' he said, 'but I can't seem to find him anywhere here.'

'You're the farmer called Omago, aren't you?' Torl asked.

'That's me all right,' Omago replied. 'Longbow the archer wants to have a few words with Rabbit, but I can't find the little fellow.'

'He's out in the harbor on board that Trogite tub called the *Ascension*,' Torl said. 'We found out that the bricks that made the walls of Aracia's throne room are actually gold blocks and cousin Sorgan put Rabbit to work melting them down and making small blocks out of them. A big gold block is worth too much to waste on little things. Smaller gold blocks work better.' He squinted at Omago. 'Do you think you could row a skiff across the harbor to the *Ascension*?' he asked. 'I'd row you out there myself, but cousin Sorgan has me busy doing other things now.'

'I can manage, Torl,' Omago said. 'I thank you for the information. I could have spent a week or more looking for Rabbit here in this overdone temple. Give your cousin my regards.'

'I'll do that, Omago,' Torl replied.

Omago went back outside the temple and located the *Ascension* out in the harbor. Then he willed himself from the beach to the ship's deck, and he could clearly hear the sound of a hammer pounding on something made of iron near the ship's bow.

'Ah, there you are, Rabbit,' he said to the little smith. 'Why are you working in the middle of the night like this?'

'Cap'n's orders,' Rabbit said sourly. 'He doesn't really trust all the sailors here on this oversized tub, and I'm working with gold, so the Cap'n would rather that I didn't do it out in the open in broad daylight.'

'I heard a somewhat peculiar sound up here when I first came up on the deck of this boat. Does gold really ring like a bell when you tap it with your hammer?'

'That was the mold,' Rabbit explained. 'The gold the Cap'n stole from Lady Aracia's temple was mostly used for disguised bricks that had been used to make her throne room. I've been melting it down and pouring it into molds. After it hardens, I tap the back of the mold to make the gold blocks break loose.'

'Ah, now I understand.' Omago glanced at the half-dozen or so gold blocks lying on Rabbit's anvil. 'Those aren't really very big, are they?'

'Four ounces each,' Rabbit said. 'That was Torl's idea. Those great big blocks Lady Zelana gave us are pretty enough, but they're too big to use for money – unless you're buying ships – or maybe a house in Kormo or Weros. Torl told the Cap'n that we needed smaller blocks if we wanted to buy food. We don't have coins over in the Land of Maag. We use plain gold blocks instead, and Torl was right when he said that bags and bags of these four-ounce blocks could be very useful.' Then he grinned at Omago. 'The size and shape suggest something different, wouldn't you say??'

'I didn't quite follow you there,' Omago admitted.

'They don't have any spots on them, but they're exactly the same shape and same size as dice. Maags are very familiar with dice, but I've never heard of a dice-game played with gold dice. The Cap'n came up with the idea all by himself. These gold dice will be the Maag version of money if the idea gets spread around.'

'Clever,' Omago said. 'Longbow sent me here to fetch you. He and Keselo need you.'

'I don't know if I can get away, Omago,' Rabbit said a bit dubiously. 'The Cap'n *really* wants me to convert a lot of the gold bricks our people are stealing out of Lady Aracia's temple into these dice-shaped blocks. If I try to sneak off, he'll have a lot of men out there trying to chase me down.'

'I'll see to it that they don't catch you, Rabbit.'

'Really? Just how do you plan to do that?'

Omago was fairly certain that Rabbit wouldn't believe him if he were to answer that question, so he went off in a different direction. 'Sleep, Rabbit,' he said quite calmly. Then he caught the suddenly comatose little Maag and carried him several hundred feet up into the air above the temple harbor. 'You look sort of tired anyway, Rabbit,' he murmured. Then he turned slightly and returned to Gunda's fort at the head of Long-Pass.

'That was quick!' Keselo declared, sounding more than a little astonished.

'I cheated just a little,' Omago admitted. 'I don't know if you'll believe this, but Sorgan Hook-Beak has filched a lot of gold from Aracia's temple. Then he put Rabbit to work melting gold and pouring it into molds the size and shape of the dice some people use when they're gambling. Rabbit told me that Sorgan planned to use those gold dice as money when he returns to the Land of Maag.'

Keselo blinked. 'Now *that's* something that never would have occurred to me,' he said.

'Sorgan's very good at doing things that other people would never think of doing,' Longbow said. Then he looked rather closely at the sleeping little Maag. 'He *is* all right, isn't he, Omago?' he asked.

'He's just fine,' Omago replied, 'and he'll be well rested come morning.'

'I don't really think we should wait until daylight before we leave,' Keselo said. 'Too many people are likely to start asking us questions if they see us going down that snowy slope after the sun comes up.'

'That raises another question, Omago,' Longbow said. 'If we start walking across the Wasteland in broad daylight, the bug-people are likely to be all over us.'

'Only if they can see us, friend Longbow,' Omago replied. 'And I can guarantee that they *won't* see us.'

'You're going to make us invisible?' Keselo asked.

'Not really invisible,' Omago replied. '"Unnoticeable" might describe it better. The bug-people will *look* at us, but they won't *see* us.'

'You can *do* that?' Keselo exclaimed.

Omago shrugged. 'Zelana does it all the time,' he said, 'and if *she* can do it, so can I. Shall we go?'

'Let's see if I've got this straight,' Rabbit said after Omago had roused him from his sleep and Longbow had told him just exactly where they were going and what they were going to do when they got there. 'Are you saying that just the four of us are going to hike out across the Wasteland, break into the palace of the Vlagh, and then persuade her children to run off and leave her there all by herself.'

'Approximately, yes,' Omago replied. 'It's probably going to be quite a bit more complicated than what you just suggested, but that pretty much sums it up, yes.'

'Have you people been drinking grog or something?' Rabbit demanded. 'The bug-people have killed thousands and thousands of people-people, and you three seem to think that you can walk right through them with no problems at all.'

Keselo stepped in at that point. 'You're going to have to adjust your thinking, Rabbit,' he told the little smith. 'Omago might *look* like an ordinary farmer, but he has at least as much power as his mate, and we've all seen the sort of things Ara can do. The bug-people won't be able to see us when we cross the Wasteland and enter the nest of the Vlagh. They won't even know that we're there, so we'll be able to do anything we want to do.'

'Butcher the Vlagh, maybe?' Rabbit asked in a voice dripping with scepticism.

'You're going to have to show him what you can do, Omago,' Longbow said. 'Rabbit needs to *see* things before he'll accept them.'

'And just for the fun of it, you might want to show us that "un-noticeable" trick that's supposed to get us safely across the Wasteland,' Keselo added.

Omago shrugged. 'Whatever makes you gentlemen happy,' he said. He rose up through the chill winter air until he was standing about forty feet above his friends. 'Does this answer any of your questions, Rabbit?' he asked the little Maag. 'Now then, I want all

349

of you to watch me very closely.' Then he reached out and touched their minds.

'Where did he go?' Rabbit demanded.

'I'm still here, Rabbit,' Omago called. 'You just can't see me anymore, that's all.'

'Are you saying that you're invisible?'

'No. You're just not paying any attention to me is all. Here, watch this.' He brushed away their insensibility, and they all seemed to be startled by his sudden reappearance.

'Are you sure that you can include *us* in this little game?' Keselo asked a bit dubiously.

Omago laughed. 'I can make a mountain range disappear if I really want to,' he replied. 'It'll still be there, but nobody will be able to see it. This isn't really all that unusual, you know. Zelana does it all the time.'

'Are you saying that you're as powerful as Lady Zelana is?' Rabbit demanded.

'*More* powerful, Rabbit,' Omago replied. 'She'll probably get better when she grows up, but she's still got a long way to go. Does that answer all the questions you have? We have quite a long way to go, so we'd better get started.'

3

The chill wind sweeping across the rock-strewn Wasteland had a distinctly mournful sound to it that Omago found quite depressing. There were several reasons why they should hurry, but Omago knew in his heart that what was really pushing him was the sad song of the wind.

After they'd gone down the slope to the west of Gunda's fort, Omago fell back to what he'd always called the 'skip-ship' method of crossing empty ground. He didn't mention it to the others, and he was fairly sure that they weren't even aware of the fact that he was cheating. When his skips reached about ten miles each, however, Longbow held up one hand. 'I don't think this is a very good idea, friend Omago,' he said.

'What was that?'

'These jumps of yours are covering too much ground. We *could* pop out right in the middle of a large group of bug-people, and they're making just enough noise to catch the enemy's attention. The jumps are all right, of course, but I'd hold them back to one mile apiece if I were you.'

'Did I miss something?' Rabbit asked.

'If you look at the mountains on the east side of the Wasteland, you'll notice that they seem to be jumping fairly often. A mountain peak that was fairly close is suddenly a long ways away.' Longbow smiled at Omago. 'I really think we should play it a little safer, don't you?'

'Do you catch *everything*, Longbow?' Omago demanded rather peevishly.

'I'm *supposed* to, friend Omago. Part of my job involves keeping my friends out of danger. If we keep going at this pace we'll arrive very suddenly at our destination. We don't *really* want to reach the nest of the Vlagh before the sun goes down, and we don't want to go inside until *some* of the servants of the Vlagh drift off to sleep, do we?'

Omago sighed. 'I guess not,' he reluctantly agreed.

It was only a few days later when they reached a peculiar-looking rock peak that jutted up out of the barren desert called 'The Wasteland.' 'I think that's it,' Omago quietly told his friends.

'There *do* seem to be quite a lot of bugs scampering around outside that pile of rocks,' Rabbit agreed.

'It looks almost like a fort, doesn't it?' Keselo said. 'I don't think I've ever seen a peak that looks very much like that one, though. What could cause something like that?'

'Erosion,' Omago told him. 'At one time, what's now called "The Wasteland" was the bottom of a fairly large sea, and water tends to eat rock. Give a sea a few million years, and it'll turn just about every rock along its shore into sand.'

'If I understand what you're saying about this peak,' Rabbit said, 'it's the "nest" the bug-people all live inside.'

'Not quite *all* of them, Rabbit,' Longbow said. 'Quite a few of them have been out in the open killing people. That's why we call this "a war," isn't it?'

'Very funny, Longbow,' Rabbit said. 'What I was getting at is that bugs don't build fires – or didn't until the war up in the north. If they don't build fires, what do they use to give them light inside that mountain?'

'Many bugs don't *need* light, Rabbit,' Keselo said. 'They find their way around in dark places with touch, not sight. Then too, there *are* certain bugs that generate light from inside their bodies. Some people call those particular bugs "fireflies," but there isn't any fire involved, and I've heard that those bugs are beetles, not flies.'

'We'll know more once we get inside,' Longbow said in a bleak voice. 'One thing, though. I want you all to know that the Vlagh is *mine*. *I'm* the one who's going to kill her.'

That took Omago by complete surprise, and it disturbed him more than a little. *He* had come up with something entirely different, but it was now fairly obvious that he and Longbow needed to talk about this – *soon*.

'That cave-mouth at the center of the peak is almost certainly the main entrance to the nest,' Keselo told them quietly as dusk began to settle over the Wasteland.

'There are a lot of bugs going in and out of that cave,' Rabbit noted. 'Even if they can't see us, we'll probably be bumping into a lot of them inside the cave.'

'I can deal with that,' Omago assured the little smith. Then he looked around. 'What *is* that buzzing sound?' he demanded rather irritably.

'I don't hear anything,' Rabbit said.

Omago glanced at Longbow and then at Keselo. 'Can either of you hear it?' he asked.

They both shook their heads.

'Is it possible that you're listening to the Vlagh herself?' Keselo asked. 'I've heard about what's called "the overmind." Maybe the Vlagh's giving orders to her children, and you're eavesdropping. You *do* have capabilities that we don't.'

'It *is* a possibility, Omago,' Longbow agreed. 'Is there some way that you might be able to understand what the Vlagh's overmind is saying to her children? If we knew what she wants them to do, we'd have a tremendous advantage.'

Omago frowned. 'That hadn't occurred to me,' he admitted. 'I think what she's telling them will be more clear once we're inside the cave.'

'This might just turn into a very easy war,' Rabbit said with a broad grin. 'If you can listen in while the bug-queen is giving orders to her children, we should be able to stop them before they even get started.'

'Let's go on inside,' Omago told his friends. 'If I can still hear the buzzing when we're in the cave, we should look into it.'

The walls of what had appeared from the outside to be nothing more than a natural opening in the side of the mountain were as smooth as the walls of Veltan's house off to the south. Polished walls – particularly in a mountain cave – seemed to Omago to be more than a little absurd, but they'd obviously given the children of the Vlagh something to do when they weren't busy invading people country.

There were many bug-people moving in or out of the cave, and even though they most certainly couldn't see Omago and his friends, they almost politely stepped out of their way. As Omago moved farther and farther into the cave, the irritating buzz became louder and more distinct. He probed at that sound with his mind, and after a few false starts, his mind captured the meaning of what the Vlagh was telling her children. 'Care for the little ones' came through quite clearly. 'Take them to a place where it is not cold, and feed them much, for they will soon grow larger and will take on their tasks. Fail me not if you would go on living, for the little ones are most precious to me.'

Rabbit had gone on ahead, and his expression when he rejoined them was a bit awed.

'What's wrong?' Longbow asked his little friend.

'You're not going to believe just how big the chamber at the end of this tunnel is, Longbow,' Rabbit said. 'I couldn't even *see* the far wall.'

'Is there light there?' Keselo asked.

'If you want to call it that,' Rabbit replied. 'There are quite a few of those fire-bugs mixed in with the ordinary ones. They don't really put out very much light, but it's not pitch-black in there.'

'Did you see the Vlagh herself?' Longbow asked.

Rabbit shook his head. 'The bug-people are all looking at some-thing that looks a lot like a large clump of spider-webs that's hanging down from the ceiling.'

'That would be a cocoon,' Keselo said. 'Certain bugs wrap them-selves in webbing when they're changing their form – or when they're giving birth to a new generation of puppies – or whatever you call baby-bugs.'

Longbow's face went cold and bleak. 'That would most likely be the Vlagh herself, wouldn't it?' he asked Omago.

'Definitely,' Omago agreed. Then he decided that it was time to clear something up. 'Don't start reaching for your bow or your arrows, friend Longbow. I have other plans for the Vlagh.'

'Oh?'

'Once you hear what I have in mind, I'm sure that you'll approve.'

'Surprise me,' Longbow said.

Omago shrugged. 'The Vlagh will live forever, and I'll see to it that she'll suffer every moment of that eternal time.'

'I'll listen,' Longbow promised.

The 'Care for the little ones' buzz was repeated over and over, even though the cocoon was still intact, and Omago was quite sure that 'the keepers' knew what they were supposed to do. It took him a while to blot out the buzz-sound, and once it was no longer audible, he reached out and began to duplicate that sound with a completely different message. 'You are the best of all who serve me,' he buzzed to the care-givers. 'Let others attend to this new hatch, for you have much more important duties. Go forth from our eternal nest and prepare to defend it from the man-things who even now approach across the land that produces no food. The fate of this nest depends entirely upon you.'

'How did you *do* that?' Rabbit whispered to Omago as virtually *all* of the bug-people rushed into the passageway that led to the outside of the peak.

'I think the most significant term would be 'cheating,' my little friend. I duplicated that buzzing noise and ordered nearly every bug in this vast chamber to run outside and hold back an imaginary invasion.'

'Aren't they supposed to take care of the puppies?' Rabbit demanded.

'They *were*, yes. But the "overmind" just gave them new orders.' Omago looked around the vast chamber that had been filled with bug-people until he'd issued his counterfeit command. 'There aren't very many of the Vlagh's servants left in here, are there?' he observed.

And then he broke out laughing.

THE VISIT OF SORGAN HOOK-BEAK

1

Commander Narasan of Kaldacin was more than a little disturbed by the sudden disappearance of the enemy army. Not even the recent blizzard had driven the bug-people back, and they'd continued their mindless charges up the slope toward Gunda's fort despite the steady rain of arrows and fire missiles and the savage attacks by Prince Ekial's horse-soldiers. But now, for no reason Narasan could determine, the bug-people had ceased their attacks, and for all anybody in Gunda's fort could tell, they'd abandoned the slope and gone back out into the barren Wasteland.

To make things even worse for Narasan, Queen Trenicia of the Isle of Akalla was nowhere to be found in the fort, and her absence troubled Narasan more than he'd care to admit, even to himself. Trenicia was boisterous, sometimes arrogant, and prone to take terrible chances when they weren't necessary, but Narasan felt a dreadful isolation when she wasn't around. She'd irritated him many times during the war in Lord Dahlaine's domain in the north of the Land of Dhrall, and it was fairly obvious that she intended to continue that here in Long-Pass. 'If she'd just tell me where she was going,' he muttered to himself as he stood on the high front wall of Gunda's fort looking down the snow-covered slope toward the Wasteland. 'I'm not going to order her around, but I need to know where she is.'

'Ah, *there* you are,' Narasan's friend, Sub-Commander Padan said, joining Narasan on top of the wall. 'Are there any signs at all of the bug-people on that slope?'

'Nothing at all,' Narasan replied. 'I suppose it's possible that they've gone back to burrowing.'

'That would take them years, Narasan,' Padan scoffed. 'I came up here to advise you that we've got company coming up Long-Pass.'

'Who's that?'

'Our dear old friend, Sorgan Hook-Beak. A runner just came up the pass to warn you that he's on his way up here to scold you about something. The runner told me that Sorgan's very discontented about something.'

'Now what?' Narasan grumbled.

'I haven't got a clue, glorious leader,' Padan replied.

'Do you *always* have to do that, Padan?' Narasan complained.

'Every now and then, yes. Shall we go down and greet him and see what he has to say? Or would you rather find someplace to hide?'

Narasan's friend, the burly Sorgan Hook-Beak, reached the rear gate of Gunda's fort about a half-hour later, and he had his shaggy Matan bison-robe pulled tightly around him. 'Is there some kind of emergency up here, friend Narasan?' he demanded.

'Our enemies aren't charging up the slope to the west of Gunda's fort,' Narasan replied. 'I wouldn't call that an emergency, though. Let's get in out of the cold, and then you can tell me about your problem.'

'It *is* a bit crisp up here,' Sorgan agreed. 'Lead the way, my friend. I'll be happy to follow.'

At Padan's suggestion they went through a long corridor that led to the kitchen of Ara, the mate of the farmer Omago. It was the warmest place in the whole fort, and Sorgan, after his long hike up the pass, was probably hungry.

'We don't want to intrude, Ara,' Narasan said, 'but Captain Hook-Beak here has been out in the cold for several days, and I'd imagine that something to eat might make his belly very happy.'

'It doesn't disturb me at all, Narasan,' the beautiful Ara said. 'Warm him up a bit, and I'll give him a lunch.'

'That won't hurt my feelings one little bit, Ma'am,' Sorgan said, pulling off his bison-hide cloak. 'Your mate has probably been away for several days now,' he added. 'That's why I came up here to talk with friend Narasan here.' Then he looked at Narasan. 'That's why I asked you if there was some kind of emergency up here. Omago came down to temple-town looking for Rabbit. I guess they talked for a little while, and now we can't locate either one of them. It's almost like they just disappeared.'

'Was Rabbit doing anything important?'

'Very, *very* important, Narasan. We found tons and tons of gold in Lady Aracia's temple, and Rabbit's been modifying gold bricks for us, but now he's gone. I've got several other men working on the modification, but they're not nearly as good as Rabbit.'

'Just where did you find this gold, friend Sorgan?'

'You're not going to believe this, but the walls of Lady Aracia's throne room were made of solid gold blocks.'

'When did that happen?' Narasan demanded. 'When I was down there, her throne room was made of ordinary bricks.'

'They might have *looked* ordinary,' Sorgan replied, 'but *somebody* down there was clever enough to disguise them.'

'How did they do that?'

'As close as we were able to determine, they sprinkled sand on the molten gold while it was still cooling in the molds. The sand stuck to the gold and made it look like clay bricks. I'd say that *one* of those lazy priests was clever enough to disguise the gold – to keep *us* from finding out that it was there.' He looked around. 'Have you got anything to drink around here?' he asked.

'I'll go fetch a jug or two, Captain,' Padan said, walking toward the door.

'How can people *live* in a place where it gets this cold?' Sorgan asked Narasan.

'Those bison-hide cloaks help quite a bit,' Narasan replied.

'I'd hate to spend much time outside if I didn't have one, *that's* for sure,' Sorgan agreed. 'Oh, before I forget, I'm going to need several more of your ships down there in the harbor before long. the *Ascension* is a nice enough ship, I guess, but she can't carry all that gold by herself.'

'How much are we talking about here, Sorgan?'

'What's the next word up from "tons," Narasan? We're a long way above "tons" already, and there's still more that we haven't pulled out of the temple yet.'

'I'd like to see some of it, Sorgan. I'm not calling you a liar or anything, but still—'

'I thought you'd never ask, Narasan,' Sorgan said with a broad grin. Then he untied a leather pouch from his belt, opened it and poured several fairly small gold blocks out onto the table just as Padan returned with two fairly large jugs.

'Pretty,' Padan said, looking at the gold scattered across the table, 'but why are you making such small chips?'

'I'm stealing another idea from you Trogites,' Sorgan admitted.

'We don't have gold coins over in the Land of Maag. We've got copper coins, brass ones, and a few made of silver, but for some reason, nobody there has ever considered gold coins.'

'Square ones?' Narasan asked. 'I don't think I've ever seen square coins.'

'It was Rabbit's idea. He said that if we put out square coins, everybody would know that they came from the Land of Maag.'

'Shouldn't you stamp a picture of somebody on those blocks?' Padan asked.

'A picture? Of who?'

'You, probably. You're the one who came up with the idea, after all, and if your picture is stamped into every one of them, the other Maags will think of you as their emperor.'

'That never occurred to me,' Sorgan admitted. 'How do people go about doing that?'

'Etch the picture on the end of an iron rod, set the rod on the face of one of your gold blocks, and then rap the blank end with a hammer.'

'How did you plan to distribute your new coins, friend Sorgan?' Narasan asked.

Sorgan shrugged. 'I'll buy things – ships, houses, land. When you get right down to it, I probably *will* be the emperor of Maag, since I'll own everything there, and I'll be able to hire an army to make everybody there bow down to me.' Then he grinned. 'And friend Narasan here will be able to buy the Trogite Empire too, since half of the gold will be his.'

'How did you come up with *that* idea, Sorgan?' Narasan asked, more than a little surprised.

'We're partners, friend Narasan, and I never cheat a partner. You should know that by now.'

'I seem to be about neck-deep in emperors,' Padan said. Then he pulled the cork out of one of the jugs he'd just carried into the room. 'Let's drink to that, shall we?' he suggested.

'I thought you'd never ask,' Sorgan declared with a broad grin.

Ara had been checking her assorted ovens, and then, with a sort of reluctant expression on her beautiful face, she joined Narasan and Sorgan at the large table where they'd been talking with each other for the better part of an hour. 'I think there's something you gentlemen should know,' she said.

'It's almost supper-time?' Sorgan asked her with a grin on his face.

'Very funny, Bent-Nose,' she replied. 'I don't want to ruin your day, mighty soldiers, but my mate has decided to put an end to this war right about now.'

'So *that's* why he came down to temple-town and filched Rabbit,' Sorgan said.

'I think you just lost me, friend Sorgan,' Narasan said.

'The farmer's clever enough to realize that Longbow, Rabbit, and your man Keselo, have made an excellent team during the previous wars. I'm fairly sure that if we looked around we wouldn't find *any* of them here in Gunda's fort.' He looked at Ara then. 'As I understood what people have been saying correctly, you and your mate can stay in touch with each other even if you're a thousand miles apart. That suggests that you know exactly what he and his friends are up to.'

'Oh, yes, and a thousand miles only begins to describe how far we can reach when we need to. Up until quite recently, he wasn't fully aware of that. Then he had a Dream that went much farther than the Dreams of the children.'

'A Dream about what's going to happen out in the Wasteland?' Narasan asked.

'No. That's sort of beside the point, though. Omago's Dream told him just who – and what – he really is. Now he knows that *he* can eliminate the Vlagh and all of her puppies. He picked up that team that's been so useful in the past, and they went across the Wasteland to the nest of the Vlagh.'

'Isn't that sort of dangerous?' Narasan asked. 'As far as we can tell, the Wasteland's crawling with the children of the Vlagh.'

'Not anymore,' Ara replied, 'and even if they *were* out there by the thousands, they wouldn't be able to see our friends.'

'When would you say that they'll reach the nest of the Vlagh?' Narasan asked.

'Actually, distance doesn't mean anything to Omago, and neither does time. They're there already.'

'What's at the core of his scheme?' Sorgan asked.

'He's blotted out the sound of her voice. She'll *try* to give her children orders, but they won't be able to hear her. Omago has usurped her voice, so now her children are obeying *him* instead of her. The Vlagh just recently laid a million or so eggs. When the eggs hatched, Vlagh's children went to the "care-givers", who are *supposed* to care for each new hatch. Since Omago had blotted out the Vlagh's orders to the "care-givers," they didn't recognize the baby bugs, so they ate them.'

Sorgan suddenly gagged. 'They're eating their own children?' he exclaimed.

'They don't *know* that the new hatch comes from the Vlagh herself,' Ara replied. 'To them, the new hatch is nothing but small caterpillars. Omago advised me that the Vlagh started screaming when the "care-givers" ate every single puppy she had created. Omago's certain that she'll scream for a long, long time.'

'How long?' Narasan demanded.

'Omago used the word "forever" when he explained it to Longbow. You might not want to accept this, but Longbow put his arrows away after Omago told him "forever." He had obviously planned to kill the Vlagh, but when my mate told him that the Vlagh would scream out her grief for millions of years, that would be much, much more satisfactory than shooting her full of arrows could *ever* be.'

'If there aren't going to be any more hatches, the bug-people will probably die out, before long, won't they?' Sorgan asked.

'Define "before long," Hook-Beak,' Ara replied.

'I don't know,' Sorgan admitted. 'A year or so at the most, I'd say.'

'No bug has *ever* lived that long,' Ara said. 'Four to six weeks is about as far as they can go. The Vlagh will still be there, but she'll be alone – and screaming – for the next million years – or so.'

'If that's what's happening, you and your men don't need to stay here, friend Narasan,' Sorgan said. 'Your men would be much more useful down there in temple-town guarding all that gold.'

'What's been going on down there since Lady Aracia vanished?' Narasan asked his friend.

'I think it's called "mutual extinction,"' Sorgan replied with a wicked grin. 'The priests have been killing each other every chance they get. That little priestess Alcevan gutted poor old Fat Bersla right in the throne room. Bersla had usurped Lady Aracia's throne, and little Alcevan came up to him and knelt down as if she wanted his blessing. I guess he was thinking it over, but then Alcevan jumped forward with a knife and gutted him right then and there.

I didn't see it myself, but I've heard that his innards spilled out all over the floor of the throne room. It's a messy way to kill somebody, but it *does* work – eventually.'

'I've heard quite a bit about that Alcevan,' Ara said. 'I think I'll make a suggestion to my mate. It might not be a bad idea to send her back home to the nest. Then she'll be able to sit somewhere and listen to her mother scream out her grief for the next million or so years.'

'She couldn't possibly live *that* long,' Narasan protested.

'Throw "possibly" away, dear Narasan,' Ara replied. 'If I want Alcevan to be in the nest listening to her mother's screams for the next million or so years, she *will*, I can guarantee that. Killing is *one* way to get revenge, but *not* killing is sometimes more satisfactory.'

It was about mid-morning the following day when the warrior queen Trenicia came up the slope that led down to the Wasteland, and she was accompanied by Prince Ekial.

'Where have you been?' Narasan demanded when Trenicia entered Gunda's fort.

'My,' she said, 'aren't *we* grouchy this morning?'

'I've asked you several times to let me know *before* you go scouting around.'

'You didn't *really* think I paid any attention, did you? You needed some information, so I went out and gathered it for you. That slope *appears* to be deserted, but it's *not*. There are thousands of bug-people down there, but they're all dead.'

'Who – or what – killed them?' Narasan asked, more than a little startled.

'I'd say that it was the weather,' she replied. 'Isn't that the way you saw it, Prince Ekial?'

'She's right about that, friend Narasan,' Ekial replied. 'The peculiar thing is that every one of them we saw was still standing up.'

'Let's go on inside,' Narasan suggested. 'Sorgan Hook-Beak is here, and he'll want to know about this too.'

'It *is* just a bit chilly out here,' Trenicia said. Then she reached out and patted Narasan's cheek. 'You worry too much, Narasan. I'm a big girl now, and I *do* know how to take care of myself.'

They went on inside the fort and found Sorgan, who was talking with Gunda and the pretty lady Ara. 'What's happening, Narasan?' Sorgan asked.

'It appears that the slope to the west of this fort isn't as deserted as we all thought it was,' Narasan replied. 'There are still bug-people down there, but they're all dead.'

'Arrows?' Sorgan asked.

Narasan shook his head. 'Cold weather, I've been told. Tell him what you saw, Trenicia.'

'It seemed a bit peculiar to me that the horde of bug-people who'd been charging up that slope for several weeks had just vanished – without even leaving any footprints in the snow,' Trenicia told Hook-Beak, 'so I went on down to have a look. The bug-people are still there, but they aren't moving. I'd say that they all froze to death.' She drew out her heavy sword and ran her thumb along the edge of the blade and winced. 'It's going to take me *weeks* to grind away all those nicks,' she complained. 'I chopped several of the bug-people into pieces, and they were all frozen solid. For some reason they just stopped moving, and the weather turned them all into blocks of ice.'

'The bug-people aren't very clever,' Sorgan said, 'but standing out in the open when it's as cold as it's been here lately is senseless.'

'Of course it is,' Ara replied. 'The bug-people don't *have* any sense. That's what "the overmind" was all about. Now that Omago has shut down the Vlagh's voice, the overmind can't contact her children. They're waiting for orders, but they aren't getting any. They don't know what to do, so they just stand there and freeze.'

'It seems that they stood there for much too long,' Sorgan observed.

'Not too long for *me*, they didn't,' Narasan said with a faint smile.

'I'd take it as a great kindness if you'd let me know where you're going *before* you go running off, Trenicia,' Narasan told the warrior queen when they were alone in Narasan's quarters. 'When I discovered that you were gone, I thought that I'd lost you, and that almost made me want to die. *Please* don't do that anymore, Dear Heart.'

Trenicia's eyes suddenly went very wide as she stared at Narasan. Then quite suddenly they were filled with tears. She threw her arms about him and held him tightly.

'Are you all right, Trenicia?' Narasan asked.

'I'm just fine,' she replied with tears streaming down her face. 'You just called me "Dear Heart," and that means that you love me, doesn't it?'

'I thought you already knew that.'

'Well, I had some hopes, but you never came right out and said it before.'

'We'd have gotten to it eventually,' Narasan told her with a faint smile. 'Please forgive me, Dear Heart. I've never had these feelings before, so I'm just a bit clumsy when I try to let you know how I feel.'

'You're doing just fine, Dear Heart,' she said, wiping her eyes. 'The only problem I can see is that I'll probably break down and cry every time you call me "Dear Heart."'

'That's all right,' he said. 'It should wash the dust out of your eyes.'

'Must you *always* be so practical?' she complained.

'Practical is what I'm supposed to be, Trenicia,' he told her. 'It keeps my people alive. Why don't I save "impractical" just for you?' Then he laughed and fondly embraced her.

THE NEST

1

Keselo was having more than a little difficulty with the true identity of the farmer Omago. He realized that he *should* have had some suspicions, in view of the evidently unlimited capabilities of Omago's mate. For some reason, however, it had never occurred to him that Omago could probably hurl disasters on the Creatures of the Wasteland in much the same way that Ara could.

The more that Keselo thought about it, though, the more he realized that Omago could almost certainly 'tamper' with those around him so that they'd all look upon him as just an ordinary farmer with no unusual talents.

Of course, if what Omago had told them back in Gunda's fort had been true, Omago had even deceived himself. In his search for understanding of the people of the Land of Dhrall, Omago had erased all knowledge of just who – and what – he really was, and he'd grown up as just an ordinary farmer who planted grain and vegetables, watched them grow all summer, and then harvested them when autumn arrived.

It appeared, however, that a certain part of Omago's mind knew exactly who – and what – he really was, and when it became necessary, that part of Omago's mind stepped over the 'farmer' subterfuge and took over. That meant that Keselo and his friends were dealing with an entirely different Omago – one who could, and would, step over 'impossible' whenever it suited him. He'd gone down to Aracia's temple-town, picked up Rabbit, and returned to Gunda's fort at the head of Long-Pass in slightly more than an hour. Then, to make things even worse, Omago had made them all 'unnoticeable' – evidently a variation of invisibility – and then had started taking ten-mile steps across the wasteland toward the nest of the Vlagh – up until Longbow had firmly suggested that those long jumps *might* cause some problems.

And so it was that late in a cold winter day they had reached 'the nest' of the Vlagh.

'Are we going to go through that cave to the Vlagh's main chamber, or are you going to "poof" us in there?' Rabbit asked Omago.

'Poof?' Omago asked, sounding just a bit puzzled.

'You know what I mean,' Rabbit replied. 'Lady Zelana "poofs" every time she gets a chance.'

'Let's just walk in,' Longbow suggested. 'If we happen to get into trouble in the main chamber, we might need to know which way to go when we run away.'

'You still don't entirely trust me, do you, Longbow?' Omago asked.

'You're doing fine so far,' Longbow replied, 'but if anything can possibly go wrong, it probably will. If it doesn't though, we can all be pleasantly surprised.'

Keselo was awestruck when Omago responded to his question about the peculiar shape of the peak that was the nest of the Vlagh by describing erosion in a manner that indicated that he'd actually witnessed something that had taken thousands of years to occur. Then he remembered that Longbow had told him that Omago and Ara had been around since before the beginning of time.

Rabbit seemed to be concerned about the probability that the entire nest would be totally dark, 'since bugs don't know much about building fires, do they?'

Keselo reached back to what One-Who-Heals had taught him and remembered something the Shaman had briefly mentioned about bugs called fireflies that generate light inside their bodies. 'But there isn't any fire involved,' he said. 'Or so I've been told. I've never actually *seen* one of them myself.'

As dusk settled down over the nest of the Vlagh, Omago led them to the mouth of the cave that almost certainly led to the home of the Vlagh herself. He stopped before they entered, however, and asked his friends if they could hear a buzzing sound. They all listened carefully, but it seemed that Omago was the only one who could hear it.

'Is it possible that you're listening to the voice of the Vlagh herself?' Keselo asked.

'It *is* a possibility, I suppose,' Omago conceded. 'Let's go on into the cave. The sound might become more clear when we get closer to the Vlagh.'

The cave had seemed to be a natural opening in the side of the mountain peak when they'd seen it from the outside, but just a few yards in, the walls were very smooth, and they even looked polished. There were quite a few bug-people moving around in the cave, and Keselo was almost startled when he saw several of them who glowed in the dark.

'Living lamps, I see,' Rabbit noted. 'The Vlagh seems to think of almost everything, doesn't she?'

'I'd say that she's been filching again,' Keselo added. 'I'd swear that I've already seen thirty or forty different varieties of bugs – beetles and ants and locusts, and flies – as well as several that have wings.'

'Then there are the ones that look like worms – except that they've got fifty or a hundred legs,' Longbow added.

'There are a lot of other varieties that we haven't seen yet as well,' Omago said.

'How does she manage to keep the peace?' Keselo demanded. 'It's more than a little weird to see natural enemies all bunched together like this.'

'That *might* turn out to be very useful,' Omago said. 'If these bugs start killing each other, we won't have to do very much except stand around and watch.'

'Those are the very best kind of wars,' Rabbit said. 'Am I going to keep on being invisible even if I go on ahead?' he asked. 'We probably ought to know what's there, wouldn't you say?'

'They won't see you, friend Rabbit,' Omago assured the little smith. 'It probably wouldn't be a bad idea for you to go have a look, now that you mention it. I don't like surprises all that much.'

As Keselo, Longbow, and Omago moved through the seemingly endless cave, they noted that the more recent hatches of the Vlagh were much larger than the ones that had preceded them. 'It would seem that the Vlagh was greatly impressed by the Maags,' Longbow observed.

'That's not really a very good idea,' Keselo said. 'Bigger children have bigger appetites, and there's not really that much food out here in this desert, is there?'

'Other bugs is about all,' Longbow replied. 'Of course, that might have been part of the idea. There *are* other nests and "queens", if we want to use that term. If the Vlagh's idea was to eliminate all the other bug-tribes out here in the Wasteland, "hungry children" could be quite useful.'

When Rabbit came back with a slightly awed expression on his face and told them about the big, open chamber at the end of the tunnel, Omago became very quiet.

Keselo explained that the big cluster of spider-web Rabbit had seen was called a cocoon. Though Rabbit and Longbow were listening to him, Keselo noticed that Omago was standing off to one side, listening to something that only he could understand.

'Don't make any noises,' Longbow cautioned them. 'We'd better take a look at this "cocoon" thing.'

Omago came along behind the rest of them, but Keselo was fairly certain that their friend was very busy now with something else.

They entered what Rabbit had called 'the throne room,' and Keselo was stunned by the incredible number of assorted bugs crawling across the floor and up the walls in the dim light given off by the few glowing 'fire insects.' Keselo turned to speak to Omago, but Omago had a look of intense concentration on his face, and he waved Keselo off.

'Where's this "cocoon" thing you mentioned?' Longbow quietly asked Rabbit.

'I'd say that it's probably in the very center of this cavern,' the little Maag replied. 'It's a little hard to see from this far back, because there are thousands of bugs between us and that silly bird's nest.'

Keselo winced slightly. 'Bird's nest' didn't exactly fit.

'Get back against one of the walls,' Omago told them. Keselo noted that their friend had a wicked sort of grin on his face. 'Several thousand of these servants are just about to leave, and we don't want to get trampled.'

'Aren't they supposed to stay here and tend to the baby-bugs?' Keselo asked.

'They just received new orders,' Omago replied.

'The Vlagh told them to go away?'

'They *think* she did, but *I'm* the one they're obeying.'

'How did you manage that?' Rabbit asked.

Omago shrugged. 'I shut off the buzz that was coming from the Vlagh, and then I buzzed a new set of orders. I told them that invaders were coming across the Wasteland, and I ordered most of the care-givers to go out of the cave and fight off all those evil people-people. A few of them will stay behind to care for the new hatch that's just about to come out of the cocoon. I'm almost certain that the Vlagh will come out of the cocoon before the new hatch does, and I want enough care-givers here in the cave to make the Vlagh believe that everything's all right. She's in for a very nasty shock before long, and her screaming will probably go on for quite a long time – a long, long, long time, if I've done this right.'

'Have you *ever* done anything wrong?' Keselo demanded, feeling more than a little irritated.

'Not that I can remember,' Omago replied with a broad grin.

After the last of the departing care-givers had left the vast central chamber of the nest of the Vlagh, Omago assured his friends that they were still 'unnoticeable' so they crossed the now virtually empty central chamber of the nest to take a closer look at their enemy.

The upper part of the cocoon began to bulge out, a fair sign that the Vlagh was squirming her way out into the open.

Keselo gasped as the Vlagh came into sight. 'That's impossible!' he exclaimed.

'Not really,' Omago disagreed. 'We probably should have expected this.'

'That's not the *real* Lady Aracia, is it?' Rabbit demanded.

'No,' Omago said. 'She's gone for good. She *was* the ruler of the east, though, and she was behaving as if she was the queen of the entire Land of Dhrall. The Vlagh thinks that *she's* the queen, so her duplication of Aracia makes a certain amount of sense. You might want to approve, Rabbit. You don't really want to see the *real* Vlagh. Nine feet tall the last time I looked and with six legs, waving antennae, and mandibles that could turn rocks into dust. Aracia wasn't quite as beautiful as Zelana, but she was much nicer to look at than the Vlagh is in her real form.'

'There's something moving in the bottom of that cocoon,' Longbow said then.

'The new hatch,' Omago said. 'They won't resemble adult bug-people – or Aracia either, for that matter.'

The bottom of the web began to give way, and a cluster of worm-shaped infants came wriggling out.

'Caterpillars?' Rabbit said in a voice charged with disbelief.

'It's the standard form of the infant bug-people,' Omago explained. 'After they've been fed for a week or so, they assume the shape the Vlagh's got in mind for them. They have plenty of feet to get them from here to there and an overpowering appetite. The remaining care-givers have a lot of work ahead of them, I'd say. But I don't think they'll be doing much "caring".'

'They're still wriggling out of that cocoon,' Keselo said. 'How many of them would you say have just hatched?'

'A quarter of a million anyway,' Omago replied. 'More, probably. The Vlagh needs a *lot* of servants just now.'

*   *   *

The new 'puppies' scurried across the floor of the vast chamber toward the greatly reduced 'care-givers,' and they were making sounds not unlike the crying of newborn humans. Keselo couldn't translate what the infants were saying, but he was quite sure that 'feed me!' was a significant part of it.

The 'care-givers' didn't seem to be very interested – at least not until the howling newborns reached the area near the west side of the chamber.

Then something happened that wasn't supposed to happen. One of the 'care-givers' reached down and snatched up one of the babies and examined it as if the care-givers had never before seen any infant bugs.

Then, evidently satisfied with what it saw, the servant stuffed the caterpillar-like infant into its mouth and bit down hard. The other 'care-givers' watched closely, and then they too snatched up infant bugs and stuffed them into their mouths.

'They're eating the babies!' Rabbit exclaimed.

'So it would seem,' the farmer Omago agreed. 'Isn't that nice of them?'

At that point, the imitation Aracia standing near the cocoon began to scream.

'Now I think you'll put your arrows aside, Longbow,' Omago suggested. 'The Vlagh's doing exactly what we want her to do.'

'How long would you say that she's going to continue the screaming?' Longbow asked.

Omago shrugged. 'Forever, most likely,' he said.

'It won't really be very hard for her to lay a new batch of eggs, will it?' Longbow asked.

'Not in the least,' Omago replied. 'Of course, the eggs will never hatch. That's the main reason we came here, friend Longbow. The

Vlagh won't produce any live servants now. I'd say that the Vlagh will never have any children – or warriors either. From here on until the end of time, the Vlagh will never produce another child, and after about six weeks she's going to be all alone here in her nest – weeping and screaming. Does that satisfy your need for vengeance, mighty hunter?'

'Her screaming *is* sort of beautiful, isn't it?' Longbow agreed, 'and I wouldn't for all the world want to interrupt her.' Then he carefully slid the arrow he'd been holding back into his quiver.

THE LAST GENERATION

1

It came to Rabbit that they shouldn't really be surprised that Omago was more than just a farmer. Omago's mate, the beautiful Ara, could do things that not even the gods of the Land of Dhrall could duplicate. A woman with *that* kind of power wouldn't be very interested in a man whose main goal in life was to grow lots of turnips. So Rabbit was not surprised that Omago understood the nature of the creatures that confronted them in the throne room of the nest.

The bulging eyes of every bug on the chamber floor, those who were part way up the walls, and even those clinging to the ceiling were fixed on the strange cocoon as if it was some kind of holy object.

'We seem to have arrived right on time, then,' Omago said. 'The Vlagh is instructing the horde of "care-givers" to take good care of this new hatch.'

Omago was staring at the cocoon, and then he suddenly laughed. 'I think that does it,' he murmured. Then he frowned again, and what appeared to be almost all of the bug-people in the vast chamber suddenly rushed toward the narrow tunnel that led back to the outside.

'Why didn't you just send them *all* away?' Rabbit wanted to know.

'I need the few that are left, Rabbit. They're going to do something that's probably going to make the Vlagh start screaming, and she'll probably keep it up for a long, long time.'

Since Rabbit and the others were still invisible to the remaining bugs, they crossed the now nearly empty chamber to get closer to the cocoon.

It was then that the cocoon split with a ripping sound as a very familiar figure came crawling through the web.

Rabbit flinched back. 'I thought she was dead!' he exclaimed.

'That's not quite accurate, little friend,' Omago said. 'What we're looking at is *not* a reborn Aracia. I'd say that Alcevan told the Vlagh that Aracia had been the queen of the east, and the Vlagh evidently decided to alter her form until she resembled Zelana's elder sister. It *is* quite a bit more attractive than the Vlagh's *real* form could ever be, and the Vlagh has always adored adoration. In some ways, the Vlagh and Aracia are very much like sisters. Even bugs have a certain sense of vanity. Then too, the Vlagh might have a certain amount of deception in what passes for her mind.'

The Vlagh, disguised as Lady Aracia, made a peculiar buzzing sound as countless many-legged worms scrambled across the nearly empty floor of the nest. They rushed to where the bugs called 'care-givers' were waiting, and they all began to make a sort of squeaky sound.

'I don't speak bug,' Rabbit told Keselo, 'but I'd guess that the puppies are all saying, "feed me, feed me, feed me."'

'That probably comes fairly close, yes,' Keselo agreed. 'Now that Omago has chased out *most* of the puppy-feeders, the baby bugs might have to wait in line for quite a long time.'

'Do you think they'd know how to stand in line?'

'Probably not,' Keselo replied. 'I'd say that we're about to see a very interesting fight any minute now.'

It wasn't exactly a fight they saw, however. The full-grown bugs looked at the tiny worms with legs for a moment or two, and then they began to eat them, snatching them up with their front claws and biting off their heads.

The Vlagh began to scream, but the 'care-givers' paid no attention and continued their feast.

'I think the Malavi call that "thinning out the herd," don't they?' Rabbit said.

'I believe I've heard them use that term, yes,' Keselo agreed.

'Big Mommy doesn't seem to like it very much,' Rabbit added.

'I think you might have spent too much time in the vicinity of Eleria,' Keselo suggested. Then he looked at Longbow and Omago. 'I'd say that our friend Longbow might be having a bit of a problem right now,' he said. 'He'd *really* like to shoot a dozen or so arrows into Big Mommy, but her screams are probably the most beautiful music he's ever heard.'

'It *is* a pleasant sort of sound isn't it?' Rabbit agreed. Then he looked around at the vast chamber. 'What do you think, Keselo? Should we stay here and listen to Big Mommy sing, or should we snoop around in the other parts of the nest and find out how all the other buggies are reacting to this disaster?'

'That might not be a bad idea,' Keselo agreed. 'I'm fairly sure that the other bug-people are filled with confusion, but maybe we should go look and make sure.'

2

'If it's all right with you, Omago,' Rabbit said to their friend, 'Keselo and I talked it over, and it seems to us that taking a quick look at the other parts of this fort – or whatever it is – might be a good idea. If the bugs are all coming apart, fine and dandy, but if they look like they're about to go charging out to kill all the people-people in the vicinity, we ought to know about it.'

'That's a very good idea, Rabbit,' Omago said. 'We've all spent so much time concentrating on the Vlagh that we haven't really paid much attention to her children. Now that her mind isn't functioning anymore, her children might try to do almost anything, and we'd better know about it.'

'They don't really live very long, do they?' Rabbit asked.

'No. Four to six weeks is about all. Now and then you might come across one that's seven or eight weeks old, but I don't think we'll ever see one that's older than that.'

'I think we're going to need a torch,' Keselo said. 'There are probably bugs out there that can see in the dark, but my eyes aren't quite that good.'

Omago reached into the canvas bag hanging from his belt and took out a pale, round object that appeared to be glass. 'Use this,' he said, handing the glass ball to Keselo. 'When you need some light, squeeze it, and it'll give you all the light you need. When you want darkness, loosen your grip.'

Keselo examined the round ball rather closely. 'I don't really see anything in this that could produce light,' he said.

'It isn't in there,' Omago said with a faint smile. 'It's in here.' And he tapped his forehead.

'Oh,' Keselo said. 'I probably should have realized that.'

'That's our Keselo for you,' Rabbit said. 'He seems to need to know how everything works. Don't let him get too close to the moon, Omago. He'll probably take her apart to find out what keeps her up in the night sky.'

'Curiosity isn't a bad thing, Rabbit,' Omago replied.

'I was only teasing,' Rabbit said. 'It's all right to tease your friends, isn't it? Come along, Keselo,' he said then. 'Let's go out and see if we can find any of Big Mommy's puppies.'

'Big Mommy?' Omago asked, sounding a bit perplexed.

'It's sort of what's called an "in-house joke," Omago,' Rabbit said. 'I'd explain it, but it'd take much too long. Shall we go, Keselo?'

'We might as well,' Keselo agreed.

The far wall of the vast main chamber was at least a mile from the place where the 'care-givers' were eating the Vlagh's babies, but the Vlagh's screams were still quite audible. 'She's got a big mouth, hasn't she?' Rabbit said to his friend.

'Oh, yes,' Keselo agreed. 'I wouldn't want to try to sleep anywhere within ten miles of this place.' Then he pointed at a part of the back wall about fifty yards off to the left. 'It looks to me like there's a sizeable hole in the wall over there. It might lead to another part of the nest.'

'Squeeze that light ball,' Rabbit suggested. 'Let's make sure that it works before we go crawling into any dark places.'

'Omago wouldn't lie to us, Rabbit.'

'I'm not saying that he would. The light ball probably works just fine when *he* squeezes it, but let's make sure that it'll work for you as well. Always test equipment *before* you need to use it.'

'If it makes you happy,' said Keselo, squeezing Omago's toy.

When the glass ball began to glow, Rabbit nodded. Then he looked around at the vast chamber that was still echoing to the screams of the Vlagh. 'This might take us quite a while, Keselo,' he suggested. 'If this mountain – or whatever we want to call it – is jam-packed full of bug-people, there could be hundreds of chambers where they hole up when they're not out in the open eating people-people.'

'We'll never know for sure until we take a look,' Keselo said. 'The more we see, the more we'll know.'

The hole in the rear wall that Keselo had seen was not exactly what Rabbit would have called a doorway, but there were many signs that it was used fairly often by the assorted children of the Vlagh. When Rabbit and Keselo crawled through the hole, they came out in what appeared to be a shaft that reached far, far up in this imitation mountain.

'I think we're in trouble,' Rabbit said.

'Oh?'

'We didn't think to bring a ladder.'

Keselo squinted up. 'The walls of this shaft aren't really very smooth,' he noted. 'It looks to me like there are plenty of handholds on the sides of the shaft.'

'Bugs have hands now?' Rabbit said, pretending that he was astonished.

'Funny, funny, Bunny,' Keselo replied sarcastically.

'Bunny?' Rabbit protested.

'I filched that one from Eleria,' Keselo replied with a faint smile. 'Let's see if we can make our way up this shaft. If it gets too risky, we'll go back and see if Omago can create a ladder for us.'

They climbed slowly up the wall of the shaft, and Rabbit noticed that there were many, many small round holes in the solid rock. Evidently generations of bugs had been climbing up and down the shaft for hundreds of years. 'It looks to me like there are quite a few openings in the walls of this up and down corridor,' he said.

'Separate quarters, most likely,' Keselo suggested. 'I'd say that the various kinds of bug-people avoid each other when they possibly can.'

'Just ahead,' Rabbit whispered. 'I just saw a bug poke its head out of that hole in the wall just ahead of us.'

'Do you think it might have seen us?'

'Probably not. It seemed to be looking *up* the shaft instead of down. To get down to the bald truth, Keselo, I'm not really thrilled by the notion of crawling into a hole in the wall that *might* just be filled to the brim with hungry bugs.'

'I'm with you all the way on that one, Rabbit,' Keselo replied. Then he leaned back slightly and peered up the gloomy shaft. 'There's a much larger opening about fifteen feet above the little one just ahead of us. That one might be a safer one to investigate.'

'I *do* like the word "safe," my friend,' Rabbit agreed.

They carefully climbed up the rugged shaft wall until they reached the larger opening. Rabbit quickly poked his head around the edge of the opening and then jerked it back. 'No bugs,' he whispered. 'Are we still invisible?'

'I think the word Omago used was "unnoticeable,"' Keselo

replied. 'I'd say that it's still in place. If any one of the bugs had actually seen us, she'd be making a lot of noise by now.'

'I'm *never* going to get used to the idea that all our enemies are women.'

'I wouldn't think of them as "women," Rabbit,' Keselo said. 'Female is one thing, but "women" is something entirely different.'

The larger opening appeared to be the mouth of a cave of some sort, and, much like the cave that had led to the vast chamber down below, this cave *also* led to a much, much larger room. When the two of them reached that chamber, they stopped. There were thousands of bugs there, but they were not all of the same variety, and the different kinds of bugs were staying away from each other, for some reason. Each group was all clustered together in the same place, and it seemed to Rabbit that there was a growing antagonism in the clusters of some varieties of bugs. Some of the groups seemed to be speaking inaudible sounds and others were reaching out with their front legs to touch the front legs of others. 'I don't imagine that you learned bug-language when you were going to school,' he whispered to his friend.

'We don't have the right kind of equipment to talk bug, Rabbit,' Keselo replied. 'Most of the time, bugs communicate by touching each other. If their language involves sound, like ours does, they make the sound by rubbing their legs against each other. Bug language would have to be quite simple, I think. They aren't really overloaded with brains, after all. I'm just guessing here, but I'd say that "kill, kill, kill," is about as far as the language of bugs would go.'

Something suddenly occurred to Rabbit. 'Are you up for an experiment of sorts, friend Keselo?' he asked.

'That might depend on just what kind of experiment we're talking about.'

'Omago can do all sorts of peculiar things, wouldn't you say?'

'I think I'd take it quite a bit farther than "peculiar." What did you have in mind?'

'Why don't you hold out that light ball Omago gave you and squeeze it?'

'Do you want to announce that we're here to about a half-million unfriendly bugs? Are you out of your mind?'

'I don't think they'll see it, Keselo. Omago wouldn't give us something that'd put us in any danger, would he? I'm sure that *we'll* see the light coming from that glass ball, but I'm just as sure that the bugs won't.'

'A light that only *we* can see?'

'Something like that *would* be sort of Omagoish, wouldn't you say?'

Keselo frowned. 'That was a rotten thing to do, Rabbit,' he complained. 'It *is* a definite possibility, and it's raised my curiosity so much that I almost *have* to try it.'

'You worry too much, Keselo,' Rabbit said with a broad grin. 'If it works the way I *think* it will, we'll have a tremendous advantage.'

'And if it doesn't work?'

Rabbit shrugged. 'We've got a clear path back to that shaft. We can escape if we really have to. Try it. Think of the advantage. We'll have light, but the bugs will still be in the dark.'

Keselo took the glass ball out from under his shirt. 'Just don't get in my way if we have to make a run for it, Rabbit.'

'Don't worry about a thing, friend Keselo,' Rabbit said with a broad grin. 'I can run at least twice as fast as you can, so I won't get in your way at all.'

'I've *got* to find out if your absurd idea will actually work, Rabbit,' Keselo complained. 'It *shouldn't* work that way, but I'll fly apart if

I don't try it and find out.' He raised the glass ball up over his head, and the growing light coming from Omago's toy grew brighter and brighter as Keselo's hand squeezed it.

'You can let it go now, Light-Bearer Keselo,' Rabbit told his friend. 'The light's as bright as the noon sun, but the bugs out there don't seem to be able to see it.'

'Oh, the poor babies,' Keselo said. He began to squeeze and release in rapid succession, and the light went on and off as Keselo's hand told it to.

'Show-off,' Rabbit scolded. And then he laughed.

They came across several familiar bug-people as they went farther back into the huge chamber. There were a lot of the snake-bugs that had made things so unpleasant in the ravine above the village of Lattash in one area, and Rabbit was a bit surprised to see several of the glowing fire-bugs mixed in with the snake-bugs. 'It looks to me like the fire bugs are almost welcome in the vicinity of nearly every other kind of bug,' he said to Keselo.

'You're probably right,' Keselo agreed. 'Light can be very useful. I wouldn't be at all surprised if the other bugs even feed the ones that glow in the dark.'

'The bug-people pay for light, you mean?'

'It's not out of the question, friend Rabbit.' Then Keselo stopped and pointed at the ceiling. 'Bug-bats,' he said.

'It's almost like old times, isn't it?' Rabbit said. 'Let's not get them excited. I didn't bring any fish-nets along this time.'

As they moved farther back into the chamber, they encountered several more of the familiar varieties of bug-people, and quite a few others they'd never seen before. 'What would you say that shaggy one whose hands drag on the floor might be?' Rabbit asked.

'Some sort of ape,' Keselo replied.

'I don't think we ever came across any of those, did we?'

'Not that I recall, we didn't. It's probably a variety that didn't turn out very well. The Vlagh experimented all the time, I'd say, and she probably turned out more useless creatures than good ones.'

'Junk-bugs?' Rabbit suggested.

'That's probably as good a term as any,' Keselo agreed.

Then a kind of roaring sound came from farther back in the chamber. 'If that's what I *think* it is, we're very lucky that we didn't encounter any of them in these various wars. It sounded very much like a lion to me.'

'What's a lion?'

'A very, very large cat. I've heard that a full-grown lion weighs about five hundred pounds, and it's got long, sharp teeth and deadly claws. It's a tropical animal, though, so it probably wouldn't have been of much use in the Land of Dhrall – except possibly down in Veltan's Domain.'

The roaring continued, but there was also another sound echoing from the walls up ahead.

'It sounds to me like there's a fair amount of "unfriendly" on up ahead,' Rabbit noted.

'That's not at all unlikely,' Keselo agreed. 'As long as "Big Mommy" was running things, her children probably tolerated each other, but Omago broke her grip on her puppies, and now her children are all trying their very best to kill each other.'

'Something to eat might be involved as well,' Rabbit added. 'This isn't called "the Wasteland" just for fun. There's nothing to eat here except rocks – and the neighbors, of course.'

'Good point,' Keselo agreed. 'Let's have a look and see just how savage all of this really is. The nest might be empty much sooner than we all thought it would be.'

'What a shame,' Rabbit replied with mock regret. And then he laughed.

'I don't think I've ever seen a six-legged cat before,' Rabbit said as the two friends moved along the chamber wall toward the violent encounter between several varieties of bug-people.

'The Vlagh probably blundered on that one,' Keselo replied. 'She's never fully understood why many creatures don't need that many legs, so it seems that six legs show in these imitations quite often.'

'She must have paid more attention when she conjured up that one called Alcevan, then,' Rabbit said. 'She looked like a real woman – a little small, maybe, but she had everything else that a woman's supposed to have.'

'I'd say that Alcevan was the best one the Vlagh ever produced. In many ways Alcevan is even better than the Vlagh herself, and when you add that odor, the little imitation priestess came very close to winning the war in temple-town.'

'You might say that she even won a war for *us* when she gutted out Takal Bersla. Torl was watching when that happened, and Torl's seen a lot of nasty things happen to people, but he told Cap'n Sorgan that he almost threw up when Alcevan spilled poor Bersla's insides all over the temple floor.'

'It couldn't have happened to a nicer fellow,' Keselo agreed. 'We might want to stay back just a bit, Rabbit,' he said then. 'I see several varieties of bugs approaching those lion-bugs, and I suspect that open war is just about to break out.'

'You're right there, friend Keselo,' Rabbit agreed. 'I see a dozen or so very large spiders on the other side of this chamber, as well as the lion-bug, some beetles that look like they're wearing armor, and some wasp-bugs flying around with their stingers held at the ready. Do *all* bugs have those great big eyes?'

'They want – and *need* – to see everything, Rabbit.' Then Keselo gasped. 'What is *that* thing?' he exclaimed.

Rabbit stared at the creature Keselo had just pointed out. 'She actually tried to imitate Longbow!' he exclaimed.

'It looks that way to me too,' Keselo agreed, 'but it has six limbs instead of only four, and it's carrying two bows instead of only one.'

'Now *this* I want to see,' Rabbit declared. 'If that thing shoots two arrows at the same time, it can kill more of its enemies than any other bug thing could ever manage.'

Keselo and Rabbit watched closely, and sure enough, the archer bug was killing two lion-bugs – or beetle-bugs – at the same time. The dead bugs with arrows in them began to pile up.

'She's good,' Rabbit reluctantly admitted. 'Longbow never misses, but he only uses one bow.'

'Look out!' Keselo exclaimed as a heavy crashing sound came from overhead.

Rabbit and Keselo pulled back from the large chamber as the overhead ceiling began to shatter. They could see a new kind of bug above them and they had big rocks in their claws.

'They're *huge!*' Keselo exclaimed. 'They have to be at least ten feet tall, and they're slamming boulders down on the top of the ceiling. The whole thing will collapse any time now.'

Then a flock of the bug-bats came flapping in overhead, and they began attacking the lion-bugs and the bug-archers.

'That's it!' Rabbit declared. 'Let's get out of here, Keselo. It's time to go on back and tell Omago what's going on in this part of the nest. Give them a couple of days, and there won't be *any* bugs left alive anywhere in this nest.'

'What a shame,' Keselo murmured, and then the two of them ran back toward the central shaft, and they didn't even laugh very much.

3

‎———◆———

When the two explorers returned to the main cavern, the Aracia creature was still screaming, but no other bugs were around anymore.

'I wasn't sure just *what* "Vlagh" was supposed to mean back in the old days,' Rabbit said. 'That's why we called her Big Mommy. But I *do* know what it means now.'

'Oh?' Keselo stepped in. 'What's that?'

'I'd say that "all alone" comes pretty close, wouldn't you?'

'Not quite, friend Rabbit,' Longbow said. 'If you listen carefully, you'll hear some other screams coming from a different part of the nest. The pretty lady delivered another screamer while you two were roaming around in the nest. The one called Alcevan is back home now, and she'll be able to listen to Big Mommy's screams for a long, long time.'

'Except that she won't *live* for a long time, will she?' Keselo asked.

'Pretty Ara took care of that before she brought Alcevan here,' Omago replied. 'Alcevan will live for as long as Big Mommy keeps screaming. Artistic screaming deserves an audience, wouldn't you say? There are solid stone walls between those two, so they won't see each other or be able to speak to each other. They'll exchange screams, and that's all.'

'Duets *are* a bit nicer than solos,' Keselo said.

'It's all over, then, isn't it?' Rabbit said, feeling just a bit sad that his days in the Land of Dhrall were coming to an end.

'Are you saying that you'll actually *miss* this war, Rabbit?' Longbow asked.

'Not the war as much as I'll miss the friends I've made here.' Then he snapped his fingers. 'What do you think, Keselo?' he asked. 'Should we tell Longbow about the imitation of him that Big Mommy made just a while back?'

'Are you sure that it won't offend him?' Keselo asked.

'It's real hard to offend Longbow, friend Keselo,' Rabbit said. 'Anyway, Longbow, it seems that you *really* impressed Big Mommy with your bow and your arrows – enough, anyway, that she made her own version of you. It wasn't at all bad, either. Of course, it was a bug, so it had six legs instead of only four. After it'd learned to stand up on its two hind legs, it had four arms to work with. That meant that it could hold two bows and shoot two arrows at the same time. It wasn't a half-mile away like you are, but up to a hundred or so paces away from its enemies, it could kill them two at a time.' Then an odd notion came to him. 'I'd be willing to bet that Omago here could modify you just a bit and give you an extra two arms – or maybe take a quick look at an octopus and give you *six* arms altogether. You could kill a whole army all by yourself if you were built that way.'

Longbow smiled faintly. 'Very interesting, friend Rabbit,' he said. 'And just where were you planning to set up your arrow factory after Omago gives me all those extra arms? I'll need a *lot* of arrows, you know.'

Rabbit winced. 'I'll forget all about this if you will, friend Longbow,' he said.

'Whatever seems right to you, little friend.' Then he looked at Omago. 'Are we finished here?' he asked.

'Unless you'd like to stay and listen to the Vlagh scream and wail,' Omago replied.

Longbow shrugged. 'After you've heard a few hours of screaming, it starts to get a bit boring. Why don't we go back to Gunda's fort and let everybody know that the war's over now, and that it's not very likely that it'll come back.'

'Good idea,' Omago agreed. 'Let's go.'

'Why didn't you just drive a dozen or so arrows into her, Longbow?' Sorgan asked the archer after Omago had described the current condition of the Vlagh to their friends in the large room at the center of Gunda's fort a few days later.

Longbow shrugged. 'Omago persuaded me not to,' he replied. 'She might have taken a minute or so to die if I'd driven an arrow into her. Now that all her children are dead and she'll never lay any more eggs that will give her other children, she'll remain in that nest screaming in agony until the end of time. In a certain sense she's paying for each and every one of our friends that the bug-people killed. I'd say that she probably *wanted* me to kill her, but I've always made a point of *never* giving the Vlagh anything she wanted.'

'So she's all alone in that hole in the ground screaming her lungs out,' Sorgan said. 'I think I'll go with Longbow on this one. Let her scream. She's not close enough to any town to keep the people awake.'

'Not exactly all alone, Captain,' Omago said. 'My dear Ara grabbed the bug-woman called Alcevan and jammed *her* into the

Vlagh's nest as well. She'll never *see* her mother, but she *will* hear her screaming. She'll scream as well – and probably for just as long. I'm sure that most of you have come to realize that you never want to do *anything* that offends my mate, and Alcevan stepped over that line when she pushed Aracia into Lillabeth's play-room. Aracia ceased to exist, but Alcevan will exist – and suffer – for all eternity.'

'That goes quite a bit farther than getting a plateful of raw beans for supper,' Rabbit said.

'A *lot* farther, yes.'

'That pretty much brings an end to all these wars here in the Land of Dhrall, doesn't it?' the Trogite Commander Narasan said as Zelana and her young brother Veltan entered the room.

'Not *yet*, friend Narasan,' Rabbit's captain declared. 'Things aren't over here until we've stored all that gold we found in Aracia's temple on board our ships.' He pursed his lips and then spoke to Zelana and Veltan. 'Why don't we just forget about the gold you two offered us to come here and fight this war?' he said.

'Generosity, Sorgan?' Zelana said with a certain surprise.

Sorgan shook his head. 'Not really,' he replied. 'Caution would be more accurate. We've got tons of gold down there in the temple, and too *much* gold would probably sink our ships.'

'Wise decision there, Captain Hook-Beak,' Veltan agreed.

Then Eleria and her big sister Balacenia came in to join them. 'Where have you *been*, Bunny?' Eleria demanded.

'Several of us had to go out into the Wasteland to put the Vlagh out of business, baby sister,' Rabbit replied.

'Isn't he just the nicest person we've ever seen?' Eleria said to the others as she climbed up into Rabbit's lap. 'You *do* owe me a lot of kisses, though, Bunny,' she said. 'Fair is fair, after all. When you all took off like that you didn't leave anybody at all here to give me kisses, so it's time for you to start paying me what you owe me.'

'I'll get right on it, baby sister,' Rabbit promised.

The discussion of what had happened in the nest of the Vlagh went on for most of the rest of that day. Then at the supper table when they were all feasting on Ara's magnificent cooking, the warrior queen Trenicia turned to Commander Narasan. 'Now that this is all over here in the Land of Dhrall, what are *our* plans, brave leader?'

'We have plenty of time to discuss that, dear Queen Trenicia,' Narasan replied.

'How much time?' she pressed.

'I'd say the rest of our lives, glorious Trenicia,' Narasan replied bluntly.

'You said *what*?' she demanded.

'I thought it was very clear, dear queen,' Narasan said. 'Get a firm grip on this, your Majesty. You will *not* leave me – not ever. You are *mine* now.'

'And *you* are *mine*,' she replied just as fervently.

'We can discuss this when we're alone,' Narasan said, looking slightly embarrassed by his own possessive remarks.

'Right,' Trenicia replied, standing up. 'Let's go. I've been waiting for *this* particular discussion for months now.' Then she paused. 'What took you so long?' she asked.

Narasan actually blushed at that point.

It was much later that night, but Rabbit found that he just couldn't sleep. His memories of all the things that had happened here in the Land of Dhrall kept coming back to haunt him. In an odd sense, he was no longer totally a Maag. He still hungered for riches, of course, but that wasn't all that unique. Keselo found gold to be at least as pretty as Rabbit did, and Prince Ekial was also attracted to gold. Longbow, however, was indifferent to it. His central goal in life had always been the destruction of the Vlagh and all her offspring. At the last moment, though, Longbow had set his arrow aside after Omago had advised him that in her current state of total isolation, the Vlagh might have welcomed four or five arrows to end her eternal grief.

'This is the strangest place,' Rabbit murmured as he wandered around the dark corridors of Gunda's fort. 'I'm quite sure that I *will* miss it – and the friends I've met since I came here. My life will seem sort of empty for a long, long time, I'm afraid.'

Then he drew in a long breath. 'This isn't going anywhere,' he muttered. 'I might as well go back to bed and see if I can get some sleep.'

He was quite sure that he wouldn't, though, but he went back to give it another try.

EPILOGUE
IN THE LAND OF DREAMS

1

'I'm not sure that this is really a very good idea, Vash,' Balacenia said to her brother as the younger gods and their elders gathered in Dahlaine's home inside Mount Shrak. 'Dahlaine's people-people have access to this place. I'm sure that they're nice enough, but this is a matter they probably shouldn't know about. There are almost certain to be some arguments, and I don't think we want people to know that the gods don't agree about *everything*, do you?'

'You may have a point there, dear sister,' Vash agreed. He squinted at Omago and Ara, who were standing somewhat apart from the others. 'I'll go mention your reservations to Mother and Father. Where would you say we should go?'

'Where else, Vash?' Balacenia replied with a broad smile.

'That place is *ours*, Balacenia,' Vash objected.

'I know, and it's so beautiful that all the others should agree with almost anything we say. We *have* had a few visitors there from time to time, and they've always agreed with anything we tell them.'

'I'll see what I can do, mighty leader.'

'Why are you throwing *that* in my face, Vash?'

'You might as well get used to it, Balacenia. You *will* be the Dominant this time. I'll go see what Mother and Father have to say.'

'Oh, bless you, Vash,' Balacenia replied.

'Bless?'

'Just practicing, baby brother. I haven't been the Dominant for a long, long time. If I remember right, blessings make the others wiggle like puppies.'

Vash grunted and went off to speak with Omago and Ara.

'Do you pick on him like that all the time, Big-Me?' Eleria asked.

'Only when it's necessary, Little-Me.'

After Vash had spoken briefly with Omago and Ara, he came back across the chamber. 'They agreed that this might not be the best place to have this meeting,' he reported. 'They'll speak with Dahlaine about it. He'll listen to *them*, but he might resent it if you and I were the ones who make the suggestion.'

'Those two can be *very* useful,' Balacenia agreed.

'I don't see what's wrong with Mount Shrak here,' Dahlaine objected. 'I can keep all the local people out of here.'

'I'm sure you can, dear Dahlaine,' Ara said, 'but it's winter here and sort of gloomy. I've seen this Land of Dreams Vash and Balacenia created out of pure imagination, and it's probably the most beautiful place in the entire universe. We have an important decision to make, and beauty will make it nicer.'

'I still don't see why it's necessary to go there,' Dahlaine grumbled.

'I learned a long time ago that it's not wise to offend the lady who runs the kitchen,' Omago said.

'I don't *need* food, Omago,' Dahlaine replied. 'Kitchens don't interest me, because I don't eat.'

'You ought to try it some time,' Omago suggested. He frowned just a bit. 'I suppose there might have been some obscure reason for that "don't eat or sleep" rule, but I think it's out of date now.'

'How do we get to this imitation place?' Dahlaine asked.

'Your Dreamer, Ashad – who's really Dakas – knows the way, big brother,' Balacenia told him. 'We had a meeting there a while back. There were several things we needed to agree about, so we all went to the Land of Dreams to make some necessary decisions.'

They all went on out through the long tunnel to the cave-mouth that opened out onto the snow-covered grassland. Then each of the Dreamers – or younger gods – took their elders by the hand, and they all rose up into the chill winter sky.

Unlike the others, however, both of Balacenia's hands were full. She and Eleria could not merge as the others did, so she was obliged to carry both Zelana and her alternate. Balacenia was quite certain that Eleria was the only possible successor for Aracia, but she was fairly sure that Eleria would violently object. There had to be something that only Ara and Omago could offer Eleria that would make the little girl willing to accept divinity. 'I think I'm going to have to work on that a bit,' she murmured.

'I didn't quite catch that, dear,' Zelana said.

'Just thinking out loud, Zelana. It's a habit I picked up back in the days before people existed.'

'That was a very lonely time, as I recall,' Zelana agreed. 'I used to recite poetry to trees and sing songs to Mother Sea.'

'Did she like your songs?'

'Some of them, yes. I could always tell which songs she liked, because she'd fill the sky with rainbows.'

'And if she didn't like them?'

'Hailstorms, as I recall.'

Balacenia winced. 'Did you ever teach Eleria how to sing?'

Zelana nodded. 'It was a mistake, though. Her voice is so beautiful that it'd fill Mother Sea's eyes with tears. It worked rather well if the weather had turned dry, though. Eleria can probably stir up a three-day rain-storm if we really need it. Is this Land of Dreams much farther away?'

'No,' Balacenia replied. 'It could be right here, if Vash and I wanted it to be. Vash is stirring up the aurora, though. Nobody argues with anybody else when the aurora's in bloom.'

The younger gods gently lowered their elders down onto the Land of Dreams, and Balacenia saw that Vash had outdone himself in the creation of the current aurora. They usually sort of lingered along the horizon, but this one seemed to be rising up from meadows and mountains on all sides of the Dreamland, and the beauty almost took Balacenia's breath away.

'Tell me, Vash,' Veltan said to the real version of Yaltar, 'what ever possessed you and Balacenia to conjure up this beautiful place?'

'It was a long, long time ago, uncle. There weren't any people – or animals, for that matter, and Balacenia and I were looking at twenty-five eons with nothing to do except maybe watch grass grow. After a few centuries of that, we really needed something else to look at. Balacenia had caught a brief glimpse of an aurora along the northern horizon, and then she and I drifted on up north – actually into the Domain of Dakas. I suppose you could say that we stole an aurora from Dakas and then planted it in a place that didn't really exist – except in our Dream, of course. We spent centuries here soaking in the beauty of our Dream. It made that empty cycle bearable.'

'I'll concede that it's much, much prettier than the moon was when Mother Sea sent *me* there,' Veltan admitted. 'Of course the moon lied to me when she told me that Mother Sea was still angry with me for tampering with her color.'

'You can't really trust the moon, uncle,' Vash said.

Dakas gently lowered Dahlaine onto the Land of Dreams, and old Grey-Beard, evidently still a bit irritated, glanced around. 'We have something very important to attend to,' he told them all, 'and looking at the imaginary scenery here is just a waste of time.'

'There's no great rush, uncle,' Dakas said. 'Time doesn't really exist here. When Balacenia and Vash brought us here last summer, it seemed like we'd been here for months and months, but that was only a dream. When we woke up again, we were all back home and only one night had passed. We can take our time making our decision because time doesn't mean anything here. A century – or even an eon can crawl past, and the world won't be a day older.'

Omago and Ara were still caught up in the glory of the aurora, but Veltan, with a slightly worried look on his face, quietly approached them. 'Just how are we going to create a god to replace sister Aracia?' he asked them.

'She's already here, Veltan,' Omago replied. 'All we have to do is persuade her to take up the position – if that's the right term.'

Veltan looked around. 'I don't see any unfamiliar faces,' he said.

'Of course you don't, dear Veltan,' Mother Ara said. 'You've probably known her since she was a baby. You *did* visit Zelana in her grotto a few times after the children arrived, didn't you?'

'Well, yes, but—' Veltan stopped, and his eyes went wide as he stared at Eleria. 'Are you saying that you're going to pile *two* Domains on poor Balacenia's shoulders?'

'We wouldn't do that, dear Veltan,' Ara said. 'Eleria and Balacenia were separated a long, long time ago.' She paused briefly. 'That's in baby-terms, of course. Eleria was too independent, and Balacenia enjoyed her company so much that she didn't put any restrictions on her. It *could* be, I suppose, that Mother Sea and Father Earth *knew* that Aracia would destroy herself eventually, so they made Eleria very special.'

'Why is everybody always talking about me like that, Big-Me?' Eleria asked.

'Because you're so special, Little-Me,' Balacenia replied. 'Isn't being special a lot of fun?'

'Not for me it isn't,' Eleria said. 'I'm not feeling the least bit goddish, so tell the others to go pick somebody else.'

'Who?' Balacenia replied. 'There's nobody else available. You spent your childhood playing with the pink dolphins, and that separated you and me so much that we'll never be able to meld into a single person again. You already have as much power – or even more – than any of the rest of us – elder or younger – have. Like it or not, you *will* replace Aracia when Enalla starts feeling sleepy.'

'I don't *want* it!' Eleria almost shouted, stamping her foot on the ground.

'"Want" has nothing to do with it, dear Little-Me,' Balacenia said rather bluntly. 'Like it or not, you *will* be the goddess of the East when Enalla goes to sleep.'

Eleria was definitely sulky after Balacenia had harshly dropped the truth on her. Eleria had always been able to persuade various people to do what she wanted them to do, but Balacenia had just deliberately slammed that door in Eleria's face. She gave her sweet little alternate some time to sulk before she moved on. 'Stop pouting so much, Little-Me,' she said. 'Zelana's coming, so don't get her all upset.' Then she paused. 'You *do* know that we absolutely *must* replace Aracia – soon.'

'What do you mean by "soon," Big-Me?' Eleria demanded. 'Enalla – or Lillabeth – will run things in the East for the next twenty-five eons, won't she?'

'Yes, she will, and that gives *you* twenty-five eons to grow accustomed to the *new* Eleria.'

'No! No! No!' Eleria screamed, stamping her foot on the ground again.

'Don't do that, Little-Me,' Balacenia scolded her. 'You're just being silly.' Then she paused and spoke more quietly. 'You *do* realize, don't you, that the *real* gods, Omago and Ara, will have to give you anything you want to persuade you to accept Aracia's silly temple?'

'*Anything?*' Eleria replied, looking suddenly more interested.

'You name it, Little-Me, and they'll have to give it to you.'

'Are you absolutely certain sure about that, Big-Me?'

'Tell them to kick down all the mountains or grab the moon and throw her away, and they'll *have* to do what you tell them to do.'

'Well now,' Eleria replied. 'Isn't *that* interesting?'

2

⟞⟝

Balacenia and Eleria went across the Land of Dreams to a nearby grassy hilltop where Ara was showing the aurora to her mate.

'It's beautiful, Dear Heart,' he said to Ara. 'It looks almost like the whole sky is suddenly in bloom.'

Ara smiled fondly. 'You have always loved blossoms, Dear Heart, but I doubt that you've ever seen the sky in bloom before.'

'When Vash and I were constructing this land, we spent a lot of time making her pretty. The outside world way back then wasn't really very attractive, so Vash and I concentrated on beauty,' Balacenia explained.

'And you did very, very well,' Omago said.

'Do you suppose we could get down to business here?' Eleria asked rather tartly.

'Mind your manners, Little-Me,' Balacenia chided.

'I'm being as polite as I can, Big-Me. I'm not the least bit interested in replacing that monster who destroyed herself trying to kill Lillabeth. I do *not* want a temple, and I do *not* want any part of a priesthood pretending to adore me. I'd much rather go back to the pink grotto so I can play with my dolphins and tend to the Beloved while she's asleep. Why does there have to be an extra goddess in the East anyway? Just tear down that silly temple and tell the fat priests that their life of luxury is over. Let Lillabeth and Enalla take care of things there.'

'It won't work that way,' Omago explained. 'They will return to being one single identity, small one.'

'That's "Little-Me,"' Eleria corrected.

'I didn't quite follow that,' Omago conceded.

'Everybody knows that Balacenia is "Big-Me," and I'm "Little-Me,"' Eleria replied. Then she gave Omago an arch – and very familiar – look. 'Now you owe me a hug,' she told him with a broad smile.

'I'd be just a little careful along about now, Omago,' Balacenia cautioned. 'Eleria's been hugging people into submission for years now. When she wants something, she'll hug it out of you.'

'Tattle-tale,' Eleria accused her alternate. Then she looked back at Omago and Ara. 'What's so important about having two goddesses in the East?'

'Balance, Little-You,' Omago explained. 'If there aren't two divinities in each region, it will be *out* of balance, it could very well irritate Mother Sea and Father Earth. You saw what happened when Yaltar – who's really Vash – unleashed those volcanos at the head of the ravine above Lattash, and they were only toys compared to what Father Earth can do if he's irritated. Let's keep things safe, Little-You.'

'I *like* him,' Eleria said to Ara. 'Does he hug good?'

Ara looked more than a little startled by *that* question. 'As far as I can remember I've never had any reason to complain,' she replied, blushing slightly.

'Good. Hugs are very important, you know.'

Omago actually looked just a bit embarrassed, and Balacenia covered her mouth to conceal her grin.

'All right,' Eleria said. 'All this talking is very nice, and now we know each other much better, so here comes the question you've been waiting for. What's in this for me?'

'You'll be a goddess, Little-You,' Ara replied.

'Why would I want anything *that* silly? If I asked my pink dolphins to adore me, they'd giggle me right out of the water and never let me go back in again. You're going to have to come up with something better.'

'Such as what, Little-You?' Ara asked.

'Don't rush me,' Eleria replied. 'I'm working on it. I'll get back to you as soon as I make my decision.' Then she turned and started on back down the hill again. 'Are you coming, Big-Me?' she asked Balacenia.

They went on down the hill and paused in a grove of blossom-covered trees.

'You did very, very well, Little-Me,' Balacenia praised her little blonde alternate. 'You were blunt enough to get their immediate attention, and then you left them both up in the air when you told them that you hadn't yet decided what you really want.'

'That's easy, Big-Me,' Eleria replied. 'I want them to leave me alone.'

'They won't do that, Little-Me. What's your next choice? Make it as impossible as you can.'

'What I really don't understand is why they want to drop this thing on me. If they wanted somebody who'd done more than anybody else to defeat the Vlagh, they'd have chosen Longbow. He's the one who actually won the war against the bugs, you know. Not only that, he's just about the best in the world when it comes to hugs.'

'Is that all you ever think about, Little-Me?' Balacenia demanded a bit peevishly.

'Hugs *are* important, Big-Me.' Then Eleria peered out through the blossom-covered tree-limbs. 'Here comes the Beloved. Maybe *she* can solve this problem for us.'

'What are you two up to now?' Zelana asked rather shortly.

Balacenia shrugged. 'Little-Me doesn't want to be a goddess, and she *definitely* doesn't want to replace crazy Aracia.'

'Be nice,' Zelana murmured absently.

'I was just telling Big-Me here that if Omago and Ara wanted to elevate somebody to godhood, they should talk with Longbow. If anybody in the world has earned immortality, it's Longbow. If he hadn't been there, all the outlanders – and the native people as well – would have been eaten by the bugs.'

Zelana sighed. 'Even if Ara and Omago offered him the position, Longbow would turn them down. He doesn't really want anything. His life has been totally empty since the death of Misty-Water.'

'That's the answer then,' Balacenia declared.

'Revive Misty-Water, you mean,' Eleria said. 'We may not look very much alike, Big-Me, but we think almost exactly the same – or hadn't that come to you just yet?' Then she turned to Zelana. 'Ara and Omago *could* do that, couldn't they, Beloved?'

Zelana frowned. 'It's altogether possible, I think. They'd have to go back in time, but they do that all the time.'

'And then we'd have a happy Longbow instead of the gloomy one we all know and love. I'd say that it's worth trying. If I tell Ara and Omago that Misty-Water is my price, they might decide to go pester somebody else.'

Balacenia had a strong feeling that she was missing something that might be extremely important, but she just couldn't put her finger on it.

'It *is* theoretically possible, Dear Heart,' Ara told her mate after Eleria had laid her demand upon them.

'I know that, yes, dear,' Omago replied, 'but won't it disrupt many, many things that have already come to pass?'

'They *won't* have come to pass way back then, will they?' Eleria disagreed.

Then several things clicked together for Balacenia, and it made everything so simple that she almost laughed. 'As I understand it, you two can move events forward or backward in time, can't you?'

'It's not really all that difficult, child. In the past we've had to correct many mistakes. Worlds are not really as solid as they might appear to be,' Ara explained.

Then Balacenia looked at Omago. 'You recently destroyed the Vlagh, didn't you?'

'No. All I did was render all the incipient eggs she'd been bearing in her abdomen for eons and eons null and void. She might still be able to lay eggs, but they'll never come to life.'

'You can move things backward or forward in time, can't you? If you'd done that a long time back, the Vlagh wouldn't have posed any threat to the Land of Dhrall, would she? *And*, if she wasn't a threat, the elder gods wouldn't have had any reason to go hire outlander armies to come here and fight a war, would they?'

'That's brilliant, Balacenia!' Ara exclaimed. 'The way things stand now, there will always be a danger that outlander gold-seekers will invade the Land of Dhrall. But if they don't even know that it's here, they'll never even try to invade.'

'And Longbow will be mated with Misty-Water,' Eleria insisted, 'and the world will be more beautiful.'

'And you will agree to accept the Domain of the East as its goddess with no more arguments, right?' Omago asked shrewdly.

'On only one condition,' Eleria answered.

'And what is that?'

'You'll give me hugs whenever I need them,' Eleria insisted.

Omago smiled. 'I think I can manage that, little one,' he replied.

'You see how easy things are when you do them right, Big-Me?' Eleria said to Balacenia.

3

There was never any question that the gods – both elder and younger, would attend the ceremony that would unite Longbow with Misty-Water, the daughter of Chief Old-Bear. One of the advantages of divinity was their ability to make themselves look familiar to the ordinary man-things of Old-Bear's tribe.

Balacenia found the deerskin clothing worn by the natives quite attractive, actually.

The one thing that startled Balacenia – and all the other gods as well – was the appearance of the young Longbow. The more familiar elder Longbow almost never smiled and there seemed to be perpetual grief in his eyes. The young Longbow smiled almost continually, and the first time Balacenia saw the beautiful Misty-Water, she knew exactly why. Balacenia had seen many, many beautiful women in her almost endless life, but Misty-Water was far and away the most beautiful Balacenia had ever encountered. Her hair was black and glossy, but her skin was pale white. Her eyes were very large, and they were almost permanently locked on Longbow.

'She *is* a pretty one, isn't she?' Zelana said between yawns. Had it not been for the upcoming ceremony that would join Longbow and Misty-Water, Zelana would almost certainly be sleeping by now.

Oddly, since this joining had been *her* idea, Eleria didn't seem to like Misty-Water very much. 'Could you maybe put a pimple on her nose, Beloved?' she asked Zelana as the day of the ceremony grew closer.

'Why in the world would I want to do something like that, dear child?' Zelana asked mildly.

'I hate to admit it, Beloved,' Balacenia said, 'but I'm catching a few hints of jealousy in Little-Me's behavior.'

'Does she *have* to be that pretty?' Eleria demanded. 'Longbow's always been *mine*, and now she's stealing him right out from under me.' Then she looked at the young Longbow. 'Isn't he *gorgeous?*' she demanded.

'I'm not sure if "gorgeous" is customarily used to describe male humans,' Zelana replied. 'He looks much nicer without that perpetual scowl on his face, though.'

It was about noon when the shaman of the tribe, One-Who-Heals, came out of his lodge at about the same time that Chief Old-Bear escorted Longbow, dressed in golden deerskin, and Misty-Water, garbed in white leather, out to the open area at the center of the village. Old-Bear spoke quite formally when he addressed his friend. 'These two children would be mated, Wise Shaman, and I have therefore summoned you to determine if it might be so.'

'And does this union have the approval of their parents, mighty Chief?' One-Who-Heals formally replied.

'I am the parent in question, Wise Shaman,' Old-Bear replied, 'and I do fully approve.'

'And is this your true wish, brave Longbow?' One-Who-Heals asked.

'With all my heart, wise Shaman,' Longbow replied in a voice much richer than Balacenia had ever heard coming from him before.

'And is this also *your* true wish, fair Misty-Water?'

'I have no other wish, One-Who-Heals,' the beautiful young woman replied in a voice that was almost musical. 'And know this, Wise Shaman. Should you refuse to join us, I will surely die before tomorrow's dawn. Longbow will ever be my heart and my soul, and without him, my life will have no meaning.'

'I wouldn't crowd *that* one,' Balacenia murmured to her relatives. 'If One-Who-Heals is foolish enough to refuse her, *he'll* probably be dead before the sun goes down.'

'I didn't fully understand Longbow before,' Veltan admitted. 'But everything just fell into place. I'm quite sure that when this ceremony is over, we'll be looking at the two happiest people in the world.'

'And perhaps the saddest as well,' Balacenia added, pointing at Eleria, whose eyes were filled with tears.

'Does any member of the tribe object to this union?' One-Who-Heals asked.

'That wouldn't really be a very good idea, would it?' Balacenia said quietly to the other gods. 'If Longbow didn't kill the objector, Misty-Water probably would.'

Then One-Who-Heals straightened and raised his hand. 'Since none objects, it falls to me to declare that Longbow and Misty-Water are now joined, and never will they be parted.'

The members of the tribe all cheered – at least *most* of them did. There were a few young men, and several young women, who chose *not* to cheer. They *were* wise enough not to denounce the joining, though.

And then the celebration began. Quite nearly every member of the tribe spoke briefly with Longbow and Misty-Water, congratulating them on their joining. Balacenia was almost positive that One-Who-Heals was really redundant. The joining of Longbow and Misty-Water had long since taken place in their hearts and minds, and nothing would ever separate them.

The congratulations of the members of the tribe continued until almost evening, and then, to Balacenia's astonishment, Zelana approached the happy couple. 'Know ye both,' she said quite formally, 'that your joining was decreed by the gods of the Land of Dhrall – both elder and younger – eons ago – for in your joining lies perfection. Love has now found a home, and she will stay with you forever.'

Then Zelana seemed to almost slump as if she were about to collapse.

'Get her home!' Dahlaine rasped. 'She should have gone to sleep months ago.'

'Take her other hand, Little-Me,' Balacenia told Eleria. 'Let's get her back to the pink grotto and put her to bed before the sun goes down.'

'I'll come with you,' Ara said. 'Zelana is our most precious child, so let's see to her well-being.'

'What were you thinking of, Zelana?' Ara demanded when they reached the pink grotto and bedded the Beloved down in her own bed.

'There was an emergency, Mother,' Zelana replied. 'I doubt if I could have slept at all if I hadn't seen it all the way through to the end. Balacenia is *good*, mind you, but *I* knew what was in the wind and how to veer it away. Of course as it turned out, she's at least as clever as I am. Toward the end of my cycle, though, I was *very* worried about what would happen if *Eleria* had to take charge. Until just recently, I didn't even *know* Balacenia.'

'We're encouraged to keep it that way, Beloved,' Balacenia replied.

'Beloved?' Zelana asked with a faint smile.

'That's Eleria's term, of course, but it seems to have rubbed off on me, for some reason. Sleep well, dear Zelana. "Little-Me" and I will keep things going as they should.'

Zelana sighed. 'It's time for me to sleep, I think.' Then she smiled at Eleria. 'Tell me "night-night" little one, and I'm sure that I'll slip right off.'

'Have some nice dreams, Beloved,' Eleria said, tucking Zelana's blanket up under her chin.

Balacenia had slowly backed away. 'It just occurred to me, Mother, that we're going to lose all of our outlander friends, since they won't be coming here now.'

Eleria quietly moved away from Zelana's bed. 'You didn't sound very happy, Big-Me,' she said. 'What is it now?'

'My clever notion has just robbed us of a good number of very close friends. Rabbit, Keselo, Gunda, Ox and all of our other friends won't be coming here because we won't need them now. The Vlagh is gone now – or at least totally alone – so she won't be stirring things up.'

'I'm going to miss Bunny,' Eleria said, 'and Keselo as well.' Then she blinked. 'Oh, dear,' she said.

'Yes, Little-Me?' Balacenia replied. 'Was there something?'

'We went to a lot of trouble to attach Trenicia to Narasan, and that just went out the window. Trenicia has no reason at all to even recognize Narasan.'

Balacenia frowned. 'You might be right there, Little-Me,' she admitted.

'Why don't you girls let *me* take care of that?' Mother Ara said. 'Narasan eventually *will* have to take charge of the Trogite Empire, and I'll arrange things so that Trenicia will pay him a call – some time in the past, I think. Trenicia's *almost* as good as anybody else with her weapons, and Narasan will be in a lot of danger if he tampers with the Empire. Trenicia *will* be able to protect him. Then, in time, we'll probably see something very much like what we saw this morning. Trenicia and Narasan *will* be joined. I'll see to that personally.'

'Isn't it handy to have Mother around like this, Little-Me?' Balacenia said. 'I'm sure that we'll want to stay here until Zelana goes deeper into her sleep cycle. Then you and I had better go talk with Enalla. I'm fairly sure that she'll knock that silly temple all to pieces before long, but you're going to need someplace to sleep. It's going to be a long, long time before you wake up and take over in your Dominion.'

'Wouldn't it be all right if I just stayed here with the Beloved, Big-Me? I know that when I wake up, I'll have to go over to the East and take charge, but until then I'd really rather sleep here with the Beloved.'

'What do you think, Mother?' Balacenia asked Ara.

'I don't see any problems with her staying here with Zelana, Big-Me,' Mother replied. 'There are many things she'll need to know, and if she's here in the pink grotto, I'll know where to find her.'

'Whatever you think best, Mother,' Balacenia agreed.

*   *   *

Balacenia was fully aware of her position as the dominant god of the Land of Dhrall during this cycle, but she was quite sure that Dakas and Vash could get along quite well without her interference for a few hundred years. Enalla was probably busy tearing down Aracia's temple and chasing off the fat men who called themselves priests. Mother Ara was there to keep Enalla from going *too* far, and that gave Balacenia some free time to consider things. She knew that she was going to miss a number of the outlanders who'd been such good friends this past year. Her suggestion to Father that he move the time when the Vlagh had lost all her children had eliminated any need for outlanders – friends or not. Balacenia sighed. 'They were delightful and very dear to me,' she murmured, 'but things are much better this way. Nobody dies, and I still have all those memories.'

She let those memories return as she sat in the pink grotto with blessed Zelana and dearly loved Little-Me while she let her mind drift back through the year that had just passed. That year no longer existed, of course, but her memories of it were precious. 'I think I'll keep them tucked away,' she said out loud. 'I'll be able to share them with children – and others as my cycle moves along.'

'Did you say something, Big-Me?' Eleria asked, emerging from her sleep.

'Just thinking out loud, Little-Me,' Balacenia replied. 'Go back to sleep and join once more with the Beloved.'

'I'll do that, Big-Me,' Eleria replied, 'just as soon as you stop all this chattering.'

Balacenia laughed then and looked fondly at her alternate. 'I really could use a hug, though,' she said.

'Why didn't you say so in the first place, Big-Me?' Eleria replied.

'Come over here, and I'll hug you all to pieces. I *am* the best hugger in all the world, you know.'

'Indeed I do, Little-Me,' Balacenia said. Then she went to Eleria's small bed and collected several years' worth of hugs.